Shakespeare's Secrets

Aaron F. Tatum

ISBN: 978-1-7927-8239-8

This work is dedicated to Inadene Rogers Tatum (late mother), Maria Reichel Tatum (late wife) and the late author and researcher exemplar, Charlton Ogburn, Jr.

The human mind cannot grasp the causes of phenomena in the aggregate. But the need to find these causes is inherent in man's soul. And the human intellect, without investigating the multiplicity and complexity of the conditions of phenomena, any one of which taken separately may seem to be the cause, snatches at the first, the most intelligible approximation to a cause, and says: "This is the cause!"

Leo Tolstoy
War and Peace

The bust, too—there in the Stratford Church. The precious bust, the priceless bust, the calm bust, the serene bust, the emotionless bust, with the dandy moustache, and the putty face, unseamed of care—that face which has looked passionately down upon the awed pilgrim for a hundred and fifty years and will still look down upon the awed pilgrim three hundred more, with the deep, deep, deep, subtle, subtle, subtle, expression of a bladder.

Mark Twain
Is Shakespeare Dead?

Contents

Prologue....viii
Chapter One....1
Chapter Two....5
Chapter Three....18
Chapter Four....22
Chapter Five....27
Chapter Six....38
Chapter Seven....60
Chapter Eight....73
Chapter Nine....88
Chapter Ten....104
Chapter Eleven....117
Chapter Twelve....131
Chapter Thirteen....140
Chapter Fourteen....142
Chapter Fifteen....161
Chapter Sixteen....181
Chapter Seventeen....198
Chapter Eighteen....213
Chapter Nineteen....220

Chapter Twenty 235
Chapter Twenty-One 250
Chapter Twenty-Two 259
Chapter Twenty-Three 272
Chapter Twenty-Four 280
Chapter Twenty-Five 301
Chapter Twenty-Six 315
Chapter Twenty-Seven 320
Chapter Twenty-Eight 336
Chapter Twenty-Nine 342
Chapter Thirty 359
Chapter Thirty-One 376
Chapter Thirty-Two 392
Chapter Thirty-Three 404
Chapter Thirty-Four 430
Dedication and Acknowledgements 442
About the Author 447

Prologue

An August afternoon—the early 1990s (just before the move to the new British Library).

Peter Stone's eyes flared from dry contact lenses and an uninterrupted stare at the extraordinary document on the table before him in the old and humid British Library's Reading Room. The hot summer day demanded irrigation of his eyes, especially now that they refused to blink in a burst of excitement.

Would the young staff member notice her error when he returned the document?

He squeezed the pencil tightly. The lead snapped. Transfixed by the discovery, he fished for another pencil in his satchel. One of his professors had alluded to such a possibility: "You dedicated legions of scholars, curious truth seekers, gadflies with iron bums, hopelessly over-trained pedants, should be ever alert to simple, unwitting allies who can't always put a foot right."

So now a staff member at the British Library Department of Manuscripts, after all these years of scholarly truth seekers, had not put a foot right. She had bragged about the new system once they moved: "It will be all electronic. No pencil on paper."

It may not have been her fault, he thought. In any event, no one really believed such a document ever could exist—except his boss who had found some evidence somewhere that indeed it did.

Eight weeks of research, he thought, and here I am—a student working six long nights a week as a concierge at the Tara Hotel and spending three hours an afternoon in the student's room—alone copying a document that might change the world. Evidently, such a document had never been intended for public eyes for it was clean, no wrinkles or smudges, so not even staff had moved it, but the document would end his employ and deliver him a bonus of three thousand pounds as promised by his employer.

Peter wiped a sweaty right hand, retrieved a new pencil, and continued the arduous task of replicating the elegant hand from the sixteenth century. Elizabethan studies at King's College, Cambridge, had given him enough experience to recognize every curve, each dramatic flourish. Dry eyes burning again, as if close to a flaming hearth, he fumbled for his small bottle of saline solution, leaned back in his chair away from the papers, and squirted two drops in each eye. He blinked rapidly then rubbed his tired eyes and glared again at the small, spiral notebook in which he regularly entered the document numbers as he ordered.

On this order he'd written "LA-LXIII-25." Positive. She must have read the checkout slip as "LA-LXII-25" when she looked under the printed notation "Collection and no. of ms." LA-LXII-25 was clearly the notation for the one-page document he was now copying.

Because of the error, he leapt to the fantasy that the wooden chair where he now sat and the misread checkout slip might well occupy an auspicious worthy status in the new British Library, off nearby Euston Road. No doubt a placard would credit his name over the historically significant find. His imagination raced on to lectures in front of large audiences about this day. Famous at age twenty-one. A chair behind him screeched, returning his focus to his mission.

As rewarding as it was, why was it happening?

"We've an enormous move ahead next week," she'd told him only the day before, "and there's much confusion in the stacks. You may be experiencing some delay in our deliveries."

No delay today, just the wrong manuscript, thank you—maybe one forever meant to be veiled from public scrutiny. Many of the large, firm cardboard binders were identical, he'd noticed, so any brief interruption could have precipitated the mistake.

He roared a sneeze, absorbing attention from clerks and monitors who were sensitive to such activity so close to ancient documents, and the one perched behind a large oak desk by the door gazed as though he might come over, but returned to his own reading. The unwitting ally wasn't at her post in front of the stacks, but somehow he felt her presence.

The fresh No. 2 pencil sliced across the spaces of the yellow legal pad, harvesting the data like the soft sound of a scythe cutting wheat. Once he could find a telephone to report the good news to the boss, what ecstatic glee he'd feel.

"We can certainly deliver you a bonus if you find something of significance," he was assured when they'd talked over the phone an evening in May, "but I doubt you'll find anything of consequence the entire summer. Maybe you have to be content in expecting £4 an hour, three hours a day, four days a week until September. Take Fridays off." A fortnight's wages virtually paid the rent in the studio shared with his brother in Grafton Way. His work at the Tara Hotel paid the rest of his living expenses.

But £3000 would be enough for the used Saab he'd coveted if it wasn't already sold. Should he wait another week? Bill another £40? He'd left behind his expensive new necktie, a bright blue Elliot from Westaway and Westaway, just opposite the museum only yesterday. Forty quid would buy five such ties. No. No. He'd have to wait yet one more week since the library would be closed and neither he nor the boss had anticipated when the move would occur. But neither had anyone else under all the annoying delays. Thus, the fortunate snafu. What if the Saab is sold, though?

Peter's boss would pay him only for hours worked. The intermediary who paid him fortnightly said the bonus would come quickly, the next day, if he'd discovered anything of consequence. He needed the bonus now.

He completed the task of copying the letter and folded the legal pad into his brown satchel, plopped in the notepad containing the itemized manuscript numbers of two months' work, and wedged his No. 2 pencil firmly atop his ear. (The pencil would be the crown of the new exhibit in the new library: "This was the pencil he used to copy the brief, but important document, in perfect replication...")

He snapped the satchel shut, caressed the forbidden manuscript binder to a close from its perch on the reading stand, and gathered the other useless manuscripts from earlier orders of the day into his arms. He stuffed his compact, black umbrella between the satchel grips and jerked them up in his left hand.

The young man's normally pale, round face flushed in throbs of anxiety. His eyes squinted unnaturally as though a limited vision could block all glowering officialdom in the silent study. Were they anticipating his march with the return of the manuscript order to the desk, then only to pounce on him? He finally coerced a trace of a tentative smile especially marked for the two staff members at the service counter.

Slower, he told himself, so he measured a deep breath and placed the manuscripts on the counter in front of the same young staffer, likely the one who had made the mistake and whom he had come to know in recent weeks. She would return them back to the stacks, or wherever she'd found them in the mysterious Manuscript Room sealed by the dark-brown paneled doors, for a final repose before transport to the new location by St. Pancras station.

Would she notice the error? Elaine? Ellen? She was about his age and they'd chatted often. Whatever the name, he was too nervous to recall it. Yes, glance at the name tag. A preemptive strike was in order. "I'm finished early, Ellen," he said evenly. "I reviewed only one manuscript."

"So you are. Done and dusted."

"By the way, you issued the wrong manuscript on LA-LXIII-25," he said, waving the order sheet. "I didn't have time to look at it, but you gave me LA-LXII-25. See. Here."

"So sorry, Peter," Ellen said. Hastily, without a look at the document, she stacked the returned checkout slips he'd just slapped down as though to say no more, work is done. "Everyone's exhausted. I should have caught it. One of several filed manuscripts we've laid out for the move. Do you recall what was in it?"

Peter glanced at the top of the stack under her hand where the ordinary, but egregious, slip of rectangular paper sparkled in his eyes. "Lansdown 62" appeared in a feminine hand penciled softly above the printed notation reading "Collection and no. of ms." Directly above the scribbling was the printed notation "Seat No. (or Reserve)" where he had penciled his seat number 6. His notation was clearly the LA-LXIII-25 he'd ordered. He instantly recalled the moment earlier of returning to his seat and casually noticing a wrong number. Now he remembered even rising to return it, until he froze as he saw the signature on the document.

How close he'd come to returning it! He looked her in the eye, grinned, and shrugged. "Like all the rest. Ink on paper."

"See you tomorrow," she said smiling. "Off you go. Oh, Friday. You don't work Fridays. Remember, we're closed for a week starting next Thursday."

"No. I'll see you after the big move." A rush of blood warmed his chest and cheeks as though he'd just devoured a steaming bowl of soup. He waved a clutch of air and pivoted to a near trot through the doors into the hallway where he opened his satchel to the guards for routine inspection. A slender, middle-aged man with platinum hair promptly grabbed the satchel, lifted the legal pad and notebook, shook once, then routinely removed a book by Kinglake and flipped its pages from the middle with both hands as he'd done in the days before. Mumbling unintelligibly, he set the items back in. No purloined document, Peter thought, just a glorious handwritten copy, highly legible for the boss. Right. Ring the boss, then Saab Motors Chelsea.

Peter bounded into the northern wing of the famous museum, soon to be vacant, past the priceless books and manuscripts by Wordsworth and Coleridge, the original letters by the hand of everyone from Elizabeth I to Marx to Freud to Churchill; around the display cases of penned lyrics and chords by Lennon-McCartney or the exacting hand of Mozart or the revisions by Verdi; through afternoon crowds hovering over the various originals of the Magna Carta; past the seemingly endless multitudes of volumes containing the painstaking notes from the quill pen of Elizabeth's treasurer, Lord Burghley (if only the supercilious Lord Treasurer had been there to read Peter's notes of the letter); and past the gift shop in the next wing teeming with congregations of French, Italian, Japanese, and Yank tourists herded by their respective guides trying desperately to herd them in or out to hotels or homes, pubs, or eateries to talk or forget about the artifacts of the British Museum.

A soft nudge against his shoulder bolted fear in his being.

"Mr. Stone." The old guard from the front portico had moved in, the one with the immense, pockmarked nose. Peter froze and squeezed his attaché handle.

"Y...Yes."

The guard thrust forward a blue wool tie, the lost Elliot. "You dropped it yesterday. I kept it for you when Wimberly told me you'd come today. You usually remove your tie whilst in there."

"Thank you so much, Mr. Paulson. You saved me about eight quid. Thanks to Wimberly as well." He bowed unnaturally in a jitter, and then adjusted the tie he'd failed to take the time to remove this day. Lifting his head, he lashed the Elliot insouciantly around his thin, white neck and puffed forcibly once before galloping onwards.

At the massive entrance to the British Museum, he danced down the concrete steps and jumped onto the expansive portico, uttering a low giggle that ascended to a falsetto silly sound, and then carelessly tossed the satchel into the air lightly above his head. Momentarily, a gaggle of German or Dutch tourists turned from their tour guide to gaze at his antics as his eyes met those of the aggravated guide so rudely interrupted. Giggling again, he returned to his trot.

In Great Russell Street, he entered a pub and rang his employer, relating one phrase he knew was the essential knowledge gleaned from a singular find. Look at the living quarters first. "That night he gathered the reward in exchange for his carefully handwritten copy of the document. His boss was satisfied it was authentic language. Apparently, it matched a clue from another letter.

"And as a bonus for your complete silence," he was told, erasing any thought of a hallowed place for Peter in the new British Library, "an envelope containing £600."

"Agreed," he fairly shouted. The Saab would soon be his.

The next day, while stacking the Lansdowns, Ellen casually mentioned to the supervisor her innocent error on the previous day. No one took particular note of it since they were so busy with the impending move.

Chapter One

Sixteen Months Later—December

Ian Scarborough dined at the club called Bookers on his father's membership once a year or so, and only for special occasions such as an important visit to London by the American Tyler Colton, PhD. Fresh off the plane that morning, the scholar was Ian's target for a quick story of how Ian's colourful grandfather (then seventy-four) had somehow whisked his mistress (fiftyish) to one of the club's third-floor bedrooms where she died of a violent heart attack during sex early in the evening. The next morning, his grandfather, after a sound sleep, had calmly dressed and fetched the manager to tell him a young woman had entered his room during the night and seduced him.

"'She expired at the height of climax,'" Ian half-mimicked the old man's sandpaper voice. "'I would have reported it sooner, but I couldn't resist her. After such a brilliant performance, I tumbled into a blissful sleep. Otherwise, I would have had her collected and swiftly removed.'"

"Incredible," Dr. Colton said, shaking his head. "Incredible."

"How dim. The family nearly lost the membership over him. My father and I play by the rules. Grandfather rarely did."

"But an entertaining life." Colton's dark, long eyebrows danced. "Effervescent."

"A life that wouldn't bear scrutiny. Shameful character. No fame, no accomplishments, only fodder for rumormongers—a wasted life. But yours, you should commit your story to print."

"My final draft of my memoirs is complete except for one brief, important span yet to be lived before I include it," said the elderly, grey-haired scholar. "I promised my editor I'd complete it immediately upon my return to Chattanooga and before the television debate filming in New York. She assured me she'd wait patiently."

"What an enviable position," Ian said, "to delay your editor... anticipating an event yet to occur." Ian sipped his burgundy, allowing it to swish gently across his tongue. His eyes raked the red, blue, green, and yellow Christmas bulbs, lone decorations spread carelessly across the dusky mantle of the cinnamon-coloured panelled dining room. The lingering hint of Christmas, just two days before, was a meager expression like that of a truant child complaining of measles based on the specious evidence of fresh crayon spots on his belly. The attempt clashed with the perfect French fare traditionally served the day after Boxing Day. Today's paupiettes de boeuf was unerring at the club in St. James Street. Dr. Colton did not lack for absorbing conversation. Admiral Sinclair had told Ian that he would open up to him based on the Admiral's mutual friendship.

Ian had helped the elderly scholar the summer before in a research trip north of London, and to the British Library where they'd discovered correspondence from Oxford's brother-in-law, Peregrine Bertie, to Oxford elaborating on the drinking rituals at court in Denmark as well as his meeting there a pair of courtiers named Rosenkrantz (with a "k" and not a "c") and Guildenstern. Bertie was an emissary for the Queen and country. "Rosencrantz and Guildenstern weren't dead," they proclaimed in their press release and in any intro in media interviews. Ian had ever noted his dry humour and endearing traits.

"Besides your excellent column this morning, two days ago we had an editorial endorsement in the *Washington Post.* Much momentum. The debate here in London should have some impact. Here's a recent article on the links of Sir Thomas Smith's books and knowledge, Oxford's tutor you know, to the acknowledged sources for the plays and sonnets." He slid a neatly folded clipping under Ian's nose near his plate and then lowered his voice. "I hope to have big news for you, Ian, day after tomorrow or so. I can't use it for tonight's debate unfortunately."

"You can't use it now?" Ian blinked, leaning forward and evincing an uncharacteristic effrontery. Ian felt he should prod since the subject seemed more taboo in the British establishment than in the States, where the retired professor maintained a frequent stream of honoraria for his tours. But Dr. Colton was a roaring gossip among fellow Oxfordians, Ian recalled the admiral telling him. "Always show heightened interest with him," the admiral had emphasized. So intent was Ian that he smashed some stray capers with a morsel of beef and squinted an eye like a sharpshooter willing a bullet to bull's-eye. The open eye then focused on his guest lingering for reassurance. "You may trust me, Doctor," Ian persisted. If an earthshaking event loomed over the quest for Oxford's candidacy, Ian desperately wanted to know in a flash.

"The fact is, son," the old man bowed to whisper over a trout and asparagus dish, "I can't yet tell you. It really is just a hint—nothing materially, yet."

"Why?" Ian asked. A bold persistence jerked his long neck back impulsively.

"Just forty-eight hours or so and you'll know." Colton pursed his lips. "I'll insist you're in on it. Sorry. Probably shouldn't have told you, but I want you to be around then."

"I'd planned after the debate to go to Torquay for three days," Ian said.

"I'll simply phone you there." He paused. "We can talk for as long as need be."

"Do ring Torquay if I go. I'll give you the number," Ian said. "It's probably worth my staying 'round. You've got my number for here."

"Yes, well, I know you're patient. I won't know anything tonight. I probably shouldn't have told you now."

"Right. I'm honored that you alerted me. I have something to look forward to. With all the grief I've had since my wife's death, I could stand some good news." He motioned to the waiter. "Morris, more bread, please." Hand and tongs clicked a tawny roll on each dish.

Colton said simply, "Thanks."

Ian nodded silently and grinned pleasantly. Colton blinked his bloodshot eyes rapidly to force a durable swallow, perhaps from embarrassment over broaching a temporarily closed subject, or jet lag or old age. He grunted, and then puffed a sigh before halving a mushroom. "It may be worth your time."

Chapter Two

Ian relied on Arthur K. Sinclair III as a friend more than any man in his life. As a sage mentor and long-time family friend, publisher of *Footloose*, a popular travel magazine, owner of a salmon cannery, World War II officer on the *HMS Ark Royal,* and yachtsman to the rest of the United Kingdom, he was vigilantly and calmly confident. But this particular evening Ian saw a different admiral solitarily pacing along the back of the stage in a worried state of expectation just before air time.

After months of artful planning, the moment had finally come and Ian patted his longstanding friend gently on the back. The admiral didn't acknowledge the affection and merely rubbed his elbow as he paced across the side of the stage in the new Queen Elizabeth II Conference Centre by the Thames. He smirked at Ian. "My arthritis again."

So the evening of the debate had arrived. Dr. Colton had arrived much earlier and now coyly approached Ian and the admiral. "I'm thrilled but jumpy. My knees are spongy."

"I can't quite weigh up this situation properly, either," Sinclair admitted, but grinned slightly. "We're all, except Ian, in our dotage. But it is, after all, a taping...only a live audience is inside the auditorium here with us. They're the ones I'm protecting from high seas for now."

Ian led them to the table marked "Oxfordians" and noticed the sound engineer shifting in annoyance as the Admiral noisily shuffled his shoes, his body swaying and arms twisting, the gait of a crusty seaman newly landed and far from sea. Ian recognized the anxious stroll of a man trying to compel the room to roll as the sea. His wide, white beard was blocked and trimmed. In the midst of a most serious debate, the admiral would retain a stolid countenance of a survivor of fierce gale forces. The lights emphasized his sanguinely weathered cheeks flanked by mammoth ears still adept at hearing the nearest foghorn. But intellectual titillation drove the admiral, no matter his age. Only a year ago, almost to the day, Ian recalled the lunch shared with his old friend, this man some thirty-five years his senior, at a Russian bistro in Yeoman's Way near Harrod's. "I know you're not on the best of terms with Vines, but ask him if he thinks such a debate would receive some ink if telly bought into it," said the admiral. "Show him my proposal and the stage plan." Editor Bradbury Vines consulted the telly editor who deemed it compelling enough, as Ian had reported promptly to Admiral Sinclair.

The admiral's ego couldn't be suppressed against the face of his bias for the Earl of Oxford in hosting the event, so Ian would be the last to stop him. Surprisingly, no one had protested. Not the BBC. Not the Stratfordians. His gravitas prevailed. "We can manage as long as he acknowledges his bias in the introduction. Then he must back away," the suits had told them.

Sinclair's voice, sonorous and raspy from the excesses of storms, Scotch and Fishermen's Friend, quieted the audience. "Quiet, please." After the cue from the director, his eyes darted over the crowd settling in seats over blue-grey carpet fading into an oblivion of lights and cameras. The admiral's hefty chest expanded like Scottish pipes, his earlier fraught puffs now gone. "Good evening. I'm Admiral Arthur Sinclair III, your host and moderator. And welcome to you who desire a resolution to one of the profound mysteries of the ages in this modern time when the *Titanic*'s sacred tomb is violated, guiding constellations are marred by the paths of manmade objects, and pirates are either radio stations or drug smugglers. As a seafaring man, I spent many a night off Calais or the Hebrides curled up with the finest works of our noble language by one Shakespeare—or Shakspere as my Oxfordian colleagues and I prefer to call him. Once ashore, I'd gravitate directly to the latest production.

"I revered the Bard's intricate knowledge of the sea, but I asked myself how a citizen of Stratford-Upon-Avon could know the sea so well? With whom did he sail? Were there any records of his experience at sea?" Sinclair paused a brief moment then shook his head.

"I found no empirical evidence that he sailed with anyone. Someone told me the Seventeenth Earl of Oxford was a suspect as the true author and had been to sea often—eventually owning an interest in the 'Colleagues of the Fellowship for the Discovery of the North West Passage'—the fate of which may have produced the line in *Hamlet*, `I am but mad north northwest.' Oxford's interest in the merchant vessel *Edward Bonaventure*, which, as in 'The Tempest,' quote 'the still-vexed Bermoothes,' end quote, eventually was wrecked off Bermuda around sixteen hundred, raising further suspicions over the nobleman.

"Those reasons were sufficient to lead me to become enthralled in a book written by an American who is on the panel tonight, and I believe if more open-minded people would read his work, then they too would adopt my conclusion. If one can't dive into this masterful compendium of rigorous research, then the next best alternative is to view this debate that the BBC is filming in two parts. The first, this one hosted by yours truly—an Oxfordian—which should have no bearing on the ensuing division of the house, and a second without a studio audience, but with a distinguished Shakespearian scholar as host at a resort hotel on a mountain in New York. The tape of that programme will be shown in the United States combined with our efforts here as a two-hour special in March. Both will be shown on the BBC in April as a combined work special, and this bit of housekeeping will be deleted in post-production edits.

"We're immensely grateful to all of those involved in bringing this project to completion." A smattering of applause erupted only to be halted by Sinclair's raised hand.

"I shall now introduce to you the advocates for Edward de Vere, hereafter referred to as the Oxfordians, and the advocates for Shakespeare known as Stratfordians. No inlet of fathomless detail or cove of syllogistic lacunae have they not visited." The crowd issued a polite rumble of patronizing laughter.

"At issue is: Resolved that the plays and sonnets ascribed to Mr. William Shakespeare were not written by him and were written by the Seventeenth Earl of Oxford, Edward de Vere."Taking the affirmative on the question is the American author Tyler L. Colton, PhD, Professor Emeritus of Elizabethan Studies at the University of Chicago; Mr. Ian Scarborough, popular music critic for the *Daily Times* of London, a songwriter, lyricist, and former entertainer—you may have seen today's edition with the superb editorial on this very subject. Also, the Honorable John B. Strawbridge, QC, barrister, and a Shakespearean scholar of particular note."

Again, the admiral stayed the crowd.

"Taking the negative argument is Professor Penelope M. Eddings, a leading Shakespearean scholar from New College, Oxford, where she is guest lecturing this term. Her numerous exegeses include a biography of the man known as William Shakespeare. Also from Oxford, Hertford College, is another equally famous scholar of the Bard's works, Professor Michael H. Quindry. Finally, renowned Shakespearean actor Sir Keith Trent, who is currently playing the lead role at the Wyndham in the Anderson Tully play, *Do You See the Rabbit?*"

Admiral Sinclair paused, grunted, and then took a quick sip of water.

Ian scrutinized Dr. Colton, first up for the affirmative as they each sat on stage left at a table lined with a felt cloth, water pitchers in front of each man. Strawbridge sat between the two men so Ian was closest to the podium. Ian dwelt momentarily on how he genuinely admired Dr. Colton for inveighing against the Stratfordian establishment his entire academic life, and writing such a splendidly complete book of detailed research on the case for Edward de Vere. Ian now bore every detail in his head, a discipline of memory practise he had mastered while studying at the Royal Academy of Music. But there was something more. Ian knew a day would come when the world would regard Colton as the scholar who shed the most penetrating light on the subject.

In fact, that credit should be shared with J. Thomas Looney, a British schoolmaster who first set out to fit a candidate for the works as the true author and found de Vere to meet the criteria. Just last summer, when Ian had spent a week with Dr. Colton in the British Library and Hatfield House reading letters written by and to Edward de Vere and Lord Burghley, the treasurer under Elizabeth I who made such a profound difference in stifling Edward de Vere as the true author (according to the Oxfordians), he saw Colton's care for truth.

The admiral nodded to Colton and continued. "Dr. Colton represents the affirmative in this first round for twenty minutes after which I'll bang the gavel. Dr. Eddings will then follow with a twenty-minute rebuttal. Dr. Colton."

Ian smiled at Colton as he rose, a rotund figure topped by a cratered, white face that looked as though it rarely held daylight, which was largely true because of his abiding penchant for late-night research and writing. Ian recalled him smoking cigarettes with recessed filters—frantically chewing on the filters and squinting at his subject between whiffs of blue smoke. At Brooker's, only hours before, he'd complained about his inability to smoke in the dining room. "But son, I play by the rules," he acquiesced, which launched Ian on his story of his grandfather not playing by the rules.

Colton's skepticism concerning the Bard and corresponding interest in de Vere began while working on a thesis on Ben Jonson's works while at Dartmouth—not surprisingly, inflaming the entire English literature department there. So soiled was his reputation, he was reviled to the extent professors would have little to do with him as he "came out of the closet." Only one opponent treated him fairly, an intellectually honest teacher who welcomed debate and recommended him to the University of Maryland for a research position where the department was much more tolerant of other views. At Maryland, one could find many historical documents in Lord Burghley's hand (thanks to a fortuitous bequest from the Vanderbilts who had married into the Cecil family in the nineteenth century) since Burghley, the treasurer for Elizabeth, played such an important role in de Vere's life.

Dr. Colton puffed heavily upon arriving at the dais and adjusted the mic, his standard practice regardless of necessity. The crowd of chiefly students, the press, and a few professors felt only the discomfort of a squeaking microphone in the modern, well-lit meeting room and lecture hall. A lighthearted atmosphere could be detected in the room as if nothing could ever go completely amiss, whether it was grating microphone sounds or scholars who dwelled on forgettable minutiae. Ian had secretly admonished his partners that Colton was habitually capable of both sins (noted particularly in the debate last summer at the Traveler's Club and an interview on a local radio program in Devon), so this performance should prove to be no exception. His teammates would necessarily lead a charge and expand. Dr. Colton even confided it in his blunt, open manner to Ian. "I've been known to race away on the track to sublime obscurity. It sounds like bilge sometimes."

Fortunately, Strawbridge, an exemplary barrister, would be consistently incisive in hitting the major points. He was organized and convincing. Ian's own particular skills stood at raising major points and then filling in with accurate, interesting detail. "A presentation as entertaining as informative," said the lawyer in a pre-debate huddle that afternoon.

Dr. Colton gaped at the full lines of a green notepad as if to meet his colleagues' fearful expectations of verbosity, then cast his eyes out to the audience, little of which he could see through the television floodlights. "You Brits refer to birders as twitches. Time for twitches to properly identify the markings of the Swan of Avon." A polite, tolerant cadence of laughter acknowledged this reference to his added reputation as a published ornithologist. "I'm a twitch who's been onto the right nest for years."

Oddly, his thoughts suddenly weren't on the Earl of Oxford, but on that of the Pied (or was it a White) Wagtail he had seen on a long plank in the Thames while taking a short walk that morning. Why wasn't he concentrating on the opening remarks? As he swiped the air once in front of his eyes, like batting a mosquito, the imagined bird flew away and his mind cleared for the task at hand. Then he felt a strong taste for tobacco surge through his tongue. "I should like to begin by stating that I will in this first segment, address several salient points to convince you that de Vere, the Seventeenth Earl of Oxford, was the true author beyond a reasonable doubt.

"Such a legal approach is appropriate here—for both sides of the issue—but particularly for de Vere, since that which was perpetrated upon him was a *criminal* wrong like no other in history. Furthermore, there is no larger irony in all history that, unfortunately, a standard for criminal conviction must be applied to the very man who wrote these magnificent works in order to prove it, thus correcting this aberration along the true vector of recorded literary history." Was he making sense? He pressed on, in spite of his confusion.

"We know virtually nothing about Mr. Shakespeare, or Shakspere as I will refer to him from now on, as far as his life. He was born in Stratford-Upon-Avon. We do not know whether he went to school since there are no surviving records indicating such. We are not certain of his occupation. There are only two references to him as an actor—one of which is altogether unclear. At about the same time de Vere is receiving an annuity from the Lord Treasurer, supposedly this same man grants another one to Shakspere. There are no manuscripts in his will, or even books for that matter—this in the face of an otherwise highly detailed will. There are only three references by contemporaries to the man as a playwright, and these for the detailed part of my presentation, are disputable, as you will see. The signatures he left behind are inconsistent, and the name, when associated with printed works during his life, is suspiciously hyphenated—`Shake (dash) Spear'—largely inconsistent with the spelling of the signatures as if denoting a nom de plume." Yes, he felt on track again.

"He dies with no eulogies, no praise. His passing is apparently unnoticed outside of Stratford. Then suddenly, seven years after his death, a monument is erected in Trinity Church with a most peculiar message to the public. Simultaneously, the *First Folio* is introduced to the world containing a wealth of new material."

Removing his handkerchief, he cleared his throat and rubbed his brow. His head was beginning to throb.

"I'll deal with a trio of literary contemporaries mentioning the name out of less than a dozen—yes—dozen during his lifetime.

"One reference is by a scholar named Francis Meres who published a book of anecdotes in 1598 entitled *Palladis Tamia*, which compared English and classical poets in a brief critique. Quote,

`As Plautus and Seneca are accounted the best for comedy and tragedy among the Latins: so Shakespeare among the English is the most excellent in both kinds for the stage.' Unquote. Meres cites six comedies and six tragedies. He also praised the sonnets, and again I quote, `The sweet witty soul of Ovid lives in mellifluous (and) honey-tongued Shakespeare, witness his Venus and Adonis, his Lucrece, his sugared Sonnets among his private friends.' Unquote. He also lists the Earl of Oxford first in the list—probably because he was a nobleman for one, and secondly, because he was willing to acknowledge him in spite of a cover-up.

"There is another public reference which was delivered in a play put on regularly at St. John's College, Cambridge, in which a character named Kempe speaks to a fellow character named Burbage as follows, `Few of the university men plays well; they smell too much of the writer Ovid and that writer Metamorphosis, and talk too much of Prosperina and Jupiter. Why, here's our fellow Shakespeare puts them all down, I(ay) and Ben Jonson too. O that Ben Jonson is a pestilent fellow; he brought up Horace giving the poets a pill, but our fellow Shakespeare hath given him a purge that made him bewray his credit.'" Colton paused.

"Finally, there was another reference in 1615, one year before the Stratford man's death, in a letter from an 'F.B.,' some say to be the poet Francis Beaumont, to Ben Jonson. I quote. `And from all learning keep these lines clear as Shakespeare's best are, which our heirs shall hear preachers apt to their auditors to show how far sometimes a mortal man may go by the dim light of Nature....' Unquote."

He paused again for a sip of water, his head throbbing more. He was aware of the Stratfordians shifting in their seats and rustling their papers.

"I will begin with the latter first. Beaumont was forecasting, correctly as it has turned out, that future generations—heirs—will hear 'preachers apt to their auditors,' in other words, the Stratfordians are suited to their gullible modern day audience. The worst part of this folly is that the Stratfordians have never read the letter from Beaumont correctly, because they do not have it literally quoted correctly, and anytime I try to deliver the above quote they become flustered, thus retaliating with the usual ad hominem."

Colton glanced at the Stratford table, and then proceeded. "The quote from the play involving Shakespeare's alleged fellow actors, Will Kempe and Richard Burbage, is most mysterious since Kempe—extraordinary actor that he was—is represented as a buffoon. He correctly identifies Ovid but somehow also identifies Metamorphosis as a writer in the same breath. The entire passage seems to be a mockery of Shakespeare.

"Furthermore, there is an irony in that Shakespeare is said to not `smell too much of Ovid' when indeed there are numerous citations by Stratfordian scholars who aver that his chief inspiration was Ovid. For example, there are five classical references in one nine-line passage in *The Winter's Tale*. Thus, the actors are making jest of the `university men' since the credit for these works is given to a country bumpkin...no small wonder that Ben Jonson is described as a `pestilent' fellow. I submit to you that this reference is not to the man, instead it is a tongue-in-cheek mockery of the pseudonym—Shake-dash-spear." Yes. He sensed the audience was with him now.

"Francis Mere's *Palladis Tamia*, from which I quoted first, was published in the month following the death of William Cecil, Lord Burghley's—the Earl of Oxford's—foremost enemy. Cecil, the Lord Treasurer of England, was also the earl's father-in-law as well as his guardian after the death of young Oxford's father. By praising Shakespeare, for the first time, Meres gave credibility to an author as a real person and not as a pseudonym for an earl too immersed in the then-current tradition of not taking public credit for authorship.

As for Meres's reference to Oxford in listing various poets and playwrights, there was simply no escaping such mention since Oxford had already published early works for all to see.

"Thus, the plot was hatched with no protest from the nobleman since it was entirely *infra dignitatem*, unbecoming, for a nobleman to be identified with his works." Sharp pain struck just behind his left eye. His head was throbbing even more.

"The quote in Meres's work referring to the sonnets is a clear tip-off that the sonnets had been written but were not published until—and we know this quite well—1609, indicating that the author was deceased. The quotation, after all, says, `His sugared Sonnets among his private friends.' Not published! Further proof of their existence at the time is the appearance of two sonnets in a poetry anthology published the year following *Palladis*—1599. The silence is deafening on the remainder of the sonnets and only slightly less so on any reference to the author among his contemporaries." Certainly hearing a flapping of wings, he didn't dare to look.

"We will proceed with other proofs that Shakespeare was not the author, that he was set up to be the author apparently after Oxford's nom de plume, Shake-Spear, was scuttled and the plot to assign the name to a real person was launched. I'm positive you will see..."

Out of nowhere, the weight of his head pulled darkness in uncontrollably. All he saw was a bustard, a heavy, meadow bird with its head down, gliding on strong wings as it occasionally beat the auditorium air in front of the fading spotlight. Why here in England? He'd only seen the bustard in Spain and once in France. It was slowly being reintroduced, but only on the Salisbury Plain. And then, more of the dark birds whisked by in formation behind the first, producing a sharp, sustained ringing. Against the ringing was a bass growl of the audience. Something heavy crashed against his head and he found only darkness. Screams pierced the buzzing crescendo. Then he heard nothing, felt nothing.

Ian dashed from his seat and lunged as the man's small upper torso deflected off the podium. He swept his arms over Colton's chest futilely while the limp body crumbled. Blood formed from a gash on his head and crawled slowly, animatedly, like a dark-red worm across his forehead. The notebook plopped as note cards drifted down like whimsical, blanched autumn leaves. Instantly, a glass of water spilled across the floor, making droplets in a concentric circle on the carpet beside the trembling knees. A miniature Oxford family crest, part of a lapel pin or tie clip, rolled defiantly to rest, inclined perfectly upright against the glass cup. Ian heard Colton mumble something like "bustards." What a bizarre utterance from a man losing consciousness, he thought.

The participants and a few audience members crowded around the still body. Sir Keith shouted urgently, "Is there a doctor present? Someone call for medical personnel."

Instantly, the admiral extended his comrade's legs and quickly loosened his bow tie and collar. "Please back away and give us some proper space," he commanded.

"Kill the lights. Kill the cameras." Muddled shouts pierced the room above the crowd's roar.

A chubby, dark-skinned, solid lady in a yellow plaid skirt and white blouse bumped Ian and joined the huddle. She held a portable phone and calmly shouted. "I'm an off-duty matron, sir. Please, don't touch him until a doctor arrives. I've fetched an ambulance. They're on the way. I'll prop up his head. Someone find a blanket. Hand me your jacket." She pointed to Strawbridge who immediately started removing his coat.

"If they don't hurry, he'll surely die," someone said anxiously from behind the huddle.

"The idea shall not die," Ian mumbled. The man may die but not the idea, he thought. Tyler Colton had been onto the truth for years but was now being cheated of a grand day.

Ian's hands quivered like so many times before in emergency medical crises. Instinctively, he cast about for a less emotional aspect of the moment and was distracted by the perfect formation of water droplets framing the crumpled chaos on the carpet. He saw the crest leaning against the glass, and next to it a note card with some scribbling in the admiral's familiar hand. The ink was smeared by some of the water, but it looked like "P helps. Try tomorrow." The Doppler sound of an approaching ambulance momentarily broke his concentration on the drops of water and the card. Why "bustards"? What is a bustard? Was he cursing as he fell? Never could he recall Colton cursing. And "P helps"? What kind of advice was that?

Chapter Three

A languid, old man slouched, chin in hand, behind a large, teakwood desk in a Manhattan high-rise and slurped a cup of loose tea made from a stash sent years ago from Bangladesh. His secretary boiled it each morning and then steeped the bell-shaped tea caddie packed with earthy shreds. He always placed the small steel caddie in the cup so it would remain warm, and he would often clang it against the insides as he savored the brew. It tasted like warm cereal with the perfunctory two spoons of sugar and about a dash of milk. Each cautious sip soothed his bones, a penetrating nepenthe for his sundry aches, making him snuggle against the leather of his large swivel chair. He carefully turned the pages of a London newspaper dated Wednesday, 27 December—now a day old—as if he were a physician carefully lifting bandages to check wounds. He loved holding the newspaper.

Still the paper smelled oddly fresh, its odor competing with the tea. While the news wasn't as fresh, in spite of arriving this morning on the newsstand from the previous day's flight, only one story he'd seen on the Internet version the night before held his interest. Ever the Anglophile, he especially loved London, since he could claim it as his birthplace and early childhood home. Long before the war, his English parents, schooled on languages, moved to New York to take German translation jobs at the League of Nations. But how he longed for London. It had been a year since his last visit and now he might well never return again. Doctor's orders, as of the day before

Christmas. A lump collected in his throat at the thought, so he took another sip of tea.

He found the editorial page and mumbled the headline he'd read on the website the night before. His half-slumbering, squinting eyes glittered as though he'd just won a lottery.

Pop Critic Ian Scarborough Jumps into the Ageless Literary Row

WAS IT SHAKESPEARE OR EDWARD DE VERE?

> This evening I shall have the distinct honor of joining Professor Tyler L. Colton (the definitive researcher advocating the Seventeenth Earl of Oxford as the true author of the works by William Shakespeare) in a debate at the Queen Elizabeth II Conference Centre for a historic taping for the BBC and, later, American television.
>
> My extracurricular crusade began over seven years ago when I read Dr. Colton's book. Colton is a retired American English professor who has turned the issue of who wrote the Shakespeare Canon on its head. His detailed research has convinced me not only that Shakspere (the way the man from Stratford most often signed his name) did not write the works, but also that the Seventeenth Earl of Oxford (Edward de Vere) did indeed do so under the Shake-Spear (the way it was presented to the public, with a dash, during de Vere's lifetime) pseudonym. De Vere is guilty by a preponderance of circumstantial evidence as cited in Colton's rather ponderous but entertaining tome—as then, seven years ago, reviewed by yours truly in the Sunday Books section.
>
> One aspect of the issue that's particularly intriguing is the debate over the monument in the Trinity Church at Stratford. At the base of the monument is the most cryptic of messages: "Stay passenger, why goest thou by so fast/read if thou canst whom envious death hast plast/within this monument Shakspeare." The monument beckons visitors to dig deeper—metaphysically and physically.

Shakspere is certainly not within the monument. His body is presumably in the tomb only some forty feet away in the floor of the church. The monument was erected some seven years (1623) after the Stratford man's death in 1616, in order, one assumes if one is to believe the worst, to coincide with the publishing of the First Folio (1623), giving the world the bulk of the works for the first time in print. No manuscripts exist now or, evidently, then.

This baffling message leads me personally to the conclusion that it's possible the works, the plays and sonnets, the original manuscripts, are the "corpus" inside the monument. Furthermore, some de Vere (Oxfordian) advocates maintain, with some credence, that the message encourages and invites the truth—a subtle time capsule from those compelled by the Queen's strict rule to abet the conspiracy to silence the earl's voice in the annals of literary history.

The monument would have conveniently reinforced the Shakspere myth to the outside world with little cost to William's meagre reputation in Stratford. Indeed, the confusion over the spelling of his name might have rendered silent the lips of his neighbors. For that matter, would pilgrimages from London in that day have been plentiful so as even to raise the issue? Especially since the literate contemporaries of Shakspere did not write about him often; the illiterates did not know enough to care about him at all. His death went entirely unnoticed in 1616.

For now the row is largely an academic one since no one has forced the issue of uncovering and exploring the monument even through effective electronic means. If a methodology could be applied also to the tomb in the chancel floor near the monument, then why not, in a phrase, proceed to break two stones with one blow?

It's not solely a mystery deserving resolution for the sake of future poet/playwrights' understanding of how the greatest of their craft (yes, he who literally defined it) devised clever plots, chiseled

> characters, and borrowed settings. It is a question that must demand whether Shakspere of Stratford, about whom we know so little, is to sleep undisturbed or if some other tortured soul, namely, the Seventeenth Earl of Oxford, is rattling about in horrid purgatory of historical obscurity devoid of the utmost panegyric.
>
> The Department of National Heritage should establish an inquest into not just the monument controversy but also the entire matter immediately. To quote the foremost candidate for the authorship (the Earl himself): "Truth is truth, though never so old, and time can not make that false which was once true."

"Remarkable," the old man muttered aloud and swallowed the remainder of the now tepid tea, eyes brightened for the first time in days. "What extraordinary timing. I pray it doesn't adversely affect our little project somehow. Scarborough. Who is this Scarborough? I've heard the name before. Where? Who made mention of him?"

His secretary rushed in as he finished reading. "What did you say?" she asked.

"Oh, nothing." His eyes rolled from a concentrated aim. "Claire, please try to reach London. It's early afternoon there and I should be able to reach him now. Oh yes, Claire, I'm definitely not able to go to London as planned. Do cancel the flight for me."

Chapter Four

The sister cast a penetrating look into the doctor's eyes. "Has he stabilized?"

"Somewhat," he said, adjusting a tube up Dr. Colton's nasal passage.

"I'll just freshen him up a bit," she said. She turned to fetch some fresh gauze for the head wound he'd sustained from the fall. Colton moaned a low note and her skillful hands checked the central line catheter where it fed into him just below the shoulder blade. "It's going to be some time before we know, isn't it?"

"He may remain in an obtunded state for some time," the doctor said as he nodded affirmatively to her question.

Even in a comatose condition, the mind sometimes has a way of wedging itself between nothingness and consciousness. It was not unlike an extended waking edge of some mornings when Colton, as a boy, would see a mockingbird or cardinal appear at the feeder each spring when all was still dark except the gleaming top of the dominating white oak in his back yard in Chattanooga, and then go back to sleep. Now he could hear voices in the room occasionally, interfering with his dreams...dreams in which no matter how hard he tried to manipulate characters in the face of odd settings and bizarre portrayals, chaos held the upper hand. A combination of methotrexate, vincristine, and a stupor induced by the clot combined to dilute his manipulations, and at this particular moment as far as he could determine, he sat among groundlings of identical men in an outdoor theatre.

Hundreds of Peter Quinces surrounded him in the audience for an evening with an actor who was debuting on stage at what could be the Globe Theatre. What a strange production of "Mid-Summer Night's Dream." The so-familiar Nick Bottom, in a French crown-colour beard, belched a lion's roar and peeled the curtain to introduce the play. "If there be no ladies in the audience, we will perform most obscenely and courageously. I shall portray the tax collector in hopes of finding evidence of valuable manuscripts. I'll be examining the will and the Will (chuckles from the Quinces) of a Shakspere of Stratford-Upon-Avon, or one of various spellings of such a name in this city between 1588 and 1596. Our play is set at the tree stump behind the Trinity Church in Stratford in the days before Shakspere's death." Another lion's roar exploded from his throat, drawing audience laughter for the ridiculous timing. "'One lion may speak when many asses do,'" he spat back, only eliciting more laughter. Then the curtain opened.

In center stage, was the lone figure of a balding man perched on a tree stump, his back to the audience. Limply, he slumped over as if the paced drift of the Avon before him was the soul of his attention. Abruptly, Bottom the tax collector, walked up to him and tapped his shoulder.

"It's time to establish who you really are for purposes of assessment," Bottom exclaimed, and picked up a yellow legal pad that lay flat on the ground by the stump. He would use it to calculate the tax. "Or, I should say, time to assess who you are in order to establish your purposes."

The bald man jerked around mechanically to reveal a vacant gaze, the look of a man who could think of nothing but contentment or money. His vacuous, non-descript face held eyes set in reverse as if the left eye should be located in the right socket and the right maybe in the left socket. With the demeanor of a man incapable of moving quickly, he signaled an intention to reply by a deliberate sucking in of wind through an open mouth ill-prepared to emit sound until thought, maybe *any* thought, had surfaced. His eyes rolled, and his eyebrows, goatee, and mustache thin as if some make-up artist had been interrupted in the midst of application—a work that hadn't been properly shaped.

"I've told you all I know," he said deliberately in a high, grating, almost shrill, twanging Warwickshire accent, and nodded once as if to convince Bottom further of his sincerity. "But I can show you a copy of my will." Instantly, from under his buttocks, he produced a document of about three pages.

"Very well." Bottom clutched the documents. "Let's see here. It's dated 25 March 1616, a revision of the one done in January the same year." Bottom raised his eyebrows looking squarely into the man's vacant eyes. "In that time it seems you had a row with your son-in-law, Thomas Quiney. You certainly had no problem in tracing the rather intricate scenarios and contingencies of bequests and inheritance. John Hall and Susanna were to be highly favored. Let me quote from the will so I might have some idea as to what estate taxes you could expect. You spell your name S-h-a-c-k-s-p-e-a-r-e in this case. How odd. You are leaving money for Judith, the one who married Thomas without license. But all real property goes to Susanna Hall, that is, the dwelling called New Place, your house at Henley Street and quote, `All my barns, stablers, orchards, gardens, lands, tenements, & hereditaments in Stratford-Upon-Avon, Old Stratford, Bishopton, Welcombe, and Blackfriars.' End quote.

"You've given your broad, silver bowl to Judith and quote, `All the rest of my goods, chattels, leases, plate, jewels, and household stuffs whatsoever...to my son-in-law John Hall, gent, & my daughter

Susanna, his wife.' End quote. You give twenty-six shillings and eight pence to four friends, two of them to buy themselves rings, and some twenty shillings to your godson."

Bottom grabbed Shakspeare's shoulder. "Here is an interesting jotting between the lines, in which you grant twenty-six shillings, eight pence each for purchasing of rings, and I quote, 'To my fellows John Hemynge, Richard Burbage, & Henry Cundell.' End quote. These are the fellows who own the Globe with you, are they not?" Bottom asked.

Shakspeare did not move...shocked, stone-faced. "Why is there no mention in this will of shares owned in the Globe Theatre? Was this lagniappe of a paltry twenty-six shillings each a mere afterthought by the drafter of the will, to interline it, for fear of sustaining any suspicions for posterity, by omitting any mention of your so-called close associates entirely? It is an insertion later between the lines by someone other than who wrote the will! Who inserted it?"

Shakspeare dropped his mouth open as if compelled to reply but could think of nothing to say and so began to suck air through his lips.

"I'll read on..."

"Please...please, don't go further." Shakspeare frantically waved a halting hand.

"'Item I give to my wife, my second best bed with the furniture.'"

"Stop." The doltish man drooped his eyelids. The muscles in his lower jaw tightened and his lower lip curled on the verge of weeping.

"I shall. That's all there is," said Bottom, lifting his palms upward, then thrusting his puffy face into Shakspeare's odd, reversed, now-tearing eyes. "Where, my dear fellow, are there any references to your books? You must have had *a* book. Where are they mentioned here?" He returned to an erect posture. "There's certainly no mention of manuscripts. Where are the manuscripts? You knew their value, did you not?"

Shakspeare was frozen in complete horror, saying nothing. Tears glistened.

"Didn't someone reconstruct this will to establish the connection to acting and the Globe Theatre?" Bottom asked as he began to roar. The Quinces laughed at the weird figure on the stage.

A tall man in a black western outfit appeared from around the prop representing Trinity Church. Colton recognized the country singer Johnny Cash. What's he doing in here? thought Colton. Why *can't* I wake up? Cash. He recalled that his late wife had loved his music.

"As Lord Mayor of Stratford-Upon-Avon, I hereby implore you to halt the harassment of this man over estate taxes. He's not dead yet and I see no reason why you should be questioning him on this matter. He'll be a valuable citizen here someday after we bury him," Cash said in his deep, smooth voice. He drew a pistol and waved it menacingly at a perplexed Nick Bottom to move off stage.

The audience of Quinces laughed in a frightful unison. In the background of the stage all could see a delighted Ben Jonson rapidly pulling the ropes to a closed curtain. "This joint is out of time," he shouted hysterically. The crowd of Quinces howled.

Located directly behind the second most popular Elizabethan playwright, Colton detected a long-faced, dour, bald man with a white, unkempt beard. He whispered in Jonson's ear. The familiar face belonged to Lord Burghley, Elizabeth's Lord Treasurer as well as Oxford's father-in-law. Cash passed Burghley hurriedly and shouted something at him as the curtain would open briefly.

"What did he say?" asked the sister. She lifted Colton's arm over his belly after completing a minor treatment on his hand.

"Junk Ass?" The doctor shook his head, puzzled. "An American writer, you say?"

Chapter Five

Ian Scarborough's long strides carried him purposefully through the front doorway of St. Thomas Hospital, straight for the information desk. From her seat behind the desk, a young woman wearing a phone headset tilted her head towards Ian. "May I help you?"

"Tyler Colton's room, please," he said. "Room 1207."

"He's recently left the operating theatre. He can have no visitors," she said, reading from a computer screen. "I do recall a lady, his daughter, has arrived from America. She should be waiting on the twelfth floor...critical care. The waiting room is down the hall. You'll see the signs."

"Right. Thank you."

Ian hesitated, unsure as to why he had come so early, the morning after the incident, since he knew he would not be allowed to see Colton. Yesterday was the only time he'd ever been so directly involved with an actual emergency as it happened. Once he and his late wife had driven up on a motor accident in Devonshire only some five or ten minutes after it had happened. The crash killed at least four teenagers who had been drinking, and had hit the side of a small bridge on a country lane. The fire in the car had probably killed two of them instantly. The other two had been thrown from the car and lay dying on the roadway. An ambulance was approaching as his wife raced to the scene and helped apply first aid to one of the dying children. He'd sat passively in the car, glued to his seat with weak wrists and knees. He simply wept—a pitiably, helpless blob. Except for a brief focus on Colton's life mission, the same desperate feeling revisited him when Colton collapsed.

Gaye, his wife, returned to the car that day seemingly as cool as a fall breeze and reported the facts glibly until she realized he was crying. "It's all right," she consoled, brushing his blond hair. It wasn't right, he'd wanted to say, it was a disaster. Her ability to remain collected under pressure was extraordinary, but he felt her disturbance over the sight as well in the aftermath when she failed to offer to drive.

Tragically, she too would fall victim to an auto accident a month later—killed instantly in fog on the new M40 from Birmingham near Bicester while returning from a legal seminar on E.U. measures. They had been married for just over six months and she had been pregnant for six weeks with their first child. The tragedy was deepened by the contrast of losing both someone he knew and loved so well and someone he did not know, but loved, too. Although his irretrievable loss was now six years removed, he still felt a gnawing grief, an emptiness, a bitter taste. A day would not pass without tapping the painful memory of the moment Brad Vines, his editor, beckoned him from a meeting with the fateful news. His work at the newspaper suffered. His drive to compose music waned. For some days the first year he wouldn't leave his bed. Certain music, in particular Gorecki's *Third Symphony*, a certain tune by Yes, or a lone cello inexplicably would move him to her memory and lugubrious outbursts—sometimes in public view at the office or once at the Sadler's Wells Theatre during an interval, in full view of his friends and a date.

Up to that point in his life, Ian had been rather lucky, he mused. A love of Old English ballads had steered him to moderate wealth at an early age. His arrangement of the traditional "Hard Times of

Old England" had earned him and his band, Falstaff's Ghost, wide recognition. Success bred comfort and they went on to produce five more albums before breaking up over sixteen years ago. For the past five years, in an effort to sustain his love of Elizabethan music—in particular that of John Dowland—he'd been jamming with three other retired rockers also enamored with lutes and hurdy-gurdies. These sessions resulted in collaborative efforts, and Ian was even inspired occasionally to write songs for other artists as well. On keyboards, flute, and harmonica he could pivot between genres. It was pop success without the massive headaches of touring and fans invading their privacy. What with prudent investments and his salary as a pop critic at the newspaper, he was quite comfortable with his flat in London and cottage by the sea in Torbay—comfortable, yes, but rather lonely.

The lift jolted to a stop and snapped him back into the present as a medical technician pushing a device on a cart entered through the back door while Ian departed the front. To learn anything about Colton's condition, he realized he would have to identify the man's daughter, a simple enough task for a devotee of Sherlock Holmes. He was suddenly reminded that as a member of the London chapter of the "Baker Street Irregulars," who met every year on Holmes' birthday in early January, he would soon be on his way to an inn in upstate New York to join the "Sherlockians," as they were known in the States, at their celebration of the great detective's birth. As luck would have it, the resort would also be the site of the American segment of the filmed debate over the authorship question if it would only go forward after Dr. Colton's stroke. He'd been told that some of the Sherlockians were debate participants. How sad, he mused, that poor Dr. Colton would not be going.

He entered the room and spotted a couple lounging in two easy chairs reading the *Guardian*. A teen was curled up in the opposite corner on a large, worn sofa listening to a CD player blaring through the headphones. A stalk of purple hair highlighted her perfectly blanched complexion. Ian felt a ripple of revulsion at the sight of a pearl pin poked through her left nostril. He guessed her to be a rebel of nineteen. Surely his long-haired days were never so shocking to others' sensibilities. He'd always felt his father had been upset at him. No real reason. The entire band, mostly from the London suburb of Enfield, was uncharacteristically politically, musically, and personally conservative. During most of their glory days, neither he or any of the members of the "Ghost," had developed significant vices on the whole. They regarded themselves as serious musicians thriving on their talents. Father threw bait from time to time, but only in sporadic fits about his son not having a normal life—usually indicating he felt a lack of control over Ian's destiny. In the face of this criticism, Ian did manage to finish school. He reasoned, we had artistic objectives; we were earnest, prolific artists, not trendy musical exploiters.

A young couple with a child of about two years old was settled on a large davenport facing the center of the C-shaped room. The little boy's mouth gaped as he looked up at Ian and enquired with resolute curiosity, "Are you Bi' Bird?"

Ian cracked a laugh, while the parents quietly laughed and shook their heads. "No, he's a nice, tall man," the mother said. "Say hello, Robert."

"I'm an impediment to modern ceilings and little people alike," Ian replied. Children, though, were rarely intimidated by his size, often delighting in his stature (although this child's choice of characters was unique). Some shorter adults, however, seemed hesitant with him as if intimidating height were all that mattered.

Despite an intellectual bent, he cultivated a distinctive tenderness upon first meeting. His interest in the opposite sex usually included an immediate subconscious evaluation of a woman's height. His late wife had been precisely five feet and eleven inches.

Ian leaned graciously towards the young father. "Have you seen a lady about who appears to be American? I would give you more of a description but I've never met her."

"An American?" The father hesitated. "Oy, yes, the lady who's here caring for her father, the stroke victim. We just met her. She's visiting his room—eh—about twenty minutes or so...." He stopped mid sentence, eyes blinking towards the doorway.

There she stood in a white smock intended for visitors to the critical care floor. Ian turned to introduce himself, feeling compelled to suggest she remove the smock and leave it in the critical care area—until her face transfixed his eyes.

Throughout his life he'd been seized by women with firm gazes. As a teen, he'd been enchanted by such a lady at Brighton Beach one early spring day while on family holiday with his parents. She was the sort who dared dive into frigid water and swim with abandon and independence, long, graceful arms and legs glistening, but who maintained a firmness of eye like his mother's while knitting. In that first encounter so long ago, aged sixteen and never having been with a girl or woman, he'd realized she had to be in her early twenties. While standing at the checkout desk, he'd overheard the bellhop relate to a friend, "That bird's from Seattle...with the American Foreign Service... the embassy in London." Later he'd encountered such an attitude, a fix in gaze from such a silky being in his late wife Gaye, which accounted for his initial strong attraction to her eight years ago.

The woman before him radiated the same engaging warmth that only intensified as he approached her. She was tall with supple legs solid beneath a simple brown dress. Her black hair was bouncing and dry—rather straight in the '60s style Ian always referred to as "pub wench" back in those chauvinistic times. Now he recognized it as nonaffected, natural hair.

She gazed at him with brown, intense eyes, and pupils surrounded by milky curlicues like in a kaleidoscope as he threw a jittery hand towards her. The enchanting contrast of insouciance and firmness in one face disarmed him, made him as nervous as one might be around a celebrity or someone greatly admired. She was enchantingly dark-skinned, much darker than her fair-skinned father, in her late-thirties, he supposed, and could have been a victim of men solely intent on conquest. How he loathed such predators, especially since his wife's death. Ian had never been that sort. But her calm, fixed eyes met his in a way making him think that he discerned a tolerance lacking in her father's mental and emotional machinery.

"Hello. I'm Ian Scarborough, a friend of your father's. I was a partner on the panel with him yesterday. I do hope he's improving. How is he?"

"I'm Veronica Colton." A lovely smile only added to her openness, her insouciance. "My father has spoken so highly of you, but I'm most familiar with your music. I must say I've enjoyed it. It...it's an honor to meet you. Yes. Just left him. He's doing somewhat better. He is moving out of intensive care, though he's still unconscious. Oh...I'm still wearing my smock." She began to remove it.

"We'll return it. Is he...?"

"He's still in a coma," she said as she removed the smock and Ian gently grabbed for a sleeve. "The doctors operated this afternoon and the clot seems to be dissolving. It's at the base of the cerebellum. He's paralyzed from the waist down, and from time to time, mumbling very unintelligible, odd stuff. They don't expect him to come out of it soon, and well, he could go either way at any time."

"When did you arrive?"

"Late this morning. After I got the word from my aunt, I caught a flight out of Atlanta late yesterday evening. My aunt is spending the year in London and she picked me up at Heathrow. I'm staying with her so I took a small nap before coming over. It's been insane."

"I can only imagine," Ian said. "Where does auntie live?"

"She rents a flat on Stourcliffe Close near the Marble Arch... teaches private voice lessons to male tenors. She said I could stay with her as long as is necessary. I was planning on coming over to visit her and my father in two days anyway."

"You need a break. Would you like to go for a cup of tea?"

"I'd be delighted."

Absentmindedly, she discarded the smock on the divan and preceded Ian out the door.

"How do you make your living?" He recalled that Americans liked to start the "getting-to-know-you" conversation with this question.

"I'm a speech writer for a senator from Tennessee. I'm very committed to his cause," she said, jerking her head erect. "The cause of keeping progressivism alive."

"My father's a Tory MP and, alas," Ian smiled, "I'm also a conservative, though he and I don't get on so well." Ian gulped, suddenly wishing he'd not brought up his father or their politics.

"My father has been totally apolitical. We've had so little in common except our love of writing." She paused. "But I do love him so."

"Your father is an extraordinary man. I've been mesmerized by his work. It's the most startling collection of circumstantial evidence I've ever encountered on any historical question. I've spent many an absorbing hour with my nose buried in his book or some of the other research. I am, as he calls me..."

"A member of the `revisionist cabal,'" she answered.

"Yes. His favorite expression."

They smiled at each other as they arrived at the counter and he poured a cup of tea. She opted for a soda. They gathered chairs seemingly scattered after a busy breakfast and placed two around a porcelain table in the center of the room.

"I've been obsessed with the Seventeenth Earl of Oxford as the author. The issue is done and dusted as for me. Shakespeare was not the man for it. The evidence is clear."

"Yes. The Stratford grain dealer seems to be a nonperson, doesn't he?" she said.

"I don't know what to make of him if he was not a fraud forced on history by Lord Burghley, the Queen, and the times."

"How can you be a good Tory if you, as a Brit, are in league with my father on such an issue, so out of step with tradition?"

"I'm interested in exposing the truth instead of preserving myths." He grinned and raised his eyebrows in mock defiance of her stereotype. "We're in touch with reality." His lips pursed in gravity, ordaining a shift away from politics. "Your father heads my thoughts and prayers."

"Good for you. I'm not totally encouraged, though, at this point. The doctors aren't saying much," she said. She smiled faintly and punched him gently on his shoulder. "We may need a tall, striking Tory from the establishment."

At her touch, Ian felt warm and slight embarrassment as he blushed and thought, how do I compose myself? Some intellectual banter, maybe. "Those fast and loose with history are not conservatives. Oxfordians are the antidisestablishmentarians." He raised his eyelids provocatively, half humourously, half seriously. He couldn't quite gauge how she was taking her father's condition. She must be as strong as she appeared.

"I've loved your music. The *Fishing For Lost Wishes* album alone was monumental, a blockbuster."

The back of his neck tweaked in a spontaneous shiver of delight at her expression of admiration. He knew she noticed the sudden giddy tremble.

"Ian." From behind them a deep voice erupted. "I have been on the twelfth floor where some parents reported I may expect to find you here looking the part of a big bird. I hope I'm not interrupting."

"Ah, Arthur. Not at all. Please join us." Ian rose and motioned towards the chair to his left at the table. "Admiral Arthur Sinclair, Dr. Colton's only and lovely offspring—Veronica Colton."

"Enchanted." He leaned close to her as he pumped her hand once. "I'm praying to the Almighty God that He'll steer your father's dory through perilous straits."

"Thanks. My father has talked so favourably about you. Thanks for phoning my aunt. She found me in Knoxville. I was able to catch a plane within two hours."

"Right," the old man said. Ian noticed his beard and hair was windblown in contrast to his neatness from the previous evening. "I've always adored your father. What a marvelous bit of research in taking on the whole rotten establishment with their rubbish—`Shakespeare would have,' `this is how it might have looked,' `here is where he could have.' The penultimate in snobbery...a veritable circumbendibus of self-serving sophistry." The Admiral mimicked the opposition by emphasizing the sibilant, alliterative S in a higher pitch, with a quick twitch of his nose and some bobs of his head. "The Stratfordians are a disgrace to honest scholarship. Even they admit they have a weak case in spite of their continued pedantry. Can't they understand it's a historical question, not a matter for literary nabobs? Your father is their complete antithesis. He's so frank and open, and he makes friends so easily. It's why, besides his penchant for detail, he was able to engage so much help among librarians and vicars and bureaucrats along the way."

"Thanks. You're right." Veronica Colton laughed at his parroting the ways of the enemy. "You are obviously cut from the same cloth. You see through them." The admiral gazed brightly into the expressive warmth of her face, even at this adverse time.

"I do so hope he pulls out of this," the admiral said. "May I fetch you another drink?"

"Yes, please. Coke."

"I'll join you in another tea," Ian said. He rose, as did the admiral. Ian hated to leave Veronica for a minute but had to corner his friend. "Veronica, I just need a quick word with Arthur."

The two men strolled towards the counter for the refills. "I have exciting news," the admiral confided, winking an eye framed by massive crow's feet surrounded by sunspots. "The shoot will be rescheduled for ten days from now, right after the New York venue, so we may yet make the spring deadline for the two-hour show. London will now be part two instead of part one."

"Brilliant."

The retired admiral softened his expression and sniffed humbly. "You are quite smitten with her, aren't you?"

"So, you noticed as always.... Well, so are you. You and I have never been able to disguise our feelings from each other."

"I believe she fancies you."

"Arthur, if you don't mind my asking," Ian said, "you wrote on a note card Colton had at the podium, 'P helps. Try tomorrow.'"

Ian observed the reddest face ever he'd seen on his friend. The admiral shook his head and paused at a rare, momentary loss of words. His eyes darted around the cafeteria. "Don't breathe a word. Acting as a locum for his doctor, he confided to me his stage fright at his seventy-eight years, which manifests itself usually on the front of his trousers. I'm eighty-two and I've never had the problem, touch wood. I wrote him a little reminder while we went over his notes merely to remind him go to the loo before the cue. Ian, I'm so glad you asked me now, away from that lovely creature over there." He motioned towards Veronica.

"Right," Ian said. "Right."

Chapter Six

To be awakened by a phone call at half of seven in the a.m. was not Ian's idea of the way to begin a Saturday morning.

"What the deuce!" he barked into the phone as he rolled to the night table by his king-size bed in his flat in Abercrombie Street by Battersea Park Road. A fearsome clutter of newspapers, books, sheet music, and CDs surrounded the bed as Ian nearly stepped on the CDs. The crisp voice on the phone was that of his editor at the newspaper—Bradbury Vines.

"Ian, sorry, you must race over to Stratford-Upon-Avon. The local authorities are holding a noon press conference at the police station. It appears someone broke into the Trinity Church last night and shattered a portion of Shakespeare's monument."

"Really?" Ian almost dropped the receiver. "My editorial must have inspired someone to explore the situation a bit further."

"I rather imagine that they would've planned a bit more in advance, although it was a provocative piece." Ian thought he detected a crackling hint of mocking laughter. He had grown weary of being in the pith and marrow of Vines's bad books.

"So, may I write the story?" Ian pricked up his ears since he'd rarely written anything other than features outside of his reviews. He enthusiastically jiggled his legs under the sheets, awaiting the "yes" he longed to hear.

"I know you don't cover hard news stories but this one is spot on your bailiwick. Oh yes, take photos. Do you have a camera?"

"Yes. No problem."

"Good luck. Do phone or e-mail the story this afternoon. Cheers."

He had barely applied two dollops of shaving cream and the phone rang again. "What the..." he answered again. It was the admiral—the bothersome old sweat.

"Ian, I'm off to Stratford this morning to survey the damage. Heard about the break-in, I take it?"

"Yes, Vines rang me about two minutes ago." He no longer drove anywhere and was about to check train schedules. "I presume you're inviting me along."

"Yes, well... I'll be over in about a half hour."

"You'll be picking up a reporter on this story," Ian said.

"Oh...who's going with us?" Ian had to pull the phone receiver away from the booming voice. "Not that bugger Thomas or his dear friend Unwin."

"Not quite." Ian, knowing his old friend's contempt for most of modern journalists, and encouraged by attacks on two of the slimiest known reporters, virtually sang his words. "Vines trusts yours truly on this one. He must be trying to be fair to me."

"I'd doubt that. He's not a fair man. I've never trusted him at all, except for his recent help." He barked, "Well, that's good enough though! I'll see you in a half hour."

The day was cold but sunny, a contrast to the recent dreary mists and rains that had hung over the Midlands and London all week. Ian tossed his grey cord jacket over the seat and slid his laptop attaché between his legs as he crawled into the admiral's new midnight blue Porsche. The two men discussed a variety of topics, but Ian had prepared a strategy for the last bit near Stratford.

"Do you mind being prefect while I prep for the upcoming debate in the US?" Ian needed to test his memory. Possessing a mind full of music from Dowland to present, and a capacity to repeat riffs after hearing them only once or twice, Ian still needed his old friend's help.

"You're so like your father. Photographic memory. But how he's been effective in his seat in Parliament with his cool personality, I'll never know."

"He's highly organized," Ian said, thinking back to his own recent lost cheques, a yearly event—last time to a petty criminal who forged signatures on numerous others before being nicked. "I'm not so much."

"Yes, you have the habit of losing clothing articles. How many overcoats have you left in the Samuel Smith pub in the Strand?" The admiral's eyes twinkled. "Or brollies?"

"Let's not count the combs, ties, belts, or rings. My command of the material in this attaché is what matters."

Included in the attaché was a ring-book containing pages of data for the debate to be held in the States in the days immediately ahead. Some of the material had been intended for the aborted television taping at which Dr. Colton suffered his stroke.

"I'm quite familiar with those works, but no, you've got the title, the author, and our man's contribution, all in," the admiral said. "Whilst I drive, allow me to test you on them if you need to memorize them for debate? I'll mind the road carefully if you'll set the notes here."

"Brilliant. As you give me the book title from this list," Ian said as he set the pad on the gearbox housing of the low-seated car, "I'll tell you everything I know about it. Can you manage to see them safely?" The admiral nodded. The page in Ian's hand was titled "Arts Patronage." Ian thought it an appropriate heading for a young earl whose father had maintained his own troupe of players and regularly performed in the Banquet Hall at Hedingham Castle. Naturally, such a culture-laden background had influenced young Edward, who had evinced an early writing talent. Upon his graduation from

Cambridge University, there appears a dedication to Edward by his uncle, Arthur Golding, in *The Histories of Trogus Pompeius*. Edward, at fourteen, is in league with Golding, especially in translating Ovid's *Metamorphoses* (often cited as a source for Shakespeare's plays). In 1567, Edward, at seventeen, was admitted to law at Gray's Inn as the second installment of the Ovid work is published.

"*The Histories of Trogus Pompeius* and the translation of *Metamorphoses*." Ian spoke automatically, absorbed in rigid concentration, and staring blankly into the windscreen.

"Of course you know these intimately. There's no reason for us to dwell on the importance of those, considering that even all diligent Stratfordians agree that Will was well versed in Ovid." The admiral pointed to the top entry on Golding. "In Oxford's case, thanks to a demanding uncle."

"What better proof he was so well versed than if we assume it was Oxford," Ian said. "No doubt, if they'd lived on, his other poet-uncles, the earls of Surrey and Sheffield, would have been similarly supportive of his talents. Two years after the Ovid translation, Thomas Underdowne publishes *Aethiopian Historie* with a dedication to Oxford. In...uh...1572, Oxford appears in Bartholomew Clerke's, his Latin tutor, no less, Latin translation of Castiglione's *Il Cortegiano, the Courtier*, writing the preface in perfect Latin. The following year Golding publishes *Calvin's Version of the Psalms of David* with a dedication to Oxford. Thomas Twyne then repeats this kindness also in *Breviary of Britain*."

"You clearly don't need my assistance. How about the title *Cardanus Comfort*?"

"The same year, 1573, the earl sponsored and wrote a preface to a translation of *Cardanus Comfort* by Thomas Bedingfield, the book which one Shakespearian scholar referred to as 'Hamlet's book,' since whole passages are sources for Hamlet's soliloquy, according to him a bang on connection. Also that year, we believe that *A Hundredth Sundrie Flowres* is edited and largely written by Edward de Vere."

"Right. Here's small beer. *The Paradyse of Daintie Devices*."

"By the time he returns from his long stay in Europe in 1576, several of his poems appear in *The Paradyse of Daintie Devices*, signed characteristically `E. O.' His juvenilia."

"Well done." The admiral looked at the notes before adjusting the heater. "*The Staffe of Christian Faith*."

"In 1577, the next year, the record shows *The Staffe of Christian Faith* by John Brooke is published with a dedication to Edward de Vere."

"Next item is the Queen's Progress in Essex," said Admiral Sinclair. "Tell us of Harvey."

"Gabriel Harvey, in the presence of the Queen and Court, specifically singles out de Vere as a prolific poet and toasts him that July evening in 1578. 'Thy countenance shakes a speare!' Double entendre, it was. While he publicly praised the earl's literary achievements, Harvey was spurned for the position of private secretary to the earl, and jealous and angry, was urging him to forsake the pen for the sword by such a double-edged admonition. Thus the pseudonym, later to be transferred to one merchant trader from Stratford. 'Thine eyes flash fire,' Harvey said. At that point the earl is anointed the chief among the Euphuist faction of poets—a group dedicated to refining the English language by combining scholarly technique with imagery and elegance of expression. While John Lyly, the man who got the secretary position, is author of *Euphues: the Anatomy of Wit*, Oxford was midwife to the publishing event. In 1579, or was it 1580, I'm not quite so handy with dates, Lyly becomes Oxford's secretary and he dedicates *Euphues and His England* to his master. Whatever the year, *Mirror of Mutabilitie* is dedicated to Oxford, published by Anthony Munday.

"It was 1579. And what did Munday also publish the following year?"

"Munday's *Zepatto* is published the following year featuring a dedication once again clearly identifying Oxford as Euphues."

"Try that title again, please," the admiral admonished through tight lips, mocking a much-imitated headmaster from a reckless and wanton matriculation at Harrow.

"*Zepaullo*?" Ian blinked.

"*Zelauto*." The admiral spoke evenly.

"*Zelauto*, like a `zealous auto.' A portmanteau, no doubt."

"So that's how you do it."

"Also mnemonics."

"What did Harvey publish the next year in praise of his would-be boss?" the admiral interrupted after consulting the notebook with a passing squint.

"That same year, yes, it was 1580, Oxford is caricatured as the `Italianate Englishman' but highly praised as `peerless in England' and without equal as `discourse for tongue' in the publication of *Speculum Tuscanismi* by Harvey."

"Si, tres excellent, mon etudiant," said Sinclair. "What an utterly frustrating relationship for Harvey, who taught him at university. How now of Thomas Watson?"

"Elementary. In 1582, Thomas Watson's *Hekatompathia* is released with yet another dedication and some evidence that Oxford may have made a contribution to the book. In 1584, Robert Greene writes *Greene's Card of Fancy*, published with another dedication to the earl of Oxford. This the same Greene who attacked Shakespeare as an "upstart crow" owning a "tiger's heart wrapped in a player's hide."

"A borrowed line from *Henry VI, Part III*," interjected the Admiral. "Greene was not green of Oxford though, given the dedication. Henry Chettle probably wrote it."

"Yes. That same year John Soowthern's *Pandora* is published containing verse by Elizabeth, Oxford's wife's poem 'Epitaphes,' and an ode celebrating his own life. If you would be so kind, spell Epitaphes. Oh, I'll check it since you're driving."

But the admiral found the notation in Ian's highly legible hand. "No problem here. E-p-i-t-a-p-h-e-s."

"Right."

"Right. *The English Secretary*."

"*The English Secretary*, by Angel Day, was published in 1586 with yet another dedication hailing Oxford as one who from `infancy' had been `most sacred to the Muses.' William Webbe in *A Discourse of English Poetry* called Oxford `most excellent' among Court poets. In 1588, *Palmerin d'Oliva* is published with, again, a dedication and two other publications by Munday."

"Hmmm, let me check that bit of data. Yes, that's `*ever* sacred to the Muses' and Munday published four, not two works. Ian, impressive. But can you do it on camera, dear boy?" He laughed and coughed simultaneously. "*The Arte of English Poesie*."

"*The Arte of English Poesie* by George Puttenham had a most striking passage upon publication in 1589. `And in her Majesty's time that now is sprung up another crew of Courtly makers (that is, poets), Noblemen and Gentlemen of Her Majesty's own servants, who have written excellently well as it would appear if their doings could be found out and made public with the rest, of which number is first that noble gentleman Edward, Earl of Oxford.'"

"Brilliant. Do omit the parenthetical statement. I assume that's what it constitutes, describing `makers' as `poets.' Refrain from rote regurgitation." He playfully trilled the Rs and shook his red face in mock pedantry, singing, "The rain in Spain falls mainly on the plain."

Ian laughed at the spontaneous, infectious roll of the admiral's voice, incapable of remotely hitting the notes. "You sang. 'Refrain, it's painful on the brain,'" he rejoined tunefully.

"Well, speaking of plains and songs, how about *Playn Song*?" The admiral was nonplused at Ian's puns, anxious with his own.

"In 1591, John Farmer published *Playn Song* with yet another dedication. Seven years later he is mentioned in *Palladis Tamia* by Francis Meres as among those `best for comedy.' This is the same publication in which Shakespeare is briefly mentioned."

The admiral raised a finger. "Doesn't that prove they were two different people?"

"They were perceived that way. Oxford already had a reputation for comedy by the time the decision was made to disguise his future works under the name of Shakespeare. That name was used in print for the first time in 1593, with the publication of *Venus and Adonis*, so by 1598 it was quite natural for anyone who wasn't personally involved in the cover-up to think they really were two different people—Oxford, the purveyor of riotous comedies, and Shakespeare, the poet who by that time was identified with some fairly serious, and indeed, bloodthirsty tragedies.

"The same thing happens today. Many writers of one type of work use a pseudonym for a different type of work, or one they consider inferior to their most important work. Michael Crichton, for example, published several books under the name John Lange. The Stratemeyer Syndicate, created by Edward Stratemeyer, produced an immense number of books in series under *The Bobsey Twins*, *The Hardy Boys*, and *The Nancy Drew* mysteries. He himself wrote some of these, but more often sketched out the stories and hired others to write them. I can cite other examples as well."

"Yes. Well done. Now, what about John Farmer?"

"In 1599, Farmer describes Oxford in a dedication as one who has `overgone' most professionals in music."

"And in 1604?"

"Edward de Vere dies in 1604, presumably of the plague."

Ian completed his mostly trance-like reverie of literary panegyric as they approached the outskirts of the birthplace of William Shakspeare.

"I've probably omitted a few publications," the admiral said, "and look at the titles by the man from Stratford appearing earlier with unusual names—*A Historie of Ariodante and Genevora* was the first version of *Much Ado About Nothing*. But let's take a break," he bellowed, "and before we do, let's remember it's often the small arrows that make an enormous impact. Barrister Strawbridge is so organized and succinct when he points out that Oxford borrowed money 'crowns' while in Italy from Baptista Nigrone of Venice and 'crowns' from Pasquino Spinola in Padua. Conflating the two names we have Baptista Minola, Katherine's father from Padua in *The Taming of the Shrew*. Spot on! If the Stratfordians could make such an argument, they'd be uncorking the bubbly."

"Yes, the same with the Gad's Hill connection of Oxford as with Prince Hal's band of troublemakers, or the use of canals connecting cities in Italy by boat as in Oxford's Italian travels that appears in the Italian settings baffling the Stratfordians but seen at least, actually traveled at best, by our man," Ian replied. "By the way, is Strawbridge joining me in New York for the debate there?"

"He has legal work in Hong Kong and should arrive the day after you get there. For now, he's the only other Englishman. There will be an American on the panel with you to replace Colton, but we don't know who it is as yet."

Ian closed the notebook and swept it into his attaché. They spent the remainder of time discussing various personalities in the world of London journalism until the last bit of the drive when the admiral broached his favorite topic.

"I do detect a certain attraction between you and Veronica," he said as they approached the bridge. "Smashing lady, if I may say so."

Ian rarely discussed his romantic life with anyone, but the closest he would come to such a discussion was with Admiral Sinclair. With less than a minute or so left for discussion, he knew the matter would probably come up again upon the return trip. Ian decided to pivot the conversation. "Dr. Colton mentioned some exciting news he had access to just hours after the debate. What do you know about it?"

The admiral scratched his head. "Little. He told me he might be on to something possibly big and he'd tell me. I hope he emerges from the coma so we'll know."

"Had he told anyone else?"

"Not that I'm aware of."

"Would he have told his daughter by any chance?"

"Don't know." He shifted again in his seat and adjusted his side mirror. "What a lovely woman."

"Yes," Ian agreed. "She's a compelling woman—one who's made her own mark in the world without the particular help of her father. An engaging personality."

Ian knew the admiral would go only so much further when he heard him grunt nervously, as if unsure of where to take the conversation. "She's most dedicated to her father nonetheless." The old man sighed. "Today's woman is fiercely independent, yet so bloody feminine. I wish I were young again."

"One can always remember the good times." Ian shifted in his seat. "I've been under roaring torture since the loss of my wife and child. Veronica's the first woman I've met who's taken my mind away from that dreadful day."

"You *will* finally get over it, Ian. You will, I know." The old man's voice cracked. "God wills it."

"Thanks."

The Porsche whizzed on the Clopton Bridge over the River Avon as Ian glanced to his left at the Royal Shakespeare Theatre. A late morning crawl of visitors was anxious to purchase the remaining tickets for the evening's performance. They cruised past pubs, shops, and stores in the ubiquitous Tudor design of white plaster framed by brown wood beams. Ian recalled the police station being to the left of the town square up ahead past the post office, and then more tourist shops. They stopped short of the square and he could see further down the street where a small crowd of reporters had gathered. The digital clock on the fascia panel flashed 11:53. The once-busy Rother Street had been renovated recently, no longer open to traffic, so it was necessary to walk three blocks to the station across from a row of two-story houses.

"Ian, it's cold," the admiral said. "Is this briefing going to be held outdoors?"

"No, it appears they're bunched together just inside. Yes, there's a klieg light."

A small crowd of reporters huddled inside the front door of the modern, brick police station. While there were a dozen milling about outside, inside there were some twenty-odd reporters and photographers, and two operators with handheld remote cameras for television.

The Admiral had trouble keeping pace with Ian's long, anxious strides and stumbled on a crack in the walk. "Slower, please."

"Ian," shouted a stoutly built fortyish man in blue jeans and a black leather jacket who held out a hand as he opened the door to the station. "How goes the crit biz, buddy?"

"Very well." He shook the hand of the American reporter who'd told him often he'd been a fan of his music. Usually they ran into each other at lunch bistros in Covent Garden or Leicester Square. Boone Phelps was an investigative news reporter of some renown. Before his London assignment in 1985, he'd been instrumental in uncovering the notorious Flick affair in West Germany, which ruined many prominent SPD and CSU politicians. "Vines woke me up with this story this morning," he said. "Intriguing."

"I agree. I've been to the church and there are yellow police ribbons everywhere. A cop at each door. Won't let me in for pictures. Maybe they'll let us in this afternoon."

"Oh," Ian jerked, a lock of hair straying across his forehead. "I forgot the camera."

"I brought one," said the admiral. "It's in the car, but will they let us in the church?"

"Probably. Thank you. We'll retrieve it afterwards. The conference is beginning, I think. Sorry, Boone. Where are my manners? Meet Admiral Sinclair. Admiral, Boone Phelps, a reporter's reporter from the *International Herald Tribune*."

"Delighted." The admiral politely shook the man's cold hand then stepped back gingerly.

"Yes." Ian held the door open for the admiral. "After this, let's go for some toke."

"Yes." The admiral smiled. "There's a great pub near the theatres. The Dirty Duck."

A short man with dark hair and a mustache, accompanied by the chief inspector, who was taller and middle-aged silver, stepped into the circle of press. Awkwardly, they stood motionless in front of a glass-encased enclosure that looked as though it served as a reception area. Microphones trailed into the enclosure from the counter, and the cameras took on angles through the only gap between the glass that was a horizontal door one could lift as it bridged the counters.

"I'm Michael Emory, spelled E-m-o-r-y, from the Shakespeare Birthplace Trust, and after a brief statement by the chief inspector, we'll take questions for about twenty minutes. May I introduce the chief inspector, Mr. Les Morton."

"Thank you, Dr. Emory. It seems there was a surreptitious entry sometime during the night, most likely while choir rehearsal was in progress and the main door was unlocked. They apparently remained hidden until the choir vacated and the unknown number of intruders—we surmise at least two—achieved the initial stages of their purpose in removing the bust of William Shakespeare. Evidently, they penetrated several areas within the bust and within the wall area below the bust. We are most certain...most certain of this aspect—they found nothing in the area because it is all quite solid and contains nothing except concrete and stone mass. Obviously, they ignored other valuables more pedestrian burglars would have nicked. They were extraordinarily tidy. After their search they even replaced some chunks of stone and concrete."

A murmur circulated through the crowd and a few reporters shook their heads. "Bespoke yobbos," one them yelled to no one in particular and some laughter percolated.

"We have no suspects. The matter was reported this morning after I spotted the main church door open while passing by on the way to this office. I frequently pass by the church. We're investigating still but we don't expect to find any significant clues. The perpetrators of this serious crime were quite thorough and professional. Uh, we'll make sure the experts can properly restore the monument to its original form. I'm told...they tell me the damage is not substantial, and indeed the stonemasons shall restore it so there's not even a trace of damage. Now for your questions." The officer swept a finger towards the gathering.

"When will we be allowed to take photographs of the scene? I just returned from there and you have the whole area under wraps," said a young stringer with the *Manchester Guardian*.

"My regrets," Chief Morton said, shifting a foot. "The scene is under close investigation and can't be accessed."

"It is a sensitive area, you see," Dr. Emory said. "The police must have total focus getting to the bottom of this matter. They can't have interruptions or distractions."

The young man persisted immediately. "We merely need photos if only from a healthy distance within the church. Would that so much as interfere?"

"Sorry, Miles," Morton interrupted. "We've a proper job to do."

"Do you not have a single clue as to a suspect?" inquired a young female reporter from Coventry.

"No. As we speak, we've had absolutely no clues. There are simply no leads. The neighbors noticed nothing. The church has been mostly closed for the last few days for the final renovation of the organ. And the vicar has been north visiting with his sick mother." Chief Morton shifted his feet again impatiently as he spoke. Sweat formed on his forehead and upper lip as the television lights warmed the small, crowded station anteroom. "The only activity was the choir rehearsal as I related to you a moment ago."

Phelps shouted, "How did the culprits gain access during the choir rehearsal?"

"The north inner door facing this direction, the main entrance, is normally left open during rehearsal. This inner door—the smaller portion of the great door, the one with the sanctuary ring—well, the choir members must be free to come and go as they please. The choir practices in the section where Lord Mayor Clopton is buried...a section largely sealed from view by walls and a separate door. Evidently, the miscreants merely sought a hiding place, and then emerged to do their deeds after the last choir member had left the church. Since the church is relatively isolated, they could then work while the town slept."

Ian had been inside the church slightly over a year ago and recalled the area precisely. Indeed, it would have been easy to hide if choir members were rehearsing in the section described. "Inspector, I'd be curious as to how you've established beyond doubt that nothing was nicked when it can't be known with certainty whether or not something, anything, was located, even secured, within the solid structure or within the bust and the stone plinth? Even a small item."

Some reporters issued a light ripple of laughter and a couple of nervous coughs. "Yeah," Phelps blurted. "You aren't too interested in why they'd pass up Clopton's halberd."

Motionless, Emory replied, "We can only surmise nothing was in the monument in the first place because pieces fit back well, and there was no evidence whatsoever of anything having fitted within the structure before. It was manifestly clear nothing was there to find, so nothing was nicked."

"But you said the area hasn't been reconstructed yet. Is it?" the pesky old man from the *London Observer* asked. "Did they try to break into the tombs on the floor beneath the monument?"

"No, to both questions," Chief Morton answered curtly.

Emory inched forward in reaction to his partner's impatience and then immediately joined in. "There was absolutely no indication of tampering with the tombs. We have the impression they were searching solely for some kind of artifacts or valuables. Any search within the tombs would have most certainly disturbed the neighbors since the tombs are buried some fifteen feet below the surface of the floor requiring extensive excavation. Besides, it's widely known that the tombs have been heavily flooded, and possibly drained, after seepage from the Avon rising through the years."

Ian saw Phelps, inimitable master of intimidation, lurch forward, virtually toppling the curmudgeon from the *Observer*. "Uh...your investigative team, Chief Inspector, has done a very inadequate job of detecting any clues. *You* personally had to discover and report the break-in. You should at least allow one reporter in with a camera, totally supervised, for about a half hour. And I'll volunteer. I'd like just a few shots of the destruction before it's reconstructed."

Other press members moaned disdainfully. All knew Phelps wanted exclusivity; most never expected anything less from him. Some laughed at his predictable behavior. "How bloody generous," one shouted. Ian saw Phelps lean forward impetuously, as though he fully expected to be appointed on the spot for the task only he could fulfill.

But Inspector Morton, unaccustomed to the press, apparently misread the disgruntlement in the room as being directed not towards Phelps, but towards him. Tiny sweat beads intensified on his forehead. A crimson flush contorted his earlier pleasant, silver-haired, statesmanlike demeanor to a slightly comical visage, complete with red bulbous nose. "See here. We've a serious investigation going here. I don't want it interrupted," he commanded.

"What are you hiding?" Phelps persisted, his bald head glistening from the klieg lights.

"We're hiding nothing. Nothing was found. There's considerable official work to be done. We shall not be distracted at this time."

Emory held up his palms to halt the proceeding and inched forward to speak a final time. "If you wish to come back in a few days, then ring me and I'll inform you as to when the church will be open for the public once again. I'll also keep you appraised of any developments the inspector may have for you." Emory paused. "Ladies and gentlemen, I believe we've answered all the questions and the matter is closed except for any information which might be discovered in the ongoing thorough investigation. We hope to nick these culprits shortly for they've certainly violated a treasured national shrine. You may reach me at the number printed on these cards after 9:00 a.m. any day this week for further enquiries." He stepped through the crowd and laid his business cards on the counter. Morton shuffled behind him.

The two hosts disappeared through a door behind the glass counter into the recesses of the station. The press corps, clearly disgruntled over an unfulfilling conference, rumbled complaints across the walls of the anteroom. Each pinched a business card from the stack on the counter below the plexiglass partition, then left.

Ian whispered to the admiral, "Something's amiss and it's not merely the bust of William Shakespeare."

"Yep." Phelps brusquely lifted his large black eyebrows. "This conundrum begs a solution. You thinking what I'm thinking?"

"There was no break-in?" The admiral was incapable of a whisper. Ian raised a cautionary finger to his lips.

"Off we go..." Ian pointed to the queue ahead, again placing a finger to his lips. He cast a furtive look at both comrades. Phelps smiled at the admiral's amusement in Ian's earnest face. They stepped off the walk onto the grass near an elm.

"Absolutely," Ian shrilled in whisper. "This is a clannish, conservative town. A chief inspector conveniently discovers the break-in, erects barricades, and orders several minions to guard the entrances to the church."

"You betcha," Phelps interjected as he grabbed Ian's wrist. "Believe me, there are four of those Nazis over there guarding the place. I'll wager that not a one of them, no one in this town, has been in there with the possible exception of the chief inspector and Emory. And tomorrow, they'll have only one guard."

"Emory's the mastermind, so he insists they have this bloody press briefing to announce to the world that there's been an intrusion" Ian said, "and nothing stolen. It's a charade."

"Since nothing's nicked, it pre-empts anyone with a grain of curiosity from ever attempting the real thing," the admiral scoffed.

"Right. As if they're not interested in the least at apprehending suspects. They were bloody defensive. The only sense of urgency they displayed was to end the briefing," Ian said.

"Ian, by this point in time next week we'll know nothing more than we know now unless we gain some kind of access to the church ourselves, or talk to someone who knows something and is willing to talk," Phelps said. "A bricklayer or some cop."

"Well...what do you say we go to the Dirty Duck and lay a scheme over a Flowers and a meat pie," suggested the admiral.

A theatre pub, the Duck held the remnants of a lunch crowd on stools at round wood tables. One such table easily accommodated the three men across from a fireplace with gently crackling coals warming the cozy rectangular room. Cluttered walls of autographed photos of Shakespearian actors—some now or always famous, and some not—brightened the room. Seven American teenagers were scattered in the large booth forged into the bay window area overlooking the Avon and within sight of the Royal Shakespeare Theatre. They were unsuccessfully arguing with the publican over whether they were permitted to play cards. Phelps laughed. Scarborough shook his head ruefully as a couple in the opposite corner looked at the three men and the woman whined, "It's so harmless. Why should he bother? They're mere children."

"Authority is on his side, unfortunately," the admiral said.

"We Americans must make adjustments when abroad," Phelps said. "I can't say I've always obeyed the rules."

"So I've heard," the admiral scoffed, then smiled politely.

Indignantly, the youngsters hastily gathered their paraphernalia and left.

The two Brits ordered chicken pies and two Flowers bitters. Phelps ordered a corned beef sandwich and ale.

Admiral Sinclair pointed to his favorite photo, located just above the fireplace. The men could barely make out the inscription scrawled across the photo of a bearded character actor of some fame posed, hand clasped over his forehead, with a look of convincing perplexity. It read in anachronistic desperation, "I can't recall being in here, much less signing this photo." Often the establishment closed to private parties in a thespians' honor after an evening's challenging performance. Ian had been to a raucous one here years ago with the late Jeremy Brett.

"I've decided to stay the weekend at this bed and breakfast I know here and phone a few masons and bricklayers, snoop around the church...you know, see if I can find anything," Phelps said.

"I have the rest of the afternoon before I must return. I can help ring a few lapidaries and try to track down the church gardener or some of the volunteers. I recall there being volunteers who provide tours of the church," Ian said, remembering his visit over a year ago to the church. "Also, I recall there was a similar incident, some damage to the monument, probably a prank, over twenty years ago. I noticed some cracks and ripples in the plinth while there."

The admiral nodded at their suggestions. "And I've made a decent contact with one of the merchants here—he and his lovely wife and I frequently dine at one of the curry establishments here. I might take them out tonight and see if they know someone in the constabulary I should chat with," he said, rising to look for the condiments.

"I should phone in my story to the paper soon," Ian said as Admiral Sinclair delivered his steaming pie. "The deadline approaches. Why don't you visit your friend while I'm writing and giving London a tinkle?"

"You must be interested in returning to the hospital." The admiral relaxed his face muscles with a knowing nod and poked his fork in the center of his own pie.

"Yes." Ian coyly nodded his head.

"It's luuuv." The admiral attempted a whisper at Phelps while raining salt onto his pie.

"At a hospital?" Phelps raised his voice incredulously. "Patient or nurse?"

"Not a sister, a daughter," the admiral said, then sneezed over his shoulder and removed his handkerchief. "The daughter of Dr. Tyler Colton, a friend of mine."

"Oh yeah, the one who wrote the book...collapsed at the Q.E. II. I read about it in one of the papers, saw the picture." Phelps tugged Ian's sleeve. "Which hospital is he at?" Ian ignored the question.

"I've met a fascinating lady. She's rather nice. She's alternating caregiver shifts with her Auntie Joan," was all Ian would allow, having instantly recalled the reason for Phelps' transfer from Bonn to London. Too aggressive, undiplomatic. The *Trib* felt he would be tolerated more in England. Abruptly, Ian sipped his Flowers IPA. "I care about Colton, too."

"That's cool." Phelps tapped the table impatiently. "Well, I need to get a scoop, desperately. I fully intend to chop down these trees here until I clear the forest. You can count on it. If you'll come back tomorrow, join me. I'll let you play Watson, Ian."

"Interesting you should mention Watson." The admiral winked and pointed towards Ian. "He's to play Holmes soon."

"Right. Not Holmes, though. Soon I'll be on a flight to your country as I prepare for the second debate in the US this week—actually, now it will be the first debate since the other one was postponed. It's a fortuitous coincidence the debate is being held at the same resort as the gathering of the Holmesians, Sherlockians to the Yanks—and the chief reason Brad Vines approved paying my way—though he knows I would pay my own way nonetheless. `The Giant Rats of Sumatra' is New York's version of the Sherlock Holmes Society of London. Looking forward to it, actually."

"So Vines is paying for it, eh?" Phelps knew the editor reasonably well. "Has he been on your case again?"

"Sort of a piece of string with him of late." Ian drummed his fork gently on the piecrust. "He thinks I'm too refined for reviewing pop music...thinks I'm prejudiced."

"He's become too prickly in his tastes," boomed the admiral. "Too much of an old party. Happens to us all, eventually."

"You will dress up for the Sherlock Holmes thing, won't you?" Phelps asked. "You have the aquiline nose and the quickness of mind...but...nearly six and a half foot tall Holmes..."

"Height can be a distinct advantage, you know," Ian said with a facetious grin. "But they've seen fit to cast me as Moriarty. I'm a villain as well to the Stratfordians."

"Ian." Phelps leaned forward. "Your editorial last week may be the reason for this charade—and something's going to pan out on it. No matter how many people we talk to, there is going to be no one who knows that *nothing* happened in the church. Emory and Morton should really know better, but for some reason they were desperate to have the issue resolved to their own and the world's satisfaction. I'll bet you the entire media in the English-speaking world runs this little story...and I'll bet you it's been staged. Paranoid productions presents, `The *Con*-cocted Caper.'" Phelps shook his head dramatically at his weak pun. "When no crime's committed, no one can possibly know one way or another. Emory, the spin doctor."

Ian pushed away his half-eaten pie. "Yes, but recognize the circumstances as they presented them to us. Can persons with the proper skills successfully remove the bust of the Bard, that monstrously saccharine hoax of an image, and perform strenuous operations with iron tools or electric bits in the middle of the night inside the church? Could they gain access? Did they? Yes, they could. I believe it's possible that it did happen. But I can't believe anyone would attempt it so soon after my editorial, in spite of the so-called inspiration I may have provided. No. I don't trust the inspector and Dr. Emory, or for that matter, any authorities in this town."

"Yes. Possibly it was they who were inspired by the editorial," said the admiral.

"Regardless of how many people we talk to in Stratford," Phelps said, "no one has been in the church except Chief Morton. No one repaired the bust and monument because nothing was damaged. I'd bet my life on it. I'm going to get to the bottom of this one quickly. I'll phone every mason in town...or whatever it takes."

Chapter Seven

Veronica sat alone in the hospital room when her father moaned, causing her to spring up from her unfocused reading. She'd been thinking about the tall Brit she'd met two days before, but now her thoughts turned to her father. Was he in pain? Could he even feel anything? Could he hear? Think? Dream?

"A stuporous state, comatose," the doctor had told her tersely that afternoon. "For now, we're undecided on whether to operate again." In other words, too risky to operate.

Tyler Colton clearly recognized the man before him pacing impatiently across a large room in his grand house north of London, Theobalds House The man had been, according to the examination of Stratfordian scholars and Oxfordians, such as Colton's own impressions after reading Shakespeare, the model for Polonius. ("Towards thy superiors be humble yet generous; with thine equals, familiar yet respective," were Burghley's words. "Be thou familiar but by no means vulgar..." advised Polonius.) Burghley's book was entitled *Certaine Preceptes.*

William Cecil, Lord Burghley, was Elizabeth I's Lord Treasurer—the most powerful individual in sixteenth century England except for, naturally, the Queen. Dr. Colton instantly recognized Burghley-Polonius as he strode thoughtfully to and fro. He was the father-in-law of the Seventeenth Earl of Oxford, but also his most dreadful nemesis.

Colton observed this powerhouse from his safe, secret spot—a face embedded in the painting above the mantle of the treasurer's library. Cecil's long white beard and hair framed a prominent, shiny, bald, egg-shaped head flowing in harmony with a blue felt robe reaching ceremoniously to the floor, noisily dragging along as he strutted peacock-like across the room. His expansive chest thrust forward as if to announce himself as a man of cautious, conservative control; a manipulator; a considerable *avoirdupois* in contrast to his carefully rationed political wracks and administrative thumbscrews. Colton thought of Burghley, not Machiavelli, as the epitome of administrative cunning: how to exert the least degree of political puissance for the maximum effect, and how to conserve the most for future expenditure at a proper time. Burghley confided to his friends that they were rewarded particularly by his actions (whether of his doing or not) anticipating he could call in a favor for its full measure and more; yet, he likewise persuaded his enemies that it was not he who had produced their misery, but if they had only, or could only, comply with his wishes they might be saved from their horrid fate through his good graces and intervention. With the friends, he might have appropriated the credit for himself; with the foes, he probably had been responsible for their misfortune. His methods were hugely successful, not only in the day-to-day execution of the Queen's policies, but in achieving the overriding objectives of her administration as well—including the public image now and forevermore. He would tweak the customs of a changing milieu, and maximize his profits by adding Wednesday to the traditional Friday-required fish for dinner, thereby doubling his own company's sale of fish. He could increase his income with the taking in of royal wards, royalty children without parents, whose enormous fortunes he managed so they dwindled like snowflakes in sunlight and poured into his own estate.

The dynamo coasted across the opposite end of the room reciting, like Polonius in *Hamlet*—as if rehearsing for the role he'd inspired—some maxims from his *Certaine Precepts*, "And that gentleman who sells an acre of land, sells an ounce of credit. For gentility is nothing but ancient riches.... Let thy hospitality be moderate; & according to the means of thy estate, rather plentiful than sparing, but not costly.... Beware of surety for thy best friends. He that payeth another man's debt, seeketh his own decay.... Be sure to keep some great man thy friend, but trouble him not for trifles.... To thyne own self be... My son, please be seated."

"True," answered Robert Cecil, entering the room, a small hunchbacked man but with a large jaw like his father's. He hobbled towards the chair facing a few feet from the small desk where his father maintained a directed, purposeful perambulation.

"Jonson will arrive any minute, I'm sure. Allow me to summarize the situation as I view it. In short, Oxford must be stopped. Jonson can help us immensely, and there's every reason for him to do so. If he resists, I'll take the necessary action. If he issues mild objections, I'm prepared to show him how Oxford is threatening the Queen's very security on the throne. If he tries to recapitulate all the problems Oxford has caused my daughter and me as a conflict of interest, then I'll raise all of the questions concerning how Oxford's plays could embarrass the Court, how he may have been an agent for us in the question over Mary Stuart—but the scoundrel may have tried to play on their side of the question as well. Those plays are great propaganda for now, but are a double-edged sword. Yes, too much revelation of our Court. Also, I've devised a means of resolving this Shake-spear pseudonym if Jonson will cooperate. It would certainly be in his interests to do so for I firmly believe we can successfully make this project work. I do want to convince him, not command him. I want...did you bring a pen?"

"Yes," the dutiful son replied, holding—Colton thought this particularly odd—a Bic pen and a green legal pad on his lap.

"You shall serve as amanuensis to this meeting. I'll show you where the secret papers will reside after we've completed this interview. You'll be the only person privy to this transaction and I demand that you conveniently forget their whereabouts until you take over this office following my passing. Then, and only then, may you safely secure them. Is that understood?"

"Yes, Father." He moved his large head in an obligatory nod.

"As I said, Oxford must be stopped. History must not record his work as his. After all of the opportunities I bestowed upon him, he's seen fit to use his sizable talents against me and my daughter, your sister—his Ophelia. He's scandalous, a mocker," he shouted. "I should have roasted him after he murdered my cook's assistant, or let him die when he was wounded in that street brawl. Instead, I covered up the murder matter for him. Was he grateful? No! His attitude is to lampoon the Queen and me, and you as well—his Laertes! Do dogs bark at you as you walk by? No! He uses euphuistic subterfuge to portray us in a bad light. The Queen herself has remarked that she was quite disturbed, although I can never seem to make her execute on this one unless I emphasize his seeming loyalty to the Catholic cause. It's as if she cares too deeply about him. Oh, I suppose he's loyal to her, but he's nothing but a worthless troublemaker!"

"How are you going to handle him?"

"Several steps. One, we'll pay Oxford an annuity of £1000 a year for the rest of his life. That should enable him to live comfortably, conditioned on the notion he doesn't squander it, and he may revise his current works and carry on with whatever else he may create. He must also surrender any identification with his works, and I may have a front man. Once the works are nearly completed, we, specifically Jonson and the publishers, shall have the option to edit out any spurious attacks on Her Majesty's government. We'll delay the publication except for the few under his pseudonym, which have been published, until after his death.

"Step two, we'll consider granting an annuity of some reasonable amount to one Will Shakspere of Stratford-Upon-Avon, who I'm told has had some ups and downs as a grain trader and has the fortuitous distinction of being relatively unknown outside of his hometown. We pay him an annuity that will allow him to live a quiet life, debt free, for his remaining years, which he has, incidentally, agreed to. We'll bring him to London for a period so we may successfully connect him with the theatre. After his death, we'll erect a monument to him in his church, attribute the works to him, declare him a genius, rework his will to further tie him into the theatre in London for that period of his life, and encourage the upper class to buy the publications after much fanfare. This fellow is younger than Oxford so he should outlive him easily—very important. He lives a quiet, sober life—contrary to Oxford's lifestyle. We may place him in charge of the Globe as a manager, so he can have a few names on contracts. Yes. Yes.... Oh yes, I've summoned and destroyed all other documents that might be traced except for a few contracts tying in Heminge and Condell, you recall they own the Rose and Globe theatres in London, with our daft "Swan of Avon" as we shall refer to him in Jonson's introduction to the publication. Our man Walsingham will continually collect his business papers until he winds it down, and hand them over to me to destroy right there in that fireplace." Burghley paused, turned to the mantle, and glanced at the painting on the wall.

Colton shivered, thinking Burghley may have noticed his eyes moving. Burghley glanced again, and then resumed his discourse.

"It's a clever scheme because Shakspere has agreed to it, and he doesn't have much in the way of public or private records in Stratford. What we've found we've mostly destroyed. There may be copies or more documents of his business records around. I've put Walsingham on it between other assignments. I'm about to tire the poor man, but he seems to thrive on his spy work. This man from Stratford isn't the most perfect man with a name resembling the Shake-spear pseudonym, but it's far enough away from London so I think we can pull it off. If only Harvey would have come up with an easier name in his toasting. There are only about seventy names similar to Shake-dash-spear in the entire kingdom, as best as we can tell."

The lord treasurer continued marching. Colton was nervous, so fearful of being detected.

"Father, will the Court and all the writers who've honored Oxford maintain a conspiracy?"

"Yes. Those that are alive will if Jonson does what he's told. I hope, and you must be aware of this if I die before either Oxford or Shakspere, I pray that you'll take care to enforce this plan. One other point, I'm destroying as much of Oxford's ongoing correspondence as I'm able to locate. That may be a hearty task since there's such a supply of it. Walsingham can't do it all himself, but we've had help. I'm skillfully selecting certain letters while we've had him sequestered in the Tower, and we've had an abundance of correspondence monitored so we know all his friends and can find out if there are copies. We've tried to intercept correspondence to his contacts on the continent, there are many. We anticipate we'll have to do this with his family as well. "

"Yet another reason to lock him and Vavasor in the Tower," Robert Cecil said as he scribbled feverishly. Robert was ever mindful of the painful fact that these were his father's grandchildren and his own nieces.

"Also—" Burghley was interrupted by a servant who opened the large, oak double doors behind Burghley and announced, "Mr. Jonson has arrived."

"Send him in," Burghley said.

The servant stepped aside and the almost best Elizabethan poet-playwright entered.

"Ben Jonson." Burghley greeted him with a swerve of his body and a right hand thrust forward. He graciously pointed to a chair beside Robert. "Please take a seat. It's a delight to have you here. You know my son, Robert, of course."

"Yes, it's a pleasure to grace this chamber again," Jonson said, and pushed a chubby right hand into the son's. "This effulgent chamber sparkles brightly with the radiant genius of two who serve as the flintlock for the conflagration against our dusky-eyed enemies—a tribute to Regina's incomparable judgment in selecting the wisest of men to devise and execute her plan."

Colton shook his shoulders, rolled his eyes in disgust, and then virtually giggled at such bold sycophancy and a well-rehearsed line. Burghley looked in the direction of the painting then returned his gaze to Jonson.

The three men chatted lightly for several minutes about a minor disruption in a performance of Jonson's *Every Man Out of His Humour* at the Rose Theatre on a recent hot night, when an actor who had drunk far too much port the night before, completely interrupted a scene to relieve his stomach. He'd retreated backstage, but his vomiting was so loud that any attentive groundling could hear him. "It was the character Sogliardo, whom I describe as `an essential clown, yet so enamour'd of the name of a gentleman, that he will have it, though he buys it....' And so I reinvented that character after this clown you've told me about from Stratford-Upon-Avon. It came to me in a dream. I've even designed a coat of arms for this bumpkin!" Jonson laughed heartily. "I revised it before that very performance, but the actor overplayed it!"

Colton instantly recalled that Jonson hated actors ever since he killed one in a duel and been imprisoned for it. He'd had a tattoo to record the episode proudly imprinted on his arm.

"Unintentional interruption, I'm sure. I wish I could have been there," Burghley said sardonically.

"That's the reason we fight for those seats," Jonson said, further noting that the "fighting for those seats" was a paraphrase of the barrister who related the incident to him. The men laughed heartily although the dour treasurer forced the jocundity in his inimitable, insincere, and practiced demeanor.

Colton noted the contrast between father and son. Burghley ever the serious, calculating man, and Robert evidently light-hearted, yet subservient and perfectly willing to conspire.

"I have mentioned to you before, Ben, this problem of the earl of Oxford, my son-in-law. While he's been an utter embarrassment to me, and I've tried to control his virtually uncontrollable behavior, I've failed. The result is, the Queen, in spite of her early attraction to him and his general popularity at Court..."

"Particularly with the fairer sex," Jonson interjected.

"...She's no longer interested in supporting him. She doesn't want his works appearing under his name for the balance of her administration, and she would like to see that he never receives credit for his work because it would reflect badly on certain aspects of Court. Yet, she believes the works are worth preserving and should be," Burghley said while reacting with the feigning of a patronizing smile, "properly published at a future date with an introduction by the greatest writer of our times, Ben Jonson."

Jonson stood proudly erect as Burghley muttered his name, relishing the flattery even though uncertain of its veracity. His ego was huge, seeking and absorbing any meager warmth no matter what the wrapping of cold calculation. Burghley apparently had so hit the mark that Jonson's face reddened and he grinned cloyingly.

Burghley continued, "Oxford's works are plentiful and acceptable enough now and, the Queen believes, of beneficial value to posterity, but the throne could be threatened in these volatile times. Think what the Catholics could do if certain plays or scenes were shown in front of their sympathizers. So it's incumbent upon you to lend your support to this cause, and all other lesser poets and playwrights of this nation will line up behind you. We'll see to it."

Robert Cecil nodded in agreement as he made notes, though Colton still could not accept the anachronism of the green legal pad with the Bic pen.

"My humble thanks to your high regard for my efforts," Jonson said. "I do consider the earl's work to be rather witty in certain passages, but it's so transparent in that he's merely transposing that which he witnesses at Court or in Europe or at that disreputable Boar's Head Tavern in London, or rendering fantasy with his incredibly undisciplined mind. It's a deplorable and lugubrious way to acquire plots. In some cases, he perpetrates a `plot' or `scene' in his daily living and then molds it into his plays with some radical embellishments—like the time when he slept with his wife and thought she was someone else..."

Burghley slapped the table in a rare display of lost composure. "How did you know about that?"

"It's common knowledge." Jonson retreated by covering his forehead with his left hand. He'd suddenly realized he was using the worst possible example—the wife in this case was Burghley's daughter, and Burghley had carefully arranged the tryst two nights before de Vere had left for Europe. Burghley was uncertain he would ever return so he wanted his son-in-law to produce a son, for the family deserved, in his mind, a titled heir. Jonson could only shift to examples even closer to home in order to appeal to Burghley's reason, not his emotions. Unfortunately, he now recalled only the matters close to Burghley. "Or his portrayal of you as Polonius or the Queen as Richard II."

Burghley grunted and then a long, tense silence ensued. Colton observed Jonson take a deep sigh of relief when Burghley forced a long puff of air through his large, hairy nostrils. Robert kept on writing.

"Such a methodology is a complete departure from your flame of imagination," Jonson concluded with an insipid grin of satisfaction referring back to his earlier metaphor. "Ah, the best example is Oxford's men accused of holding up travelers at Gad's Hill—the same Gad's Hill where Prince Hal perpetrates the same crime in *Henry IV*, part 2. Or, the fact that Rosencrantz and Guildenstern were two names on Danish astronomer Tycho Brahe's frontispiece of a work, as two of Brahe's ancestors and Oxford's brother-in-law Peregrine Bertie, Lord Willoughby, was none other than the English ambassador to Elsinore in the 1580s."

"Let's not get carried away," Robert Cecil said.

Colton nearly spat at him from his frozen vantage point.

"The Queen has devised this plan and your part is most clear," Burghley ordered. "Your introduction, Ben, will highlight the nom de plume of Shake-spear, which should be perpetuated forever. Any revelation could ever threaten the throne by inciting the papist hordes."

"Why Shakspere?" Ben Jonson asked. "I've forgotten. Why not another name?"

"It's simple," Burghley replied. "We've already referred to him at Court and in the few publications under this pseudonym, and we have this stand-in, a real person, in Stratford, who has spent a great portion of his life there and easily, suffice it to say, could be maintained as the author. The pseudonym was given to Oxford after Harvey's toast, *hasti vibrans*, 'thy countenance shakes a spear.'"

"Think," said Robert. "Think, momentarily, about how this ruse will aid your place in literary history, with considerable thanks to the numerous plays and poems by Oxford praised by contemporaries. I know you're fond of Oxford, but those Italianate airs, his upper-crust background—he doesn't respect you. In spite of an upbringing in the nobility, the earl mingles with poets, musicians, and paupers. He's jealous of you, sir."

Colton knew Jonson had witnessed the jovial earl drunk and wearing a blindfold at the Boar's Head one night and correctly identifying a half dozen different types of port. There were wagers all over the tavern and many of the tavern patrons had bet on the earl and won. The seventeenth earl was an exceptional individual in every respect, and in the face of wanton recklessness, he was as endearing and charming to men as a "hail-fellow-well-met" man as he was dashing and romantic to the females of the species. He treated everyone, except for a few in his inner circle, with equal temperament, relating well to commoners. Ben Jonson lacked that quality in spite of coming from the lower classes and fighting his way to the top.

Colton could read Jonson's thoughts. Jonson, increasingly jealous of the earl's success, desired a degree of control in this scheme. Colton detected, even from his patinated perspective inside the painting, a willingness by Jonson to devise a way to mollify the devious, paranoid pair before him while satisfying the demands of history and truth as well. The key was in his craft. He had to control the introduction to the *First Folio*, and plant a few hints around for historians if the publication is indeed seen to completion. That would give him a way out in case the plan falls on its face. His introduction could then be interpreted as an inside joke.

"I shall write the introduction, most assuredly, for Queen and country, and I insist on the freedom to write it in precisely my own style and expression." Jonson leaned forward in his chair, his belly nudging his round thighs. "By retaining such freedom, why, I'll lend more credence to the plan and," he felt Burghley would appreciate this further manifestation of ego, "enhance my own standing in the eyes of future generations."

Burghley grasped the importance of the latter point immediately since he assumed in everyone fulsome self-interest as a chief motivation.

"Agreed," Burghley beamed. "Ben, the Queen will grant you a consulting fee from the treasury until we accomplish the task. Her Majesty insists on the amount being about £100 a year..."

Again, the footman burst through the door, this time announcing, "Rumpole of the Bailey."

Awed, Colton stared through the door at the appearance of the modern pear-shaped barrister whom he knew so well from his late night reading. What was his purpose here? Clearly, Rumpole was in the wrong century. Powder snowed from the barrister's white wig as he stepped front and center, his bulbous ruddy face gleaming. Colton uttered, "Horace Rumpole" and Burghley, Robert Cecil, the servant, and Jonson looked up at the painting in complete bafflement and shock. Then, they vanished along with all in the entire room, including Rumpole, an erstwhile friend from fiction.

The nurse shook her head in some amusement emptying the Foley while she heard the man mumble something inaudible, and then blurt out again slowly, "Hor-ass Rump-hole."

Veronica's soft brown eyes squinted in puzzlement as she looked up from her book. "What'd he say? Did you catch that?"

"Something entirely obscene," replied the nurse as she dutifully carried the bag to the loo. "It can happen given his condition," she added nonchalantly.

"Father has never used such language." She shook her head slowly, evenly. "He's a man of taste and refinement." Her forehead wrinkled as she looked up at the nurse for aid and comfort.

"It's the clot, dearie. He's not himself, I'm sure."

Chapter Eight

Ian awoke with an earache. It was an uncommon malady for him, but the previous day's penetrating cold had injured his right ear and now the eustachian tube conducted searing pain to his throat. His head movement to the right felt restricted. He went to his cluttered medicine shelf and fumbled for a tiny bottle of eardrops his mother had given him over twenty years ago. He hesitated, fearing the ancient drops may be worse than the disease, then squirted one drop in for a trial basis.

It being Sunday, he could stay home and force himself to listen to a new release by the Tamales due for review in Tuesday's edition. Fully dreading the task, he recalled they were as loud and as graceless as a horde of hyenas. His vital hearing was diseased, soon to be assaulted by noise exasperating to ear and mind.

The phone rang at the precise moment he dropped a second eardrop from the squeeze tube. As he held his head sideways to answer, he heard the unmistakable, unctuously smooth voice of Brad Vines.

"What the deuce," he answered, his ear throbbing.

"Ian, I'm sorry to bother you on such a lazy morning, but I've some startling news for the second day running. I don't know quite what to make of it. You must return to Stratford."

"Tell me more." Ian blinked in curiosity. The phone remained steady over the good ear. Only a small portion had spilled from the sore ear as he reached for the bedside phone. "I have an earache. I'm in no mood to travel to an exotic cold spot such as Stratford or even the office."

Vines cleared his throat. "There's the Shakespeare Express to Warwickshire, so that's where you should go again if you want a good story. They nicked a fellow who was part of the gang that broke into the Trinity Church last night. And the officials are refusing to release a name."

"Last night? That doesn't seem possible." Ian Scarborough never knew Vines to joke. "The police had to be alert to guard the church after the so-called break-in two nights ago. You mean a fugitive from the break-in you believe happened two nights ago."

"No. I do mean last night. I ran your story the way you reported it. If you saw the morning paper, you'll see that we kept your phrase `alleged break-in.' Personally, I believe the break-in was bona fide two nights ago. But I stood by your report."

Ian grunted to begin reiteration of his opinion then suppressed a protest. Evidently, Vines truly had supported him in print.

Vines paused, then continued. "It will take most of the morning to go by train and one leaves from Paddington in just over an hour. E-mail or phone a story from Stratford for tonight's deadline. These reports are coming from the Beeb, so that's all the information I have, but it does appear that someone actually broke in last night and nicked something, or maybe, if you're correct, the authorities concluded their hoax wasn't authentic enough on the first go."

"So the BBC is out front. I'm dressing as we speak." He gathered two scarves to wrap his neck and ears then slid his slippers off, reached for his thermal socks, and hung up the telephone. Reminded of his trip with the admiral the previous day, he rang him at home in Kensington, and then the magazine office in Chelsea. No answer. The two men had returned to London during the night after failing to find the admiral's Stratford friends so they might chat with the local police off the record. Ian's calls to the locals had produced no results.

Impulsively, he again grabbed the phone and dialed the number to Dr. Colton's room where Veronica was probably still asleep. She'd begged him to phone her upon his return and they had talked for nearly an hour that night. The admiral's urgings in the last five minutes of the ride back fulfilled Ian's expectations that he would return to the subject. "Lad, as particular as you are and as lonely as you have been, if you have any interest at all, and I believe you do, have a go at this bird! Stay serious."

The admiral then launched into a soliloquy about some zaftig kiwi he had become infatuated with in his early days—a well-known New Zealand radio celebrity who would repeat a hackneyed sailor's line of his on her show each day as he rang or wrote her to tell her he was floating in the vicinity. "She was damn fetching," he roared, convinced he had adequately shifted subjects. "'Hello to you on the downhill run!' she would say over the airwaves, addressed to me." He laughed until his heavy cheeks turned blood red and the laugh went deep in his stomach becoming a cough, as he frequently was infected with in recent years. Ian had spotted a tear in the corner of the old man's left eye. His wife had died of cancer nearly five years ago.

Veronica answered, her voice cracking on the first syllable of her surname. "Hello. Veronica Colton." He'd awakened her.

"Veronica, I'm so sorry to wake you." He paused, curious and excited to hear her voice at such an hour. "I must go to Stratford-Upon-Avon again even though I've a dreadful ear pain and I would like to see if you might come along."

"I...I...Dad had a very restful night except for some brief moaning and mumbling earlier...and so did I. Excuse me, but I'm not quite awake. I...yes, yes....Yes, I would love to go along. Aunt Joan is with him today and she should be here within a half hour."

"Have you ever driven in England?"

"No. Not at all."

"Please meet me at Paddington in an hour. That's on the Circle line from Westminster tube station that you catch in front of Big Ben. You simply walk down Abingdon Street towards Parliament or hire a taxi. Veronica, there was apparently a second break-in last night, or truly, I believe, a first break-in at Trinity Church. They nicked one of the culprits, it seems. No one knows whom they're holding. It's quite unusual so I'm popping over to cover it. I'll be in front of the large train schedule board sitting in one of the four-directional chairs. If it's too cold there, find me standing in the information booth very nearby."

"I'll call my aunt and then leave immediately. I'll see you then. Oh yes, did they print your story like you wanted? You're saying this one isn't a hoax."

"As I said last night, the first one was a hoax. This one may be. I would cancel because of the ear. If it weren't for you coming along, I wouldn't go at all," Ian said. "I was printed as submitted, Vines informed me. Shall we go?"

"I wouldn't miss it for the world. Congratulations, Mr. Reporter."

He stood and stretched his long frame. The thought of her on a train with him alone made the throbbing of his ear and the dreaded Tamales less horrifying. The sensible approach would be to write the review en route.

His first step upon arriving at the station was to buy a newspaper to assure himself that Vines had not tampered with his story. Thumbing to the section, he lifted his eyebrows excitedly to notice no change in what he had submitted as he stood in the quay for his tickets.

"Yes, dear, you change in Reading and Leamington Spa," said the woman at the Paddington Station ticket window. "You'll arrive in a little over three hours from now."

Ian felt out of place as he walked to the plastic chairs just in front of the schedule board near the platforms. He mused on the awkward spectacle of himself—a man six foot six inches wearing small plastic headphones and the scarves, and an occasional sway of improper balance. Earmuffs he'd found on a closet shelf would replace the circular, orange, foam headphones after he sufficiently panned the Tamales. He'd finished the second listen. Time to write. He opened his laptop.

Music critics find some assignments unfathomably repugnant, he thought as the pretentious lead singer screamed most of the words, some obscene and virtually all unintelligible. This was one. Most tunes were some slight variation of the all-too-familiar one-four-five chord progression, and the guitarist chiefly relied on "power" chords to give the music a very linear dimension. Occasionally, at the end of a verse, there would be some clever time changes, but the majority of the music was in a square four/four time. It was a hellish sound—repulsive to a man who knew that rock music was once rebellious because it blended and contrasted time-honored music techniques with newer sounds and concepts. Totally lacking in any semblance of refinement or subtlety, this banal noise wasn't sufficiently artful for rebellion. It was the same old predictable noise he'd been reviewing the last several years—a couch potato's invitation to oblivion. To deservedly obliterate the rubbish, he lifted his long fingers to type the kill. Text virtually complete, excluding some minor rewriting, he sensed a caress of his right shoulder and removed his ear phones and scarf as he looked into Veronica's dark eyes and ever-present wide smile that said "yes."

"How's your ear, Ian?" Her voice drifted onto the good ear like a wisp of cotton.

"Barely bearable." To combat the pain he focused on the antidote of her sparkling eyes.

"Have we missed the train?"

His heart fluttered in panic as he gaped at the large clock in the center of the platform entry. "It's almost time now. Sorry. We must make a dash for it. Platform seven! Off we go!"

He leapt from his seat and she caught his stride like a shadow. They broke into an athletic gait towards the platform. Her light brown overcoat, streamlined stride, and long hair complete with bangs gave her the alluring appearance of a Cold War lady spy. Obviously in superb physical condition, she drew long, evenly paced nostril breaths while he was beginning to puff through his mouth. His portable CD player bounced rhythmically on his side; her woven wool handbag freely swung under her shoulder. Her black leather lace-up boots did not hamper her long, gliding strides from legs that Ian recalled from two days ago that were smooth and muscular. Her legs, he thought, were a source of lingering curiosity on his part, an aspect he rarely ever noticed in the opposite sex, but the impression of strength and beauty intensified his desire. He'd already made an estimate of her keen mind. Now he indulged in the exotic beauty of an energetic, inspiring woman of grace.

"All aboard for the 9:03 to..." They heard the announcement as they entered the train and stalked first class. They rambled to the second compartment, which was empty and would likely remain so since the train began to move slowly out of Paddington at that instant. Ian was puffing heavily, his ear beating with pain. Veronica was diligently searching through her handbag as she sat across from him by the window.

"Take this extra-strength aspirin. Two of these."

"Bollocks!" He puffed angrily. "Of all days to crit the Tamales. One more obit for rock and pop."

"Sounds like an impossible assignment. What's the solution?" she asked.

"I'm not sure there is one. An Elvis or the Beatles could never catch on today. The creative side, a cutting edge, would have no viable opportunity to be legitimately heard. These days it's formula-driven, prefabricated, and hyped uniformity. The western ear is being subtly conditioned to hear only certain types of sounds, and the same sensory deprivation conditioning is beginning to permeate higher art forms as well."

"Yes." She folded her overcoat and carefully set it with her handbag on the overhead rack. "In literature, I don't recall reading a modern writer who is a realist. The days of Hemingway, Fitzgerald, Faulkner, Greene, Bellow are over. You have the rise of minimalism or totally new universes or the illogical plot or post-modernism or surrealistic characters, and no end to this wild bend of so-called experimental creativity. It's all escapist literature!" She sat next to him.

Ian leaned against the window. "I take your point. One can't find a modern novel about, say, modern London in the same way that Dickens wrote about his London. It's not something a writer would want to tackle for fear of being labeled as `dull, boring and unoriginal.' There's an obsession with this neo-creativity that defines itself in terms of format, outlandish characters, and story, and basically ignores the intrinsic purposes of good fiction that I maintain is to strengthen and expand valid experience. Where are the heroes and heroines as writers?"

"Ian, I firmly believe there will be a new influx of former Eastern bloc writers who have no choice but to inject a new realism based on a long, desperate sequestration behind the Iron Curtain. There will be a wealth of new talent, eventually, assuming all didn't escape before the walls came tumbling down. It'll give—at least the written word, maybe music—a Renaissance..."

Enthusiastically, he interrupted, but caught himself. "Veroni—. Sorry, carry on."

"It's so ironic that much sustaining art emanates from areas where oppression exists...or historical aberrations. Elizabeth I, according to the Oxfordians, repressed and manipulated de Vere, controlling not only the history as it was being made and recorded, but a subsequent view of posterity. She and Burghley never wanted the truth to be known so they wouldn't embarrass themselves, and certainly not tarnish future Brit royalty. That's the case according to my father."

"Right. I'm not ready to leap onto that tangent as yet, but I concur with your major point. Control!" His pulse raced from the invigoration, their sudden sustained intellectual compatibility. Something he longed for. Their eyes locked in concentration. "Perhaps a society dominated by commerce produces generally evanescent artistic values. That which sells most usually lasts the least and degenerates into fad and whim. I admit, my own arrangements and compositions during the seventies met the immediate desires of the public, albeit with some occasional superbly tasteful judgments on my part. I believe the little ditty I wrote with Blake entitled 'The Blackbirds' Choir' will last. It's been covered over one hundred times. It's now lift music. You hear it at the Lord Mayor's Parade. Other critics have compared it to Monk's 'Serenade To A Cuckoo.' There I go again, though. It's incessantly inescapable. I can't help but define what I believe to be my best composition except largely in terms of commercial success. This in spite of my knowledge of how so classically constructed the piece is—the cadence, the use of counterpoint, the simple but satisfying melody, the sudden timing of interlocking arpeggiated patterns of 15/8 over 17/8—the same approach I used on the tune `Cloud Mattress.'"

She yawned involuntarily. Evidently her understanding of musical lexicon was limited.

"No," she said and stretched her graceful arms majestically. "There's absolutely nothing wrong with universality of composition. In spite of all the pretensions of publishers or producers, an exquisite work can't be ignored. It must rise to wide, sustained praise and acceptance."

He paused to rub his sore ear as if unable to talk until doing so.

"Don't rub," she admonished. Ian nodded obediently then took the aspirins and washed them down with water.

"Yes, but we are referring to that overwhelming mass of representations which pass for art out there, aren't we? Think of the money spent, billions of pounds and dollars, on appalling rubbish ultimately. Ultimately, art is best when conceived for the inner self."

The conductor entered to punch tickets as they rolled towards the English countryside.

"What ever happened to Blake, Blake Hummel, wasn't it?"

"Yes. Guitar, mandolin, vocals, and some flute. He now lives in Paris…owns a recording studio and doing quite well recording jazz and blues. When the band broke up, he became wildly addicted to nitrous oxide, of all things—claimed it made him more creative. He fell arse over tip in love with a lovely and brilliant Ibo girl, the dental assistant administering the doses. The dentist didn't mind, but alas, his license was suspended over it. The Nigerian girl eventually ran off with a farmer, a Yorkshireman, and Blake nearly lost his mind. Furthermore," Ian forced a sardonic, toothy grin, "all that dental work early in the courtship nearly ruined his perfectly marvelous teeth."

"Crazy." She widened her smile and blinked fascination. "Was it exciting in the sense of groupies and drugs?"

"No. Very little except for Blake and his wild love for Pep as she was called, and the nitrous. He maintained that it instilled creativity until he realized the true source of inspiration is in the heart as well as the mind. Once he came to that conclusion he was home and dry again."

"We were quite serious musicians and most intent on not believing too much that was written about us. We had only a year of playing locally before we recorded and had a hit, so we adjusted quickly. The other fellows were older than me and, at first, my mother would sometimes tour with us. It annoyed me occasionally, being the protected nineteen-year-old, and it made my father extremely jealous. Things have never been the same since. He was particularly upset over all of this money-spinning at such a young age and my dear mother's absences. She took over some of the scheduling after we began to hit. Since then, no one else had problems. Blake has solved his, and is wealthier than any of us thanks to the studio. He married a Parisian lady in international trade and they have two adorable children."

"Why did you decide to become a critic?"

"Pressures of producing music for a living are so unnerving. I would rather rely on salary and interest from investments, which together make things rather comfortable, and I write only when I feel I have something worthwhile to offer. It's so hard to try to live up to the successes of the past unless you know you have a certified six. What counts is the music for its creativity."

"You're an excellent pop critic, but don't you think you could offer the world more by continuing to write prolifically rather than tabling your musical ability?"

"Tabling?" he repeated, quickly recalling the Americanism, a word completely opposite in meaning in British parlance. "Currently, I'm working on a Dowlandesque-style tune that I intend to either record myself on an album of Elizabethan music or I'll find an artist who I believe would do justice to the song. It's quite melodic and I intend to compose a lyric version. All of this work is at my own pace. Besides, if I'm a crit, I should be especially circumspect of my work. Also, my critiques are good if I may say so. I've certain values based on a technical knowledge of the music, not merely a vague idea of what a listener hears, so I relate to the sounds in a purely musical way, too."

She coughed lightly. "By the way, how did you meet my dad?"

"I was attending *Do You See The Rabbit?* on opening night over two years ago as a guest of Sir Keith Trent, who is also a friend of your father's. He also knew the admiral. We met at the opening night party. He listened closely as I told him of my studies in Elizabethan music, and I lent a diligent ear to his obsession with the Seventeenth Earl of Oxford. We had dinner the next day and I started reading his book later that week. I couldn't leave it on the shelf. I still carry it on trips and make it a practice to rehearse certain arguments, because I, too, am obsessed with proving the case. So your father enlisted me as a guru for the younger generations. That's why I'm off to New York in a few days, and my part of the debate is now more important because he is ill."

"Sir Keith came by the hospital yesterday while Aunt Joan was there. She was delighted. Such a sweet man." Veronica crossed her long left leg over the other leg and leaned forward, smiling with her hand cupped over her chin, elbow resting on her knee.

"Too bad he's on the other side of this issue, and yet it hasn't prevented your father and him from a dear friendship. Veronica, it's remarkable how some on each side of this issue, by and large, like and respect the other. Oh, I think the Stratfordians consider us to be the same sort of cranks as, say, astrologers, but all recognize the overwhelming greatness and sustaining power of the works of Shakespeare—Shakspere—Schakspeare—de Vere. That..."

"Pardon me for interrupting, but what's the difference between the three pronunciations?"

"Right. Shakespeare is the name, of course, which history has settled on as politically correct. Shakspere is the fellow from

Stratford and how he signed his name sometimes, and how the name was spelled throughout the family at the time he was living. The name, probably the correct spelling, is used only by the Oxfordian persuasion—a catchword, a shibboleth so to speak. Schackspeare is also another way he signed his name. I pronounce it throatily merely in order to overemphasize the difference. But the second spelling, S-h-a-k-s-p-e-r-e, is usually how he signed his name of the six signatures known to history.

"There's also the appearance of Shake-dash-spear, which we maintain was a pseudonym for de Vere in the early days of Elizabeth's reign, and when he was in mostly good favor with the Queen. Also, it was verboten for nobility to be published under their names—especially since Oxford drew much material and verisimilitude directly from deep experience at Court. Some of the experiences could be corroborated in, frequently, Lord Burghley's meticulous records."

"A `kiss and tell' of the sixteenth century."

"Quite right. Between Lord Treasurer Burghley and Elizabeth was concentrated virtually the entire power of the kingdom. What was most difficult was de Vere's relationship with Catholics. He was born into the centre of this controversy as a Protestant, although not a very well-behaved one, and it was to his credit and skill he survived as long as he did in the Queen's good graces since she was so fiercely obsessed with Mary, Queen of Scotland. You see, he preferred the pomp and history of Catholicism. He never inserts the word Catholic in any play. For another thing, Thomas Howard, the Fourth Duke of Norfolk, was the son of the Sixteenth Earl of Oxford's sister, Frances Vere, in other words..."

"Edward's Aunt."

"Right. His father was the Earl of Surrey, Edward de Vere's first cousin. That longstanding coalition, the Earls of Northumberland and Westmoreland...

"A la *Henry IV, part 1*," she said, and tilted her head like a charmed schoolgirl in revelation.

"Yes," he replied as he adjusted his scarf over his ear, "but Norfolk was, well, dim. He was an ardent Protestant, in love with Mary, who was in hot pursuit of the throne, and he was convinced he would be a moderating force if she took the throne. His problem was that he lied to Elizabeth about his impending marriage to Mary. After they found him out, they tossed him into the Tower. In spite of Howard's protests to the two northern earls, the northern rebellion ensued. Our man, all of nineteen years old, was ill when the rebellion began, but he demanded from his guardian, Lord Burghley, that he be sent to the front. It was four months before Burghley granted permission, but the young Oxford saw excruciating action under the valiant Thomas Radcliffe, Third Earl of Sussex, particularly at the siege of Hume Castle, which was because of the capitulation of Lord Hume and the magnanimity of Lord Sussex, voila, a scene in the play—*Henry V*."

"*Henry V*," Veronica said simultaneously, enthralled at his devotion to the subject. Ian returned her wide smile, pleased by her incisive knowledge of the plays. He fumbled for his notebook.

"I keep my notes handy at all times for I must read you these quotes from Elizabeth Jenkins's *Elizabeth the Great*. Let's see...he `Dazzled the Queen and absorbed the attention of her leisure moments. Edward de Vere, Seventeenth Earl of Oxford, was a young man of high birth, arresting presence and exceptionally disagreeable temper...'"

"`Thy countenance shakes a spear,'" she interjected.

He vigorously nodded his head and he read on. "`A pathological selfishness did not deprive him of attraction, and though very poor, he attained for a short time the peak of fashionable celebrity; spoiled and ruthless as he was, the Maids of Honor were wild about him.' Conyers Read, the modern Elizabethan scholar, called him a `young, unwhipped cub' who `dared to write' back to the Queen's chief minister—Lord Burghley.

"While some of this is accurate, the portion concerning his wealth isn't entirely. De Vere had periods of debt and much wealth appropriated by Burghley and the Crown, but while in favor at Court he was quite wealthy." The ear throbbed more.

"Nonetheless, to return to Thomas Howard—Oxford utilized his then good relations to delay his cousin's death. It's possible Oxford married Anne Cecil, Burghley's daughter, so it might increase his influence while Howard had now come under house arrest for supporting the disastrous Ridolfi plot—a scheme to place Mary on the throne, thus deposing Elizabeth. Howard was doomed, but his life was preserved at the behest of his cousin. In fact, it was Burghley, Oxford's guardian and now his father-in-law, who prevailed upon Elizabeth, after months of vacillation on her part, to behead Thomas Howard. From this moment on, the fortunes of Oxford went to a dicey end."

Ian clutched his throbbing ear. Veronica patted the seat with her fingertips and said, "You have room to lay down. Why don't you and I'll place some extra drops in your ear?"

"Thank you. There's so much more to tell, but we'll be changing trains in a few minutes and I should rest some." He stretched across the seat as he waved his right hand in a gentle, pontifical fashion. "The artistic culture was corrupted in my estimation of the facts, corrupted then by a repressive regime, so that while this splendid work surfaced, it was never attributed to the proper author and we don't know the methods by which such genius was articulated. They would want us to believe the author was an unknown from a quiet, small town who left no books in his will, who couldn't consistently sign his name, and who had dubious, scarce praise from his contemporaries. But the identity of the author is synonymous with the author's works. J. Thomas Looney proved that."

"If it hadn't been for Looney, my father says his words may never have been written." Veronica stood and clutched her overcoat, and rolled it to form a pillow for his aching head.

"Thank you," he said. "Yes. Looney was the beginning of the path towards truth."

"Moreover, our society may not be able to replicate such genius when there's an empty paradigm like one William Shakespeare." She slid the first class compartment door to a snapping close. "You need to be quiet now until we change trains." Her voice soothed like a ray of penetrating warmth over his aching ear. He would doze until the stop at Reading.

Chapter Nine

The rails to Stratford-Upon-Avon from Leamington Spa bore a quaint, antique train (circa 1940) with freshly upholstered aqua-coloured seats, for which Ian was most gratefully in comfort as he slowly, painfully raised his head from Veronica's lap. She shared with him, as an ever alert first-time visitor to England, her fascination with the old vehicle, which featured doors holding latches made of old metal cranks. A door to the outside was adjacent to each set of seats. While the new seats were firm, Ian groaned when a rollicking motion, as on the previous train, exacerbated the pain escalating through his head. His entire auditory canal throbbed severely and his throat was sore. The discomfort and awkwardness of his long legs running uncomfortably perpendicular to the seats caused them to stiffen upon rising. Some teenage girls sitting in the corner of the car giggled unabashedly at his rubbery legs as he stretched and yawned. He groaned again at the annoying sight of their amusement.

"Ian, we have to take you to a doctor. You're miserable."

"Right," he replied listlessly, shocked at his own willingness to capitulate. "Right. There's a small clinic only a bit from the station. We'll go straight away in a taxi if necessary."

The train arrived and Ian and Veronica gingerly stepped from the door next to their seats. They ambled arm in arm through the small station and came to the portal opening up to the town. A wide drive lay before them with what looked to be a fairground just beyond. A one-story brick building was the first building after the fairground.

"I believe that's the clinic." Ian pointed. "I do hope someone's there to treat me."

"Taxi?" A large man in his late forties stepped from the driver's seat of a black taxi idling a few steps away.

"Yes," Veronica said and nodded. "It's only to the doctor's office over there. This cold weather has brought on an earache for my friend. I know it's a short..."

"No bother t'all." He dashed to the boot. "Any luggage?"

"No." Ian smiled wryly. "Just the small case. I can manage. Thank you."

They sped off to the hospital and arrived in less than a minute. Ian leaned over and kissed her cheek for the first time, as much out of gratitude for her tender care as affection.

"I want the driver to take you to a Salterham House, 51 Rother Street." He had memorized the address from the day before when Phelps had told him of his plans to stay in Stratford. "There's an American reporter there by the name of Boone Phelps. I believe he's still there. Link up with him and see if you can gather some information for me. I'll try to prepare a story by this evening if I'm able to recover. Book rooms there if you can. If I don't show up by say fivish, call me then. It's a B and B directly across from the police station so it's easy to find. Oh yes, watch out for Phelps, a most aggressive reporter. Before he talks you into doing anything, make sure it's ethical or legal. He's quite a hound, but he has been known to find things in spite of his clumsy bodacious behavior."

"We'll do whatever is necessary to heal your aching head," she whispered. "I'll take care of everything."

He staggered into the front door of the small brick clinic. Luckily, someone was on duty, and he waved and shouted, "The bed and breakfast owners will know the phone number here."

The two-story Victorian house in Rother Street was indeed directly across from the police station. The owners, who lived next door, smiled convivially at the commanding American woman.

"Have you a vacancy?"

"Yes, we do. For you alone?" the lady asked.

"Yes and no. My friend has come down with a terrible earache and he may even remain overnight in the clinic near the station. If not, do you have other vacancies? By the way, I'm Veronica Colton." She reached out her right hand.

The barrel-chested man with heavy eyebrows counterpointed by a strong Hapsburg chin grinned and extended a hand. "I'm Clive Cook. This is my wife Angela."

"A pleasure," Veronica said.

"So far, yes, we do have rooms. A tour group from Ireland cancelled so we have only one room occupied." Angela Cook glanced at her husband. "Sort of occupied."

"That wouldn't happen to be Mr. Phelps would it?"

"Why yes, that's right," Mr. Cook nodded quizzically.

"He is a friend of my friend. They are both reporters."

"I see." Cook was visibly relieved by the answer. "Miss Colton, I don't know quite how to tell you this, but it appears Mr. Phelps is in a bit of trouble as I'm told that reporters have a tendency to step into from time to time."

"What...what kind of trouble?"

"Come in and have a sit down on the sofa." He ushered her and his wife to a hallway lit up with bright light from the many windows along the exterior wall. They came to a sitting room dominated by large bay windows and a breakfast table beside a dark, old, upright piano. There were sofas around each wall except for the interior wall that held the piano and a fireplace lit with small dollops of burning coal, an added coziness. Veronica felt relaxed, as though among trusted friends, removed her scarf and coat and carelessly sprawled them atop the sofa.

"Mr. Phelps, it appears, was nicked last night by the police." He raised his large eyebrows in sharing the secret. "Chief Inspector Morton secured a warrant this morning and searched the room himself. You may be of great assistance to Mr. Phelps, especially if he is a reporter, since Mr. Phelps has been, according to the chief, quite feisty, refusing to answer any questions. Indeed, I heard he's been himself rather full of testy questions to the chief."

Veronica fleetingly envisioned a prisoner slumped in a crude wooden chair under a solitary, swinging light bulb casting hideous shadows across a cold, empty room except for the commanding figure of a policeman smoking cigarettes—only in this case the captor was asking questions of his torturer in response to each question.

"My friend could probably handle this much better since I've never met Mr. Phelps, but he's too sick now to become involved."

"Should we check you in?"

"Give me until about five o'clock if you will. Ian, my friend, asked me to call him then and I promised I would try to resolve anything that came up. You surely must understand that Mr. Phelps, if he's like most American reporters, is quite aggressive when it comes to getting a story. Did he strike the police chief?"

"No, but I'm afraid it's somewhat worse than that." Mr. Cook shook his head as if he might have regretted sharing the news. "He's the bloke who broke into the Holy Trinity Church last night. Keep it quiet, please."

"I shall. Really? My friend is a reporter, a critic actually, but he volunteered for this job and now he's relying on me to gather the facts for him since he is incapacitated for the moment. So maybe I should try to help Mr. Phelps."

"I do suggest you go over and try to talk some sense into the poor man," Mr. Cook said. "So many reporters don't respect limits."

"I'll call my friend. By the way, his name is Ian Scarborough, in case he happens to call while I'm there."

"Oh yes?" He paused. "The gent who used to be with Falstaff's Ghost."

"Oh, right." His wife leaned forward. "We know his music."

"He's also the same fellow," Clive said in a slight growl, "who writes for the *Times*. We read his editorial a few days ago."

"His music is splendid, but he seems to be starting a hare about who wrote the works," Mrs. Cook blurted, looking nervously about the room as if shocked at her own sudden unrestrained bluntness.

"The *Fishing for Lost Wishes* album...a crowning triumph," Mr. Cook said, resuming a higher pitch as though the chorus might soon follow. "I've a copy of it in my own old vinyl collection as well as the new CD reissue."

"Well, I must get to a phone," Veronica said. "Excuse me."

"It's down the hall and to the right," said Mrs. Cook. "The phone number is 67301."

When Veronica called, the doctor was still examining Ian, but she could hear him in the background insisting on taking the call.

"Veronica, dear, I intend to remain here for at least another few hours on a cot. The doctor gave me some better drops and a painkiller. I'll kip down for a time, after which I should be improved. Then I hope to join you and Boone. By all means go have a bite."

"Ian, I have some important news. Boone was the one who broke in last night. They are holding him at the police station." Silence, then she heard him grunt.

"He's known for his marvelous investigative exploits. Please, go see what can be done for him. Have a word with the authorities and ask if you might chat with him...tell them you represent me...that you're my assistant. If they ask for press credentials, tell them I have them and suggest they call me. Inspector Morton will remember me if you describe me to him. He knows I'm the editorial writer, but he knows I'm not a monster like Boone Phelps. After you talk to Boone, ring me back and I'll assess the situation, and then go to the station myself. By then I shall be feeling much better, I hope."

"What if I'm not allowed to see him?"

"If not, call me immediately and I'll join you at the B and B. Veronica, I thank you. The doc says it is a somewhat serious ear infection made worse by this bitter cold."

"I do hope you recover soon. I'll call at five. Call me here if you need to. Bye."

She returned to the sitting room where Mr. Cook was lighting a cigarette and Mrs. Cook was scanning the telly with a remote. Hastily, Veronica surmised that the best objective would be to free Phelps somehow. If the chief was capable of pulling the type of hoax he had perpetrated the day before, he was also capable of being reasoned with before any charges were formally placed, provided the public records did not reflect who was arrested and being held—an American reporter. If the chief was so certain about his captive, then why hadn't he trumpeted his achievement? Did Phelps know something that was a problem for the good officials of Stratford?

"I may be able to help Mr. Phelps out of his dilemma. Ian said Phelps is quite famous for these kinds of exploits," she related to the concerned couple.

"Mr. Scarborough's joining you soon, is he?" Mr. Cook asked.

"Yes, at some point." She picked up her coat. "I'll see you in about an hour—I hope with Boone Phelps in tow. Thanks for your help."

She strode purposefully through the doorway. Low, wintry grey clouds now canopied Rother Street. Without breaking stride, she swung open the glass doors of the station and glided up to the window separating her from a front desk where a young man sat stamping a stack of papers. She pinched a business card lying on the counter with the name Michael Emory, Director, Shakespeare Birthplace Trust emboldened in black on the front.

"My name is Veronica Colton, assistant to Mr. Ian Scarborough of the *London Daily Times*, and I believe I can help Chief Morton in this matter concerning the break-in if he would be so kind as to allow me to see Mr. Phelps. Mr. Scarborough and he are friends and were together at yesterday's press conference here. Mr. Scarborough is very ill and asked me to try to meet with the chief."

"Another reporter. One moment, please." The young man rose from the desk and smiled graciously. "Inspector Morton may be out of his office."

"I'll wait." Veronica smiled with a patronizing wink as she stood at the glass windows knowing full well Morton was in. Such determination and a formidable intellect propelled her to become special assistant to Senator Wade Langston, a position she had held for six years as his speechwriter. His "aerosol is air assault" speech (her concept) before the recent Democrat convention had almost secured him the vice-presidential nod from the Democrat nominee. Veronica had been acknowledged by most leading Democrats, and some media movers, as the speechwriter to watch, the next wizard of the thirty-second sound bite. But there had been nasty rumors about her and the handsome, young, quite liberal senator (married with four children). Untrue. The selection didn't go to Senator Langston partially because of those vicious tales perpetrated by several competing camps. The result might have been disastrous since the senator could have lost much favor among the voters of Tennessee (if the ticket lost), in spite of his somewhat disguised liberal record, had he appeared on the ticket with the openly liberal nominee. "These southern Democrats will never change their views on race," he often lamented, "and I have to play along when I'm out at the barbecue stand." Fortunately for him, enough voters ignored his voting record. "It's the image that counts," Langston always maintained, and so his speechwriter could do wonders.

"Inspector Morton will have a word with you," the man said to Veronica as he floated back to his desk. "His office is through the door to the left. Carry on until you come to the third door on your right."

She thanked him, pleasantly surprised at how casual the young man's attitude was towards her. He hadn't asked for press credentials or identification. Well, she concluded, it's a small town. Morton certainly must have recalled Ian after his strong editorial and the press conference appearance.

Morton's bulbous nose projected a hint of comical ambience while his grey hair exuded a regal air. He stood calmly at the doorway, a hot beverage in his hand, evincing an air of authority in an upward thrust of his firm, thin lips.

"Miss Colton, I presume."

"I am pleased to meet you, Chief Morton." No one had bothered to correct her use of "chief" as opposed to "inspector."

"Will you join me in a cup of tea? Coffee?" he asked.

"Certainly. Tea."

"Do you take it English style or American?"

"Two sugars and a teaspoon of milk."

He had obviously anticipated her acceptance of the offer, for she saw a tarnished silver tray on a table between the two wooden chairs facing each desk. The tray held a black, ceramic pot with matching dainty teacups, a bowl of sugar, a cup of cream, a spoon, and two napkins, strikingly elegant for a police station in spite of the modern building. He poured the tea as he prepared the accompaniments to her satisfaction. No bare, dangling light bulbs here, she thought.

"I'm sorry Ian Scarborough couldn't come by, but he's incapacitated with a terrible ear infection. He's presently at the clinic. I took him there right from the train station. He was too sick to join me when," she paused for special emphasis, "he was told about Phelps being the suspect."

Inspector Morton took a deep breath and rubbed the area beneath his ruddy nose. "Mr. Phelps is helping us answer some inquiries. So the press knows it's Phelps, do they?"

"No, Chief, they don't. Only I know and Scarborough, and maybe his editor."

"Mr. Scarborough was just here yesterday with Mr. Phelps and that's why I'm here to listen to you...since you're his assistant. How can you shed some light on this matter?"

"Ian warned me that Phelps has always been a most rambunctious investigative reporter. You see, I've never met Phelps, but I can only imagine the lengths he might go in order to obtain some hard facts. I'm sure he will eventually cooperate. How did you figure it was he who broke into the church, and how did he allegedly carry it out?"

"We nicked him just inside the Trinity Church. He was high on a ladder replacing a section above the bust in the monument. He was apparently rather clever in that he called to report an electrical fire at the Royal Shakespeare Theatre earlier last evening, which caused the distraction necessary to achieve an entry into the church. Evidently, he had cleverly used some kind of utensil to pick the lock on the small door from the outside of the church's sole entrance, and somehow gained a rapid entrance to the inner door of the porch. Again, he found nothing, but we must hold him for questions, and we shall file charges against him Monday morning."

"How do you know he called the fire in?" She sipped the tea with a gentle slurp.

"We don't really know it was him except the dispatcher said it sounded like an American."

"I'm not surprised at his aggressiveness—typical for an American reporter." She thought back to her one year of law school before joining then-Congressman Langston's campaign for the Senate. It would take some skill to bluff her way along. Then again, what if Phelps had indeed performed the break-in? Would one year of law school make her a lawyer here? "I've been out of the practice of law since working for Ian Scarborough. However, my law school preparation should allow me to at least talk to him and make the necessary arrangements for him to hire legal counsel in case of arraignment."

"Sorry, Miss Colton, but I simply can't allow a briefless barrister, unlicensed as you are in this country, to see him. It's a problem and I don't know quite what to do since the BBC has reported the incident already. I've turned away four others, all newspaper reporters. They don't know who he is. They simply know we have a man in custody."

All along she noticed his face flush. She'd bluffed. He must have realized his mistake by reconfirming the last bit of information: she knew the identity of the man, whereas, no one else did except Ian and she.

He raced on, trying to obliterate it from her speedy mind. "He's most uncooperative and it is so tiring." He huffed with exasperation. "Here we say he's helping us with the inquiry." The hole deepened. He clamped his lips shut and gripped them inward, like a turtle's final shutting of the shell.

She pounced on the error. "As I told you, Ian and I are both well acquainted with his nature, his reporting style. When Ian told his editor, he merely mumbled, `He's at it again. You'll have to negotiate.' So now you see us as we are. Ian will, I know this to be a fact, reveal who this man is to the world." She noticed sweat forming on his upper lip. "Unless you allow us to cut a deal with him. You obviously want the story to die. We want him out of the slammer. If I can convince him of the necessity of neither of us writing stories on this incident, then will you let him go? You have everything to gain by letting me negotiate with him privately and nothing to lose except a little time, which just means more aggravation for you."

Morton's feet shifted nervously as his sanguinary face tensed. "I allowed him briefly to call his newspaper and a barrister is on the way from some east London wine bar." He sipped the last drops of his tea and placed the cup and saucer off to the side of the tray. He could not very well hold her there, Veronica realized, although he would try to talk her out of the notion of a chat with Phelps, and she sensed most viscerally that he surely knew damage had been done. The previous break-in was a likely hoax and Phelps had exposed it. But even with access, would she be able to talk sense into Phelps?

Now his stratagem was to try to divert the entire troublesome subject.

"How's Mr. Scarborough doing?"

She stayed silent for several seconds. "Chief, please decide what you intend to do so we might accomplish something." She glanced at her watch. Two o'clock. "We have a deadline in just over an hour." The deadline was actually at six-thirty p.m.

"Could you return in an hour to allow me to give this serious thought?"

"No, sir. Ian asked me to call him in thirty minutes. If you give me an hour with Phelps, then we'll miss our deadline and I can convince Phelps in that time not to run his story. We'll threaten that we will run a story on how he got caught breaking the law if he tries to run the story himself. I know Phelps can reason with his editor. Otherwise, someone out there, eventually, is going to run a story."

Chief Inspector Morton puffed a baffled sigh at the determined woman before him, and then shook his head in resignation. "If you are unsuccessful in preventing him from running a story, then I'm going after him all in! You had better succeed." He glared at her soft dark eyes. "As far as I'm concerned, he was caught nicking the most valuable of antiquities."

They both rose. Veronica caught a whiff of his nervous sweat as he passed in front of her towards the door. She was so excited she almost forgot to set her teacup back on the tray. Her knit handbag banged against her arm and she spilled tea onto the saucer as she set it down noisily. So far, she thought, success. But the true test was ahead.

"Did you recover anything he took?" she asked. He didn't answer for what seemed like a minute.

"He has broken the law, remember that as you talk to him. This one seems to believe he's above the law. He feels his only duty is to have answers from *me*."

He walked down the hall to a door on the left and pushed in the key. It clicked and opened to reveal a windowless room of some twenty square feet with a large wooden table and four chairs scattered at various intervals on its two long sides. The chair on the far corner held a very erect and nervous man, not looking like a somewhat famous reporter for the *International Herald Tribune*. His attitude was surly.

"I hope this lady is either a barrister or an incentive for me to talk. Otherwise, you may show her the door until you answer a few of my questions."

"Mr. Phelps," Morton uttered in a surprisingly civil tone, "this lady is an assistant to your friend Mr. Scarborough, whom I recall was with you yesterday. She tells me she can help us resolve this matter. I'm willing to give her a chance. Otherwise, you're in for the hard."

Neither American understood, or they were unfazed, by the British slang for prison. Phelps shrugged in a mild consent and Morton took a seat.

"Chief Morton, I believe you implicitly promised you would exit the room for some time so we might talk in private," Veronica said. Phelps said nothing.

Morton had played his hand out. He rose from his chair and turned to Veronica. "You have thirty minutes, love."

An hour later she burst out of the police station and marched across the street with quick, purposeful steps. She couldn't wait to call her "boss" to report the news.

"Good party?" Clive Cook asked.

"Good show," she laughed, mimicking the idiom. "Very good show. Your guest will be returning through these doors in, oh, say about fifteen minutes. He's taking the back way out of the cop shop to avoid being seen. Excuse me, I must call Ian."

She dialed the clinic and was transferred to a nurse. "He's asleep. Should I wake him?"

"Yes. It's urgent."

"One moment, please." She heard the phone plop down noisily.

Then she heard a loud yawn and heavy steps approaching the mouthpiece. "Veronica?" He was hoarse with sleep.

"How do you feel?" she asked.

"Better. My head and throat pain are gone. I'm about to chat with the doctor after we're finished. Bollocks, we're going to miss the deadline!"

"No. There will be no story. Morton is letting Phelps go and the city fathers are dropping the charges."

Ian's voice skipped. "How can we manage to do that?"

"There is a larger story here, so Boone and I decided there would be no reportage of this story." She lowered her voice to virtual whisper. "We're sitting on a big one. Let me explain. Boone followed, yes, *followed* three burglars into the church last night while hiding outside and contemplating a break-in himself. No wonder he seemed so guilty, Ian. He's so predictable. He mulled over breaking-in at the church for over two hours. There were no guards, no police—just the yellow police tape. Morton must have figured their break-in hoax had worked in scaring off potential burglars so they simply called off the detail after all the media seemed to have left town. Boone assumes that the three burglars were professionals because they picked the lock perfectly. He hid behind one of the large grave markers and watched them do it in less than five minutes. He believes their lookout was further away from his position. They locked the inner door behind them, and as one of them came back out to grab a tool or something, Boone dashed into the church and hid near the pulpit on the south aisle so he could peek at them. Now, here was our bargaining chip—the monument and bust were totally undisturbed until one of the intruders carefully climbed up a ladder and took a sledge hammer and pick and smashed a portion of the monument about two feet above the bust. It appeared to be the coat of arms—the shield shape. As they worked, Boone crawled over to the wall at the south transept near the entry to the chancel, the better to observe without being observed."

"Did they find anything?"

"Yes," Veronica said adamantly. "They pulled out a small box containing some kind of artifacts or documents, or so Boone thought. They obviously knew where to look. They were in there for no more than twenty-five minutes Boone told me."

Ian's voice climbed ecstatically as he repeated his question. "So the monument, had it been disturbed?" His sore ear demanded to hear the response again.

"You were right...not on the first break-in. The first break-in was a complete hoax. But as for the second one, the police had been either on patrol or over at the theatre where a so-called electrical fire had been reported as out of control. Evidently, when they realized it had been a false alarm probably phoned in by one of the three burglars who Morton said used an American accent, they came upon Boone in the church up on the ladder trying to determine what had been in the space in the box! They thought they'd caught him red-handed and arrested him since the trio had, naturally, already left, although he was about to try somehow to follow them. He believed they had at least two other accomplices, a lookout and a get-away driver, but the beauty," she exclaimed, trying to whisper, "was that Boone kept his cool. Morton knows Boone followed them in. One person couldn't break the bust of Shakespeare while on a ladder. Morton also knows Boone knew the first break-in was a hoax perpetrated by the local authorities, of which Morton is one." Veronica could hardly contain her glee.

"But, Boone Phelps told Morton that he was the sole perpetrator and was merely curious about what was in the damaged area above the bust since Morton had told the world at the press conference that the area had been broken into. Morton couldn't very well deny a break-in since that is what he had maintained only the day before. Boone kept asking why the bust of William Shakespeare wasn't broken into as they had attested to in the press conference. Boone, of course, told him nothing about seeing the trio. But Morton had to know Boone followed the real perpetrators in. There were plenty of different footprints and clues. Morton seemed quite confused. Oh, hold on, here's Boone now. There's more!"

"American ingenuity strikes again," Boone Phelps shouted. Veronica grabbed him and held her finger to her mouth with a "shhh" to shield the information from the Cooks just visible in the nearby living room. "I had no idea your lady friend was so, what was the word you used the other day—'fetching.' Veronica, you were great in there. What have you told Ian?" Phelps turned to see if the Cooks were listening.

"She's told me about the break-in, the arrest, your witness to the burglary, and your witness to an undamaged bust beforehand. Is there more?"

"Yes...Yes! I didn't tell her while we were in there at the police station working on this deal. I simply said I saw evidence of what they retrieved from the monument. You never know when cop shop walls have ears, old buddy. The document," he fell into a complete whisper, "the scroll, the cloth...whatever it was...I heard one of them say as they read from it. It was not perfectly clear to me. `Now we know we can go to Hat Fill—Hat Fill— tomorrow night.' That means tonight. The problem is, where's Hat Fill?"

Ian's hands squeezed the phone receiver. "I'm on my way to scheme the next bit. Tell Veronica to ring the paper...no, I'll ring them to inform them there was nothing to the story about the break-in. While I'm on the way, order fish and chips from the take-out just round the corner. It may not be too late to catch up with whoever is behind all this."

"Okay."

"Boone, do you have a car?"

"I do. I'll pick you up in a minute. So let's skip the snacks."

"Then it's off we go to Hatfield, north of London."

Chapter Ten

Aunt Joan sat at the hospital bedside, silently reading a book and occasionally staring through the narrow ceiling-to-floor window at the green courtyard far below. This pleasant view would surely be the last look ever at the outside world for her brother, she thought, if he ever awoke from what the doctors described as a lingering coma. She hoped, in her morbid outlook, that she at least would get a final word with him.

Tyler Colton would mumble from time to time, words barely intelligible and bizarre, and uncharacteristically obscene. Never once had she heard him use such language. "Verbal pollution" he would label such utterances in his normal life. His vices had consisted of overworking, smoking, and a lack of exercise. In light of these deficiencies, it was a great wonder to her that he'd not suffered a stroke before now since he was nearly eighty-one years old.

She returned her gaze to reread a paragraph she had not absorbed before her brief reverie. Her brother interrupted her concentration again with a snort through his nostrils and a quick puff through his lips. His breath was uneven, but deeper, as the fingers in his left hand twitched briefly.

The movement in his left hand was a reaction to a breeze so refreshing, so quenching, he could see himself against the darkness of his mind. A penetrating, narrow beam of light riveted on his movement so he could see, clearly, his own body in its entirety.

Colton watched himself move through the pale, wide-open doorway of a gabled schoolhouse in the late afternoon of mid May. It was somewhere in England—maybe County Durham. The air swirled around as he crossed the threshold and smelled the saccharine odor of sweat that he instantly identified with his own youth and school days. Carefree children were bursting from the schoolhouse in untamed fits of energy and noise. As all children will do, they ignored him except to avoid his space. He was a mere temporary obstacle to their long-awaited pleasures, an afternoon of dancing, singing, scuffling, roaming, and shouting with no particular purpose except to indulge in youthful, blissful, frivolous fun. He could remember those days when he understood so little and found curiosity in so much, never becoming attached to any particular effort for any span of time. His childhood had been an exceptionally happy one, occupied by Civil War battle games, fishing, baseball, bird watching, reading, and horseback riding.

He turned around from the passing dervish of children to face a man about his own age. Eerily, he physically felt about ten years of age but with a mind of an octogenarian, so the old man across from him would surely prove intellectually accessible.

"Dr. Colton, it's so refreshing to see you again." The short man with round, wire-rim glasses gazed sincerely into his eyes, then blinked into the bright afternoon light. He wore a black, three-piece wool suit and held a large, dark-blue book. With certain crispness, he laid the book on the school desk behind him, and stood in back of the small wooden schoolroom that curiously cast a quaint atmosphere of Queen Anne Revival.

"Where have we met before?" Colton brusquely broke with his usual formality of greetings.

"We've never met before. I have seen you, though. I'm J. Thomas Looney. Pronounced `Lon-e,' not `Loon-ey' as it's spelled." The schoolmaster raised his chin as though instructing a young student.

"Yes, I visited your grave once." Colton realized that the man he was talking to was dead, but must have seen him (from the grave?) when he visited it during a prior visit to England. "I read your remarkable book!"

"You're in a coma, I believe," Looney said as though he might be stating an obvious status like being an American, or a visitor.

"Yes, I can't recall precisely what happened, but I have been dreaming extensively and running into all sorts of friends. I'm glad to have happened along on you because I owe you so much. Mr. Looney, most royal of swan-uppers, thank you for reviving this matter. Your *Shakespeare Identified* was a brilliant exegesis on the subject of Edward de Vere."

"Thank you," the gentleman said, bowing tightly. "I owe it mostly to an inquisitive mind, a keen eye for prose, John Stuart Mill, the games of logic and philosophy, and a compelling sense of historical justice. Historical justice is more important to a reputation than the esteem of contemporaries since, if one maintains an instinct for democratic fairness about the matter, exponentially there are more people in the generations to come than there are of one's contemporaries."

"I've never viewed it that way. May I sit?" Colton asked.

"Certainly."

The two old men settled opposite each other into the small wooden chairs with writing desks attached. The black iron braces connecting the desks to the wooden chairs issued squeaks as the two pressed their weight against the slanted, wooden desktops replete with vows such as "Patrick loves Christine" surrounded by a large heart, or proclamations like "Hardy is full of rubbish," or "Mr. Looney is looney."

"Ah, Professor Looney, I hope while you've been resting you read some of the reviews of your book. I believe my favorite was from Hamilton Basso of the *New Yorker*. His contention, put forward in nearly five hundred sober, modest, heavily documented pages is... 'that Shakespeare was not the Shakespeare that Mr. Bliss, Mr. Cooper, Mr. Brown, Mr. Pearson and Miss Chute take for granted...Mr. Looney is no crank. He is an earnest level-headed man who has spent years trying to solve the world's most baffling literary mystery.... If the case were brought to court, it is hard to see how Mr. Looney could lose...the various mysteries that surround Shakespeare...are mysteries no longer if the man we know as Shakespeare was really Edward de Vere...' That was written in 1950."

"I have read it, but it's so gratifying to hear it again." The wiry man lifted his thin eyebrows gleefully. When he spoke, Colton felt a warmth penetrating his heart as though meeting a long-lost kinsman. "Tyler, if I may call you that, if you awaken to your world, please include the argument that historical justice can only be achieved in a court of historical evidence. Not a jury of English professors and Shakespearean scholars. They aren't historians, or even writers. Historians and writers know whom to convict of the crime of writing the works. Is that another review you wish to read to me?"

"Yes," Colton said, suddenly aware of the magazine he was holding. "Edwin Bjorkman's review in *The Bookman*. `It is impossible to do justice to the wealth of evidence collected by Mr. Looney, or to the ingenuity displayed by him in its coordination...the most remarkable aspect of his labours is that they affect not only the central problem of William Shakespeare's relation to the work named after him, but a whole series of literary enigmas that have puzzled every painstaking student of this period for nearly two hundred years. There is the problem of the lyrics excluded from the plays of Lyly, author of *Euphues* and private secretary to Oxford, on their first publication—one of which is practically identical with one of the lyrics in *A Midsummer Night's Dream*. There is the problem of Shepherd Willie in Spenser's *The Shepheardes Calender*, 1579. The peculiar thing is that all these problems seem to fall into place and form a consistent picture the moment you accept the theory of Oxford's connection with the Shakespearean plays.' Mr. Looney, leads will be followed up." Colton continued quoting. `The days are past when a new Shakespearian theory can be laughed out of court.... We should be moved solely by a desire for truth, and nothing that may be helpful in finding it should be despised.'"

"Yes," Looney said, "that was written during my lifetime."

"Please, as the one who initiated the research, tell me how you were able to accomplish this achievement."

"I established a paradigm, a scientific and historical paradigm. Shortly after reading and teaching *Hamlet* to my students during the autumn session of 1913, I read a most compelling book by Max Wertheimer that dealt with establishing models or paradigms as a true reflection of reality—even in historical research. It means when we observe a phenomenon we must observe it in an objective sense. We must look at raw facts together and interpret the data without the bias associated with casual observation. Observe these lines."

He grabbed a pencil from the slot on the top portion of the desk and slid a small card from his coat pocket. He drew four vertical parallel lines and carefully filled each line with alternating slanted parallel lines at about thirty-degree angles so the first and third parallel lines were filled with upward slants to the left, and the second and fourth parallel lines were filled with upward slants to the right, each line starting at the same horizontal point. Colton knew it as the Muller-Lyer optical illusion.

"The slants make the parallel lines appear to be not indeed parallel. If one accurately measures them, one finds they are equidistant at the top and the bottom. That's precisely the problem in the Shakespeare case. When one starts empirically to measure the man against his knowledge, his experience...even if he was a genius... there is so little there, that a scientist, an empiricist would reject his authorship. The non-empiricists drew the horizontal lines, the myths and legends, without evidence." He traced the lines with his fingertip for emphasis.

"The world accepted the schema of Shakespeare writing the works based on casual, prima facie examination much as the flat-worlders or the creationists would have us believe things. While the matter isn't scientific, it does lend itself to certain measurable proofs so the historian can exercise detective instincts and judgments, and deductions after the manner of Conan Doyle."

"Yes." Colton squirmed in the creaking desk. "Were you familiar with the arguments for other authors?"

"Only pedagogically. I would mention in lecture Bacon, Marlowe, and Jonson as possible authors because I had read occasional passages in the *Encyclopedia Britannica*. I inserted these tidbits as a means of perking up the lecture and I always noticed that even the youngest boys would suddenly prick up their ears. Children, and it's true in every generation, we know this, our children can recognize a fraud more quickly than we can. They have the innate ability to be objective because their biases are undeveloped and every subject appears to them in a fresh and meaningful perspective. It's particularly true in this controversy.

"I show the paucity of facts about the Stratford man and my students become immediately suspicious. When I offer the alternatives to him, they are most curious as to which one fits the author. One young man wrote a paper devoted to Bacon as the true author, making me curious enough about the subject to spend more time on it. And so I constructed, as much as I could, a paradigm, a model, and a profile of the man or woman who wrote the works. I delved into the sonnets and plays for over a year with a mind towards listing the traits of expertise and knowledge a person would own—most of which required a wealth of experience. Genius alone couldn't supply much of this background. If such was the case, then all one needs on a tour of unfamiliar territory is to hire a genius as a tour guide. The guide would have had no need to have actually visited the sites before setting out. He would know every brick, every blade from having read about it. Landmarks would become meaningless."

"Ah, but landmarks." Colton waved the fingers on his left hand as if one finger would be impolite and too pontifical. "The landmarks of his travels, his life and associations, his experiences are those which take us directly to the destination marked the Earl of Oxford."

The small man nodded and giggled from deep within as if overcome by the puerile simplicity of the discovery. "After I made these conclusions, I tried to erase my knowledge of Bacon, Marlowe, and Jonson. I arrived at `some legitimate surmises as to what we might expect to be the conditions of his life, and the relationship of his contemporaries towards him,' to quote from my book. I reconstructed the biographical lapidary of the true monument to the man and I concluded it should contain the following engravings..." He rose from the tiny desk and paced the floor next to Colton's desk, counting points off on his fingers. "One, a mysterious, recognized genius—possibly the record of wasted genius. Two, a person who was not merely necessarily eccentric but probably capable of dramatic whims. Three, an aloof person who might have suffered the envious hostility of other lesser beings. Four, an individual who may have had his works inadequately presented given the limitations of theatre at the time—thus, not personally appreciating the full value of his or her creation. Five, yet he or she would have had extensive literary knowledge ranging from classical and Italian literature to a more than casual knowledge of history—and be recognized as a strong, lasting force among contemporary literati. Six, almost without saying, a lover and devotee to the theatre. Seven, a poet of some substantial consequence—even if unable to use his own name. Eight, a widely educated individual who continually associated with the intellectuals of the day.' Yes. These are the general features."

Colton laughed in unfettered delight.

"As for particular characteristics, I had nine specifically listed based on my extensive readings of the plays and sonnets. `One, a man with feudal connections. Two, a member of the higher aristocracy. Three, connected with Lancastrian supporters. Four, an enthusiast for Italy, and especially the literature. Five, a follower of sport, including falconry. Six, a lover of music. Seven, loose and improvident in money matters. Eight, doubtful, and somewhat conflicting in his attitude to women. Nine, of probably Catholic leanings, but touched with skepticism.'" His hazel eyes danced in the sunlight. Colton held the widest of smiles.

"How did you come around to de Vere?" Colton asked, leaning forward on the desk as if never before hearing the story.

"I marked Oxford down as the author after reading *Venus and Adonis* again because it was, for whomever the author, an `early work,' to quote from my book, `kept in manuscript for some years....' and `it seemed to stand just where his anonymous works begin.' It appeared to me that `the facility with which he uses the particular form of stanza employed in this poem pointed to his having probably used it freely in shorter lyrics.'

"Therefore, when I discovered a small anthology of sixteenth century poetry in the London Public Library and Archives, which featured most all young suspects of that day before *Venus and*

Adonis was published, only two poems seemed to match in style and substance. One was anonymous and the other was on *Woman's Changeableness* and was signed `E. of O.' I said it was `enhanced by the force of contrast with other work of the same period, and on the other hand emphasized by a sense of its harmony with Shakespeare's work.'"

Colton's memory was now working overtime on the discovered lines. He shared his observations. "The line `How oft from Phoebus do they flee to Pan' reminds us of Queen Gertrude's flight from `Hyperion to a satyr.' Women as `haggards' that `fly from man to man' so one would `shake them from the fist/and let them fly...which way they list' bears a strong resemblance to Othello's threat `If I do prove her haggard/...I'd whistle her off and let her down the wind, / To prey at fortune.' Oxford also uses the metaphor of the falcon lure, a training device, like Petruchio does in training Kate, `For then she never looks upon her lure.'"

"Dr. Colton, you have an exquisitely incisive memory. I must read your book soon. At any rate, I was absolutely shocked to find one of the leading Shakespearian biographers, Sir Sidney Lee, contributing an article to the *Dictionary of National Biography* about Oxford and it read, `Oxford, despite his violent and perverse temper, his eccentric taste in dress, and his reckless waste of his substance, evinced a genuine taste in music and wrote verses of much lyric beauty.... Puttenham and Meres reckon him among the best for comedy in his day; but though he was a patron of players, no specimens of his dramatic productions survive.... A sufficient number of his poems is extant to corroborate Webbe's comment, that he was the best of the courtier poets in the early days of Queen Elizabeth,' and `In the rare devices of poetry he may challenge to himself the title of the most excellent among the rest.'"

Colton interrupted. "Thomas Babington Macaulay wrote that he `shone at the court of Elizabeth, and had won for himself an honorable place among the early masters of English poetry.'"

Looney rubbed his chin ruefully. "My downfall was the dating for *The Tempest*. Thank heavens you rescued me."

"Ah, the 'still vexed Bermooths,'" Colton said, "when we discovered the wreck of the *Edward Bonaventure*, from an account in *Hakluyt* dated 1600, three years before *The Tempest* was written. Yes, de Vere had held a fiduciary interest in it, so when it shipwrecked in Bermuda, de Vere knew its fate."

"If only I'd gone to the National Maritime Museum where the ship had been registered in the names of the investors, including Oxford's." Looney's eyes tracked lugubriously across the stained wood floor as though it concealed the secrets of the doomed *Edward Bonaventure*.

"But the end of that episode is likely that the Bermooths was a seedy section of London where Vermouth became popular, thus the early suburb's name. The ownership of the sailing vessel is still salient—especially given the fact that it was wrecked," Colton said.

The late afternoon sun had been dipping beyond large oak trees surrounding the schoolhouse. A cool breeze swept through the open windows jutting flower boxes and through the doors where the children had rushed by the man, deep in thought and forgetting his placement here from future time and place. Energetic pixies burst in, a subtle inspiration to their master, bolts of youthful strength to the visitor, reminders of now forgotten notions of unlimited seconds ahead and afternoons then forever. With a jolt, Colton realized these simple, roytish innocents, with clear eyes and perfect complexions, were his own contemporaries—many of them now dead from the wars and upheavals of the century ahead, lives irredeemably lost. Survivors' hopes and idealism would be wasted along the way, discarding the ability to acknowledge other's ideas with open minds, behind which stood the curiosity about great books, art, philosophy, and even religion. Most were in the fervid pursuit of commercial affairs. Commerce, as wedded to their adulthoods and the devotion to their recreation on this sunny, spring day in this northern town on the Tyne. One or two might retain the vision, the fascination, the willingness to explore deep thought, to write, to compose, to create. These few would certainly be the exception in a busy century. Some of them might have made a difference. Tyler Colton hoped he had.

Now they ignored him as if he were a tired old man, yet he had been in their time the same age as they, though his play was on another continent. But he was equally in wonder at life begun. He had not accomplished enough, he reminisced in his old man's body and mind, to satisfy an eager, intelligent, insatiable mind. Why did he feel as though he were dying? Why God? No further pursuit of knowledge. Or was he afraid that all life's mystery would be revealed in the afterlife? He did not know what motivated his fear; he only felt its persistence. What caused this current bodily predicament? He couldn't recall. Was it snakebite? He'd always been deathly afraid of snakes. Was it his heart? No recall. Determined, he prayed for Divine Providence to delay death so he might accomplish one more thing—he could not know or remember, for the moment, what it was.

Colton saw Looney in quiet tears. He must have felt his sadness and know about the dilemma of death. This is absurd, Colton thought, now Looney's smiling.

"Here's one of our cheery friends. I believe he intends to recite young Edward de Vere's *Woman's Changeableness*."

A trim, well-groomed, elderly man with grey hair in a dark suit stood before the two seated men. Several children, tired from playing, scattered shyly against the stark grey-green walls of the schoolhouse to hear the new arrival. "It's Wodehouse," yelled one of the brighter boys. "Where's Psmith?" The British voice was a gentle, clear, baritone capable of gratifying any radio listener or any audience appreciative of stentorian sonority.

"I'll read to you Psmith some other time, lads. I'm going to recite a poem from a youthful nobleman." He grinned and jerked his head back as he began:

> If women could be fair and yet not fond,
> Or that their love were firm not fickle, still,
> I would not marvel that they made men bond,
> By service long to purchase their good will,
> But when I see how frail those creatures are,
> I muse that men forget themselves so far.
>
> To mark the choice they make, and how they change
> How oft from Phoebus do they flee to Pan,
> Unsettled still like haggards wild they range,
> These gentle birds that fly from man to man,
> Who would not scorn and shake them from the fist
> And let them fly, fair fools, which way they list?

"Who is he?" whispered Tyler Colton as he pointed to the man reading Oxford. "Wodehouse?"

> Yet for disport, we fawn and flatter both,
> To pass the time when nothing else can please,
> And train them to our lure with subtle oath,
> Till, weary of their wiles, ourselves we ease;
> And then we say, when we their fancy try,
> To play with fools, Oh what a fool was I.

"P.G. Wodehouse," answered Looney, which Colton repeated.

The day sister was puzzled and concealed a grin. "What did he say this time?"

"Odd." Aunt Joan slapped her knee with the book. "Was it Piggy? Piggy Whorehouse? How odd"

Chapter Eleven

"Hatfield House," Scarborough lectured as they passed through the north suburbs of London in Phelps's VW Rabbit. "Specifically the Royal Palace of Hatfield and the enormous grounds around it are where, according to Lord Treasurer William Cecil, Elizabeth sat when she first heard the news of Queen Mary's death. All of twenty-five years old, her first act was to summon Cecil to seek his advice."

"Lord Burghley was William Cecil?" Phelps's normally husky voice rose inquisitively. "De Vere's father-in-law?"

"Right. The property remains in the family, the current Marquess of Salisbury. One of them was PM three times. Veronica's father and I toured the place several months ago. It has numerous paintings—William Cecil, Lord Burghley, ever the grey-beard of Polonius; Robert Cecil, the hunchback son who appeared to be an old man; and Queen Elizabeth in two extraordinary portraits that probably reveal as much about her as any artist was allowed. There is a most famous portrait by Sir Joshua Reynolds of Robert Cecil, First Marchioness of Salisbury, who was ennobled by George II. Sir Robert, Burghley's son, became the First Earl of Salisbury. Oh yes, he's buried in a church just a stone's throw away. You can see it up on the hillside from Hatfield."

"I wish we'd had a bite while in Stratford," Phelps said. Why don't we stop? I haven't eaten since lunch and it's nearly 8:00 p.m."

Veronica was sympathetic. "Good idea. Ian, can't we at least have some fish and chips somewhere or a sandwich?"

"Time is not on our side. Those three intruders may have already accomplished their mission by now. I suggest we carry on."

"How's your ear?" Veronica asked.

"Much better, thank you. It's clogged with ear medicine but I believe the infection is abating." Ian was speaking louder than usual because of the ear and his station in the back of the noisy compact car.

Phelps glanced at the gasoline gauge as he drove. "How much further do we have to go? We're on empty. So's my stomach."

"About twenty kilometers, I suspect."

They pulled over to a small petrol station. Phelps pumped, Veronica gathered snacks, and Ian paid. "I'm surprised at Phelps's willingness to slow the chase," Ian told Veronica. Had the temporary confinement made him contrite and tamed his zealous nature?

Veronica resumed her position in the front passenger seat and tore open bags of crisps as they continued along the route to Hatfield. Ian nudged her elbow playfully. "Your father and I had the good fortune of receiving a personally guided tour from the librarian of the Burghley archives, a Mr. Banfield Smith. He was most helpful. He took the trouble of retrieving a letter in de Vere's hand addressed to Lord Burghley asking him for money while visiting the continent. De Vere heard the news of his wife's delivering a child shortly after he'd arrived in Italy. Remember, she was Burghley's daughter."

"My father told me that because of Oxford's suspicion that he had not produced the child, that message caused his complete falling out with Burghley," Veronica said.

"This singular row with Burghley," Ian said, "launched his life into a ghastly state of personal turmoil in which the two men, in spite of an earlier close relationship, were never to thoroughly make up.

Take a left here and carry on about six kilometers. We're approaching the grounds."

Ian leaned forward to grasp some crisps from the bag Veronica offered, and then continued sharing his knowledge. "In 1607, ten years after Burghley's death and three years after de Vere's death, Sir Robert Cecil had the quadrangular palace torn down except for the remaining sides, which you'll see. It's the Old Palace Hatfield and was made into stables by Robert when he built the sprawling house. The house, finished after his death, hold much of the works and letters of all the Cecils who matter, many prominent to this day.

"Has anyone been through the letters with a mind towards a cover-up on de Vere writing the works?" Phelps asked.

"No, not to our knowledge. We Oxfordians believe Burghley was such a careful administrator and held such firm power that all direct clues were destroyed by him or by his son. But no one has really attempted such a search. A scheme like that would cost much time and money. If there's enough awareness among young scholars, then possibly some corpus delicti might turn up some day.... Maybe that's what the section in the monument in Stratford held."

"Now when did Shakespeare die?" Phelps asked.

"1616." Veronica and Ian replied in unison.

"Plenty of time, after the death of Oxford in 1604, for Robert Cecil to assign a real person named Shakespeare to the works and allow time for that person to `complete' the works in 1623," Veronica observed.

"And construct a monument in Stratford in 1623 once the local legend had been established about the man who was off in London `writing,'" Phelps added.

"With the monument erected in the church, it brings to mind a compelling question. Namely, who would place clues to Oxford's authorship in the monument about seven years after Shakspeare's death and nineteen after Oxford died?" Veronica asked.

"Most of us believe all was done and planned long before then with Oxford's tacit approval and it was thought to be an open secret at Court," said Ian. "But before the *First Folio*, arrangements were made with the brothers Herbert, James the First awarded the title of Lord Chamberlain to one of them. That title had charge of the Royal Theatre, a title de Vere inherited as Earl of Oxford, until death. The Herberts published the *First Folio* in 1623, some say the exact year the Shakespeare monument was erected."

"Who were the Herberts, again?" Phelps asked after a healthy sip of soda.

"Phillip was the Earl of Montgomery and his elder brother William was the Earl of Pembroke. Together they published the *First Folio* with the blessing of Robert Cecil, the Treasurer. Pembroke was Ben Jonson's patron and paid him an annual stipend of £25 to write the introduction to that most important collection of plays and sonnets. Here's the scoop—Phillip married de Vere's daughter Susan de Vere in 1605, so they wanted to see her father's works published even if he could not receive proper credit for them. Both brothers occupied the Lord Chamberlain position during all of the crucial years before and after publication. They were offered other positions, even more powerful ones, and declined—Pembroke would not budge unless his brother took his place. Another brother eventually was awarded the Master of Revels, which oversaw the day to day operations of publications.

"Hmmmm, married a year after Edward de Vere's death." Phelps raised his eyebrows. "To the perfect husband for the mission, no less."

"Boone, hang a right here and we should see...there it is. Well, as you might imagine, the Herberts might have been unwilling coconspirators in this cover-up. But their motive was to have the works published under their guidance, hoping Jonson would leave enough clues in the introduction to the *Folio* so a member of some future generation would discover the fraud. Also, half of the works would have been lost forever. They were fearful of someone else publishing first. Here we are."

The car entered a wide drive with a guardhouse to the right. Large black iron gates partially stood open flanked by two parked police cars, their lights flashing. Two men, one a police officer and the other a guard, emerged from the two-story guardhouse with its old, orange brick, the same colour as the four-foot high brick wall on either side of the iron gates. The officer immediately walked towards the boot of their car to inspect the license plate while the guard marched up to the driver's side as Phelps rolled down his window.

"Looks as though we didn't make it in time," Ian lamented.

"There's been a break-in. Sorry, we can't allow you in here presently." The guard was nervously clutching a large torch.

"We're press," Boone bellowed and flashed his press card. "I'm with the *International Herald Tribune* and these two folks are the *London Daily Times*. We're covering this story."

The policeman walked around to the open window and bent down to peer in. "I'm not sure there's a story here. No one entered the building."

Ian leaned forward to speak out the window. "Sir, I know Mr. Smith very well and I would like to have a brief word with him. If you'd care to ring him, I'm Ian Scarborough of the *Daily Times*. I don't think he would mind at all."

"I'll ask him." The guard nodded, walked back to the guardhouse, and reemerged after about a minute. "Go ahead. You must wait 'til he's finished an interview with the inspector, however."

They drove through the gates and down the wide road sheltered by large, leafless trees. The Palace of Hatfield directly faced the drive and stood three stories tall, all yellow brick with a limestone trim. The imposing towers spoke the assurance of a formidable

Elizabethan palace. Indeed, this estate was where the young princess spent much of her childhood, and where she later held her first Council of State. They marveled at the larger Hatfield House, built by Robert, which had apparently not been the scene of the crime as evidenced by the activity of cars and people in the drive at the older palace.

A low, concrete latticework minimally protected the grounds. In the winter air, bare trees and bushes framed the grounds, casting eerie shadows over the moist, green grass splotched with what appeared in the moonlight to be occasional brown patches of dead grass. Small pools of water surrounded by stone borders interrupted the tidy, manicured grounds. The open spaces and immaculate gardens, replete with daisies even in dead of winter, emphasized a relative lack of development on these grounds north of London. The location fulfilled an aura of tradition, defying the ever-burgeoning creep from the south where foreign money and the mellifluous expressions of a dying empire were daily imposed on a culture which had been in years gone by the very seed of one of history's foremost empires. An ambience of majesty lingered in the nocturnal shadows.

"It's quite imposing even without the three sides of the quadrangle," Veronica said. "Older, elegant but much smaller."

Four police cars parked on the east side of the structure sat with lights penetrating the backside of the park, emphasizing that the action had taken place there. A small crowd stood around the cars as an even smaller group of men stood near the side entrance where a portal accepted autos.

"Boone, you've been in enough trouble today," Veronica said. "Why not wait here while Ian and I check this out?"

"Let's not run any risks that the flatties here have communicated with your friend at the Stratford police station," Ian implored him. "Please wait here. I know Mr. Smith."

"I'm not going to miss a story." Phelps anxiously twisted his lips in determination as he grabbed his ubiquitous notebook. Veronica reached for his shoulder when he jumped out of the car and whipped out press credentials before the two cooler mouths could issue another protest. Ian and Veronica dashed from their seats and fell in behind him.

"Officer, I'm Boone Phelps of the *International Herald Tribune*. Have you apprehended the perpetrators?" He flashed his credentials boisterously in the inspector's face. Red swirls of police lights flashed the group, underlining some sense of urgency.

"There seems to have been some sort of explosion here earlier this evening and three men made off with a small box from the back wall. No one knows exactly what was taken except it may have been a box of some sort." The officer paused. "You may read the crime report tomorrow morning. Nothing valuable was taken, apparently. They failed to enter the building."

Ian noticed Banfield Smith standing next to the officer as he apparently recognized Ian. "Hello, Mr. Smith, you may remember me, Ian Scarborough of the *London Daily Times*. I visited with you months ago with Dr. Tyler Colton. Did you see anything?"

"Hello, Mr. Scarb'ro," answered the slender old man with a warm smile and a handshake extended. "No. Unfortunately, the archives were closed. The cleaning maid, Mrs. Dorse, saw three blokes race for the back way—one carrying a small box—after she heard the explosion."

"Where was she?" Veronica asked.

"On the ground floor in the kitchen preparing to clean dishes. She had a view of the escaping men. That is, she heard them."

"Please, we're performing an investigation here," the officer shouted. "You may read the police report once it is filed. I insist tha—."

Banfield Smith interrupted. "Mr. Scarb'ro', you may accompany me after the police have completed their investigation. You may either wait in your auto or meet me back here in a half hour." He glanced at the Americans. "I prefer you come alone."

Phelps protested. "I'm a reporter as well."

Ian gripped Phelps's arm forcefully. "I'll see you soon, Mr. Smith. Let's go, Boone." Phelps was seething.

"Let's go have a meal," Veronica said, tapping him on the shoulder. "We'll find a place."

Phelps shrugged. "Let's go. Take me to the best in town. I guess it's been one of those days...but I'm not quitting. Ian, I want a story, too."

"You have my word. I'll share my notes."

Hatfield had an excellent restaurant that Ian remembered from the visit he made with Veronica's father. It was no more than five minutes away, not far from the famous pub where Dick Sikes of *Oliver Twist* was alleged to have retired for a drink after his heinous murder. The Markham offered fine English and Continental cuisine, and the three were lucky to find good seats in a lit corner.

"I knew I should have called the bureau in London and had them send someone out," Phelps grumbled, staring at the menu.

"You knew bloody well that you couldn't resist scooping the piece yourself," Ian said. "Boone, you required weeks of cultivating so many German politicians in the Flick matter. How did you expect to take up the running when I'd established sufficient prior contact with Smith?" Ian was clearly miffed. "I knew he'd remember me immediately."

"I'm sorry, but I'm afraid I'll never have a story again as big as Flick. It's been tough years," he mumbled.

"You won awards." Veronica's voice conveyed her impatience in clipped finality.

Phelps face turned white.

"I'm really afraid it'll be my last great success. I'm a reporter. Damn it. I love this. It's my life." He fidgeted with a pen.

A waiter appeared. "I'll have the loin of lamb covered with the basil and garlic mousse," Veronica said and smiled pleasantly. Ian adoringly watched her wide mouth as he sipped a Chablis. "For starters, I'll have the barley soup," she added.

Phelps shifted his weight in the large wooden chair. "Mushrooms for starters, the filet of beef with caramelised shallots, barley soup with extra watercress. Make my beef rare. Ah, a carafe of Beaujolais."

"Sir?" The waiter looked at Ian.

"I'm sorry. I must leave to meet someone. When I return," he placed his plastic on the tray, "charge these meals to that card. I'll see you in an hour or so. Cheers." Ian quickly rose before either of his companions could raise a protest.

He truly believed Phelps would not focus on the events of the day in the presence of such attractive company and sumptuous food. He also hoped Boone Phelps would order more wine.

Upon his return to Hatfield House, Ian sighted Banfield Smith conversing with the same inspector. Both sat inside the police car, each with a leg out of the opened doors. The other cars had disappeared.

"Thank you for allowing me to return and interview you," Ian said as Mr. Smith stepped out of the passenger's side. "I'm most grateful."

"I didn't care to talk to someone from the *International Herald Tribune*—especially since it's American. I trust you, Mr. Scarb'ro', because I read your reviews from time to time. In fact, I read with immense interest your editorial concerning the Shakespeare controversy and I cannot help feeling that this episode had something to do with that very subject. I heard a brief report on the Beeb concerning a break-in at Stratford last night and the night before."

"Perhaps. I'm not surprised since some of de Vere's letters are here." Ian coughed and rubbed his ear.

"Shall we retreat into the kitchen here? It's warmer. Mrs. Dorse is inside still." Smith was a small man, so thin his hips twisted slightly as he walked. He bundled his arms against a cold wind that intensified and caused Ian's ear to hurt once again.

"How is Dr. Colton getting along?" Smith suddenly asked. "He's a good egg."

"Not well, I'm afraid," Ian replied as they passed over the threshold into a cozy warm kitchen, ample succour to big feasts. "He suffered a clot four days ago, in a coma ever since."

"Oh dear. Most sorry to hear that. Wish him well if he wakes up. May I introduce Mrs. Eileen Dorse, ably serving as the cleanup expert who works frequently in this kitchen during special events." He pointed a slender, elegant right hand towards a large woman who wore an olive green sweater stretched around her rotund figure. In her sixties, she stood nearly six feet tall with very rosy cheeks and forehead as if embarrassed about something, although it appeared to be a permanent, natural condition. "Mrs. Dorse, meet Mr. Ian Scarb'ro', a newspaper reporter with the *London Daily Times*. He has only a few questions for us and I'm cooperating because I want the public to know the truth on this matter. None of the other media bothered to show except for the locals."

"A pleasure to make your acquaintance, Mrs. Dorse." Ian felt she was immediately charmed and at ease with him. Her engaging smile indicated that she clearly wasn't intimidated by his height or his purpose.

"Likewise," she said.

Ian whipped out a notebook and pen from his shirt pocket. "Could you merely describe for me what you saw and heard?"

"Yes. Well, I was cleaning up the fridge, overdue for a defrost, when I heard loud drilling for a while. It raised my curiosity so I went to the window and listened." She pointed to the window above a large table. The glass was cracked open about an inch. "I heard it through the window so I swung it open a little and listened for a bit. I couldn't determine where the sound had actually occurred and turned around to work again on the fridge when I heard a loud explosion and sensed it was somewhere at the rear of the building. I rang the guard gate, and they rang the police who came in about five minutes."

Ian was writing furiously. He nodded at her pause. "And then?"

"Well, I believed the horrid noise came from the back of the house so I was frightened. I decided to turn off these lights because I had only been inside the kitchen for five minutes. I'd been in the hallway closet before I came in here, removing the cleaners and toilet articles for distribution. I work once a week." Her already ruddy cheeks were turning redder in her excitement. "I explained to the guards that I was inside the kitchen and would remain there until they or the police arrived. About a minute after turning the light off, I heard some voices and one sounded either Aussie or American. He said something like, `Did anything fall out?' Another, a cockney, said. `It's not damaged all that bad.' The first one, or yet another one, yelled, `Papers can't fall out as long as we didn't do much damage.' The other one, either Australian or Yank, clearly said, `Yeah, but in the box old papers can crumble.' They were on foot and apparently rendezvousing outside my window." She drew a steady, deep breath. "It happened very quickly."

"Did you have a look at any of the men?" Ian inquired.

"No. Certainly not! They were passing right beneath the window...I...was afraid. Oh, I forgot to mention what one of them said. It was rather odd. The fellow who may have been cockney said something like, `Ale need your 'omes cat for this li-ul caper, chief. I'ull take more than a clod.'" She perfectly mimicked a cockney accent. So well, Ian thought, that even he wasn't quite sure he got what was said.

"Clod, yes, a policeman. What the phrase `omes cat' would be." Smith raised his wiry palms, "I do not bloody know."

Ian could not imagine how a cat could be involved.

"Officer Burns believes the men knew the area very well," Smith continued, and he's having a go at the grounds behind the palace tomorrow at daybreak after his routine check tonight. He surmises they escaped on foot, joining a getaway car nearby. We're enquiring throughout the neighborhood for any other reports on the men."

"Do you recall any other remarks?" Ian asked her.

"No. What I described was quite close to what I heard."

"Are you sure the one was American? Or Australian?"

"No. But the rest I heard were English, except for that one Yank, or he could have been an Aussie. He was not from here."

"Where, may I ask, is your transportation, Mrs. Dorse?"

"She lives just by the pub on Church Street down the way with her son and daughter-in-law," Smith said. "She usually walks here."

"It's good exercise, you know," she said jovially.

"Right. You've been most helpful, Mrs. Dorse. I'm to file this story by telephone for Monday's edition. I won't use your name. I'll only identify you as `a witness overhearing.' Much thanks."

"I'm delighted to be of any help." She bowed her head obediently.

"I'm depositing you home tonight," Smith said. She nodded.

Ian shook her hand warmly and turned to Mr. Smith. "Do you mind, sir, if we have a look at the damage to the tower?"

"Not at all. I'll fetch a torch I returned to the boot just before you arrived. I should've planned to leave it out for us. Please wait here, Mrs. Dorse."

As Ian followed him to the auto, the wind began to howl around the ancient stone building. Smith turned the key in the boot and lifted it, immediately locating the torch. He flipped the small switch and the beam shot to the sky and infinity.

"The ground is somewhat soft since we had all the ice and snow, so do step carefully." The torchlight danced to the tempo of the little man's jerky gait as he walked and talked. "We'll have to stay outside of the police tape, of course."

The soil squished as they plodded along some one hundred feet towards the tower that jutted out from the base of the back wall. Ian could see a solid silhouette in the radiance of a half-moon now peeking over the dramatic slope of Jacobean roof, a renovation since the seventeenth century. Two small round chimneys sat on top of the tower like antennae to the stars in the clear, frigid, windy night. As they approached the rear of the tower, Ian noticed a doorway topped by two rectangular openings. Smith's beam settled on the side area of a gentle buttress creeping up the tower until the structure was even with the second open window where it abruptly ended.

"They obviously knew what they were looking for and precisely where to look," Mr. Smith announced firmly. "We believe they scouted this area earlier today, maybe marked the brick for a quick drilling and then had a go at it with some well-placed miniature explosives. Well planned and well executed, I'd say."

"Do you have any idea what they were extracting from that space?" Ian leaned forward just over the tape, his neck stretched. "It's amazing more damage wasn't done here. It was as if the explosives were set to topple the area above where the alleged box could have sat so as not to damage the box or its contents."

"I have only one idea." Smith looked up at Ian's light blue watery eyes as he paused. "Is this totally on a lobby basis?"

"You have my word I shall not print anything which would prevent me from solving this mystery. I'm having a go at the bigger story, unlike Phelps, my American friend. I see no need to print anything beyond this point and I'm relating that to my editor. I'm not relating this aspect to Phelps or anyone else."

"There was a rumor that Sir Robert Cecil had something placed there when he demolished the other three quadrangles of the structure and left only this side. Some say it's why he built the towers to begin with, aside from aesthetical considerations."

"Who are `they' who say that?"

"Oh, there's nothing written in the archives. I can't recall who specifically told me. It's mostly a legend—like the proverbial haunted castle or resident ghost."

Ian felt a slight shiver spill down his spine. He could not wait to return to the restaurant to tell Veronica Colton, and only her, that "the game was afoot" now more than ever.

Chapter Twelve

The culprits had been thorough in fashioning an escape from the grounds of Hatfield House in a getaway car rented with false credentials to a Henry Hooper of Leeds. Hooper had died in a plane crash, but his wallet had been found in the wreckage and placed via black market in a Soho porn shop where the manager did such things as were necessary to earn extra pounds.

Two of the accomplices were dropped off at St. Albans where they took a train back into London. The American paid the two men the balance of their fee of £3,000 each in cash before they boarded. The short, cockney bloke chauffeured the tall, angular Yank, who worked diligently in the back seat.

Dressed in a dark grey double-breasted suit, he sat calmly amidst a small Samsonite suitcase and an ancient box. On the floor lay a variety of large books, several old record album covers from the forties, many architectural tubes, a large map-carrying case, and two old-style computer binders. He selected the binders as perfect for the task. Indeed, only one binder, referred to as a 20-point cover, was necessary. The computer printout, in its standard alternating green and white horizontal stripes, referred to as "unburst" in computer parlance, would fit perfectly when one of the documents was slipped between the folds. It had worked well with the box from the Stratford break-in. He'd placed them in the binder in less than an hour after photographing them at his hotel near Picadilly.

As they drove towards Gatwick, he dutifully removed the documents from the remarkably well-preserved bronze chest that stood only about four inches in height and was about nine inches square. This box had a darker hue, probably due to moisture, but it was identical, as far as he could tell, to the one found in the Trinity Church monument. He proceeded to pry a small metal hinge off the side. There were no locks, only hinges. He anticipated the box's contents as he completed his work with a hammer and screwdriver in about five minutes.

The box revealed documents he had expected to find by virtue of his contact's revelation to him only days before in spite of his meticulous planning over the past six months. "What am I after?" he'd implored in every meeting.

"Please, bear in mind that it's not the least bit important to you because it's nothing more than a small box," came the reply. "Likely, you'll find old documents that could be as large as about a square foot. Take good care. That's all you need to know."

The first document, a letter on brownish-white parchment, contained a signature he couldn't quite make out in the dim light of his flashlight. Most papers were about eight inches long by ten inches wide, and the entire stack was about four inches thick according to a razor-thin ruler he slid along the edge of the trove. A black, steel-hard wood filled the box around the documents, a most impenetrable wood—perhaps that of the Yew tree. The handwriting would probably be legible to an Elizabethan scholar, although there was evidence of a few wormholes. The documents, at first, appeared to be in more than sufficient condition for photographing, a duty he would soon fulfill during his journey as the clock approached 6:30 p.m. If he failed to make the 8:35 p.m. flight from Gatwick to Kennedy, then he would stay at a nearby bed and breakfast until the mid-morning flight. However, he wanted desperately to leave the country as soon as possible—before the police figured out what was missing and where to look. Traffic was flowing steadily down the M30 as smoothly as several days before when he and the driver had made a practice run. So far the police scanner had made only one mention of their incursion into the wall of Hatfield House—the original report at about 5:00 p.m.

A shiver slid down his back at the prospect of being caught. In spite of his serious demeanor, he resolutely lacked an interest in antiquity. But it dawned on him briefly as it had the night before, "I'm the first person to see these documents, and touch them, in probably four hundred years!" Then he went back to work.

He set the box next to his feet on the floor and retrieved a self-developing Polaroid Spectra camera—a simple way to photograph the documents once and be assured the final product would be of such quality to allow his employers to ascertain the substance of his treasure trove. In case he was apprehended while leaving the country, he would send the photos to them by dropping them in a mailbox upon arrival at Gatwick. The packet of photos from the night before was already stamped and sealed for mailing. Meticulously, he lodged the camera onto a special close-up lens attachment designed for use with the Polaroid. It included a ten-inch strap that could measure the proper distance for perfect focus when deployed.

Ever alert for any news on the radio of their exploits earlier that evening, the tall man sat in the back seat and pulled curtains closed on his windows—wire curtains he had rigged to prevent light from entering while allowing little light to escape. Many times he had practiced the photography on samples of small-print computer paper with nearly illegible print thanks to a frazzled old computer ribbon. To further block light to the outside world, he'd stretched an overcoat formed like a tent over his head—a maneuver that had worked marvelously while testing the procedure. In the partly cloudy night, he imagined the odd sight of cars passing and seeing occasional flashes. Would this precipitate a suspicion he had stolen something? He didn't think so. His partner drove silently at 75km an hour. He had nearly five hundred shots in the rolls of film inside the suitcase. He turned off the inside car lights as he worked, and placed a small bright lamp next to him to accomplish the tedious and important task of placing each document inside the computer cover after completing the two photos per document. The lamp provided just enough light for the photographs. The entire time he wore latex gloves to maintain traction on the documents and, of course, leave no fingerprints.

After photographing the first document, he noticed there was a thin layer of cloth between the first and second documents, which he removed. "Better keep it," he mumbled aloud.

"Wot'd you say?" the driver asked.

"Nothing, Tom. Just whispering to myself. Keep on driving. Can you see these flashes?" he shouted above the radio.

"Only a li'ul," he said.

The tedious process was necessary to manifest an appearance to airport security that the computer binder, ancient as it was, was a normal American tax receipt register. From all outward appearances, it was. His passport, under the name Marvin N. Morris, would show him to be affiliated with the tax assessor's office in Brock County, Colorado. He would say he was getting advice on modern tax reportage in a conference. But the exercise was simply a precaution against airport security being alerted to what was taken from Hatfield House and, especially if the information received from his superiors was accurate, that no one would understand the contents of the tax binder. No inventory. Besides, the tip about the laxity of the Stratford police had been right on the money.

Interested solely in completing the mission and collecting a fee, he failed to notice any further particulars about the documents. He would hopefully hear of the outcome, in favorable terms, afterwards.

Each photo developed remarkably well, but he was surprised at his impatience. He'd practiced the procedure often and his expectations were disturbed only by the sense of it not being a drill. He numbered each photo consecutively to coincide with the exact order of the documents as they sat in the snug, ancient box. He would place the photos inside four large, bubbled manila envelopes to be mailed from Gatwick. He briefly thought again about the documents, resting and folded seriatim, starting with the first one at the front—to be placed inside the computer sheets so that when the documents were removed, the computer paper would simply need to be torn at each perforation. He'd also write corresponding numbers on the computer paper. Perfect. After rote repetition of the photo procedure and placing them inside the unburst sheets, that is, sheets still doubled up, housed in the green binder, his driver snapped his fingers and shouted, "Take it you're finished. Well, we're almost 'ome."

While placing the final documents inside the binder and the four envelopes of photos in the attaché case, the gaunt American could see the lights of Gatwick and the occasional float of a commercial airliner through the curtained windows. He had little to do now but wait until he stepped out of the vehicle. His suitcase was carefully packed and contained spartan necessities for the trip, except for his blue sweater and a deerstalker hat bought specifically for the upcoming meeting. He would leave it out for fear of it being crushed. He might even wear it at some point. No, on second thought, it would need to remain in the case. Gingerly, he placed it in the center and rolled up four balls of white socks as ballast and delicately closed the suitcase. He would set the attaché and the suitcase on an empty plane seat beside him. If there weren't an empty seat near, then he would merely find one—certainly no problem on a red-eye to New York.

The envelopes were sealed and ready for delivery. The driver was to take the scraps and other detritus home to burn in the fireplace, including the old boxes. But Michael McCann (his real name) had photographed the outsides and interiors of the boxes after inspecting them and finding nothing except scratches from wear and tear and small pockets of moisture.

As the car approached the airline entrance he reached into his inside suit pocket and withdrew an envelope stuffed with £3000. "Thanks, Tom. "

"Righto, chief." The cockney smiled brightly. "'Ave a good life. But wait a second while I to'ul up." He counted and nodded.

After checking flight information at the flight desk and a scurry to the loo, grips in hand, he emerged from the toilet just as a bobby was entering. McCann stared icily ahead. He'd seen a mail slot on his practice run, but for the moment he completely forgot where it was. He was certain it was in the toilet's vicinity. He kept circling the area. The bobby emerged from the loo, heading in his direction. His palms began to sweat. It was one hundred yards to customs. He broke into a slight trot as if concerned over missing his plane. His mind began to race—was the cop on to him?

Nervously, he circled around the lobby looking for the mail chute as several seconds, seeming like hours, ticked away. If caught, at least he would have tucked the envelopes of photos inside the mailbox, hopefully undetected before the bobby nabbed him. Where was the infernal round, red Royal mailbox?

He mustn't disturb the priceless contents of the tax binder, which he held under his arm and would carry onto the plane. Furtively, he glanced back towards the restroom. The cop was following, gaining ground. No use, he thought, I must look elsewhere—near the bar.

No, I'll ask at the newsstand. He crossed the lobby and heard a voice from behind. It was the bobby.

"Pardon me, sir."

He turned around and felt his face fall, his heart racing. He now saw, only thirty yards away, the familiar round, red Royal mailbox directly around the corner from the newsstand.

"Pardon me, sir," the bobby repeated as he broke into a grin, holding something over his right arm. "I saw this as I left the toilet. I believe I did recall seeing you with it as I entered. It's warm enough to leave a woolly. I found it on the floor there, sir."

Woolly, he thought. Yes, his sweater.

He grabbed the sweater. "Thank you," he said and puffed heavily in relief for the recovery of a simple sweater. He managed a weak grin. "Sweaters are like umbrellas. I leave them everywhere I go. Otherwise I would be a wealthy man. My wife always nags over the habit."

"A woolly and a brolly cost some lolly." The bobby chuckled. McCann smiled nervously, not understanding brolly and lolly. "What part of America do you hail from?"

"Colorado," he lied. They turned to continue walking towards the mailbox. "I've been in London for a week and had a super time. I love the theatre. As a matter of fact, I'm about to mail some photos to some of your fair citizens whom I met backstage when I met one of your famous actors after a recent performances." The mailbox was now within ten feet.

"Who was it?"

"I've forgotten his name, but quite big over here."

"Yes." The bobby reached for the mail slot to assist him. "The West End isn't Hollywood."

"Fortunately. Acting is better here. Thanks." He dropped the envelopes face down so the bobby would only see the writing of PHOTOS and DO NOT BEND spread across the back.

"I'm sure they'll enjoy the photos." The bobby waved as if to end the discussion.

"Thanks again."

"Have a safe return."

"Thanks." The bobby walked towards the lobby, and the lofty "Colorado theatre buff" sighed in relief.

McCann placed identification on his small suitcase and confirmed his seat on the 7:15 flight to New York. He dreamed of downing at least four whiskys and going to sleep with the tax receipt register carefully connected to his wrist by a strand of dental floss to awaken him if someone grabbed the documents. Thus, he could catch up on much needed sleep.

British customs proved no problem. The officer merely glimpsed at his identification and asked if he had anything to declare. McCann said no, and the officer nodded and handed him his passport.

Only two security people per machine manned the two X-ray machines at the international terminal. He chose the machine on his far left because it was closest and would draw no particular suspicion about him as he sought to give the impression of a typical, loquacious American tourist—a little insouciant chatter to create a relaxed atmosphere.

"Great night to fly, bad night to drive," he said, glancing at both guards.

"Sparkling day. Splendid," replied the fellow behind the machine, focusing on the screen as the tall Yank laid the attaché and the full binder of computer printouts on the rubber roller. A short, wide-bellied man in uniform stood on the other side of the machine and ran a round electronic rod up and down McCann's rangy body. It was all he could do to reach the top of his shoulders. "It's a good thing you're not wearing the hat," he grunted.

The American did not reply but heard the young machine operator laugh quietly, wink, and say, "Of course, Holmes."

It instantly dawned on McCann that the young man had seen the deerstalker hat and made the joke, unprofessional as it was to do so, probably failing to closely observe the register. What a clever distraction, he thought. I couldn't have had a better one if I had planned it! He felt elated. Now—home free.

Confidently, he knew he was past customs as his vocal chords tightened like a boxer's pectorals set to strike. Only customs in New York remained. Calmly, but resolutely, his strong left hand clasped the wide, black attaché. He would celebrate his accomplishment with five, no six, whiskys. He would arrive at Kennedy Airport in little over eight hours, relieving himself of his burden of ancient jottings into the hands of a few celebrants later in the week. They would be ostensibly anxious for his treasure trove to be delivered at a secluded perch in the Shawangunk Mountains in the great state of New York. Soon he would be home free.

Chapter Thirteen

"All we know is this—three or four men, one with a cockney accent and one with an American or Australian accent, although we lean towards him being a Yank, and one of the group is a large man. That last bit is according to the size of one of the shoeprints. Artifacts are involved, some sort of treasure, probably old documents possibly relating to Shakespeare," said the detective between puffs on a long-stored nonfilter Sullivan. "Of course, if there's an American involved, I had to alert you, Joe. Even if he left the country last night right after the incident, I'm sure he's been through customs. We failed to spread the word until this morning. The Hatfield officials weren't too pleased by all this."

"Adam, if you'd called sooner, we could have alerted all the major airports first," Joe said. "Same old story. This isn't terrorism, evidently, so it doesn't get priority."

"As I said, no one took the crimes very seriously at the local constabularies. The one in Stratford had just been broken into two nights running and they had no clues. They held some reporter who wandered in and was idiotically questioning whether there had been a break-in in the first instance. In Hatfield, the authorities didn't know quite what to make of it since the penetration was on the outside of the building. Much confusion, regrettably, on our end."

"Do you have any other clues whatsoever?" Joe asked.

"We're working on one...something about a cat. Do ignore that spot of information until we have it all sorted out." The detective stretched, blowing smoke out his window overlooking morning traffic. "It may be, pardon the pun, much ado about nothing. Possibly some coincidence of vandalism, although I'll say something was secreted in the two spaces. The mustiness suggests they hadn't been disturbed in some time."

"All's well that ends well," Joe replied dryly. He couldn't resist. "I'm getting on the horn to New York after we hang up. I'll alert them. As for greater matters, we've found Mulcahy at an apartment in Boston. He's the contact on the arms shipments and we think he was behind that bombing in Sligo years back. I'll tell you more about it at the confab in Manchester next week. My wife's anxious to meet Amy. She is coming?"

"Yes, she is. We've already selected a restaurant. Great curry. We shall be so delighted. Oh, Joe, I'm sending some more data on the Sligo bombing—through crypt. A code P."

"I'll read it. Good to hear from ya. See ya in a week."

"Likewise. Cheers."

"Good-bye."

Chapter Fourteen

"An enormous disappointment," Ian said to Veronica from a straight-backed chair in the cramped hospital room two days after returning from Hatfield. He'd spent the previous day filing a story, then rested. Now he fidgeted and chewed his cuticles nervously, rueful and daunted at the prospect of leaving the chase just as things were heating up.

Veronica stared at the tubes in her father's nose and mouth. Not much she could do about that, but she sensed Ian's need for soothing an emotional wound. That she could provide. "Ian, you know Vines is playing `editor-who-knows-best.' He knows you're on to something, but there aren't any clues beyond your housekeeper witness at Hatfield House. So he wants you to leave for New York and enjoy yourself. You know yourself that there isn't enough evidence to print a large story on the speculation as to what was in the secret spaces in either Trinity or Hatfield, because...well...it'd be nothing more than speculation. He's hoping for a bigger story. You said you told Smith that, too. That's what you—you—and only you, Vines assured you, will cover if new clues come forward. He even promised to bring you back instantly from New Paltz if that happens."

"But I'm the one who initiated the subject, who began this crusade. Now that I've developed the case and have some clues, he removes me from the local beat and installs Emmitt. What rot! Brian Emmitt—plain dotty—that bloody, dimwitted curmudgeon. Vines is trying to force me to resign. He knows how vital this issue is to me.

He hasn't trusted my judgment beyond reporting that small story on page twenty-three yesterday morning on the Hatfield incident. He doesn't want me to have a go at the larger story, just as he doesn't trust my judgment on reviewing that rubbish they call music. It's a ruse, a setup, so he can sack me." He rose and took two giant strides to the window and gripped the plastic curtain rods. The room was compressed as though it was too small for him and his anger.

"No. Don't believe it. Emmitt is, you told me this morning over the phone, the best old investigative reporter on the paper if not on the entire street. But the culprits aren't in England with the artifacts. I'd bet on it. He won't find them here. The American is probably in some exotic place like Nice or Bangkok or Walla Walla, selling those artifacts to some billionaire who'll in turn reveal their existence while on his deathbed after the statute of limitations has run out sometime in the next generation." Veronica lowered her voice and planted a flashy, feinting smile at a uniformed lady who had suddenly appeared to close the half-open door. Now she fell to a whisper, like a child caught shouting in class. "Go and have a good time. Besides, Ian, if the Yank went to Walla Walla instead of Nice or Bangkok, you are only five or six hours away in case Emmitt's connections at Scotland Yard pay off. Vines won't send Emmitt. He'll call you and send you. Otherwise, where do you look? There are no clues. The police don't seem that interested. Go to New Paltz. Ian, go to New York. I chatted with Admiral Sinclair about this. He agrees wholeheartedly."

"Nobody is taking the scope of this story seriously." He exhaled and returned to the uncomfortable chair. "I'm going to be sacked... back on the streets."

"Ian," she said, "just go to New York. Trust me."

He had to hand it to her. Her levelheaded demeanor under the circumstances did have a calming effect on him. On the other hand, he knew she was still an achiever while he had settled into a bland routine of review work for the newspaper with an occasional assignment like the current one. He'd made some money and was comfortable while she was yet moving down the runway. His life was music, the Oxford debate, composition, reviewing, investments, writing, Holmesians, dating, and reading. Her life was politics, society, speechwriting, American media, and public debate. Music was still his forte, words were hers.

He would concede on the immediate issue because there would likely be no developments as Veronica and Vines maintained. But Vines's stance to suggest he carry on with his trip was Ian's utmost concern—as if he wanted him out of England—and made him feel as if their relationship was further deteriorating. Ian was positive there were some clues. Someone, somewhere, had come across the precise knowledge to unearth some key artifacts. Desperately, as an afterthought, he resolved to try another tack.

"I'll go, but only if you accompany me." Of course he knew her answer upon speaking.

"I have to stay." She watched her father's chest rise and fall slowly. "I have no choice for at least two more weeks while Congress is out of session."

Dr. Colton's feet shuffled as he leaned against the heavy double doors and, with some effort, pushed them open to reveal an old banquet room. The floors creaked as if tattling on his late arrival and he hesitated, scanning the back rows for an open seat. Naturally, there was only one, in the front row of the audience. As in any meeting, most of the audience had congregated at the rear like recalcitrant sheep before the sheepdog appears, so he would have to take the seat near the front of the old hall on the second floor of the Hotel Peabody in Memphis.

Memphis, where he'd matriculated a year at Rhodes College before going to Dartmouth. As a boy, his mother once took him to the lobby to see the ducks that arrived at eleven each morning prancing off the elevator to gaily swim in the hotel fountain. Then they would return to the elevator at five to go to a night's rest on the roof. This time, for some reason, he'd managed to pass up the lobby. How had he suddenly arrived here in the ornate conference room on the second floor?

The words on the white banner above the wide head table read in two red lines, "'Folks Against Strokes' Roasts William Shakspere." Never had he heard of the charity, but the spelling of Shakspere made him comfortable. These were right-thinking people, for both causes, and he deserved to be up there with them unless.... He would listen and see what the event was about.

Men and women of disparate dress and age sat at the two head tables divided by a podium with the insignia "F.A.S." A microphone with an adjustable neck pointed innocuously into the space below the banner until the lofty Ian Scarborough popped in from behind the blue curtains and began speaking in his familiar voice.

"Welcome, ladies and gentlemen, and special greetings to those of you who've been so gracious as to interrupt your convalescence with your precious presence tonight. It shall be an exciting evening, for we've assembled those who've made marks in the world, particularly in literature. We've chosen to question the authorship of the works attributed to the man known to literary history as William Shakespeare. We Oxfordians, however, prefer to refer to him as Shakspere—without the second 'a' and the first 'e.' We also have a handwriting expert present to offer testimony. Please do be aware of the fact that many of these folks are coming to us from a time when the Seventeenth Earl of Oxford wasn't considered a prime suspect, as he is now. Some of these roasters consider Sir Francis Bacon as the true author. While the Baconians have been swept aside in this century, it does us no harm to hear their arguments—especially when they effectively debunk Shakspere. To quote from Leo Tolstoi's General Kutuzov in *War and Peace*, 'He knew how ready men are when they desire anything to manipulate all evidence so as to confirm what they desire; and he knew how readily in that case they let everything of an opposite significance pass unheeded.'" The audience stirred softly.

"Appropriately, here's a man born on Russian soil, and who finished his life in this marvelous nation, and who will relate his thoughts on the elusive, mysterious, invisible William Shakespeare or Shakspere. Please welcome the superlative author, poet, and essayist Vladimir Nabokov."

An imposing man in a dark brown, double-breasted suit rose from the table to the right of the podium. A firm, resolute face featured dark eyes resting on double bags of grey skin. He stood briefly and nodded to acknowledge the heavy applause, then strode cautiously to the podium, never smiling. He produced a folded document from his left inside suit pocket and adjusted the microphone downwards with a supple jerk. The applause died and he cleared his throat.

"Truth is best reflected in fiction when practical logic and proof is less than adequate. I do not know about the Seventeenth Earl of Oxford. I maintained to my wife and closest of friends that Sir Francis Bacon was the true author. I do know, instinctively, that the man we call William Shakespeare, or Shakspere of Stratford, was not the author. I do know he didn't own the experience of a writer, and nothing in his scanty background suggests a man of a writer's soul." He took a sip of water and cleared his throat again.

"I shall read from my 1947 novel entitled *Bend Sinister*.

A fluted glass with a blue-veined violet and a jug of hot punch stand on Ember's bedtable. The buff wall directly above his bed (he has a bad cold) bears a sequence of three engravings.

Number one represents a sixteenth-century gentleman in the act of handing a book to a humble fellow who holds a spear and a bay-crowned hat in his left hand. Note the sinistral detail (why? Ah, `that is the question,' as Monsieur Homais once remarked, quoting `le journal d'hier'; a question which is answered in a wooden voice by the Portrait on the title page of the First Folio). Note also the legend: `Ink, a Drug.' Somebody's idle pencil (Ember highly treasures this scholium) has numbered the letters so as to spell `Grudinka' which means `bacon' in several Slavic languages.

Number two shows the rustic (now clad in the clothes of the gentleman) removing from the head of the gentleman (now writing at a desk) a kind of shapska. Scribbled underneath in the same hand: `Ham-let, or Home-lette au Lard.'

Finally, number three has a road, traveler on foot (wearing the stolen shapska) and a road sign `To High Wycombe.'

His name is protean. He begets doubles at every corner. His penmanship is unconsciously faked by lawyers who happen to write a similar hand. On the wet morning of November 27, 1582, he is Shaxpere and she is a Wately of Temple Grafton. A couple of days later he is Shagsper and she is a Hathaway of Stratford-on-Avon. Who is he? William X, cunningly composed of two left arms and a mask. Who else? The person who said (not for the first time) that the glory of God is to hide a thing, and the glory of man is to find it. However, the fact that the Warwickshire fellow wrote the plays is most satisfactorily proved on the strength of an applejohn and a pale primrose.

He folded the sheets of paper slowly and carefully, and cast a concentrated gaze over the audience. "My wonder and amazement is that the Shakespeare scholars will support their fellow based on his knowledge of 'applejohns and pale primroses,' indigenous to Warwickshire. Yet, when it comes to his infinite knowledge of court, war, politics, Italy, law, music, hunting, sailing, falconry, medicine, French, Latin, and Greek, not to mention history, there is no evidence. There is only surmise.

"I have selected some quotes from a review I wrote for The New Republic of Frayne Williams's book Mr. Shakespeare of the Globe. `The biographical part of this book will not disappoint the imaginary not-too-bright giant for whom blurbs are fattened and human interest lavishly spread.' End quote. Also, I wrote, `Finally, it is interesting to learn that it takes two to make a conversation and the same number to make love—which fact, together with the second-best bed, "the most intimate monument of her life," is about all we and the voluble author really know concerning that particular marriage.' End Quote.

"I have here also," he said as he reached into his right inside coat pocket and produced another sheet of paper, "a poem I never published. My son Dmitri translated it into English in 1988. I wrote it in 1924.

Shakespeare

`Amid grandees of times Elizabethan
you shimmered too, you followed sumptuous custom;
the circle of ruff, the silv'ry satin that
encased your thigh, the wedgelike beard—in all of this
you were like other men...Thus was enfolded
your godlike thunder in a succinct cape.

Haughty, aloof from theatre's alarums,
you easily, regretlessly relinquished

the laurels twinning into a dry wreath,
concealing for all time your monstrous genius
beneath a mask; and yet, your phantasm's echoes
still vibrate for us; your Venetian Moor,
his anguish; Falstaff's visage, like an udder
with pasted-on mustache; the raging Lear...
You are among us, you're alive; your name, though,
your image, too—deceiving, thus, the world—
you have submerged in your beloved Lethe.
It's true, of course, a usuere had grown
accustomed, for a sum, to sign your work
(that Shakespeare—Will—who played the Ghost in `Hamlet'

who lives in pubs, and died before he could
digest in full his portion of a boar's head)...
The frigate breathed, your country you were leaving,
to Italy you went. A female voice
called singsong through the iron's pattern,
called to her balcony the tall `inglesse',
grown languid from the lemon-tinted moon
and Verona's streets. My inclination
is to imagine, possibly, the droll
and kind creator of `Don Quixote'
exchanging with you a few casual words
while waiting for fresh horses—and the evening
was surely blue. The well behind the tavern
contained a pail's pure tinkling sound...Reply—
whom did you love? Reveal yourself—whose memoirs
refer to you in passing? Look what numbers
of lowly, worthless souls have left their trace,
what countless names Brantome has for the asking!
Reveal yourself, god of iambic thunder,
you hundred-mouthed, unthinkably great bard!

No! At the destined hour, when you felt banished
by God from your existence, you recalled
those secret manuscripts, fully aware
that your supremacy would rest unblemished
by public rumor's unashamed brand,
that ever, midst the shifting dust of ages,
faceless you'd stay, like immortality
itself—then vanished in the distance, smiling.

He stepped back from the podium and the audience applauded enthusiastically. Colton had forgotten about Nabokov's later expressed doubts. He now fully recalled re-reading the new poem only a few months before. Scarborough moved the microphone as high as it would stretch and leaned his head towards its center to achieve proper volume.

"Our thanks to you, Mr. Nabokov." The applause tapered off. "Now, I shall introduce a man born a few hundred miles up river from this charming city and over a hundred years ago. Samuel Clemens, also known as Mark Twain, doubted the man credited as the author of the greatest works in the English language was Shakespeare. Mr. Clemens, or Mr. Twain as you prefer." Ian raised his arm to summon the speaker and the crowd stood, roaring cheers as if welcoming a sports hero.

A short man with silver, wavy hair and a large moustache scrambled from his seat on the audience's far left of the head table. A white three-piece suit highlighted the shimmering hair colour, and a red bow tie floated slightly off-center on his blanched shirt, emphasizing his pink face. Colton noted the overly large head in proportion to the smaller than average body. Twain momentarily smiled, but the grin was soon replaced by a wry smirk under the brush of white lip hair as though he'd just been told of some private fraud. The applause intensified while he silently stood at the podium for some five minutes.

"Thank you. You're so kind," he finally said in an oddly endearing voice, and the room stilled so as not to miss a word. "I'll begin by telling you a little story. Once I'd been asked to speak on this subject before the Baconians of London where I was approached before the speech, rather annoyingly, by one of their members, who asked who I thought wrote the works since I so heartily agreed with them that Shakespeare didn't. I replied that I didn't know, but I fully intended to ask Shakespeare about his secret ghostwriter when I arrived in heaven. The Baconian rather snootily informed me that I wouldn't find Shakespeare in heaven. Then *you* ask him, I said, and got on with my talk."

The room quaked with roars of laughter, and then more applause as Twain smirked.

"Shakespeare, Shakspere of Stratford-on-Avon, couldn't have written Shakespeare's works for the reason that the man who wrote them was limitlessly familiar with the laws, and the law courts, and law proceedings, and lawyer talk, and lawyer ways—and if Shakespeare was possessed of the infinitely divided stardust that constituted this vast wealth, how did he get it, and where and when?"

He paused and smacked his lips twice as he cast his eyes in a deliberate, mocking stare.

"From books."

Scratching his head, he paused again and scanned the audience, then shook his head. The crowd laughed.

"From books! That was always the idea. I answer as my readings of the champions on my side of the great controversy had taught me to answer, that a man can't handle glibly and easily and comfortably and successfully the argot of a trade at which he has not personally served. He will make mistakes. He will not, and cannot, get the trade phrasings precisely and exactly right, and the moment he departs, by even a shade, from a common trade form, the reader who has served that trade will know the writer hasn't." Some people in the audience nodded in agreement.

"So far as anybody actually knows and can prove, Shakespeare of Stratford-on-Avon never wrote a play in his life.'" Twain arched an eyebrow at the audience, defying someone to differ. "So far as anybody knows and can prove, he never wrote a letter to anybody in his life. So far as anyone knows, he received only one letter during his life." Murmurs floated among the crowd. "So far as anyone knows and can prove, Shakespeare of Stratford wrote only one poem during his life. This one is authentic...he wrote the whole of it out of his own head.

> `Good friend for jesus sake forebeare
> To digg the dust encloased heare:
> Blest be ye man yt spares thes stones
> And curst be he yt moves my bones.

Twain raised a pointed finger.

"The historians *suppose* that Shakespeare attended the Free School in Stratford from the time he was seven years old till he was thirteen. There is no evidence that he ever went to school at all. The historians *infer* that he got his Latin in that school—the school they *suppose* he attended. They *suppose* his father's declining fortunes made it necessary for him to leave the school they suppose he attended...but there is no evidence that he ever entered or retired from the school they suppose he attended...."

The great man sipped some water from a glass, and then smoothed his moustache before continuing. He moved his lips near the microphone and lowered his voice almost to a whisper as though confiding a secret.

"Experience is an author's most valuable asset; experience is the thing that puts the muscle and the breath and the warm blood into the book he writes. Rightly viewed, Shakespeare's calf-butchering accounts for *Titus Andronicus*.'" His voice then climbed back to the formal level. "The historians find themselves *justified in believing* that the young Shakespeare poached upon Sir Thomas Lucy's deer preserves and got hauled before that magistrate for it. But there is no shred of respect-worthy evidence that anything of the kind happened.

"The historians, having argued the thing that might have happened into the thing that did happen, found no trouble in turning Sir Thomas Lucy into Mr. Justice Shallow...

"If he began to slaughter calves and poach deer, and rollick around, and learn English, at the earliest likely moment—say at thirteen when he was supposedly wrenched from that school where he was supposedly storing up Latin for future literary use—he had his youthful hands full..." He bobbed his head at the chuckles from the crowd.

"He must have had to put aside his Warwickshire dialect, which wouldn't be understood in London, and study English very hard... incredibly hard, almost, if the result of that labour was to be the smooth and rounded and flexible and letter-perfect English of *Venus and Adonis* in the space of ten years, and at the same time learn great and fine and unsurpassable literary form.

"However, it is *conjectured* that he accomplished all this and more, much more. learned law and its intricacies, and the complex procedure of the law courts; all about soldiering, and sailoring, and the manners and customs and ways of royal courts and aristocratic society; and likewise accumulated in his one head every kind of knowledge the learned then possessed, and every kind of humble knowledge possessed by the lowly and ignorant, and added thereto a wider and more intimate knowledge of the world's great literatures, ancient and modern, than was possessed by any one man of his time—for he was going to make brilliant and easy and admiration-compelling use of these splendid treasures the moment he got to London. And according to the surmisers, that is what he did...

"It is surmised...that the young Shakespeare got his vast knowledge of the law and his familiar and accurate acquaintance with the manner and customs and shop-talk of lawyers through being for a time the clerk of a Stratford court.... But the surmise is damaged by the fact that there is no evidence—and not even tradition—that the young Shakespeare was ever clerk of a law court.

"Shall I set down the rest of the conjectures which constitute the giant biography of William Shakespeare?" Twain adjusted the red bow tie. "It would strain the unabridged dictionary to hold them. He is a brontosaur, nine bones and six hundred barrels of plaster of Paris..." The audience howled with laughter over spontaneous applause swelling to a crescendo. Twain smiled gently at the swell of the crowd. As its voice began to ebb, the white moustache twitched.

"Am I trying to convince anybody that Shakespeare did not write Shakespeare's works? Ah, now, what do you take me for? Would I be so soft as that, after having known the human race familiarly for nearly seventy-four years?"

Colton looked for a calendar. He knew Twain was dead longer than even Nabokov—and was that Churchill puffing a cigar at the head table?

"It would grieve me to know that anyone could think so injuriously of me, so uncomplimentarily, so unadmiringly of me. No-no, I am aware that when even the brightest mind in our world has been trained up from childhood in a superstition of any kind, it will never be possible for that mind, in its maturity, to examine sincerely, dispassionately, and conscientiously any evidence or any circumstance which will seem to cast a doubt upon the validity of that superstition...

"Ladies and gentlemen of F.A.S., is it any wonder we are here to roast the ghost of such an obscure man?"

The audience stood again. Staccato yells and cheers elicited a joyous bedlam. Scarborough shook Twain's hand. He recaptured the microphone, shouting to the crowd still on its feet, roaring in admiration.

"Now, ladies and gentlemen, you shall hear from a man who can ever peer into the soul of the author who wrote the best works in the English language. I'm delighted to present to you Dr. Sigmund Freud." Scarborough kept the applause going as Freud rose.

The man known as the father of psychoanalysis lifted himself from a seat to the right of Twain. He had a large forehead, further enhanced by baldness on the entire front top, and a firmness of his right eye. The stern eyes rigidly anchored waving brows, the left brow like a capsized "s" only to be rectified to a gradual curve. The dark hair above the expanse of skull above the ears and at the back of the head was complemented by a white goatee that thickened as it spread across a large, round chin. Freud gingerly dropped a half-smoked, dark cigar into a nearby ashtray as he stepped towards the podium. He adjusted a gold pocket watch chain trailing down a black vest covered by a matching wool suit coat, and strode in a directed gait of a man abundantly assured of purpose. Although Freud could not command the populism of his predecessor, the crowd clapped respectfully, for his presence was intimidating if not overbearing. Quiet fell upon the room.

Colton, amused at the spectacle, thought mischievously why expect anything else from an audience so adeptly read and systematically psychoanalyzed as this one must be?

"I first heard of the Shakespeare authorship question while studying under that great teacher of the last century, Theodor Meynert." Freud's clipped, sonorous Austrian accent penetrated the silenced hall. Enough frivolous banter spoke his demeanor, and let us absorb the facts. "It wasn't until 1881 that I doubted the beliefs of Professor Meynert and other Austrian and German scholars who maintained that the true author was Bacon. Besides the seeming paucity of evidence concerning Bacon, I stated that he `would have been the most powerful brain the world has ever produced, whereas it seems to me that there is more need to share Shakespeare's achievement among several rivals than to burden another important man with it....' So I concluded this without a substitute based on my meager research up to that point. The problem continued to perplex me to the extent of being an irritation.

"Nearly seventy years ago I came across a book by John Thomas Looney that gave me the impetus to declare in my work of 1927, *Autobiographical Study*, that I no longer believed `William Shakespeare the actor from Stratford was the author of the works which have been ascribed to him. Since reading *Shakespeare Identified* by Looney, I am clearly convinced that the assumed name conceals the personality of Edward de Vere, Earl of Oxford.' At this stage, I no longer had a smidgeon of confidence in traditional Shakespeare scholarship."

Colton thought he heard a "Hear, Hear!" from the mouth of Henry James.

"In 1940, the German edition of my *Outline of Psychoanalysis* contained the following footnote, which incidentally settled for good the question of where I stood on the issue: `The name *William Shakespeare* is most probably a pseudonym behind which there lies concealed a great unknown. Edward de Vere, Earl of Oxford, a man who has been regarded as the author of Shakespeare's works, lost a beloved and admired father while he was still a boy, and completely repudiated his mother, who contracted a new marriage soon after her husband's death.'

"Needless to say, my followers were chagrined at such a pronouncement. In spite of the latent uproar from the incipient swirl of whispers, my desire for the truth was unwavering.

"Also in 1940, I read a book by Gerald H. Rendell further reinforcing my firm belief. I shall read from a missive I wrote in 1932 to Dr. R. Flatter, a renowned Shakespeare scholar of the day.

> What you say in your letter about the appreciation of the Sonnets seems to me to be obsolete, by which I mean there can no longer be any doubt concerning their serious nature and their value as self-confessions. This is, I think to be accounted for by the fact that they were published without the author's cooperation and passed on after his death to a public for whom they had not been intended.
>
> The contents have been used to ascertain the poet's identity, which is still doubtful. There lies in front of me a book by Gerald H. Rendall, *Shakepseare's Sonnets and Edward de Vere* that puts forward the thesis that those poems were addressed to the Earl of Southampton and written by the Earl of Oxford. I am almost convinced that none other than this aristocrat was our Shakespeare. In the light of that conception the Sonnets become much more understandable.

"In 1934 I wrote to J.S.H. Bransom,

> I have already taken the liberty of hinting to you by my belief in the identity of Shakespeare with Edward de Vere...Let us see if this assumption contributes anything to the understanding of the tragedy, *King Lear*. Oxford really had three grown-up daughters (other children had died young, including the only son): Elizabeth, 1575; Bridget, 1584; and Susan, 1587. I will call your attention to a striking change Shakespeare made in his material. In all accounts of the sources the daughters are unmarried at the time of the love test and got married later. In Shakespeare the two elder are married

> at that time (Gonreil already pregnant) and Cordelia still single. When we date the composition of *Lear*—surely with right—in the poet's late years then we have a striking agreement. Elizabeth married Lord Derby in 1595; Bridget married Lord Norris in 1599. Since Oxford died in 1604, and Susan, our Cordelia, married Lord Montgomery only in 1605, she was single throughout her father's lifetime. We have, of course, to take it that *Lear* was composed after 1599, naturally before 1604...
>
> Is it not curious, by the way, that in the play that deals with the father's relations to his three daughters there is no mention of the mother?...If Shakespeare was Lord Oxford the figure of the father who gave all he had to his children must have for him a special compensatory attraction...oppressed by debts..(he) left the education and care of his three daughters to their grandfather, Lord Burleigh.

"In '36 and '37 I wrote the following to the poet Arnold Zweig reproaching his firmly entrenched belief in behalf of Shakespeare.

> "'Dear Meister Arnold: You must bring Looney back with you. I must try him on others, for obviously with you I have had no success. Your Shakespeare theory seems to me to be as improbable as it is lacking in foundation. The most personal of Shakespeare's works, his sonnets, show an elderly man who regrets much that has happened in his life and who pours out his heart to a younger man he loves. This youth is an aristocrat, probably H.W. (Henry Wriothesley) Earl of Southampton. Actually the poet reveals himself unambiguously at once when he mentions that he once carried the baldachin (i.e. over the Queen's head in a procession). So I warn the poet A.Zw. against building fantasies about Shakespeare on untenable premises. Yours, Freud. 22 June 1936.'"

The assembly was spellbound at the spectacle of Freud reading his own letters as a witness in de Vere's behalf. Freud never looked up to observe his admirers as he read. Colton was himself transfixed with concentration. He'd read this letter and inserted a portion of it into his own copious research, aware of this mind, this severe, powerful force projecting a straight vector as strongly on the matter as anyone ever could. The psychoanalytic reasoning and insight linked with the thread of logical circumstantial evidence and verisimilitude was a mind-altering concoction. No great leaps of faith were required.

Freud briefly made eye contact with Colton before continuing.

"I wrote a second note to Zweig after a belated reply from him yet in favor of the Stratford man. I'll read you only an excerpt.

"'Dear Master Arnold:... We will have a lot to discuss about Shakespeare. I do not know what still attracts you to the man of Stratford. He seems to have nothing at all to justify his claim, whereas Oxford has almost everything. It is quite inconceivable to me that Shakespeare should have got everything secondhand—Hamlet's neurosis, Lear's madness, Macbeth's defiance and the character of Lady Macbeth, Othello's jealousy, etc. It almost irritates me that you should support the notion. Yours, Freud, 2 April 1937.'

"When I was forced to flee Austria, I received a letter of welcome after arriving in England from J.T. Looney. In June of 1938, I wrote the following letter to him in reply: 'Dear Mr. Looney: I have known you as the author of a remarkable book, to which I owe my conviction about Shakespeare's identity as far as my judgment in this matter goes and confessing myself to be a follower of yours...S. Freud.'"

Freud's eyeglasses scanned the room, flashing like a beacon as he spoke, and stopped to stare at one bearded man near the front who he immediately recognized. "Walt Whitman, you wrote concerning the history plays: 'Conceived out of the fullest heat and pulse of European feudalism—personifying in unparalleled ways the medieval aristocracy, its towering spirit of ruthless and gigantic caste, with its own peculiar air and arrogance (no mere imitation)—only one of the wolfish earls so plenteous in the plays themselves, or some born descendent and knower, might seem to be the true author of those amazing works, works in some respects greater than anything else in recorded literature."

"If I'd only had the opportunity to have Mr. Looney as a contemporary and have read his work, it would have proven me correct in identifying that 'wolfish earl,'" he replied.

"With that observation, I shall take a seat," said Freud as laughter and applause swept the room.

"There is yet another torch carrier in our marathon who deserves recognition, for he is alive and with us now, although perilously near death. I would like for him to merely wave if he can. I would have been delighted to know him if I had been alive when he published his excellent research. I am speaking of Dr. Tyler..."

Every famous head at the dais, from Washington Irving to Sidney Lee to Henry James to Benjamin Disraeli to Justice Henry Blackmon to Dr. Mortimer Adler, moved simultaneously to spot him. Somehow, Colton found himself lodged in a hospital bed at the rear of the room.

Instantly, Tyler Colton snapped into a catatonic state. Not only was he unable to move his arm, he was hypnotized, paralyzed by Dr. Freud's performance. His eyes locked on the podium where he saw Freud's face change as he stepped down to the distinct visage of a famous architect he remembered meeting once at a cocktail party on the waterfront in Gloucester, Massachusetts.

"I.M. Pei," was all he could mumble.

"What did he say?" Veronica said aloud to herself. Ian had just left her alone with her father. She spoke louder as if he were still there. "I am pee?" She called for a nurse to check his Foley.

Chapter Fifteen

Ahead of Ian Scarborough was a seven-hour direct flight to New York. He settled into his comfortable aisle seat with his portable CD player, a note pad, and his deerstalker hat on the empty seat next to him (the better to prevent its crushing).

Whilst the rest of the passengers boarded, he listened to a CD he'd recorded concerning the literary doxologies to the Seventeenth Earl of Oxford. After some ten minutes, the batteries were running low so he turned the machine off and opted to read the duty-free catalogue in the seat compartment in front of him. Once airborne, he could allow the batteries to recharge, and then search for replacements in his attaché in the overhead.

With a light jolt the plane backed onto the runway. Each time Ian felt this movement and heard the drone of the engines, he was reminded of the very instant he conceived of his (and Blake's) marvelous tune, "Blackbirds' Choir." The tune had occurred to him on a quick flight from London to the Isle of Wight for what proved to be a disastrous outdoor festival that promoters had billed to be the English version of Woodstock. Their manager, not always the clever promoter, had predicted wide media coverage and heavy crowds. In spite of all the right names and positive pre-event publicity, the venue bombed thanks to unruly, nonpaying fans who interrupted the performers to heckle them on the evils of money and selling out to the labels. The cost of plane tickets, hotels, meals, equipment shipping, and labour devoured the entertainers' profits. None of the festival organizers thought to buy rain insurance from Lloyd's and, in the only similarity to Woodstock, it rained when they were finally allowed to play after long sessions of jeers.

Though the event was then a loss to everyone else, it was not to Ian, strangely enough. The airplane drone, that boring, monotonous repetitive note—somehow he heard an A or A flat—had given him the tableau for a catchy, but bathetic, serpentine tune for his flute and recorder. How deceptively simple it was, except for some toe-tapping percussive beat accents and a completely haunting chord progression led by a very tame tenor sax gently suggesting a moonlit, rural mood before a return to the stable, predictable, magnetic melody. Blake had fashioned the sax bridge melody over an unusual chord progression and time signature on his guitar while they were waiting in the airport for a taxi. Ian roughed it out on a portable recorder until they were able to put it down at rehearsal. The result was a gold mine. Royalties in the hundreds of pounds per month still poured in thanks to covers by other artists the world over. The reviewer for *Times Magazine* called Falstaff's Ghost the "most important English classic-folk-rock band ever." The band quickly developed a cult following (their fans were called "Ghosties," and carried large beer mugs with many males with beards dripping suds at concerts) for years. Recently, "Blackbird" had received renewed interest via the reissue on compact disc of their blockbuster *Fishing For Lost Wishes* master. The vinyl album itself was now accorded collector's status if in reasonably good condition.

The discovery of that one lilting, mysterious melody had made him hungry to tap the essence of his own creativity. If he could divine such an elusive trickle, this Pyrrhic spring of inspiration, he felt he could consistently replicate his art. He could attain some genius in the age of tabloids and artistic decline—even if it was merely through the medium of popular music. Some of it would last beyond his lifetime. He knew "Blackbirds'" would. Was the song a result of a brief moment of genius? Was it luck? Was it simply a gift presented to him from above? After all, when he conceived it, he was floating above a storm in bucolic, nocturnal heavens. Perhaps it was science—the mere confluence of positive and negative ions flashing through the brain as a reaction to the lightning below. As far-fetched as it had seemed, he wanted to believe in a combination of all of these factors. He knew he would never actually know the answer. Never could he experience that moment again in the same way. Inspiration had never been so facile and perhaps would never be so again. As often as he sat down and replicated a "found tune" on keyboard (his primary instrument while in the band), no other creative moment had occurred to him since in such an instantaneous spark. He was always longing for the understanding of genius.

For himself, he could never find a similar facility for expression in words. De Vere had had a mountain range of learning, an ocean of sorrow and self-pity, and a continent of experience in composing the most intricate works of literature ever. Ian sensed he and de Vere shared the commonality of work as being its own intrinsic reward.

The plane crawled down the runway as Ian hummed the melody to the famous bridge, his mind totally immersed in capricious thought. Ah well, time to focus again on the sonnets for the upcoming debate, since they were so fascinating to him as the source of the mysterious mind of de Vere. Let me see, he thought, how would these points surface in debate? He opened his notebook to the sonnet section and reviewed notes culled from Colton's book.

Who was Shakspere's so-called "dark lady"? Never had the Stratfordians offered adequate theories as to who she was. As far as history records, there was no "dark lady" in Shakspere's life, yet we discover one in the sonnets. Ian had committed the entire passage to memory, but of these, Sonnets 127 and 132 were most convincing.

Therefore my mistress' brows are raven black,
Her eyes so suited, and they mourners seem
At such who, not born fair, no beauty lack,
Sland'ring creation with a false esteem.
Yet even so they mourn, becoming of their woe,
That every tongue says beauty should look so.

Then will I swear beauty herself is black
And all they foul that thy complexion lack.

The plane thrust into the grey clouds while he turned to a passage from *Love's Labour's Lost* that he'd scribbled in the margin next to the two sonnets.

Where is a book?
That I may swear beauty doth beauty lack,
If that she learn not of her eye to look:
No face is fair that is not full so black.

O! if in black my lady's brows be deck'd,
It mourns that painting and usurping hair
Should ravish doters with a false aspect;
And therefore is she born to make black fair.

He was always struck by the poem "Anne Vavasor's Echo" from the book *Verses Made by the Earl of Oxford*. The book, published in de Vere's youth and with little sympathy for his name being so unfashionably included, underlines the dedication the earl had to this widely acknowledged court beauty.

O heavens! who was the first that bred in me this fever? Vere.
Who was the first that gave the wound whose fear I wear for ever? Vere.
What tyrant, Cupid, to my harm usurps thy golden quiver? Vere.
What wight first caught this heart and can from bondage it deliver? Vere.

Yet who doth most adore this wight, oh hollow caves tell true? You.
What nymph deserves his liking best, yet doth in sorrow rue? You.
What makes him not regard good will with some regard of ruth?
Youth.
What makes him show besides his birth, such pride and such
untruth? Youth.
May I his favour match with love, if he my love will try? Ay.
May I requite his birth with faith? Then faithful will I die? Ay.
And I that know this lady well,
Said, Lord how great a miracle,
To hear how Echo told the truth,
As true as Phoebus' oracle.

Here the young artist was seminally acknowledging to the world his remarkable ability—before his downfall, before his discovery of the Italian sonnet, before his affair with Anne Vavasor, before his disfavor with his father-in-law, Lord Burghley.

Ian reread his notes on Anne, a woman destined to become de Vere's mistress. They were derived from a most prominent Stratfordian, Dr. E. K. Chambers.

"Anne Vavasor was born sometime in the early 1560's, the daughter of Sir Henry Vavasor of Copmanthorpe in Yorkshire. Her mother was Margaret, who was the daughter of Sir Henry Knyvet. He was a cadet of the Knyvets of Buckenham in Norfolk and the family had been a part of the royal household since the days of Henry the Eighth. Thomas Knyvet, Anne's uncle, had been a Groom of the Privy Chamber. Aunt Katherine Knyvet was a Maid of Honor and a Lady of the Bedchamber to Elizabeth. In 1500, Anne was appointed a Gentlewoman of the Bedchamber."

Ian vividly recalled the portrait of Anne by John de Critz in the Paul Mellon Centre for Studies in British Art in London. She was slender, with a quick, alert, somewhat feline face featuring an aquiline nose complemented by rosy cheeks against an ivory complexion. Ian could appreciate her attraction, but she wasn't his particular cup of tea. Modern beauty clearly held a different standard than the Elizabethan age, or maybe it was simply his unique, particular tastes. Nonetheless, she was, for Oxfordians, the inspiration for the "dark lady" of the *Sonnets*. She lived past the age of ninety and buried three husbands—two of whom she was married to at the same time, according to a conviction of bigamy in 1618. When she was eighteen, the twenty-nine-year-old Edward was much taken with her and suffered grief in spite of the joy she evidently gave to him.

Ian revisited a letter to Lord Burghley written by his spy, Sir Francis Walsingham, concerning the entire affair surrounding the Catholic rebellion of Henry Howard and Charles Arundel. While Oxford had been instrumental in helping to expose the rebellion, also known as the Throckmorton Plot, it was clear that Burghley wanted his son-in-law imprisoned for a liaison with Vavasor, who was a cousin to Howard—as was Oxford! The Plot was designed to rally Catholics on the continent behind Mary, Queen of Scots. The letter was written almost two months before the uprising occurred. "On Tuesday at night Anne Vavysor was brought to bed of a son in the maidens' chamber. The E. of Oxeford is avowed to be the father, who hath withdrawn himself with intent, as it is thought, to pass the seas. The ports are laid for him and therefore if he have any such determination it is not likely that he will escape. The gentlewoman the selfsame night she was delivered was conveyed out of the house and the next day committed to the Tower. Others that have found any ways party to the cause have also been committed. Her Majesty is greatly grieved with the accident, and therefore I hope there will be some order taken as the like inconvenience will be avoided."

Elizabeth would stand for no sexual liaisons outside marriage, and Lord Burghley must have had *some* dissatisfaction. (Ian grinned at his own propensity for understatement in his notes, since it was Burghley's daughter to whom de Vere was still married).

In the previous year, 1582, Anne's uncle, Sir Thomas Knyvet, was disturbed enough to challenge the earl in a brawl, in which both men were injured severely. Edward de Vere received a dangerous wound which may have been the source of the duel on the field of honor referred to in the *Sonnets*: "Speak of my lameness, and I straight will halt," or "[I], decrepit, made lame by fortune's dearest spite," but having "comfort" of a young man's "worth and truth.../So then I am not lame."

Ian stood up briefly to stretch, his long back popping. It was still too early in the flight for him to get away with stretching his long legs out into the aisle, but once food and beverages were served and people settled in for the movie, he'd take advantage of that modicum of extra space. The Vavasor-de Vere affair would be enough to captivate him until then.

Knyvet had carried on the feud by killing some of Lord Oxford's men over the next few months. In the face of these conflicts, Lord Burghley, as discontented with his ward as he was, nevertheless found ample words to plead sympathy with the Queen in a letter to her on his son-in-law's behalf:

> But I submit all these things to God's will, who knoweth best why it pleaseth Him to afflict my Lord of Oxford in this sort, who hath, I confess, forgotten his duty to God, and yet I hope he may be made a good servant to her Majesty, if it please her of her clemency to remit her displeasure; for his fall in her court, which is now twice yeared, and he punished as far or farther than any like crime hath been, first by her Majesty, and then by the drab's friend in revenge to the peril of his life...When our son-in-law was in prosperity, he was cause of our adversity, we only are partakers thereof, and by no means, no, not by bitter tears of my wife, can obtain a spark

> of favor for him, that hath satisfied his offence with punishment, and seeketh mercy by submission; but contrariwise, whilst we seek favor, all crosses are laid against him and by untruths sought to be kept in disgrace....

Ian laughed spontaneously at Burghley's reference to Anne as a "drab"—an Elizabethan word for prostitute—in this letter. De Vere was certainly no loyal family man, as Burghley painfully knew more than anyone. On the other hand, Vavasor had been having an affair with de Vere's rival poet, Edmund Spencer, even at the time she was carrying de Vere's child.

His notes were meticulous in the category of the *Sonnets*. Colton's research had prepared him well. The elderly professor's muddled, tangential arguments in debate were so vastly overshadowed by his abundant, incisive research that it rudely occurred to Ian the one redeeming element of the man's unfortunate stroke was the fact that he would not be able to participate directly in the debate in New York. It was ironic—the old man was so adept at providing the grist for any aspect of the argument. Colton had spent several hours with Ian, pouring over the sections of his book dealing with the *Sonnets* to better prepare a second area of expertise for Ian for television. Colton dwelt so painstakingly on the so-called "Will" sonnets (numbers 135-136) in which the name recurs frequently and to the confusion of the Stratfordian scholars:

> Whoever hath her wish, thou hast thy Will,
> And Will to boot, and Will in over-plus;...
> More than enough am I that vex'd thee still,
> To thy sweet will making addition thus.

And in 136:

> Make but my name thy love, and love that still,
> And then thou lovest me, for my name is Will.

Colton believed "Will" here to be the Earl of Southampton, while other commentators proffer theories ranging from a friend of Shakespeare's also named Will to—what seemed to be the most remote—the ribald reference to the sexual organ. Ian told the professor that the lacunae of hard facts made anyone's speculation concerning the "Will" sonnets only pure speculation. Ian maintained that it was a prima facie case for the pseudonym the earl was resigned to accept as a consequence of fate perpetrated by Elizabeth and Lord Burghley. Still, he recalled the vacuous look and slow steady blinks Colton gave him. Maybe this was too simple for him to have seen or, if he had seen it, maybe he didn't care to linger on seemingly specious arguments. For him, such author impressions might only disrupt time better devoted to detailed research. Ian was bold enough to declare to Colton that there was a striking similarity in the two warring factions, and perhaps, because of their aggressive position, the Oxfordians may have been more addicted to detail than the Stratfordians. After all, the Oxford cause had abundantly more details to work with considering the paucity of facts about Shakspere. Oxfordian scholarship, however, until the appearance of a smoking gun, would never be acknowledged as more refined since they were protagonists of the antiestablishment cause. Some Oxfordians often hurt the cause by attaching their imagination to dodgy, or even good, data.

At any rate, he must now, for the camera's consumption, prepare a hard case for Ms. Vavasor. The flight attendant appeared and he ordered a wine as he lowered his tray.

Anne appeared to be Rosaline of *Love's Labour's Lost*. One indication of this is her lover exclaiming in an attack on her virtue:

> A whitely wanton, with a velvet brow,
> With two pitch-balls stuck in her face for eyes;
> Ay, and, by heaven, one that will do the deed
> Though Argus were her eunuch and her guard!

Am I to sigh for her! to watch for her!
To pray for her!

Whereas *Love's Labour's Lost* closes with Rosaline sentencing her lover to a "twelve-month term" away from her if she is "to be won," Beatrice says in *Much Ado About Nothing* that her lover should "marry, once before he won it of me with false dice." Both characters were modeled after this high-spirited woman who captivated the earl over a fifteen-year period in an on and off again relationship. She would make many demands on the earl, even while married to the sixty-year old Sir Henry Lee.

Next, Ian decided to focus some attention on the earl's favorite male, since the Stratfordians also had no explanation as to who this could be in the *Sonnets*. The dedications to *Venus and Adonis*, published 1593, and *The Rape of Lucrece*, 1594, were to Henry Wriothesley, Third Earl of Southampton. He was the "fair youth" of the *Sonnets*, worshiped by the Earl of Oxford who, if one accepts Oxford as the true author, avers "to take advantage of idle hours, till I have honored you with some graver labour."

In the *Rape of Lucrece* dedication:

> The love I dedicate to your lordship is without end; whereof this pamphlet, without beginning, is but a superfluous moiety. The warrant I have of your honourable disposition, not the worth of my untutored lines, makes it assured of acceptance. What I have done is yours; what I have to do is yours; being part in all I have, devoted yours. Were my worth greater, my duty would show greater; meantime, as it is, it is bound to your lordship, to whom I wish long life, still lengthened with happiness.
>
> Your lordship's in all duty,
> William Shakespeare.

On one point, Colton was incisive and unrelenting. All of Southampton's biographers (one a prominent Stratfordian) concur that he was indeed the "fair youth." Stratfordians couldn't produce any evidence whatsoever that Shakespeare ever met the Earl of Southampton, even though one Southampton biographer, without documentation, produced this most heady fiction as fact.

Southampton and Oxford had much in common. He was born in October 1573, and attended St. John's College, Cambridge (like Oxford), graduating (like Oxford) in his fifteenth year and then received an MA. He entered Gray's Inn, the law school (like Oxford who also preceded law studies with an MA.). Before his matriculations, he'd been a royal ward in Lord Burghley's house (like Oxford and the Earl of Essex, Robert Devereux, in whose rebellion late in the century Southampton was to be implicated and almost lose his life). He had a strong interest in drama and was a patron of poetry—again like de Vere.

Professor George Phillip V. Akrigg reports that he "lacked stability" and was "slapdash and careless...hot tempered and sudden in quarrel," and "within four years of attaining his majority he had so dissipated his fortune as to have to sell land, turn over the administration of his debt-encumbered estate to the family's old men of business, and retreat to the Continent." *Sound familiar?*

In spite of "all the follies of the young earl, he attracted people." According to Akrigg he bound them to himself and his fortunes. Even as a young boy he must have had something singularly attractive about him. When Southampton was only fifteen, his brother-in-law, writing to Burghley, noted that `your lordship doth love him` and added, for himself, `My love and care of this young Earl enticeth me.' William Camden, who as master of Westminster School had learned to appraise boys and young men, seems to have had a decided liking for young Southampton. Mountjoy, the conqueror of Ireland, trying to get for him the governorship of Connaught, wrote, `I can name no man that I love better than the Earl of Southampton.' ...Sir Charles Danvers, after the Essex rebellion, could declare that his chief motive for joining it had been `the great obligation of love and duty' that bound him to Southampton.

He was "passionately loyal to his friends.... He could be selfish and unkind, seducing Elizabeth Vernon and then leaving her amid tears, he did finally marry her," at a time when "every consideration of Elizabethan common sense demanded that he repair his ruined fortunes by taking some rich heiress, not penniless Elizabeth, for his countess."

He was "an exceptionally handsome man...with a particular brilliance of the eyes." (In Sonnet 16: "If I could write the beauty of your eyes.")

In the face of such agreement among scholars, however, there was the nagging question—Why were the *Sonnets* dedicated to a mysterious Mr. W.H.?"

The only likely candidate would have been William Herbert, the Earl of Pembroke, who was anything but a "fair youth" in spite of being a famous personality.

Why the initials W.H.? H.W. would have been as plain as spelling it out: Henry Wriothesley. A simple reversal of the letters allowed the publishers of the *Sonnets* to carefully satisfy the author in his poetic dictum that Southampton's "name from hence immortal life shall have." Since the *Sonnets* were written, as most scholars agree, after 1594 and the *Rape of Lucrece*, then such subversion in the dedication was timely—especially (as Stratfordians and Oxfordians largely concur) because of Lord Burghley's desire to have Southampton marry Oxford's daughter. After all, Burghley was the guardian, being grandfather of Elizabeth de Vere. The Stratfordians believe Burghley prevailed upon Will Shakespeare to write the first seventeen of the poems for the purpose of encouraging the relationship.

Many Oxfordians believe de Vere wrote them to encourage the relationship because of his fatherly affection for and identification with Southampton. Some instead maintain the link was sexual, or Southampton was de Vere's son by Elizabeth. How does one prove such suppositions? Ian could not dwell on them.

"That in black ink my love may still shine bright" in sonnet number sixty-five; "So long as men can breathe, or eyes can see,/ So long lives this, and this gives life to thee," in sonnet eighteen; and "Your praise shall still find room/ Even in the eyes of all posterity" combined to reinforce the adulation which the poet insisted to express for a wide and long readership.

A series of the sonnets admonishes the young man to recoil from associating too closely with the poet:

> O! lest the world should task you to recite
> What merit lived in me, that you should love
> After my death—dear love, forget me quite,
> For you in me can nothing worthy prove. (Sonnet 72)

> I may not ever more acknowledge thee,
> Lest my bewailed guilt should do thee same,
> Nor thou with public kindness honour me,
> Unless thou take that honour from thy name. (Sonnet 36)

The poet's name has been disgraced, for whatever reason—perhaps his theatrical works. "Alas! 'tis true I have gone here and there,/ And made myself a motley to the view... (Sonnet 110), and "Thence comes it that my name receives a brand,/ And almost thence my nature is subdu'd/ To what it works in, like the dyer's hand." (Sonnet 111)

The two men not only knew each other well, Ian thought, they adored their shared experiences, much of it identical. De Vere acknowledges his obscurity and his inability to link his name with

Southampton's, and much less have him identified properly in Sonnets 72 and 81 respectively.

How could Shakspere be so utterly capable of ignominy in light of his ensuing fame at best and, in the least, his contemporary success? Why is the record of this important man so empty? "My name be buried where my body is,/and live no more to shame nor me nor you./For I am sham'd by that which I bring forth,/And so should you, to love things nothing worth. I, once gone, to all the world, must die." (Sonnet 72)

The reason for such dark remorse was that the author was a nobleman and he knew his fate was sealed to oblivion because he was writing for the hoi polloi...the masses, not just nobles.

A nobleman, such as Oxford, would cite falconry and equestrianism:

> Thy love is better than high birth to me,
> Richer than wealth, prouder than garments' cost,
> Of more delight than hawks or horses be. (Sonnet 91)

The Earl of Oxford, who inherited the title of Lord Great Chamberlain, carries the canopy (as shown in a print from the period) over Elizabeth I:

> Were't aught to me I bore the canopy,
> With my extern the outward honouring,
> Or laid great bases for eternity,
> Which proves more short than waste or ruining?
> Have I not seen dwellers on form and favour
> Lose all, and more, by paying too much rent,
> For compound sweet forgoing simple savour,
> Pitiful thrivers, in their gazing spent? (Sonnet 125)

The sonnets abound in clues, of course, but an essential one in Sonnet 76: "That every word doth almost tell my name,/Showing their birth, and whence they did proceed." Is "every word" a jeu de mot on the name "Vere," which is Latin for truth?

Was he the fallen nobleman as reflected in Sonnet 25: "Let those who are in favor with their stars/Of public honor and proud titles boast,/Whilst I, whom fortune of such triumph bars...." If his life had proven anything, it was that he had not been able to overcome the powers of Elizabeth I and Burghley, or much less stay in their favor for any sustained time. Sonnet 29 expresses the notion succinctly: "When in disgrace with Fortune and men's eyes/I all alone beweep my outcast state..." In Sonnet 111, the poet defines "Fortune" as "The guilty goddess of my harmful deeds."

Thus, Ian mused, the sonnets reveal much of their protagonist-poet who experiences the tug of carnal desire versus impassioned reason, the dialectic of erotic beauty measured against the pulchritudinous intellect, the conflict of an obscure future in repentance from past transgressions, a blemished life contrasted by the synecdoche of a sparkling, innocent youth represented by Southampton. Sonnet 144 succinctly presents his inner conflicts:

> Two loves I have of comfort and despair,
> Which like two spirits do suggest me still;
> The better angel is a man right fair,
> The worser spirit a woman colour'd ill.
> To win me soon to hell, my female evil
> Tempteth my better angel from my side,
> And would corrupt my saint to be a devil,
> Wooing his purity with her foul pride,
> And whether that myh angel be turn'd fiend,
> Suspect I may, yet not directly tell,
> But being both from me, both to each friend,
> I guess one angel in another's hell:
> Yet this shall I ne'er Know, but live in doubt,
> Till my bad angel fire my good one out.

Ian set aside the notebook and folded his tray against the rear of the seat in front of him. He forced the now empty plastic wine glass into the pocket below the tray and rose to dash to the toilet. Again, his own composition occupied his active mind and he suddenly recalled a sonnet from his initial days at Eton—two lines of a couplet that fit the simple melody well. He hummed them softly as he walked: "Not marble, nor gilded monuments/Of princes, shall outlive this powerful rhyme...." It was from Sonnet 55.

Before returning to his seat he looked longingly towards an empty block of seats at the rear of the plane. While Business Class had been somewhat crowded, Coach was sparsely populated—there were not over sixty passengers on the late intercontinental flight. He resolved to stretch all six feet six inches across the middle seats and sleep the balance of the flight with a small drop of medicine in his ear. The pain had abated greatly, but he felt some occasional residual throbs. On the whole, he was feeling better. It amazed him how the grace of health returning surged through his otherwise spent body. At the moment, he felt he could climb mountains. But he knew he should, would sleep.

He slid the notebook back inside the carry-on and retrieved three pillows from the overhead, along with one large, black wool blanket. He raised the seat arms in the middle section and promptly fell soundly asleep.

When he awoke nearly three hours later, his famous tune was still there, the ubiquitous leaky faucet. He'd also retrieved the lyric from Sonnet 55: "Not marble, nor gilded monuments\Of Princes, shall outlive this powerful rhyme." Actually, it fit rather well. He would be patient; maybe a new tune lurked just beyond the drape of discovery.

That was how the creative process worked—a synthesis of experiences and art. The new tune did not need a lyric, but that particular sonnet could be adapted to it. The collision of the melody against that lovely lyric produced an entirely new appreciation of his musical abilities. The freedom to associate these two concepts gave him a fresh entity. The ability to create was of a God-given nature in his opinion, yet it required experience. Melville could study at Oxford or Cambridge all he may, but only the sea's infinity would satisfy his curiosity and allow him to encapsulate hearty firsthand inspiration.

Ian had nearly always considered himself a deist. The deistic creed gave him a kinship with all humankind, superseding all the petty schisms of organized religions and allowing him to rely on reason and enlightenment. Besides, when one creates tunes on a fairly regular basis for worldwide consumption, one senses how each sound is in one of God's many hemidemisemiquavers.

The concept that "the ordering of events constitutes a general providence," among others, gave him a justification to carry on his creative activities—he was merely sifting the golden nuggets of tunes from the pan of discovery and further serve as a critic. He maintained—indeed, even introduced his critic's column with such a statement—that his purpose in criticizing modern music, from minimalist to (God forbid) rap and "evy me-ul," was to uphold a certain standard, to inveigh against pretentious art, and to advocate that art which was, he had actually said it in his first column, godlike.

Lately, his editor, Vines, had increasingly failed to see Ian's mission as being as important as satisfying the whims of the music world, particularly the rock and pop categories. "You have to meet the public halfway," he'd admonished. What made their relationship so difficult was Vines had agreed, when he'd coaxed Ian to work at the newspaper over seven years ago, that he would answer only to Vines and be allowed to have other duties, such as occasionally expressing himself editorially on music and art issues. Ian had read Vines's willingness to grant him flexibility on the Oxford debate as being motivated by giving him a chance to hang himself in the eyes of the cultural establishment's tight noose, where he was, in spite of status as a semiretired, popish musician, well received and respected for his largely conservative views.

To Ian, truth was paramount. Truth was what he was pursuing in the case of de Vere, and his resolve had not changed an iota. He was having trouble getting a firm grip on the fact that criminals had stealthily whisked away some form of truth for their own purposes. If they held documents relating to the Oxford debate, he could only imagine the pounds, dollars, yen that might be commanded by some idiosyncratic, old billionaire who could impress his wealthy friends on some egocentric binge at a New Year's party in America. He shuddered to think of the task ahead as he again made his way back to the toilet.

What if the thieves were in America as Veronica said? He would be on the right lines for the kill. After all, she was probably correct. The ringleader had to be an American. The maid at Hatfield House felt reasonably sure on this issue, too. Money had to be the motivator and Ian would steel himself to this sad assumption.

He returned to his seat and placed his deerstalker cap carefully on his head. He knew he would attract comments wearing such an odd hat, even in the wide world of New York. It certainly never looked like "Old York" to him, he reflected as he peered at the endless, electric sparkles peeking through the fog like fireflies defiant of an overcast, snowy day.

As he marched towards the baggage pickup area, Ian noticed a few curious heads turn to stare at the floppy deerstalker. He was annoyed that the neatly tied brown ribbon had fallen off of its top position, making the earflaps flop somewhat at the sides of the cap. When the hat was placed properly, his prominent cheekbones and pointed nose made him resemble Basil Rathbone's Holmes. But now he looked comical in a way that contradicted his serious mood.

Ian saw his large black suitcase come through the chute and nudge itself squarely onto the oval carousel like an animated box. He waited for it to make the turn where he stood, and then lurched forward into the line of people encircling the rack and grabbed it off in one fluid motion. As he proceeded towards customs, a short, young man in uniform approached him. Behind him stood a tall, stately, dark-skinned man in a black suit, fixing him with serious, piercing eyes. Without breaking eye contact, the man reached inside his jacket and produced a badge. "My name is Morse and I'm from the Federal Bureau of Investigation and I just need to ask you a few brief questions. If you will step aside here and follow us to a more secluded area..."

Ian's mouth twitched suddenly. "What the deuce!"

"It should only take a few minutes."

"Right." He wasn't one to resist the demands of law enforcement, especially in a foreign country, and particularly knowing he had done nothing wrong.

"Is this your only visit to New York in the past three days?" the agent asked after they had entered a small office which served as a security station.

"Yes. What's the meaning of this?" The room was spare, so he was forced to stand while the airport policeman sat. Morse propped a leg and buttock on the side of a brown, wooden desk.

"May I see a passport?"

Ian fumbled inside his tweed coat pocket for his passport. The detective flipped through the document to locate the photograph and identification.

"Mr. Scarborough, you're a reporter. Do you have any particular business in New York?" His eyes were cold.

"I fail to see why I must answer these questions. I...I shall do so only to this extent— I am spending three nights at the Mohawk

Inn in New Paltz, New York, with the Holmes—," he corrected himself, "Sherlockians, who are the Sherlock Holmes Society. I'm also taping a literary debate for telly, scheduled to be shown on the state-owned broadcasting system. After the meetings, I'm returning home to England."

"When does the conference begin?"

"This evening."

"Don't be too upset over this. We're looking for a man who matches some of your description—we merely mistook you for someone else." Ian swallowed with some relief as the man continued. "I have one more question for you. Will others at the conference typically be dressed like Holmes?"

"They most likely shall," Ian answered curtly.

"Thanks for your trouble," the agent said, "and you're free to go as you please. You've been cooperative and we apologize for any inconvenience. Have a pleasant visit."

Ian picked up his luggage and walked through the door. Adjusting his hat, he realized at that instant why he had been questioned at Kennedy Airport.

Chapter Sixteen

The anticipated snowfall had just begun when the black limousine carrying Ian Scarborough hit the open stretch of Route 299 just west of New Paltz, New York. Large flakes blew a horizontal slant of occasional swirls from a fierce, whistling wind out of the Canadian icebox.

"The forecast is for a very heavy snow tonight—blizzard conditions for the next twenty-four hours at least—in a band from Buffalo, as far north as Albany, down to the outskirts of New York City," the weatherman reported on the radio. "A low is expected locally of about twenty degrees tonight, and will probably rise only to about twenty-seven tomorrow. Winds are from the north at fifteen, producing a windchill of six, so bundle up. Chain laws will be in effect for elevations above five hundred feet tonight. Driving will be hazardous."

When the limo left the freeway, the heavy snow instantly covered any tracks in the road.

"Looks like we'll arrive in the nick of time, friend," said the young driver. "We should be able to get you to Mohawk in another fifty minutes. Just relax and enjoy."

The traffic jams on the Thruway had been annoying and the limo had been delayed in its approach to Route 299. It was already mid afternoon, Ian was surprised to discover. He'd been sleeping in the back seat on the long journey so he hadn't been aware of the delay from Kennedy, where finding the limo service had not been easy. Delays, especially while queuing at the exchange, combined with habitually poor jet lag adjustment, had made him very tired. Figuring this limo ride would be the last sanctuary of solitude before plunging into America's crème de la crème of Sherlockians on this eve of Holmes's birthday, he'd hoped to focus more on the notes during the ride, taking the opportunity to study for the upcoming debate. Ian knew it would be a wonderful social occasion. Though he had always been curious about the American fixation on such an English creation, he did feel a keen sense of kinship with them on this score. Yanks lacked the inherent stuffiness exhibited by the rigid class system of his country, and he relished the spontaneity he often had with them.

He cast his memory back to a three-month tour with a sensational American folk-rock group from New York. He enjoyed their company of joking, pranking, ad libbing, and word play. Falstaff's Ghost was the opening act for the Catfish Forks, and they were a perfect complement to each other since the two bands' guitarists were blues aficionados and were constantly mimicking blues licks. Most English groups were far too timid to blatantly imitate legends like Mississippi John Hurt or Muddy Waters. Falstaff's Ghost played mostly English traditional music in a rock format. The Forks drew from American blues, country, and folk. It worked. Both bands drew somewhat different audiences, which broadened their mutual appeal.

Next to a golf course at the foot of the mountain, a sign partially covered with snow read "Mohawk Inn" with an arrow beneath.

"If you've never seen this place you are in for a treat," the driver said.

Ian watched the snow envelope the car. He was captivated by the sparkling, mesmerizing sight unified in the wind drifts like tiny pale minnows shifting tumultuously wherever the leader led. It was a night for snores, since the snow whirled in defiance of all extraneous force save for the baying bellows. Childhood memories flashed of playing in the snow with friends for hours and never wanting to go indoors.

The tires crunched as the limo made its way up the snow-covered road to a small entry booth. An attendant wearing a wool parka stepped out to greet them and wiped a clump of dirty snow from beneath the windshield wiper.

"Welcome to Mohawk Inn," he shouted from behind a clipboard guarding his face from the weather. "What's the name?"

The driver partially rolled the window down and a burst of wind-propelled snow coursed into the back seat, invigorating Ian with the fresh air. His ear was much better. "His name is Scarborough."

"Yes. The musician. Cool. Welcome, Mr. Scarborough. A pleasure to have you here. I'm a fan," the attendant shouted.

"Thank you," Ian said, and thought if only the FBI had recognized his fame.

A serpentine road holding a disappearing trace of tire tracks guided them to the entrance of the massive inn. Big snow-covered trees, some evergreens and probably some old Scots pine, punctuated the creamy, blanched grounds rolling playfully ahead. Ian squinted through the translucence and around a bend to discern a massive shadow, a hulk like some looming freighter with lights rendering the odd appearance of movement because of the dervish of snowflakes and the car's steady climb through the turbulent, frozen sea. The impregnable sight signaled a sense of comfort, warmth.

As they drew closer, Ian noticed the remarkable contrasts of shapes. There was the considerable stretch of a lower building, maybe four or five stories, nearest the approach, topped by a roof layered with white flakes splotched with occasional orange-red roof tiles where heat was emitted or a miniature avalanche had occurred. The architecture became unusually familiar when he noticed a steeple—only recognizable from photos because he had never been there—maybe the Kremlin, but definitely Russian. How delightfully odd. The steeple, a visual introduction to the resort, stood in front of a variety of Victorian towers, two of which dominated the view and were topped by the twin peaks of roofs now virtually white. Behind them were two loftier chimneys shooting puffs of black smoke into the late afternoon sky. Ian noticed a more diminutive tower further behind the chimneys holding an icy American flag aloft, defiantly jerking against a flagpole. Closer to the ground, bifurcating the two polar building styles as if it were a perverse but exotic afterthought, stood a two-story Japanese lake house jutting out onto a lake. Ian cast his gaze over the icy lake, smiled, and absorbed the entire sight. Taken separately, such architectural anomalies were anachronisms, a contrast too strong, but as an ensemble, they worked splendidly.

A tune came to mind that he'd recorded recently with his jam session friends. It contained a simple one-four-one-five chord progression coated with an almost totally atonal melody incorporating minor notes. The tune meandered as though attempting to find the rhythm, virtually off time, tantalizing and exotic. The song resolved itself with a violent atonality that gave it a tragic climax. Similarly, the admixture of elements before him remained suspended, no resolution, as the snow emphasized the architectural juxtaposition—a counterpoint. His jet lag and recent awakening summoned the haunting tune as the sights engulfed him, trance-like. Then the limo arrived at the hotel.

Ian walked quickly up the steps to the porch and through the entryway to the front desk. The driver, ignoring the concierge, boldly followed with his luggage and set it at Ian's feet.

"A pleasure, Mr. Scarborough," he smiled blankly. "I had no idea you were famous."

"I am, quite apparently, not famous if indeed you had no idea I was famous." Ian couldn't resist correcting this frequent tautology as he handed the driver his fare and a tip.

The driver continued his vacuous smile. "I'll say one thing. You look famous to me."

Ian managed a wry grin as he turned to young woman behind the front desk, "You're Mr. Scarborough?"

"Yes."

"Welcome, sir. You're in room 513, a tower room. Here's your key and a message from Dr. Vernon of the Sherlockian group. He'd like you to phone him in his room, he told me."

"Thank you."

Her captivating eyes reminded him to phone Veronica—he'd promised to do so upon his safe arrival. He decided he would phone her each day, not only because he wanted to hear her voice, but also to assure himself that he was up to date on the news about the stolen artifacts back in England. A special longing for her was abetted by the great distance—the first time he'd experienced a very heartfelt emptiness for a woman since his wife died. And with that, fear came over him. Fear that while he was in rural New York, even for this brief period, he might lose her, never to see her again. Since his wife's death, his feeling towards women had ossified—fear of attachment then possible loss. His father had been of no help whatsoever because his life of politics was paramount. His mother had been mildly helpful, but she tended to dote and mother him. Her smothering, as he called it, was a continual source of embarrassment as he approached age forty-eight.

Entering his tower room, he felt anxiety over the call. It was 9:00 p.m. in London, a perfect time to call. She would be in the hospital room.

"Ms. Aldridge," he whispered to himself. He'd suddenly recalled he was supposed to have phoned her upon his arrival at Kennedy, but the jet lag, FBI incident, and general excitement had blocked it completely from his mind. The admiral had admonished him just the day before to call upon arrival since she was the producer for the debate that was taking place in two days at the inn.

"She will be difficult to ring over the weekend since she keeps a busy social schedule and produces segments on some enormous telly news or feature program on one of the networks. Otherwise, ring her Monday morn. She has all the details. I do know she will arrive Monday evening." The admiral winked carefully and lifted his raspy voice two or three steps. "She's gorgeous, slender, Bermudan American, and single, I think. She's a former Olympic track star. She can run circles round you." Yet another trite joke tossed by his elderly friend.

Ian smiled at the memory and decided he would indeed call Ms. Aldridge, the lovely track star, on Monday and only for the business of the debate. Veronica was uppermost in his thoughts now that he could prop up his feet.

Ian paused in the doorway and scanned the room as he turned on the light. Two medium beds (neither were over six feet long so he would have to sleep crosswise and curl his long legs) were topped with immaculate white spreads neatly covering what looked to be two layers of blankets. The sight of a fireplace, topped by a cherry wood mantle and framed by a rectangular mirror, comforted him. A gold, ornate light fixture with four tulip-shaped globes hung from the ceiling. The room was slightly pentagonal because of two sets of French doors leading to a small wooden balcony on the tower overlooking the lake. Each door, framed by aged, raspberry-red drapes, held six sets of square, clean windowpanes from tip to toe, filtering a faint light from the snowstorm as the beams crept across the light brown carpeted floor. A thin veil of pale frost was forming on the borders of the lower windows. An antique, red felt loveseat stood awkwardly blocking one of the sets of doors leading to the balcony, and he thought as he moved into the room, that seat must be moved shortly.

Two bright red sofas flanked by floor lamps stood on opposite sides of the doors, defining a cozy sitting area. A small chest of drawers with a marble basin on top lined the wall next to the farther bed. For once, he opted to unpack his luggage and use the drawers since it seemed endearing and inviting. The entire furniture ensemble was from the previous century. Ian was shocked at the tasteful splendor of such American antiques. Whatever gaudiness had once been imposed on weary travelers a hundred years ago, had been touched by the ravages of time, yielding the softer reds, and in the case of the undoubtedly once glossy wallpaper, a dainty brown flower pattern blending more with the pliant yellow. A simple black coffee table held a large pot of poinsettias—a vivacious reminder of the recent Christmas season.

He stepped to the fireplace, tore up pieces of the *New York Times* and wadded them into the fireplace. Fresh wood and kindling lay in a log holder beside the ample supply of newspaper. But before he lit the fire, he recalled the message from Dr. Vernon, a professor from the University of Texas at Austin. Instantly, his brain locked onto Veronica. In spite of his anxiety being abated momentarily by the qualities of a snug room, he'd ring the woman with whom he could now reliably say he was falling in love.

A fragile, antique nightstand next to the bed nearest the entryway to the room held the telephone. After ringing, he stretched out on the bed. The line crackled a couple of times as if the weather was interfering with the connection. After two rings, Veronica's unmistakable voice answered, uplifting him.

"Ian here. I've wished you were here from the moment I arrived," he gushed uncharacteristically.

"How nice. I miss you, too. Father's doing no better, no worse. Spent the night reading. I couldn't go to sleep, but I slept this morning at the apartment. Auntie relieved me. I dreamt about us on a boat, in Cuba, of all places, dancing to your music and eating shark. Strange."

"That's quite a contrast to my situation here at the inn. It's snowing rather heavily and we're in for a blizzard. I may be snowed up for the entire three days. It's a lovely old inn. The appointments are so tasteful. My room is cozy but grand. I haven't even bothered to venture a look out the balcony since my first objective was to talk to you, but it has a vista over an ice-covered mountain lake, and I'm certain it would be complete if only you were along." He knew he sounded like a lovesick puppy.

"How sweet of you," she laughed. "I do really miss you."

"Have you heard from Vines?" he asked. "Give him my number tomorrow."

"I called him to see if he needed you to check in. He said you could call tomorrow afternoon, about five, but said there's no news. All's quiet. Anything interesting to report?"

"I most certainly do. Ghastly. I was detained by a gentleman from your Federal Bureau of Investigation while fetching my luggage at Kennedy. Veronica, love, I've a feeling that the culprit who made off with the artifacts, papers, whatever, is at this conference of Sherlockians. I divined what the cockney meaning of 'omes cat' is, as heard by the cleaning lady at Hatfield House. She must have heard 'Holmes cap' or 'hat.' Evidently the FBI figured it out, too."

"Yes. Could be. But how'd you arrive at such a simple conclusion?"

"Elementary, my dear." He heard her laugh politely and thought maybe he'd do better next time. "I'm convinced that the reason the FBI questioned me is that the deerstalker is the only clue they have, and even in Kennedy, one can't help but be noticed when wearing one. I held on to it and wore it so I wouldn't crush it. It would have been spiflicated inside the luggage."

"Yes! How exciting. The FBI. I said you might be on the trail."

"I'll try to determine who it is tonight when all of the Sherlockians arrive. It will be a bloody mammoth task."

"How was your flight?"

"Splendid. I reviewed the arguments concerning the *Sonnets* and then slept a bit. I rode here in the hotel limo so I could review the other portion of my arguments for the debate, but I fell asleep most of the ride. Nackered."

"Ian, please, please find a way to tape the program. Ask the network if they'll provide you with a copy. If my father ever awakens, he would love to see it. It would...it would be the grandest thing for him to see it...especially if..."

"I understand. I'll try to make a contact on Monday. I was so nackered I forgot to call my contact, a producer, in New York. A Dr. Vernon from the University of Texas is coming to my room soon. I'll ask him. He's the gaffer for the Sherlockians. I hope also to discover a little about who is coming and try to determine who our suspect might be. He may have arrived already."

"Ian, do take care. I miss you. I wish I could be there with you, but I know you understand."

"I miss you, too. I'll ring again tomorrow afternoon after I chat up Vines."

"Goodbye."

Ian placed the phone in the cradle and walked over to the French doors, staring wistfully out the windows at the hard-driving snow accumulating on the lake. He noticed for the first time the ascending rock on the lee shore fading into a cloud of snowfall that was momentarily slanting from a forceful wind. His longing for Veronica consumed him again and he faulted himself for a too platonic, too cautious relationship. He resolved to rid himself of his former fears that had made his life too restrictive, too predictable, too boring. His obsession with steering the music world back to where it had been in his heyday had made him cynical. Vines knew that, which might be why he made the bold decision to allow him to express himself on the editorial pages and to cover a hard news story, to travel to this remote getaway. Was Vines such a bad bloke? Maybe not. A light bulb flashed in his mind. Maybe all he needed was this new perspective.

Arms stretching towards the tall ceiling, he yawned and moaned from jet lag. The room darkened. He heard a loud roar in his head and nearly fainted as a vertebra popped.

He sat down on the bed again, taking a deep breath and closing his eyes to restore his equilibrium. When he opened them again, the empty fireplace beckoned for a flame. He longed to hear its reassuring crackle against the raging blizzard outside.

The fire blazed suddenly as he lit the paper in four strategic corners, unleashing the latent energy. Now he felt sanguine, hopeful about this trip for the first time. The FBI had given him the clue he needed. Those fellows, or Scotland Yard, must think nothing of translating cockney after decoding all manner of messages, and the context helped, he thought. An aspiring upper crust Brit-twit should at least know enough cockney to recognize "`omescat" as "Holmes cap/hat." Strange his two American partners, Banfield Smith, or the cleaning maid had not made the connection while on the site.

Darkness was falling as he dialed Dr. Vernon's room. A resonant, distinguished, baritone voice answered in what Ian recognized as a southern American accent. "Fitz Vernon."

"Dr. Vernon, Ian Scarborough replying to your message. I arrived a half hour ago."

"Yes. Thanks. Would you like to come up?"

"Do you mind joining me in my room? I have a nice fresh fire roaring, and I'll order some hot buttered rum if you'd like."

Vernon cleared his throat. "I can't resist such an invitation in this sort of weather, but you must excuse me, I've already had two Jack Daniels on the rocks since my arrival. What's your room number, Mr. Scarborough?"

"I am in room 513."

"Wonderful. I'll be right down."

In the early darkness, Ian searched through his satchel for a quart of rum he'd bought on the plane. If Professor Vernon were an imbiber of Jack Daniels at mid afternoon, then surely he'd enjoy hot buttered rum at this hour.

Shortly, the room resounded with a quick, firm knock at the door. When Ian opened it, there stood a neat, well-groomed man in his mid-fifties with sandy-to-grey hair and a youngish face except for two dark circles under crisp, hazel eyes. His trim body stood straight and tall in a pair of blue jeans and an over-sized aqua-blue wool shirt left unbuttoned over a thick, white turtleneck. Handsome black cowboy boots bespoke a laid-back Texan taste for fashion. He held a glass in his right hand, a bottle in his left. Ian perceived immediately that this was a man who had the talent and flexibility to be patrician and formal, but the heavy whisky and his casual attitude prevailed for the moment.

"Fitzhugh Vernon," he said with a thrust of his right hand as Ian reciprocated.

"Do come in and take a seat. It is indeed a pleasure to make your acquaintance."

Ian motioned eloquently towards one of the red sofas and plopped down on the opposite one facing the professor. He set the bottle of Jack Daniels firmly on the table at the end of the sofa. Vernon crossed his legs.

"Call me Fitz. I've been looking forward to your arrival today, especially since we've had so many cancellations because of the horrendous weather. Also, I've composed a pastiche, a one-act play, for the evening dinner that I hope all will enjoy. Have a good trip?"

"A lovely flight. I'm active as an Oxfordian besides being, as you call it here, a Sherlockian. I'm Ian, by the way."

"Oh yes, the Shakespeare question. The lady at the front desk this afternoon was telling me about the filming of the upcoming debate. I've read a lot about the controversy. There's one fellow in particular in my department who's absorbed with defending Shakespeare and believes you guys are nothing but gadflies. You should be happy to know that I haven't formed an opinion one way or another, except as a mystery fan and an ardent devotee of Poe, what I publish and teach mainly—nineteenth century lit. I do find the lack of biographical information on Shakespeare disturbing. Saccharine Shakespearean scholars are the scourges of English departments, in my opinion. I adore a good mystery, and I love to get under their skin just to be a contrarian."

Tell me, Professor...Fitz," Ian stuttered as he could never easily adjust to relaxed American informality, "is there anyone else among our group who'll be attending the Oxford debate...besides you?" Ian probed, by assuming Vernon planned to attend, to uncover any veiled knowledge of the issue. Was this the man behind the break-in? Did he own a deerstalker?

"Well, as you might imagine, I intend to return to Texas, weather permitting. I'm not a snow aficionado. I'll return on my regularly scheduled flight on Sunday."

"So, will anyone else in our group be likely to remain?"

"Not that I know of. We have a newer group this year. Ian, you realize that these folks are sort of the upper crust. You're with a bunch of celebrity-mogul-literati types. They change each year. A few, the New Yorkers and one or two of us from the hinterland, are consistently a part of this. And Forsythe, the innkeeper, doesn't believe half of us will arrive, thanks to weather. It may be a sparse turnout. Thus far, only six of us have arrived and I happen to have six characters in my one act play."

With that he unfolded several long sheets of paper produced from the back pocket of his jeans. "Here's the whole play, and I've highlighted your parts in yellow. If you don't mind, would you memorize the lines? If you do mind, of course, you may simply write on small strips and read aloud from them. You'll be mostly sitting at a dinner table—Lord's Supper style. I've got most of the lines in the play and I long ago committed them to memory. You're Moriarty."

"Yes, so you said in your letter." A short knock sounded at the door and Ian let in a porter with a tray of cinnamon sticks, butter in a small dish, and a steel pot of hot water. Ian motioned towards the coffee table and handed the man a tip.

"As Moriarty, I can't reliably say you look the part except for your imposing height. But we're not very serious, as you may imagine," he muttered and sipped his whiskey. "It's all good fun and we have no time for rehearsal."

"Care for some rum?" Ian motioned towards the table.

"No. I have all I can handle right here. Go right ahead."

Ian poured some of his Jamaican rum into an eight-ounce glass. He sliced a tab of butter, slid it into the glass, and then poured hot water from the pot to fill the glass. The butter disappeared after he stirred it once with the cinnamon stick. The fragrance combined with the crackling fireplace invigorated him.

"Cheers," he said and they raised their glasses. "You're due an apology from me. As I recall in your correspondence, it was our duty to find a certain Sherlockian artifact to bring along to discuss with the group. Fitz, I'm sorry to say that I failed abjectly. Didn't even look into the matter. I've been very busy with a story I'm working on and simply forgot."

"Oh, it's all right. As I say, the session this year is going to be very abbreviated. A real shame. This is undoubtedly the most appropriate setting we've ever had for our meeting."

"Right." Ian smiled. "The inn resembles the Master Detective himself, elegant and smart."

"It's a unique inn, isn't it? No television, an extensive library, fireplaces in each room, the nineteenth-century decor. The perfect place for my little one-act mystery."

"Oh, by the way..." Ian cupped his hands around the warm cup, "do you think the inn has any means of recording the Oxford debate so I might have a taping of it?"

"You probably need to ask Forsythe, the owner, but if it's live, I can ask my wife to tape it when it airs...or the film crew itself may do it for you. Forsythe said they're having problems leaving New York. I do hope they make it up here."

"Right. I'll speak to him. Repeat the Holmes...the Sherlockian schedule please, Fitz."

"We have dinner and the play in an hour and a half." He glanced at his watch. "It's five-thirty now. Then we have a quick tour of the inn from Forsythe. He told me it might be cancelled due to the snow. Tomorrow morning is free time until noon when we meet for lunch and then watch a film from your own Granada television. Then Judge Armstrong from Memphis is reading a paper if he makes his way here. Someone else is reading a paper or two. We'll then take an afternoon break and meet for cocktails at six, followed by dinner, then the show-and-tell of Sherlockian artifacts. Sunday morning we have a brunch, and then we're off to our respective homes, I hope, safe and sound."

"You've prepared an interesting program, Fitz. I wonder—"

The telephone rang. Ian leaped up and almost spilled the rum as he answered the phone.

"Hello, is this Mr. Scarborough?"

Ian was startled by the sound of a female voice with an English accent, a hint of Yorkshire. "Yes it is. Who's speaking?"

"The British Embassy in Washington. Please hold for Ambassador Crain."

Ian leaned away from Vernon.

"Mr. Scarborough, such a delight to have made the connection. Cedric Crain here. I'm so sorry to have to bother you, but I have a most urgent message to relate to you. I hope you don't mind, sir."

Ian felt annoyed, yet curious enough to allow the ambassador to continue. Never before had he been contacted by his country's embassy. "Carry on."

"As you may have gathered by your inconvenience at the airport a few hours ago, we're searching for someone who somewhat fits your description and could possibly be with your group of Holmesians there this weekend. That individual, we strongly believe, is a male American. Incidentally, you have our humble apologies for our asking the FBI through our channels to involve itself and interrupt your progress. As I was saying, that person is likely a part of your group and could be there with you in the Holmes conference..."

Ian immediately recognized where the discussion was leading and decided he must have the ambassador call him when Fitz, a possible suspect, however remote the odds, was out of earshot.

"...And we believe he may have stolen some quite valuable papers relating, in fact, to the debate you have been so involved with. We assume his purpose is to either destroy the papers or to sell them to some American tycoon with no intention of having them released to Her Majesty's Government. I implore you to consider, especially since Queen and country are counting on you, and it appears that no one from any law enforcement agency is able to arrive there in the blizzard you are currently having."

Ian struggled to think up some sort of code so they could talk more freely about the details concerning the suspect. Was there a British idiom that Fitz, thankfully a Poe man and maybe not a Wodehouse scholar, wouldn't understand so the ambassador would ring back later?

"Mr. Crain, I'm sorry that I must interrupt, but the penny may drop here any second." He intentionally left off the title ambassador.

Fitz did not seem to notice the expression. He was staring out the window at the snow falling on the lake.

"I see," the ambassador replied in a lower tone. "You obviously have someone with you."

"Right."

"Brilliant. I'll call back. Would it be wise to ring you again in, say, a half hour?"

"Right. That would do quite well. The weather here is horrid and I must await a better connection to call in my story."

"Thank you, Mr. Scarborough. I shall ring you in a half hour then. You're most clever and our government will be most indebted to you. I met your father, whom I had the honor of joining in cocktails here at the embassy, about two years ago. Please stand by. Cheers."

The ambassador hung up but Ian continued to talk on the telephone. "I'll ring in that story once I have it ready, although I think it would be most propitious for you to ring me since the weather is so abysmal. Try again in about a half hour. I did not bring my computer and there may not be one here that I can use." That should allow his guest time to leave if he took the hint. "Yes. Right. Until then."

Ian faced his guest.

"My newspaper is trying to ring me to turn in a story even though it's getting late in London and I don't believe the phone lines are adequate to properly hear my voice. I suggested they try again in about a half hour. By then I should have my copy entirely ready. It's very close now."

Fitz nodded. "It's not a good time to receive an overseas phone call—especially with your kind of deadline. I'll head back to my room and get ready since I do need to wash up. Ian, I look forward to this evening. Thanks for your hospitality and accepting the part of Moriarty."

"I look forward to it, too. It'll be most pleasurable. What room are you in?"

"Seven nineteen." The Texan rose from the sofa.

"Do join me in about an hour and we'll go down to the dinner hall together—Holmes and Moriarty." Ian laughed forcefully. "I do so look forward to this evening."

"I'll see you then." The Texan shut the door behind him.

"A bloody spy on Her Majesty's Service," Ian whispered as Fitz closed the door.

Chapter Seventeen

Ian waited in vain for the phone to ring within the appointed half hour. After an hour, he wondered if he should ring Vernon to delay his appointed return. He weighed the risk of Vernon, even remotely a possible suspect, eavesdropping during the important conversation.

While mentally debating the matter, he knelt in front of the fireplace to stir the coals with an old iron poker, chipping at the burning wood. He was reluctant to take on the role of detective for Her Majesty, especially since his duty was as a journalist, reporter, and critic. For now, he was intent on the goal of securing the letters, manuscripts—whatever the contents—for the purpose of exposing the truth of de Vere as the author of Shakespeare's works. Otherwise, how could he face Veronica, or her father if he ever gained consciousness? On the other hand, his father, were he ever to get wind of it, would never forgive him, patriot that the old MP was, if he didn't protect the interests of England first. Patriotism was one of their few common traits. "What if the papers show Shakespeare was in fact Shakspere of Stratford-Upon-Avon?" he ruminated aloud. Then he recalled the quote by Oxford he'd used in his own editorial, "For truth is truth, though never so old, and time cannot make that false which was once true."

The possibility that the documents or artifacts were being secreted away by some egocentric American tycoon, or even destroyed by someone, maybe an American Stratfordian, to perpetuate the myth in the face of sudden exposure, literally chilled him. Spine quivering, he turned his back to the healing warmth of the fireplace. It was unnecessary to decide which role he would take for now. The desideratum was to find the culprit as soon as possible. Such constant musings might even hinder his train of concentration so he decided to delay the decision concerning whether to remain loyal to the de Vere cause or safeguard the interests of the government. Instinctively, he placed the deerstalker firmly on his head despite not needing it for his role as Moriarty. In either role, he would be wearing the master sleuth's hat to achieve the goal: truth. Whether he was the investigative reporter or a loyal citizen in traditional bowler, the goal was constant. Hold that thought, he told himself. The difficult conclusion was what to do when the truth presented itself—especially if the evidence was about to be destroyed, or secreted away, in the clutches of a carefully guarded ego-parlor of some millionaire. Or if the horrid truth was, it was Will.

It had now been over an hour. Vernon was ten minutes late for their appointed rendezvous. He rang the front desk to ask to connect to the information service for DC. A young man answered. "I am sorry, sir, but the phone lines, incoming and outgoing, have been down for nearly forty-five minutes. The only service is within the hotel."

"I see. How do I ring another room?"

"Dial seven and then the room number."

"One more question. Would you leave my message light on once the lines are restored?"

"Yes, sir. Certainly. Let me say, it may be hours. Last time this type of blizzard came through we went for over two days. Cell phones don't work, either."

"I see. Right."

"I'll be glad to leave a message when that happens, though, and I'm writing a note to that effect. Is there anything else?"

"No. You've been most helpful."

He dialed Vernon's room. The line rang twice before the man answered in a thick voice. "Fitz, I humbly apologize for not ringing you sooner, but I patiently waited for them to ring when I should've been ringing them at the earliest opportunity since the lines are down."

"Incredible. I was supposed to call my wife minutes ago. I simply forgot. You reminded me, but now I have an excuse. I don't suppose a fax machine would work since they are on the telephone lines."

"I expect not."

"We should inquire about a mobile phone or shortwave."

Ian weighed the suggestion and quickly decided against the prospect of having someone, even Vernon, the owner, or even the radio operator, aware of the new reason behind his mission to the old inn. How could he and the ambassador discuss such a sensitive matter in solitude without someone knowing? He would defer a final decision by brushing it off, although Fitz's suggestion was a worthy consideration that he could take up with the owner later if he felt it entirely necessary. He spoke quickly. "No cell phone service according to the front desk. I don't believe it's as urgent as that. Before I left London, I booked an evergreen to my account and I'm not due for another one for two days so maybe the lines will clear by that time."

"Oh well, at any rate, I'll be right down, Moriarty."

"Never forget that you are dealing with the `Napoleon of Crime,'" Ian warned against Vernon's chuckle, then took a quick gulp of his drink and hung up with a hearty, "Good-bye."

Ian donned a large, luminous black cape loaned to him by none other than his friend, Sir Keith Trent, actor and Stratfordian. Ian adjusted his deerstalker and grasped an inexpensive, but authentic looking, meerschaum pipe. In Moriarty's role, he'd have no opportunity to use these latter two trademarks, or the less significant but ubiquitous magnifying glass. Impulsively, he removed the hat again, sweeping his hand to brush back his hair and allow his forehead prominence—an effective stroke since his wide, smooth forehead was a phrenological paradigm secreted for twenty-five years behind blond Beatle bangs that were lately tinged with grey.

Vernon entered clutching a glass of whisky. "Shall we go, Napoleon of Crime?"

"Right." Ian shut the door behind him.

"I'll ask Forsythe about a shortwave."

Ian wondered if Vernon's hospitality was sincerely expressed or was it a ploy to eavesdrop? Was Ian so anxious about the matter that he'd become overly cautious, even paranoid? "I'm most grateful for your concern, but I believe the paper will survive without my latest effort. As I say, I've booked one article to my account for tomorrow and..."

"I find your Briticisms charming. `Booked one article to your account' and `the penny may drop any second.' Hollandsworth, the Shakespearean scholar in our department, and I frequently discuss hilarious expressions or idioms in the various branches of English."

"Really?" Ian self-consciously sounded more keenly interested than he cared to express as his voice slipped vulnerably into falsetto.

"Yes." Vernon pushed the elevator button and the door opened immediately from where he had come only moments before. "The term `account' simply means you have one `under your belt' as we would say—an evergreen article which can run at any time. The `penny dropping soon' implies something would soon `dawn on you.'"

Vernon dashed to the next observations, Ian noticed. Was it diplomacy, or an intentional cover-up of his provocative explanation in his knowledge of the last phrase?

"You say `gump,' we say `horse sense.' Your `monkey-freezing' is our `bitter cold.' Fascinating."

They stepped off the elevator and snatched their name tags from a long, blue-draped table. Sadly, too many tags remained uncollected.

"Looks as though attendance will be light, regrettably," Ian said.

As they entered the room, a fist playfully struck Vernon's right shoulder. The hand was attached to the body of a man in a blue pinstripe suit whose white hair was the only signal that he might be pushing forty. The man exuded an extraordinary presence. No other man in the room held such attention. The room looked different, livelier, with him in it.

"Ian, Congressman Lloyd Rogers from Kentucky. Congressman, I'd like you to meet British critic and musician, Ian Scarborough."

"What a pleasure to meet you." The tall, handsome lawmaker's smile revealed an engaging row of top teeth, "I listened to your music the whole time I went to undergrad and law school at UK," he said and extended a graceful hand.

"My pleasure. You matriculated in England?" Ian looked puzzled at the sound of UK."

Vernon nudged the congressman and laughed heartily. "He's referring to the University of Kentucky, then known as the University of Rupp. You may know, the basketball coach."

"Right." Ian broadened his smile as they strolled further into the dining room. Eight round tables were set to accommodate about forty people, while the head table contained about seven place settings. Small groups of people dressed in capes and deerstalkers, accompanied by frequent clouds of tobacco smoke from varying designs of pipes, clustered about the quaint brown-paneled Victorian room. Aromatic logs and hot coals crackled in the large fireplace behind the head table.

"Your music is immortal—right there with the Everly Brothers, Roy Orbison, the Beatles," Rogers said. "I still listen to it. You fellows were refined—like classical musicians."

"Thank you very much," Ian said.

Vernon grabbed his arm. "Ian, meet Shelton Stallings. He'll be playing Mycroft this evening. Shelton, Ian Scarborough."

Ian faced a heavy, sixty-plus man with a spreading waist. The man looked familiar, especially the large nose and ruddy complexion in his well-preserved face.

"Hello." Ian extended his hand and the man shook it. Ian was embarrassed because he felt he'd known this man before yet was certain he'd never met him. "Holmes's only brother," he said.

"Yes." Stallings then extended his hand to the congressman. "Good to see you again, Congressman. I'm Mycroft tonight."

"You knew him, if the television show or movies ran in England, as the `Long Stranger,' the masked Cherokee who cleaned up the Wild West." Vernon could hardly detect Ian's embarrassment, as the show had indeed run in England. Ian knew it well as a child. "Now you know what he looked like without the mask."

"Yes," Ian said, face reddening.

"Where is your faithful sidekick, Honko?" Vernon asked.

"Him find out what `Kemosabe' means. Him left." Stallings delighted in the adulation as the four men laughed. Stallings never tired of the line, Ian perceived, as the Indian's mouth widened in mock anticipation of their laughter. "Now it's incorrect politically and out of fashion"

"Ian is a critic, musician, and Sherlockian from London," Rogers said. "He's playing the evil Moriarty tonight."

"What character are you?" Stallings asked Rogers.

"Inspector Lastrade."

"You'll make a good one." Vernon smiled and sipped whiskey. "We'll start soon. We're about ten minutes late now, but I want to delay the festivities since we're having a light turnout."

"It hasn't stopped snowing," Ian said. "I believe it's intensified."

"Yes, indeed," Rogers said. "The telephones are out. I tried to call my office but no luck. My car phone wouldn't work, either—there are no towers close by to adequately support them."

"Dr. Watson." Vernon greeted a bald man who possessed a cheery, comical face befitting Holmes's companion and biographer.

"Hi, Fitz...Lloyd, I've been talking with Shelton. We've been discussing a trade," the man said, winking at the retired actor.

"Ben, meet Ian Scarborough, a Holmesian first and foremost as well as a noted critic and talented musician," Vernon said.

"Ben Aronson, Ian. You need no introduction beyond that since someone told me you were coming. We've played your music, ASCAP of course, through the years at the ball park..."

"Ben owns the Chicago White Sox," Shelton explained. "They're a baseball team."

"Some years they're not," Ben said. "Some years I believe they're winos or vagrants. It's the reason I'm bald and have," he knocked on wood below his knee, "this peg leg. They're the great white whale and I, Captain Ahab, forever lashed to it and sometimes sinking to the deadly depths of the American League."

Two waitresses entered from a door at the left side of the head table and began placing large menus at the front table. This cued Vernon that the event was to begin soon, so he checked his watch, gulped the remainder of his drink, and walked quickly towards the front table. He turned around to face the entire group as he knocked loudly on the table behind him. Ian judged that this was one professor who had a remarkable propensity to hold whisky. He discerned that his heavy tongue had lightened up in his public persona. There were now about twenty people at the tables.

"Gentlemen, if you'd take your seats, we'll be placing orders. Then we'll begin our play this evening. A lighthearted pastiche."

The waitresses moved from the head table and returned to a menu rack next to the warm fireplace.

"These two charming waitresses will be delivering paper menus to your table. Circle your selections on the menu with the crayon in front of your plate, and once done, place the menus near the center of the table. Print your name on the selection sheet for proper identification when they return with your meals. In a few minutes, they'll come around to pick up your orders.

"Also, near the center of each table you'll see the various Sherlockian relics, the subjects of lectures by some of you. I have here in my hand," Vernon raised a manuscript protected by a tight, plastic case, "the original manuscript to *A Scandal in Bohemia,* which the University of Texas at Austin's librarian has been kind enough to lend me. It's," he hesitated for emphasis, "a most valuable item, for it contains the signature of Sir Arthur Conan Doyle. I'll be giving a brief introduction to its history during the play while we wait for dinner to be served." He reverently placed it in the center of the table close to his plate and sat down.

The five other actors took their seats behind nameplates bearing their character names as well as their real names. Sitting behind his nameplate "Ian Scarborough as Prof. Moriarty," Ian unfolded his script and reread the stage directions and cues. Would the play work on such short notice? He began circling his menu selections: Chicken Kiev, baked potato, peas, and cheesecake.

A stocky, elderly man with long white hair took the seat "Zelton Prossor as Baker St. Irregular." Vernon waved pleasantly at him as he removed the script from his shirt pocket underneath his large brown cape.

In the rear of the room a man suddenly stood up. "To Irene Adler—who deserves the title of 'the' woman."

The group repeated in unison, "To Irene Adler," and sipped a toast to Holmes's only true love.

A photographer entered and began taking pictures as toasts went out to various Sherlockian characters. He was using nothing more than a self-developing Polaroid that made a noisy whirring as he snapped each shot. He would rip the film off the camera then place it carefully in the outside pocket of his gaudy green sports coat.

The waitresses began retrieving menus with marked order sheets. They carefully separated the marked sheets from the menus, returned the menus to the rack by the fireplace, and then carried the sheets to the chef. As Dr. Vernon rose to deliver a toast, the waitresses rushed to the head table. The photographer turned around to take aim at Vernon.

"To a thespian who has redefined the Holmes character on stage and television the world over, the late Jeremy Brett," Vernon shouted.

"To Jeremy Brett," came the refrain.

Dr. Vernon threw his wine glass into the fireplace after the toast. The photographer caught the toss with a perfectly timed camera shot. The two waitresses and some of the audience were genuinely startled at the sudden disturbance. Some laughed. One of the women reached to retrieve Ian's menu just as he stood to deliver a toast. Ian had read this section of the script meticulously. A small piece of green tape was attached to the base of the fake, easy-shatter glass, which was made of sugar for Vernon to hurl "with force" as the script directed.

"To the man in whose true footsteps Sherlock Holmes followed in a real life—Dr. Joseph Bell of Edinburgh." As Ian pronounced *Bell,* he unleashed the wine glass at the roaring fireplace. The toss was vigorous enough to cause the broken sugar glass to ricochet back onto the floor around the fireplace pit and even onto the backs of the nearby occupants. The photographer caught the moment from a vantage point several feet away. One of the waitresses shrieked and nearly dropped her armload of menus as the fake glass scattered around the hearth and near the table.

"Are you hurt?" Vernon asked, handing her a stray menu he'd retrieved from the floor.

"N...N...No," she replied loudly. Ian noted that the waitresses were part of the script, as was the photographer.

"She's scared speechless," hissed Vernon's Holmes to Ian's Moriarty as she moved away from their table to return the menus. "Your heavy hand is harm's handiwork, Moriarty!"

Despite the laughter, the danger of the breaking glass (the sugarcoated prop donated by Stallings had been effective) had made some of the audience wonder if Ian's Moriarty was overplaying his part somewhat. Ian was so glad he'd been able to carry the role off at all since he'd not taken the time to read much beforehand, and was now cribbing from the copy of the script just to the left of his plate. According to the script, Moriarty was to nod his head at the waitress as she retreated to the kitchen. He did so. She acknowledged with a quick bob of her head.

The script indicated there were approximately five minutes before the first plate would be brought out. Ian noted that the timing of the service was apparently integral to the plot, so as the crowd settled down, Vernon walked out to a spot in front of the table as if to interrupt the scene while waiting for the serving. He began a lecture on the history of the manuscript entitled "A Scandal In Bohemia," describing how such an original heirloom had arrived at the University of Texas. At one point he achieved the pith typifying an English professor from Texas. "When all is said and done, it's extraordinary what oil and cattle money can accomplish." He rambled on about the physical aspects of hauling a valuable manuscript around, including the security it entails. "When I went through Kennedy today, I was appalled at how I was questioned and treated. They insisted I show them the letter of authenticity from UT's library."

Ian jerked up his head, his heart skipping a beat as he heard the ad lib. Was it indeed an ad lib? He scanned the audience to see if anyone else had the same reaction. No. There were a few blinks but they seemed to be routine. He then looked at his script to see if it was an unrehearsed, extemporaneous line. Yes. "Vernon ad libs on origins of authentic manuscript" were the words on the page. Was he serious about an inconvenience at Kennedy?

"I was stopped by the FBI, no less," he continued, but the crowd was evidently not taking him too seriously concerning the comment. Ian scanned the room to see if anyone was.

The waitresses and other kitchen personnel appeared bearing trays of plates. A heavy aroma of beef, chicken, fish, vegetables, and gravy instantly permeated the hall. At each table, wine stewards began pouring either clarets or blush Zins. Vernon continued to prattle on as the serving crew delivered to all attendees except Vernon. Most participants had begun eating.

"So it was with much gratitude to the head librarian that I made it a point to make mention of this valuable...The papers are gone!" he gasped as he turned to reach for the manuscript behind him on the table. "Where are they? Someone has stolen them!"

Stallings's Mycroft said, "Perhaps the packet fell on the floor."

Prosser's Baker Street Irregular turned on the overhead lights. The other play characters looked under the table and in the immediate vicinity. Some in the audience were craning their necks as they glanced over the room while others laughed at the spectacle of some of the actors crawling under the table in an impending orgy of overacting.

"No one leaves the room," ordered Rogers's Lastrade. The group continued to search. Vernon's Holmes puffed vigorously on his pipe while he studied the photographer's Polaroid prints through his magnifying glass. He brought one particular photo close to his eye to catch more detail, then slapped the photos onto the table and walked stealthily over to Aronson's Watson.

Grabbing Watson by the elbow, he escorted him to the area in front of the head table, closer to the audience, and removed a set of keys from his pocket. While the other characters continued their search, Holmes handed the keys to Watson and said in a stage whisper loud enough for the viewers to hear, "Watson, go to the parking lot where my old yellow car is parked and get two smoke bombs from a small shoebox beside the umbrella in the back seat. They should be in good condition. When you return, you'll see me raise my hand thusly..." He lifted his left hand to the top of his deerstalker's ribbon. "Then toss the bombs into the coals at the front of the fireplace." He looked furtively at the others to see if they had been within earshot—they studiously ignored him as they were continuing their search. He said to Watson, "Don't move till I order you to apprehend the perpetrators."

Watson sneaked out the door to the kitchen without the notice of a distracted Lastrade, who was busy examining the top of the mantelpiece. Holmes tapped on the table with his smoking meerschaum. "Gentlemen, I believe you'll see some important evidence in these photos. I would like for you to gather around the table here."

He returned to his seat and gathered the stack of photos from the front of the table where he'd placed them before sending Watson on his mission. He intentionally reshuffled the photos to purchase more time and give Watson a chance to return.

Ian's Moriarty protested. "What ever does this have to do with a missing manuscript? We're standing here observing photos while someone has traversed all Devonshire."

"Yeah," the Baker Street Irregular agreed innocently with Moriarty, "we're wasting precious time."

Holmes blew pipe smoke above the group as he flipped through the stack of photographs and held one out at arm's length. "You may find this most worthwhile, gentlemen."

At that moment Watson emerged from the kitchen and approached the fireplace. Holmes touched the top of his hat and Watson tossed the smoke bombs into the flames. Some smoke rolled over the room as the group scattered towards both sides of the table.

"Fire!" Holmes yelled. "Evacuate. Don't forget your valuables!"

The audience had been quietly going along with the play while eating, drinking, and laughing, but the smoke aroused concern—two even rising from their seats to leave. Holmes stopped the action immediately, anticipating a minor stampede by part of the audience.

"False alarm, false alarm," he yelled, dashing into the smoke-filled area in front of the fireplace to push the smoke bombs further into the draw. "Lastrade, Watson, snatch the perpetrators."

Everyone stared at Ian's Moriarty who was standing just to the left of the fireplace with his hand fumbling in the menu rack like the proverbial child in the cookie jar. Ian's height rendered him a look particularly awkward as he leaned over the very low menu rack on the wall and the audience roared at the entire amateurish spectacle. Watson blocked Moriarty's path as Lastrade grabbed the thief firmly.

Scene frozen, Stallings's Mycroft raised his right hand and turned to the audience, asking simply, "How?"

The audience roared at the famous old Native American's stereotyped utterance and stoic pose.

"Elementary, my dear Watson," Holmes replied as the audience laughed at the inside joke of the apocryphal cliché, since the group was so familiar with the canon of Doyle to know that the phrase had never been used except in film. "I noticed that one of the waitresses lingered for some time while placing the menus in the rack. This wasn't so much of a problem until I noticed that my order was either very late or hadn't been turned in at all. When the manuscript disappeared and we couldn't find it anywhere, although no one bothered to look in the menu rack since it's an obscure place, I decided to test my theory by applying the actual plot contained within the manuscript of "Bohemia' to allow the miscreant to find the missing artifact for us. I gathered that the glass scattering incident was precisely the distraction the waitress needed to snatch the manuscript. Moriarty executed it well, but didn't count on the photographer being here to document so inadvertently the exact moment the waitress grabbed the manuscript. This photo," he shuffled to the correct snapshot, "was proof."

"Yes. I can see the sides of the menus, but there is one rather thick area between them which is shorter and doesn't have those metal reinforcements on the corners," Watson said.

"Furthermore," Holmes said, "to quote from the actual manuscript itself, the perpetrators' instinct was quote, `To rush to the thing which [they] most value', end quote, when I used the fire evacuation ploy. Ironically, it was a photo that Irene Adler retrieved when I yelled `fire' in the story itself. Tonight, it was a photo that corroborated."

Prosser's Irregular snatched up his script since he couldn't recall his line. He held it up to the lights as the crowd laughed. "The moral is, `You should shout fire in a crowded theatre,'" he read, the audience hissing at the cliché. With a grin he asked, "What's Moriarty's motive?"

"Moriarty paid the waitress handsomely to assist him, I'm certain, because he could command a very high price for such a valuable manuscript. An autographed original manuscript could do well in front of the right Texas oilman or Jersey gambling tycoon. Moriarty, you're no petty furuncle, you're the Napoleon of Crime."

Ian smiled as the audience applauded the perfect resolution of the crime and the motley thespian pretenders bowed. After this display, Ian was somehow confident now that he could trust Vernon enough to probe him about the incident at the airport and perhaps go even deeper about the make up of the Sherlockians in attendance. As the applause died, he crept over to Vernon, grinned, held out his congratulatory hand, and whispered, "Well done. Please do come up to my room as soon as this evening's events are over and we'll have a drink."

The applause muffled the conversation. "I most surely will," Vernon concurred with a wink. "An excellent job, Ian."

The crowd had barely sat down to finish the meal before Vernon announced, "I've just received word from Mr. Forsythe, the innkeeper and owner, that all phones are down, the cellular phone station is out and without emergency power, and an old shortwave is about all we have to communicate with—and it's not up and running yet. He hopes to repair it within the next twelve hours. If anyone has a CB in his or her car, please let Mr. Forsythe or me know. Thank you all for coming, and thanks again to our marvelous thespians. Enjoy your meal and your company."

Somewhere out there in the audience, Ian thought to himself, there just might be a man capable of selling artifacts even more valuable than all of those penned by Sir Arthur Conan Doyle. And now Ian's singular mission was to stop him, for it would compound the tragedy of the loss of proper recognition for a desperate, forgotten, and tortured soul.

Chapter Eighteen

"Veronica, dear, I'm so delighted you're here." Auntie Joan rose from the seat by the window to hug her niece, whose coat and umbrella dripped from a trek in London's winter rain. "Dr. Sims just left. Said he saw some improvement. He thinks the drugs are reducing the clot.

"Wonderful. But there's still risk of the clot hitting the brain, right?" She propped her umbrella in the corner and draped her raincoat across the back of an old wooden chair.

"Unfortunately, yes. It's a risk we'll have to bear." Her voice trailed off slightly.

"Did you sleep well on the cot?"

"Yes." She sighed. "But I did lose my blankets during the night and nearly froze to death. Maybe we should move the cot away from this window while the wind is heavy. It must be affecting the temperature over here, although it seems to be quite comfortable this morning."

"Why don't you go home? Take a nice break," Veronica urged. "I can handle it until tomorrow around noon. Turns out I have to write a speech for the senator—he called last night after I talked to Ian. He has to speak next week before the New York Longshoreman's Union concerning the US trade deficit and I'm not sure I can put this one down to their level without many rewrites...a tricky insert. Oh...Ian's going to call here, too."

"How do you like Ian, dear?"

"He's most unusual for a retired rock star. He's...he's quiet, reserved, intellectual, and unassuming, but his mind's constantly working. He's created his own world. I'm taken with him—his warmth, his sensitivity, his solitude." The attributes came in a rush, as though she'd never thought of them before, then she knew subconsciously there was something in life to look forward to again and it was quite simply his presence.

"Do you think the drugs made him so introspective?" Her Aunt squinted superciliously like the time she'd asked her why she worked for a Democrat.

Veronica momentarily glared at her. Was she merely showing her age and narrow mind, or had she seen enough of the scourge even among her serious opera students over the past thirty-odd years? She smiled glibly. "I know most of them have a reputation for a wanton lifestyle," she replied evenly, "but he comes from the conservative edge of the English progressive rock movement. He's a gifted musician who joined a band on its way up. He contributed some magnificent compositions and revised certain early English folk songs like `Wildecombe Fair' and `Hard Times of Old England,' so they had wide appeal in England and North America...even Europe. He's very accomplished. Some rockers were too serious for drug use. He was one."

"Oh, yes, I remember `Hard Times.' It was delightful," Joan squeaked, then maintained the pitch for a brief hum. "One of my older students used to sing it incessantly as a warm-up."

Professor Colton groaned and mumbled gently. Aunt Joan stared at his lips and moved hers slightly as though coaxing a student for a note just past his range.

"You are a bird lover I understand, professor." A stout red-haired man of about fifty stood next to him on the front steps of the keep at Castle Hedingham overlooking the peaceful sweep of Essex countryside. Colton looked at the man, and then returned his gaze to the open field below the steps where a red-haired boy held a falcon on his arm. Then he stared at the monstrous Norman tower behind him, rising over one hundred feet in the air. It was made of white limestone and loomed against a placid backdrop of trees. The only interruption in its facing was small portals every twenty or so feet, equidistantly spaced on either side of the doorway by some fifteen feet. The two men stood in front of the doorway under a noonday sun. Another dream, thought Colton.

"Yes, I've even contributed heavily to the literature on the subject of ornithology. It's a shame there is so little left of the sport of falconry in my age," Colton lamented. "You must be that boy's father. You're John de Vere, the Sixteenth Earl of Oxford."

"You're correct, of course. A pleasure to meet you, and how kind of you to visit us this special day. We'll be expecting no less a personage than the Queen herself in a half hour. My good friend William Cecil will be accompanying her, along with the entire royal entourage."

"I see. You're blessed to have a son such as Edward. He's a most brilliant young man."

"I must nurture his great talents because he has so many—more than any young boy his age I've ever observed. So I'll make absolutely sure he has nothing but the very best England has to offer. I have a most extensive library here, and my troupe of players is renowned throughout the land. In fact, drama is one of Edward's greatest fascinations—as well as the Queen's. He's constantly composing rhymes and poetry as well as plays. It's not for his station, but he is so enthusiastic and talented. Good recreation. I'll see that he's trained well in tennis, falconry, jousting, Latin, Greek, poetry (for his private friends), and the manners of court. I want him to study law and take some lessons in anatomy. Already he's demonstrated that he's a prodigy of the highest order and I have no reason to do anything less than encourage him to succeed in these areas. Dr. Colton, would you agree that my vigilance is crucial over this, my greatest legacy—my son, who will become the Seventeenth Earl in a long line of notable men?"

"Yes, your Lordship. There's no question you should pursue all avenues of opportunity. So much so that I'll warn you about some important events that may happen soon. The first event...I hesitate to mention because...it's quite personal...you see, you..."

"What are you trying to say? Out with it, my friend. Don't hesitate."

"It concerns your own longevity on this earth."

"You're saying I may die soon?"

"Yes, in about a year. It'll be the most unfortunate circumstance in the boy's entire life."

"You may rest assured, Colton, that that very subject is on this afternoon's agenda. I shall be making full arrangements for Cecil to take care of any contingencies in case something unforeseen should occur concerning either me or his mother—or both. While William Cecil has no rank above knight, he's the shrewdest man in the nation and he owns the Queen's ear. His star is the brightest and I shall ask him to hitch young Edward to it. To become his guardian, if necessary, should both of us, God forbid, fall into the hands of the Scots."

"It's an extremely delicate matter for me to advise you on this point." Colton watched the brown falcon light softly on the young boy's outstretched arm. "But you're quite correct about Cecil's ascendancy. However, he is...he will be the second major tragedy to occur in the boy's young life. While discipline of studies and regimen is important—he will excel in all the areas you mentioned—he'll also wage a certain rebelliousness against Cecil, even against his station as an Earl. It'll be the most tragic arrangement in the history of arts and letters. He'll never re—"

"What am I supposed to do?" John de Vere was incensed. "If he's without the security of this castle, I want the boy as close to the Queen as possible. It would be a far greater sin if we didn't place him within the Queen's inner circle. I wrote Cecil on this subject nearly a year ago after Queen Mary met her fateful death. I intend to seal this agreement tomorrow while the Queen and Cecil are here. Dr. Colton, you must understand my position."

"Your Lordship, do you understand mine? Anyone, anyone but William Cecil. He'll manipulate your son's life to his own gain. He'll tutor him well, but the consequences will be disastrous. He *will* try to prevent him from going to the continent."

The Sixteenth Earl of Oxford shook his head. "Elizabeth will allow it. She's enthralled with European learning. She writes with an Italianate hand." He pretended to scribble, demonstrating the Queen's delicate hand, across the wispy, cool wind of a summer's morning.

"Your son will murder a servant. The saving grace will be that Burgh..." Colton corrected himself since Cecil had not been elevated to Lord Treasurer, and thus was not yet titled. "Cecil will cover up the incident but it'll surely haunt your son's life."

"We can't manage every detail of the young man's life. He'll make mistakes." The father's crimson face was hardening.

"Cecil will arrange for him to marry his daughter. It will be disastrous and Cecil will hold this against him for the rest of his life. Even the Queen won't be able to stop all of the malicious manipulations he'll be forced to endure. Your son will allow most of your lands and possessions to escheat to the Crown. Bur—uh—Cecil will place your son on an annuity for the remainder of his life. Your son will write the most magnificent works in all the English language, past, present or future, and then Cecil will deny him the right to authorship and bestow it on an idiot who can't even spell..."

"Dr. Colton, he's a nobleman," the elder de Vere protested. "Any of his compositions will be written under a pseudonym like anyone else of such high birth. The Royal Family couldn't stand for such nonsense. Besides, what are you doing here?" Losing his patience he bolted for the large front door of the keep. "You're prying into family affairs. We Oxfords, sir, carry the title of Lord Great Chamberlain to the Crown. You've no right, with your strange accent, to come here and foist onto me your wild visions about my son's future."

"Very well," Colton said, physically blocking the man's movement. "Lord Chamberlain, before I leave, I'll read this poem by your son."

"Read it if you must," the Sixteenth Earl barked through tightly clenched teeth. "Afterwards, I implore you to take leave as soon as you've finished or I'll have my servants show you the road back to your omniscient future."

Colton puffed his cheeks and unraveled a small sheet of paper from his right trouser pocket and read,

> "Help Gods, help saints, help sprites and powers that in
> the heaven do dwell,
> Help ye that are aye wont to wail, ye howling hounds of
> hell,
> Help man, help beasts, help birds and worms, that on the
> earth do toil,
> Help fish, help fowl, that flock and feed upon the salt
> sea soil,
>
> Help echo that in air doth flee, shrill voices to resound,
> To wail this loss of my good name, as of these griefs the
> ground."

"That, John de Vere, will be written after your death in Edward's fourteenth year. He'll sign it `E.O.' and its title will be `Loss of Good

Name.' Your daughter, Catherine, and her husband, the Third Baron Windsor, will sue for your entire inheritance based on whether or not Edward was your legitimate offspring, harkening back to your affairs with a `Mistress Dorothy.' What's the truth there? Luckily, the Windsors won't steal your title. Edward held on to it by the skin of his teeth. Shall you tell us the truth about Edward or will it forever be a mystery? You owe it to him and to history, you know." Colton folded the paper.

"That's quite enough." De Vere shoved him away. "Take your prophecies and poetic drivel back to where you belong. Mr. Ashburn! Ashburn!"

From behind the large door appeared a well-built baseball player in a 1950 circa Philadelphia Phillies uniform. Colton remembered him. Richie Ashburn, outfielder.

"What did he say this time?" Veronica asked her aunt.

Aunt Joan shook her head in disgust and called the nurse to check for bedsores.

Chapter Nineteen

"May I compliment you again on a fine performance with so little rehearsal time?" Fitz Vernon's sweaty, odorous orbit swirled from the gravity of Jack Daniels circulation, but incredibly the host didn't appear to be inebriated. Texans live the legend indeed, Ian thought.

"Thank you. It was a rich experience for me as a critic—a fun luxury to perform in a medium besides music," Ian said.

"You obviously had not one whit of stage fright."

"I did, actually, but it was entirely intended. On my best nights of performing before live audiences, I found it advantageous to conceal fear while maintaining a bit in reserve as a source of energy. I always imagined there was a superior musician in the audience. It works easier in music because there's the sound and the melody to carry the voice along. Treading the boards, you have the naked voice, raw emotion, and physical movement against a stark, silent stage. You can't cover up your mistakes or eliminate them before they happen just by staying in rhythm."

Ian placed another log on the rejuvenating fire in his room.

"You're so right, sooo right," Vernon said. "I enjoy taking something like that pastiche and making it work. Work, yet lighthearted fun. If we'd spoiled the execution and forgotten our lines and cues, the audience might have enjoyed it just as much. Since the TV features reporter from the station in New York called and canceled coverage because of the storm, it went without a hitch. If they'd shown up, well, we would've flopped."

"Knowing the sort of amateurs we are, except for Stallings who was brilliant, they'd probably have laughed even more. You didn't bother to warn us about telly," Ian said, raising his eyebrows provocatively.

"I didn't intend to tell anyone but Stallings." Vernon laughed. "A better answer is they called before most of you arrived. They have an advantage with in-house meteorologists. We probably got bumped for man bites dog. I'm glad they didn't show—too nerve-wracking for me."

"By the way, that was an excellent ad lib concerning the history of the manuscript. Were you actually halted in Kennedy because of the deerstalker hat?" Ian took a deep breath and licked his bottom lip before biting it gently as Vernon sipped more whiskey. Would the direct approach work?

"Ahhh yes!" Vernon answered. "I assume that's the reason. I came through this morning and an agent, a tall, black fellow, pulled me aside." Gingerly, he shook his glass, ice rattling the sides, and he peered into the amber liquid as though it held the remainder of his memory. "He was nice, but seemed very interested in knowing why I was wearing the hat. I gave him identification. I replied that I wore it because I was a proud Sherlockian. I made a little joke out of it and proceeded to tell him where I was going. He wanted to know where I came from. I told him I was from UT at Austin and had flown in from Dallas. He wanted to look at the manuscript in my attaché. I told him it was loaned specifically to me for this event, though the one in the play was a copy. He finally sent me on my way after I let him look at it. It was bizarre. Ian, you would've thought they were looking for a murderer. I believe he watched me pick up my suitcase so he knew which flight I'd taken. I came in before the heavy snow."

Ian decided to provoke first, then probe. "Your country is replete with horror stories of police abuse. Was this bloke indeed a police officer?"

"FBI. He flashed his badge or papers in his wallet. I really didn't bother to look. It happened about noon, eastern standard time, and that's too early for me. I'd taken an early morning flight because my brother and his family are staying with us while he's moving for a new job in California. He's a city planner from Sarasota, Florida. We'd stayed up with Jack," he grinned good-naturedly and lifted his half-full glass.

"He obviously didn't believe you were the culprit."

"No. Maybe it wasn't the hat. Maybe...he didn't even mention any other...he didn't ask any other questions. Odd. I laughed while talking to him concerning the reason for wearing the hat and he smiled. Then he politely waved me on. Were you stopped, too?"

"No." Ian instantly decided not to relate the truth. He instinctively trusted Fitz Vernon, PhD, and imbiber of Tennessee whiskey, but he was ever the last one to show a hand. "I find it interesting that the police have such a way with citizens in this country."

"Oh, we've learned to put up with quite a bit of inconveniences. Terrorism and the drug thing is much of a problem."

"It's a problem in England as well. Too many unsecured boarders and coastlines."

Vernon nodded, finished his drink in one large gulp, and stood. "Forsythe says to check with him tomorrow morning about the shortwave. He says he's not going to bother with it tonight even if he even got it to work, except to check with the New Paltz police on routine reports. He wants to make sure no one was stranded coming up the mountain. Apparently, it's happened many times before. Cell phones are just out of range here in bad weather, he says."

"Right." Ian raised himself from the sofa to pour himself a rum and 7-Up. "It's not necessary for me until tomorrow. Surely the faulty phones will be back in service by then."

"Forsythe says the phone problem has occurred before, too. He claims he's as prepared for these contingencies as much as anyone—even the City of New Paltz. He has generators, a Land Rover in the garage, and two snow sleds. If you ask me, he's a hearty guy for his early sixties. Did you know that he chops all of the firewood for these rooms himself? He works on it year round, starting the day with thirty minutes of wood chopping. He said he never got along with his father and it's who he thinks of with every blow."

"His father's dead?" Ian took a sip of rum.

"Yes, he told me his papa always wanted him to leave the family hotel business and go into medicine. He had the grades and money, but he loves this hotel and nature. He studied geology and worked briefly for the National Center for Atmospheric Research in Boulder, Colorado, before coming back to the family business. He's an amazingly independent fellow for an old-money type. Aronson's been nagging us for years to come here instead of the Harvard Club in Manhattan. He said he loves the ambience as well as Forsythe's hospitality."

"I look forward to meeting him. Tell me, Fitz, you didn't quite answer me when I asked if there are any among us who are also interested in the Shakespeare-Oxford question besides me. It's ironic both events were scheduled almost simultaneously. I'd like to engage in conversation with someone like me who finds Sherlock, Shakespeare, and Oxford to be a compelling lot."

"No, I suspect it was all arranged independently. Forsythe has been pushing the inn for years as an oasis of learning. He has a language seminar here, a mystery weekend, an author's lectureship, business and government retreats, medical meetings, and nature retreats. He told me that he even got a call last week from a bunch of child molesters who wanted to take over the hotel and meet to discuss lobbying strategies for next year in Albany and DC. Can you imagine that? He rejected them. He's now worried about the ACLU.

Ian returned to his agenda. "Do you have many new faces in the crowd this year out of those who have appeared thus far?"

"Yes, about half the crowd I've never met before or seen on any lists. Four or five simply showed up from the surrounding area, mostly New York. They registered last night or this morning. I suspect they're friends of some of the longstanding members, or upstaters."

"And you don't know of anyone who's a fan of these two issues?"

"No, not that I know of."

Ian was convinced now that Vernon knew nothing about why he was enquiring so carefully on these subjects. However, he didn't care to jeopardize his future position by revealing his intentions. It was clearly time to shift the thrust of the conversation. "How often do you have this debate with your colleague at Texas University?" Ian could never overcome his confusion with the names of universities in America, and ever aware that he was usually wrong, he rarely attempted to sort it out. ("It's indeed a pleasure to be here at Louisiana State's Tulane University," he'd announced one night in Baton Rouge years ago before a crowded audience of concertgoers before they were booked the next night at rival Tulane. The crowd roared their displeasure and howled mockingly. He apologized later when he discovered a fight had broken out in the audience over his faux pas.)

"Oh, every few weeks. I do it mainly to incite him. He's one of those weaseling fellows we love to pick on. Schadenfreude, you know. He reminds me of the old Farkle family on *Laugh-In* if you've ever seen the show. He is a..." Vernon realized he had probably not connected with the Farkle analogy since the old show may not have run in the UK, "a jerk...as you say, a twit...a yes…a twit."

"How extensive are your discussions?"

"I have a very good student who joins me in our little banter with Hollandsworth, and he has read the book by...what's his name?" Vernon snapped his fingers, trying to recall the name.

"You mean Colton, of course."

"Yes. I usually stay with my knowledge of the issue concerning the paucity of detail concerning Mr. Shakespeare, or Shaxsper with an 'x,' I believe..."

"Sorry, usually with a 'k,' although out of the six signatures we have extant, only three are complete, and in every case the pronunciation is with a short 'a.' Carry on."

"Since my area is Poe and nineteenth century American authors, I'm very aware of Washington Irving's publication in 1819 entitled *The Sketch Book*, in which he recorded a conversation with a sexton at Holy Trinity Church who had no bias in the whole matter. I might add that the sexton had guarded the open grave diligently while workers dug to fashion an adjoining vault and the earth caved in, creating a vacant area like an arch so one could peer into his grave."

"Right, I am familiar with the passage."

"Yeah. The sexton guarded it for two days since there is such an admonition on the tombstone above..."

"'Good friend for Jesus sake forbear, to dig the dust enclosed here, blessed be the man that spares these stones, and cursed be he that moves my bones,'" Ian recited, "but with an application of proper spelling and pronunciation, of course."

"Yes, excellent, Ian, and the sexton attested that there was nothing, *nothing* but dust in the grave. Irving had no axe to grind. He was calling it as he saw it."

"What was Mr. Twit's reaction?"

"Oh, he always starts squirming in his seat and babbles something about deterioration of bones and caskets, especially those constructed out of cedar or cypress. But one day we brought in Professor Joyer, an expert in scatology, who spent a life of summers in the Middle East. He is the most knowledgeable man in the southern US on remains, and he says two hundred years are nothing—though he did submit there might have been a very minor problem if seepage had occurred from the nearby Avon."

"Whilst there's no real evidence either way on that score," Ian insisted.

"No, not really. But he maintained that the remains tend to simply settle to the bottom of the grave and never crumble—usually they ossify in spite of moisture. Old Hollandsworth, Olin is his first name. Olin sat there and started bawling. He cried." Fitz giggled like a little boy under the bleachers, and Ian laughed at the childish sounds from a grown man. "The student, young Potter, changed subjects. He pivoted to Poe's obsession with death and my own habit of visiting cemeteries so as to lighten up the conversation and it failed. Olin took out his polka-dotted handkerchief and wiped his tears. He blew his nose with that ridiculous hanky that he never washes. I left the room I was so tickled. Joyer cracked up, too. It was soooo damn funny."

"What type of argument does he offer?" Ian was relaxed and entertained with this unorthodox, yet engaging Texan who'd run out of whisky. "By the way, do you want some rum?"

"Oh, he's very big on the dating of the plays and sonnets. If you don't mind, let me go upstairs and get old Lawrenceburg Jack. I'm going to get my Uppmann's, too, if you don't mind."

"Uppmann's?"

"Cigars."

"Oh dear. Better not. My apologies, but I can't bear that smell in my room."

"No problem. I'll smoke on the way down and douse it in the hallway ashtray."

"I have no problem with that. I'll see you in a few minutes. Oh yes, would you be so kind as to fetch another 7-Up?

"Certainly. See you then."

As he left, Ian turned to the fireplace and lifted another log, chopped and split so cleanly by his host, onto the roaring fire. It was nearly eleven o'clock and he was fatigued from jet lag, yet he wasn't sleepy. His body was rested, his mind was tired, but his emotions were effervescent. The telephone rang.

"Mr. Scarborough, this is Bill Forsythe, the innkeeper."

"It's a pleasure to greet you even if merely over the telephone, Mr. Forsythe. Dr. Vernon has told me splendid things about you. Your inn is exquisite," Ian said.

"Thanks. A treat to have you here. Do call me Bill, everyone does. Is Dr. Ver... Fitz there with you now?"

"No. He's just gone upstairs to fetch something, but he'll be returning shortly."

"Fine. I'll call him there. I look forward to meeting you. You turned in an excellent performance downstairs. I was busy, but I caught the first part of the play. I'll phone him in his room. I look forward to meeting you. Good-bye."

Ian finished his glass of rum. The phone jingled again.

"Mr. Scarborough, Forsythe again. I'm so sorry but I didn't seem to reach Fitz. Would you ask him to call me as soon as he returns? I may need his help on something important."

"Yes, I'll ask him to ring you when he returns. He was going to be in his room for less than a minute."

"I'm in Room 201. I'll be here for another twenty minutes."

"Very good."

Vernon had left the door slightly cracked and he burst into the room, forcing a held last puff of his temporarily abandoned cigar, holding a half-full quart of Jack Daniels, a can of 7-Up, and a glass of ice. "Ian, I propped the cigar in an ashtray near the elevator. I'll pick it up when I return to my bed. A delicious brand."

"Pardon my not indulging. Forsythe rang while you were gone. Ring him at 201."

Vernon immediately went to the phone and dialed.

"Bill, I...I...I'm sorry I missed you.... Noooo...the television crew cancelled before the storm hit. They weren't willing to risk the drive and get stranded up here." He laughed. "It's obvious they've heard about the remoteness of this place...I would like to go, too. I think it would be exciting.... No, don't worry, I'll sign a release.... I will! You get me a good warm down jacket, long-handle underwear, and a thermos full of coffee and I'll be troopin' right along. I'll bring along a tall bloke as well. Let me ask him."

Vernon raised his left eyebrow as if to challenge his newfound friend.

"There's what appears to be another television crew about three-quarters of the way up the mountain."

"That must be the crew designated for the Shakespeare-Oxford debate. Rather early, I should think, if that's them," Ian surmised.

"Would you like to join Forsythe in a rescue mission? He and some of his student bellhops are scrambling down the mountain in a Land Rover. He knows the roads perfectly."

"Likely, I would," Ian said, curious over the crew's early arrival. "I'll join in."

"Ian believes it's the crew for the shoot and they didn't want to miss their story. He'll be happy to join us. I promise.... We'll see you in about ten minutes. We'll need to change into some much warmer clothes. I'll be down in a second to pick up the underwear. Ian will need an extra large. Bye." Vernon laughed as he replaced the phone in its old-fashioned cradle. "He's paranoid about lawsuits. Wants us to sign releases. He must have been in one recently."

"There's a risk to our safety, I would say," Ian said.

"Forsythe knows the lay of the land. You know the sort of machine the Land Rover is, Ian. He's counting on us, and he doesn't need university kids on Christmas break helping him alone."

Ian rose, gulped down his drink, and began to select a jersey, T-shirt, and wooly as reliable layers. "We'd better pull our socks up and make way for 201." The telephone rang again.

"Mr. Scarborough, Bill again. I'm sending one of the employees up with warm clothes."

"Yes.

"Have you a problem with going on our little expedition?"

"Actually, I look forward to it. It should be invigorating."

"It's not a difficult mission as long as we go slow and leave enough room for the three stranded men. One's injured. I'll have a doctor along. One of the Sherlockians, a Dr. Barlowe."

"Perfect. We'll anxiously await our new clothes."

"I do thank you. I'm sending the down jackets as well. Oh yes," Forsythe seemed to be driving at the real reason for his call, "is Fitz okay to go with us? Has he had too much to drink? Reply simply `yes' or `no.'"

Ian didn't know which question to answer and hesitated. "All seems well with us."

"Uh, thanks. We'll see you both in a few minutes."

Ian turned to face Vernon with a wry grin and an arched eyebrow. "This fellow is quite well organized. He has a barrister and a physician at his beck and call—both through the good graces of the Giant Rats of Sumatra. Good deeds performed for free."

Vernon cackled heartily. "He told me he's had every kind of predicament imaginable at this inn—especially in blizzard conditions. He told me Poe would have had a field day up here."

"I believe it. This inn is an amazing find, a throwback. Poe, A.C. Doyle, and I are all in."

"'All in.' You Brits are so clever with the language. I wish our writers could accomplish what you do in mere conversation."

"There's no difference in terms of substance, there's only the gulf of perception between the two cultures." He believed, in fact, the cultures were a constant reflection of each other since they were both English based. The mirror image extended to the written word, too.

"Yes, but isn't it all in such a state of decline? Isn't it this monstrous commercialism of books, bands, agents, and record—I mean CD—promoters? You've got the video with the recording. You've got the author on the morning talk show. Hype has overshadowed the art." Vernon poured another drink as if time was running out, which it was since they would be dressing for the mission at any moment. "Seems to me, there have been enough books about loveable villains, enough who delight in the most hideously imaginative repulsions, enough songs about divorced truck drivers, enough inane oxymorons, and not enough...not enough... ohhhhh....well, heart."

"Precisely. When I wrote my music I tried to avoid a glib lyric or the...you said `inane.' I did write some banal melodies, of course. They were usually consigned to album fillers or the 'B' side of singles. We had no idea we were giving in to the trendy producers. They pushed us to make good use of studio time and we had to produce, so we would listen to the engineer or the record company executive for filler ideas. Often they—"

Four rapid knocks echoed across the room. Ian opened the door to find the efficient, blonde woman from the front desk, now holding two grocery sacks packed full of clothes. "Here are your clothes. Let me know if I can be of any further help."

Ian thanked her and politely offered a tip, which she refused with a smiling nod and quickly shut the door.

Vernon's whiskey was prompting him. "I wish she stayed around to help me get fitted."

Ian ignored the remark. "I presume we shall be going the way towards New Paltz."

"Yes, the only *way* from here is down. I hope whoever it is down there is reasonably safe. This could be a matter of life and death." Vernon took another sip and unbuttoned his shirt.

"That's what's missing," Ian said, removing his black leather shoes and stepping gingerly to the seat to sit and remove his socks.

"What's that?"

"Urgency, life and death, crucial issues, morality."

"Yes. There's some sort of fixation on the idiosyncratic, leaving no room for the sublime. Books can no longer possess a moral to the story. If they doooo, they should be convoluted and highly subject to interpretation." Ian wondered if Vernon's sustained vowels meant he'd had too much to drink for the trip. "No more Tolstoys or Dostoevskys. The days of clarified truths are simply gone."

"Is it the buying public? Is it the fault of us as critics? Are you professors responsible? Editors? Publishers?" Ian asked, tugging at the long johns.

"It's aaaall of us." Ian concluded Vernon was probably still sober, but allowed himself certain inflections such as the "aaaall" when he dropped some inhibitions. "We've forgotten the simple morality of Singer or Hawthorne or Melville or even Shakespeare—I'm sorry—de Vere to you. Maybe publishing became infected with a scintilla of corruption with Homer and intensified to a degree that the Oxford cover-up was possible under Elizabeth's and Lord Burghley's tight fist. Censorship extended most dramatically in this century under Nazism and Communism to the point that some of the best moralistic and critical oeuvres emanated from Solzhenitsyn or Boll. What happens if there's no longer a war to flush out the greatest writers? Is repression necessary to nurture creative minds who judge, who believe, who care?" He burst out a staccato laugh and pointed at Ian's torso. "Sorry, buddy, but your underwear is on backwards!"

Ian, smiled lamely, uttered "bollocks" and stepped out of the long underwear to begin anew. "Pardon me, Fitz, but music is no better. In rock and pop music today, there are mainly imitators out there. This has always been true to some extent, but the record people have devised in their own drugged minds, and I mean that literally, a notion, a preconception of what the buying public wants to hear based on what they assume has been successful in the past. They're not too curious about new approaches. A song with an occidental chord progression and melody has not a good chance today. A Jimmy Webb style of composition, or works like the Beatles or the Doors, would rarely reverberate in a studio today. There are exceptions, but not many. Most certainly, there's no room for such esoteric talents as the Left Banke or a Focus or a Premiata Forneria Marconi. If these artists do secure opportunity, they're generally deigned in jazz or new age categories now so they're no longer a part of mainstream rock. So rock is not, artistically, `here to stay.' It's losing appeal. As far as I'm concerned, I don't care for most rock today. It's no longer a category at the end of the day."

The two men were lacing up their black army boots, preparing to head out the door when they heard a knock. Fitz slung it open and smiled, greeting Bill Forsythe.

"Bill, we were just leaving," he said, stepping aside. "Meet Ian Scarborough."

"Such a pleasure." Forsythe looked rather solemn, a short, alert man with a full head of white hair of about sixty and remarkably fit.

"My pleasure as well," Ian responded.

"I'm sorry to seem rushed, gentlemen, but I do fear for those guys down there on the road. They're cold and one of them has a broken leg. Have either of you ever driven a Jeep before?"

"I have," Vernon said, "but never in a blizzard."

"That's no problem," Forsythe answered, "as long as you're able to drive back after I drive down with a snow plough attachment. If we're able to use the winch to pull them out, then you can follow me back here. If not, then I may ask you to drive back yourself with the injured man and the other two who are stranded, and either return to pick us up or we'll walk back since the plow should clear a path. It's only about two miles or so according to their description of the tree and the snow bank they drove into. They weren't operating very wisely by attempting such a trip as late as they did. Gentlemen, shall we go?"

"What prompted such a desperate attempt?" Ian asked. They each made for the door.

"I don't know." Forsythe's grey, glassy eyes softened momentarily, then seemed to snap into sharp focus. "Except they have some irascible, old lawyer on board who's obsessed with arriving here by tonight, according to the driver on the CB before it went out. I think it's some battery-powered walkie-talkie. If I can charge it, we're bringing it back with us."

"Old lawyers don't die, they just nag away," Vernon said. "Why's a lawyer with a camera crew?"

"I'm not sure," Forsythe said as they stepped off the elevator and were joined by a chubby man in his late fifties. He was evidently Dr. Barlowe, whom he introduced around as Congressman Rogers appeared, holding a coffee cup and dressed in an orange, down ski jacket like the other three men.

"Welcome to the mission. This is about as close to a mystery as we may get, except for your excellent pastiche," Rogers said.

"The congressman has graciously prepared some releases," Forsythe said, guiding the group to the front desk. "Excuse me for relying on such a formalized legal instrument, but I was sued several months ago when a guest and I rescued a young girl drowning in the lake and the guest inadvertently broke several of the girl's ribs. No good deed goes unpunished. We were sued. So before we go, I'll ask you to sign them. If you decide not to go, that's fine. You shouldn't feel compelled to go at all. I have several willing college boys working here, but I would prefer your mature judgment in case I have to stay behind with their Jeep in order to try to drive it up. I have full insurance coverage on all passengers."

"I don't object to signing," Vernon volunteered.

"I will sign, too." Ian read the brief release and scribbled his signature, then handed the pen to Congressman Rogers who signed with a flourish.

"Gentlemen," Forsythe announced, "we're about to embark on an important task. I thank you in advance for your generous help."

Chapter Twenty

The five men waded towards the barn through snow approaching two-foot drifts. Forsythe had to manually open the garage door, and then rattled a gratifying laugh. "I told my family this vehicle was going to be perfect for a night like this. It has electronic fuel injection, a 3.9-liter aluminum V8, and for the man with the broken leg, a double-folding 60/40-split rear seat with armrests. Wool army blankets are in the back. I've radioed down there and asked them to leave their lights off until I give the order. I don't want the battery to run down, although I did ask them to leave the engine running to keep the car warm."

They piled into the newly acquired hunter green Range Rover with its odor of new plastic and vinyl. It reminded Ian of the smell he encountered as a teen upon opening a new record, or a bit like the time he watched the waxing of the band's first album. Ian managed to stretch his long frame towards the space between the two front seats and place his buttocks on a wide board cleverly positioned as a bridge between the two back seats, thus creating room for him between Dr. Barlowe and Congressman Rogers.

"There's a first aid kit under the back left seat, Dr. Barlowe," Forsythe said. "I have two small pillows back there and a stretcher as well."

Everyone buckled their seat belt as Forsythe turned the ignition. The vehicle shot directly forward onto the crunch of snowy road, the chains on the tires causing characteristic uneven bumps before hitting the snow. The clumsy snowplough created a trace of drag on the Rover's progress, but they moved along at a steady six or seven miles an hour.

"This is as bad a storm as we've ever had up here," Forsythe shouted over the noise of the chains. I believe only a few of the Shakespeare people checked in. I don't see how we can have a debate. There's no media except for those three guys down the way, and one of them has no connection with television as far as I can tell."

"What debate?" asked Barlowe. The doctor fidgeted with the zipper on his down jacket.

"There was to be a debate over the issue of whether or not Shakespeare wrote the works attributed to him," Ian replied. "Apparently the injured bloke had something to do with it."

"It's the lawyer...the old man...name is Reichol or something," Forsythe said. "He called me this morning, leaving a message that he would probably attempt to come up. Said he had to wait for two others to join him. Laura at the front desk advised him to hurry since she felt concerned about the road conditions."

He turned onto the highway leading towards the bottom of the mountain. Ian looked back to see the red tail lights interrupted by intermittent flashes from the emergency blinkers. The snow sprayed out frozen wakes as if the Rover was a longboat moving down the Thames.

"Did he ask if the debate was postponed?" Ian asked.

"No, Laura said he simply hung up after saying he'd get up here and to hold the room. He called mainly to ask about conditions and if a certain guest had arrived."

"Did she happen to mention who the guest might be?" Ian blurted.

"No. She talks to so many people. Probably of no consequence to her."

"That was the cute blonde, I take it," Fitz said. "The one you sent up with our clothes."

"Yes. She's one of the best employees I have. I'm going to make her head of personnel next month, although she doesn't know it. She's worked the front desk for two shifts since her replacement was stranded in New Paltz. She's very bright and efficient."

Ian shifted the focus to the old lawyer. "So the lawyer's involved with the Shakespeare debate?"

"I suppose he is somehow. There were many lawyers booked for both groups," Forsythe commented. "Sherlockians and this Shakespeare controversy must attract them like flies."

"I'll saaay." Fitz couldn't halt an intoxicated tongue.

The vehicle rounded a small sharp curve on about a fifteen-degree incline. As the men slid slightly in their seats, they heard a dull *clunk* across the snowplow. It was rock against metal. Forsythe shifted to low gear.

"We hit a nice-sized boulder," he observed. "I hope we don't run into more like that."

"How big was it?" the doctor asked.

"Maybe a couple of feet in diameter. It could mean there are a few larger ones but we would have hit them by now. I want to stay right in our path on the return. Remember that if any of you are the ones to drive back." Forsythe hit another curve and maintained his speed at a snail's pace. The heater was on full blast and Ian was roasting in his clothes. He removed his down jacket. The defroster had been working well as had the windshield wipers sweeping the thick snowflakes off. They could see about twenty yards ahead. "I'll probably have to drive back up. May be too perilous."

"Right," Ian agreed, baffled at how anyone could drive with such a blizzard obscuring his vision.

Forsythe activated his CB. "Forsythe to Otis Wainwright. We're rounding the last curve above your position. Any second now you should see the lights. When you do, turn on your lights. It's not necessary to leave your vehicle. Do you read?"

A deep, resonant voice replied like the low roar of a campfire through the freezing darkness. "This is Wainwright. I can hear you. I see your headlights. Can you see mine?"

The five men caught sight of a reflection against the snow some forty yards away. Forsythe slowed the Rover down to a complete crawl on the steep incline. Soon they could see the vehicle pinned against a large old tree where the road had curved slightly outward.

Forsythe could read every inch of the road. "Fellows, it's obvious to me exactly what happened. The driver didn't notice this subtle bend in the road and steered into a drainage area where ice normally accumulates...usually for days. Fortunately, the tree stopped them in their tracks, or they might have driven up on the side of the mountain and turned over. Perhaps even careened to the opposite side of the road and over the cliff. That tree may have saved them."

"They did some pretty bad driving there," Fitz said.

"Not really. You get up here in this blinding snow and you simply can't see two feet in front of you at certain crucial turns," he said. "Their fatal mistake was in deciding to come up in the first place. Of course it didn't help that the county failed to replace the snow markers this fall. I warned them about that. But, clearly, those guys should have stayed down in New York."

"Not quite enough to snow up these chaps," Ian said.

No sooner had Forsythe stopped the Rover than Dr. Barlowe quickly leaped from the back door and waded towards the vehicle. "This reminds me of my house call days back in Iowa." He laid the emergency first aid kit on the snow beside the vehicle, then picked up two sawed-off broom sticks he'd devised for splints and a large brown bandage with two silver pins.

Fitz held the stretcher with the two aluminum poles as Ian grabbed the thick wool blanket. Forsythe whispered to Ian, "Our friend Fitz seems to be a little soused. Do you mind staying here with the two stranded men while I drive back with the victim and the other volunteers? I'm afraid I used bad judgment on Fitz. I didn't notice his condition until the ride down. He seemed to be sober enough in the room."

Ian shrugged. "He appears a bit squiffy but I think he's capable of all *but* driving." He tried to imagine an answer that would relieve him of staying at the site since he now was interested solely in returning with the injured man. Surely this old man had to have a connection with the mysterious papers or artifacts since he was so intent on arriving at the inn despite the danger. Ian hoped to carry the old man to his assigned room on the chance of examining personal effects for clues. "Where—"

"Doctor, where should we take him?" Vernon interrupted as he lifted the stretcher out.

"Near me, of course. The adjoining room is 408, I believe, and he can convalesce there. Dr. Poole didn't show up because of the weather, so I don't think they've booked anyone in 408." Barlowe turned toward Forsythe. "If you have, then you should send them on a hike or switch my room. It's a connecting suite, though, so if we have any others, that's where they can go, too."

"No problem," Forsythe replied. "I'll radio Laura and have her handle it."

The door on the driver's side opened to reveal a very stout, thick-necked black man with a stunning white goatee. He and his front seat companion obviously had been out of the car several times, judging by tracks in the snow surrounding the disabled vehicle. There were small branches and rocks wedged under the front wheels as if they had tried to back away from the tree. That they hadn't made any progress in doing so was evident by the car's front hood glued to the large white oak.

"Greetings, gentlemen." His voice was sonorous and soothing against the swirling snow. "You're all we want to see. I've become short on patience and my friend's thermos is bereft of tea."

"I'll save the introductions," Forsythe said. "The only important name for now is Dr. Barlowe."

"A pleasure to meet you all, to say the least...especially you, Doctor. I'm Otis Wainwright." The wind whisked away their short puffs of greetings into the gelid night. Otis Wainwright shook his head once upon catching a whiff of Vernon's whisky breath even in the swirling weather.

"It's our pleasure," Vernon said. "You're the film documentarian whom I've enjoyed so many times on the *Daybreak Show*."

"That's me. For the past forty-five minutes I was beginning to think of myself as the 'late' film documentarian for the *Sunset Show*."

"Wainwright, stop your socializing and let's get the hell out of here." A high, nasal whine emanated from the window of the back seat where the rescuers could see a thin, wiry frame of a man in a worn, but warm looking, A-2 leather-flying jacket from World War II. He stared up as he held a white thermos cup in his unsteady left hand. He was completely bald.

"That's our man," Forsythe smiled.

"Yes, and I think he has a break in two places," said a young man emerging from the front door on the passenger side. "We'll need to move him very carefully."

"Gentlemen, if you will remain on this side with Mr. Scarborough," Dr. Barlowe gently ordered, "Bill and I will enter the back seat from the opposite side and carefully, very slowly...we will lift his body. Your name, sir?"

"Randle Richtol."

"Mr. Richtol, bundle up your arms. See if you can move your legs into the fetal position. Let me look at the leg. It's the right one?" He gently felt the area directly below the knee, all the while staring into the man's bloodshot eyes.

"Yes. I must tell you...it's most painful. I'm a bone marrow cancer patient."

"Incredible. Are you warm enough? Do you need a blanket?"

"Yes. Warm enough. It's wretched when I move. As long as I'm motionless, it only throbs."

"Take this painkiller. Do you have some coffee left?"

"It's tea. I have one swallow." He pinched the two pills from the doctor's palm, placed them in his mouth, and swallowed them with the remaining chase in the cup.

Barlowe handed his flashlight to Forsythe and began to fashion a splint out of the pair of two-foot broomstick handles. He slowly wrapped the brown bandage snugly around the man's leg held rigid by the splints. Richtol uttered a low moan. Barlowe grabbed the flashlight from Forsythe and examined his work approvingly.

"Fine. Now, Dr. Vernon, please hold that stretcher steady, and here," he shoved the large flashlight into the professor's right hand, "you hold the light for us until we're ready to place him on the stretcher. Someone help him with the stretcher."

"I'll help." Wainwright took a crunchy step towards Vernon.

Barlowe slipped and almost fell as he rounded the sloped side of the Jeep Cherokee. "Damn. I've never seen such snow—even in Des Moines." Forsythe grabbed the doctor's jacket to steady him.

Richtol doubled up in a fetal position while Barlowe entered the back seat. "Bill, brace his back after I get positioned on the floor here. I'm going to hold his legs between my elbows and we're going to move his entire body very slowly toward the other side. Now, I want you to slide his body very gently while you elevate his back. Let his butt drag along the seat. Mr. Richtol, I want you to wrap your arms around my neck and pull towards me a little so you'll glide smoothly. Do you understand?"

"Yes."

"Gentlemen...you two will take over on his butt and back once I'm out of the door there on your side. Hold him there until Vernon and Wainwright can carefully slide the stretcher under him and then I'll lay his legs down. Does everyone understand their task?"

A chorus of "right," "yes," "yes," and "yep" banged his ears.

"I'll count to three. On three we move, Fitz. One...two...three." Richtol grunted as the process began. It took only three or four seconds to move him to the opposite door, but it seemed longer since his body was so motionless and the doctor was straining to make sure he did not move the legs any more than was necessary. Dr. Barlowe's face grew red, his eyes bulging when he dashed over to support the victim's light body on the other side of the car. He was determined to cause as little pain as possible, but he wanted to move him quickly in order to place him onto the stretcher for closer examination.

Ian and Congressman Rogers took charge of the small man's upper body as the doctor held the legs ever so steady. Ian was reminded of the crisp motion of a ballet. Forsythe relieved Fitz of the flashlight as he and Wainwright slid the thick, army green stretcher under the old man's weak body. The young man stood by holding the brown bandage.

"Good job," Barlowe shouted. "Hold the stretcher perfectly still and let me in here so I can get to the leg. When I place it in position, son, you hold it for me perfectly still...perfectly still."

Richtol looked up at the doctor. "Doc...I want you to assure me that you will take my attaché case up with me. You may leave my suitcase behind until the next trip or with the car if you can drive it out of this mess. I *want* my attaché case."

Wainwright leaned over. "Randle, I promised we'd take care of it for you. They may not have room. These very brave men have taken..."

"It goes, or I don't go!" Randle Richtol screamed above the engines. Ian thought calmly about the play they had just completed that evening. The perpetrators reveal the contraband when the pressure is turned on. It was a large, black case, typical of barristers.

"We have ample room in the back," Forsythe assured the old man. "If the suitcase isn't too big, we can place it in there as well. Relax, my friend. You're going to the doctor's adjoining suite for some treatment."

"Thank you." Richtol looked immensely relieved.

"Wainwright...and I don't believe I have caught your name." Forsythe turned to the young man in the ski mask.

"I'm Steve Doerflinger. I'm a cameraman," said the young man. He seemed to be smiling, although it was hard to discern under the mask.

"How do you two feel? Are you cold and exhausted?"

"We're in good shape," said Wainwright, revealing perfect teeth as well as an indefatigable spirit. "Except for my faux pas behind the wheel and a lack of confidence in my driving through this kind of weather, of course. I take it we'll have room for the camera and lights when you return to pick us up."

"Don't worry about the accident. It could happen to anyone," Forsythe said. I'm going to leave you two down here to try to cope with this for another forty minutes or so while the doctor, the congressman, Dr. Vernon, and I carry him back. Mr. Scarborough will remain here with you. Then we can return to pick up you gentlemen and the camera stuff. Is it very large?"

"No. It's a handheld job," Wainwright said.

"I suggest you start the engine and warm up every ten minutes or so." He glanced at his watch. "I have 11:05. Turn your CB on channel 11 instead of 9. I came down here okay, so we should have no problem returning since my snowplow has done its job. What in the world compelled you to start up here in all this weather"

"Determination and a persistent back seat driver," said Wainwright calmly.

"I hope you get what you want because I don't believe we will be witnessing a Shakespeare debate. Very few have arrived who are related to this thing."

As Forsythe returned to the wheel of the Rover, Wainwright said nothing. Ian decided to launch his own inquiry while in the relative warmth of the disabled Jeep. "Mr. Innkeeper is a bit nastier than when we started," he said. "It's been a hard day for him. This could have come to a sticky end, I imagine. You seem to have kept your pecker up."

"I view this as one more adventure, Mr. Scarborough. My mind is totally occupied with the current project. Besides, I don't allow myself to get daunted for a moment, not after what I filmed a few years ago in Rwanda, more recently in Iraq and the Sudan, and in other places. No frozen skid into an oak tree is going to shake me up after seeing the utter Hades created by mad regimes."

"Right. I recall your docs have won awards. I saw the Sudan on ITV. It was brilliant...shocking. I'll never forget it as long as I live." Ian shivered at the thought of the wanton starvation and neglect.

Doerflinger had just started the engine to heat it up and the warmth spread quickly through the interior as they shut the doors. Ian sat in the middle of the back seat and leaned forward to watch the sides of their faces. He didn't want to delay in embarking on an investigation of Richtol.

"I suppose you are interested in a documentary of this whole question concerning Shakespeare, but unfortunately so few of the participants have arrived," Ian said.

"We can't really talk about our work," Wainwright said.

"There must be some silly twits who believe that Shakespeare didn't write the works and that the Duke of Oxford did instead." Ian tried the tactic of feigning ignorance as to de Vere's title.

"Earl of Oxford," Doerflinger corrected. Wainwright coughed. "He was the Seventeenth Earl of Oxford." Ian's heart raced.

"I just do my job," Wainwright said, trying to neutralize the discussion.

"Is there any proof?" Ian asked.

"L..L..Loads of it," Doerflinger stammered. Wainwright coughed again and Ian detected an abrupt motion of Wainwright's left hand from near the steering wheel. It may have been a reaction to the cough, but it came across as a quick jerk of the index finger towards his cameraman to caution him against further conversation. "We're just here to do a job. Right, Steve?"

Ian spotted the camera in the space behind the back seat. Two 12K lights lay beside it and the stands were next to them. That would be the next line of questioning after he gave them some relief. What exactly were they here to do? Was it for telly?

Ian kept spinning his fiction. "I've been in the States for three or four days on business—arrived here this morning for the Sherlock Holmes birthday event. It was a smashing affair. The doctor, the professor, the congressman, Forsythe, and I are members of the group. Mr. Forsythe informed me only about half of the expected guests arrived, the last ones shortly after three."

"The state police warned us not to try it." Wainwright yawned. "We probably should've taken their advice."

"Richtol insisted," Doerflinger said. Wainwright turned off the engine. The car was almost too warm.

"What do you do for a living, Mr. Scarborough?" Wainwright asked as he unzipped his green parka and untied his yellow scarf.

"Please call me Ian. I write music from time to time."

"What sort of music?" Doerflinger turned around to face him.

"Rock mostly, although it's jazz and early-English folk oriented. I'm not composing as much now, not as demanding of myself as I approach my fifth decade. The Muse doesn't visit quite as often."

"I filmed a documentary about a year ago on American rock artists of the Sixties—a sort of `where are they now?' piece. Fascinating. It ran in Britain as well." Wainwright smiled.

"Really? I would love to have seen it. I knew some of the artists here of that period and I've lost track of them."

"You must have been somewhat of a star yourself if you knew them," said Doerflinger. As he removed the ski mask from the top of his head a wave of blond hair stood straight up.

"Actually, I toured with my own band, Falstaff's Ghost, back in '78. We had two hits here in America and an album that was a smash. We toured for nearly six months here, twice."

Wainwright turned to face Ian. "What were your hits?"

"`The Blackbirds' Choir' and a ditty called `Come Ye Over From France,' here in the States. I wrote `Blackbirds' and borrowed the other—public domain. We had one more tune that sort of made it in a few markets from that one album."

"I remember both hits." Wainwright whistled the "Blackbirds" tune and stopped after the first two bars. "It was great."

"Yeah, I remember it." Doerflinger nodded with a bright face as if he'd been presented an unexpected gift. "Aardvark Boogers just did a fantastic heavy metal cover of it."

"That's one reason I'm here," Ian began his fib. "I'm meeting with the record company lawyers to make sure I'm receiving all royalties due me. There are so many covers to it and I'm still making some healthy quid on it. Sales are doing well, thanks to the CD and downloads."

"That must have been an exciting time." Doerflinger's face blazed with admiration. "I'm only twenty-three, too young to remember it, but I believe my mother had one or two of your albums. What was the name of the big album here in the States?"

"That would have been the *Fishing For Lost Wishes* album. Big worldwide."

"Yes, I remember it! I think she still has it."

Wainwright yawned again. "I remember it, too. I was at UCLA film school. Very popular."

"Those were the days," Ian mused. "Right. Do you think you will still film while you're here?"

"We have nearly three and a half hours of film to use in one of the suitcases," Wainwright replied. "That's about all I can say."

Ian nearly fell off the edge of the seat he was leaning so far forward. They were doing something quite involved if there was that much film. His legs shuffled involuntarily and he leaned back in order to collect himself. He simply had to find a way into room 408 no matter what the cost. What he would do once inside, he didn't know, but he would gain entry—by furtive design if necessary. What was Richtol's motivation? Ian wondered. What motivated these two men? Were any of them capable of destroying important art or artifacts, as the British ambassador would have it? Would the impetuous Richtol, if his character was as rash as he displayed during the rescue, destroy such historical objects belonging to Shakespeare or de Vere? The British ambassador may have been limited in what he could relate—after all, the phones went dead.

"It's time to turn on the engine again. I'm shivering," Doerflinger said. It was 11:20.

Wainwright yawned and moaned. Ian felt inspired to yawn twice and rapidly. Soporific jet lag was about to blindside him with a vengeance. He'd been awake for almost twenty-four hours, so the alcohol, fresh air, and coziness of the jeep were beginning to make him sleep. He had to decide what approach to take in gaining access to Room 408, but he could not, would not, decide until he'd had some sleep and the present was an opportune time. After all, he may not have a chance for the next twelve to twenty-four hours. His ear began to ache lightly. An earache would be the final blow. "Gentlemen," he said and yawned again, "I'm going to kip down until our rescuers return. Jet lag is about to overcome me."

He decided he would feign sleep as long as possible so he might eavesdrop on the two men in case they discussed their mission. As much as a six foot six man could do so, he stretched out and soon, in spite of his plan, fell into a deep slumber.

Some twenty minutes later he awoke suddenly to the shouts of the two men in the front seat. For a moment, Ian couldn't remember where he was.

"We thought *we* were fools!" Doerflinger yelled.

"Looks like there's actually someone more determined than us to get to the top of this mountain," Wainwright said. "He was driving like a maniac."

Ian moved his head but faked sleep, listening intently.

"It's probably him," Doerflinger whispered. "I thought Richtol said he'd phoned him from up here and he was at the inn already."

"Keep quiet." Wainwright raised his left hand, whispered, and then shook his head once in a stern, cautionary nod. "We've already said too much, although I can't believe this," he slung his thumb in Ian's direction, "is any kind of a risk or problem here."

"Otis, whoever that was is either our man or someone possessed. He was hauling some serious ass for a slippery slope like this," Doerflinger said.

"Did you see what he was driving?" Wainwright leaned over to turn on the CB. "Wainwright to Forsythe." He heard a click and no answer.

"No, but he did have chains. He had some sort of spotlight on the front hood or inside the windshield. I don't think he saw us."

"He was probably concentrating on the path Forsythe's Rover cut. Wainwright to Forsythe." Again, a click and no answer.

Ian stretched and yawned. "What seems to be happening?"

"Some kind of Jeep or Rover just passed through in a big hurry. He was going too fast in this mess. It was like he didn't care whether he was on the road or not," Wainwright said. "And our guys at the top of the hill must be on the way down."

"I hope there's no collision or we'll be walking," Doerflinger said.

"Forsythe's very likely in the center of the road." Wainwright sighed. "I had him on the horn a minute or two ago. I just tried to raise him and there's no answer. Either our battery is low or there's been an accident."

Ian was wide awake now. His ear throbbed harder. Yes, he thought, this ear is too painful.

Chapter Twenty-One

Veronica shifted on her cot to face the window in the cramped hospital room. Beside the window, her watch was flashing 4:40 a.m. Outside the pane, a blowing and frosty sleet was falling. What was her newfound love doing right now in New York? Probably in bed with a heavy rest from jet lag, she told herself, remembering his difficulty with overseas travel. She wondered about his ear.

She turned to face her father, who lay in bed parallel to her cot. Just before she'd lain down, he'd moaned twice and opened his eyes in nearly imperceptible slits for some ten seconds. She'd called out, "Dad. Dad. Can you hear me? If you can, moan again." Nothing further happened. She had remained awake until midnight, reading a novel, then turned out the light and fell immediately fast asleep. Now as she sneaked into the bathroom, she heard a slow puffing, and maybe a trace of a moan during one of his exhalations.

Dr. Colton found himself standing in a shop full of printing equipment—primitive, yet oddly new. He was alone in the work section, but he could see several people dressed in Elizabethan resplendence standing in the front office, which was located behind a partially open door. Another dream, he thought, this one set in a sixteenth-century printer's shop. When will these dreams end? When would he awaken?

A man who appeared to be the owner, or manager, was leading three Elizabethan, well-dressed visitors into Colton's work area, pointing directly at him while talking to them. I don't belong here, he thought. I know nothing about this machinery and I've no idea who these people are, much less the owner, whom I suspect I'm supposed to be working for.

"Dr. Colton," the owner said, grinning as if he'd seen him every day for years, "I want you to meet some very special folks. We've recently contracted with them to work on a most noteworthy project and they want to discuss it with you briefly." He lifted his hand towards each guest as he introduced him or her. "This is the Earl of Montgomery, Philip Herbert, also his wife, the Countess of Montgomery, Susan de Vere Herbert." Both extended their hands, which Colton thought unusual for Elizabethans. "Also, please meet the Earl of Pembroke, William Herbert, the Earl of Montgomery's brother. And this is Dr. Colton, our chief compositor."

"Delighted to meet you." Colton resigned himself to play along since he had no other choice. He knew these people from his copious research, but had no idea who the shop owner could be.

"This genial man is going to be running the presses for the *First Folio*. They want to discuss the nature of this project with you and I believe, since the Lord Chamberlain has such total control over the project, it's imperative that you listen carefully to him. You should feel free to chat with them and ask any questions pertaining to the practical aspects of the publication. They've laboured for years to bring the *Folio* to this stage and you must know how important it is to them."

"I'll be most happy to listen to them and answer any questions. I may have a few myself. Have a seat." His boss must be one of the Jaggards, or Edward Blount—the printers. Colton looked down beside his desk to find four black Volkswagen seats, circa 1970, next to the press. What are they doing here? He didn't seem to notice any details about the remainder of the room for now his attention focused entirely on the beauty of Susan de Vere, a daughter of Edward de Vere's union with Ann Cecil, Burghley's daughter.

She had rosy cheeks and a perfectly blanched complexion, another aspect consistent with the Elizabethan age. Her eyes were a deep brown, and light auburn hair fell straight and long down her back. He noticed a small mole on her left cheek, which gave her a wanton allure, a flaw of sensuality inconsistent with his perception of Elizabethans. After all, King James I, "the wisest fool in Christendom," was on the throne since it must be 1622, the year the printing of the *First Folio* began. That was six years after Shakespeare's death and eighteen years after the death of Susan's father. Maybe the style was changing in the direction of Queen Anne.

No, it was a dream, he thought, as Susan (did she resemble her father or her mother, Anne Cecil?) sat nervously, her folded hands opening and closing restlessly, alternating in a rhythm of slow sways like the wings of a butterfly on a flower. He wondered how the seat supported her, detached from the car as it was. He would mull over the physics later since he couldn't fathom it, or for that matter, how to operate the printing presses.

"Our brother, Henry," William raised a supercilious right eyebrow as he spoke, "has bought a lease to the Office of the Master of the Revels, which will be charged with the day-to-day details of this project. The three brothers now have complete control. You are to speak to him about the logistical details—the choice of fonts, the layout of the frontispiece, the artwork. On matters concerning the content of the sonnets and plays, seek out Ben Jonson, who has spent some of the last nineteen years patching up the manuscripts of all the available plays—well over half the total output, and certainly the best and most mature of the lot. This volume will double the number of the author's plays to see print. Mr. Jonson has done a yeoman's service for the nation."

"At a hundred pounds a year since 1604," Colton retorted with a knowing wink. "The services of the second-best poet in England are dear and well documented."

"He's earned it, indeed. He'll be coming by later this afternoon to deliver the first manuscripts for typesetting and discuss any special instructions. You'll greatly appreciate his efforts," said the Lord Chamberlain, glazing his eyes imperiously.

"You've set on a substantial task as well," said Phillip Herbert, who was more engaging and congenial. "What you print will be the only edition intended for posterity. But we must abide by Jonson's request for him to retain the original manuscripts. It's a rotten scheme, but it was the only means by which we could save these works by virtue of printing this *Folio*. The King has saved the day for us. You must understand, my friend."

"I don't understand entirely, but I'm sure I will soon if not in this life," Colton sighed, "so fleeting, maybe the next one."

William Herbert slapped his own left cheek gently in sincere disgust as he rolled his grey eyes. "You know most of the story of how Susan's father was deprived of the gargantuan legacy he left the world. Why should we delve into the matter with you, the printer?"

"William, Dr. Colton made a very innocuous observation. Don't raise an argument when there's no issue. Please," Phillip admonished as he looked to Colton and away from his brother. "William's become so very weary of this subject and he merely wants us to get on with the project and see it to completion."

William rose from his VW seat. "Precisely. We should leave these details to Henry. I, as Lord Chamberlain, simply have the duty of overseeing the theatre. I'm not going to allow myself to discuss the minutiae concerning the publication of the plays. I'm content with knowing it's in capable hands. Thank you, Dr. Colton, and I shall now excuse myself." He pivoted and marched out of the room.

Phillip shook his head. "He's had such a difficult time with the project. You see, the publication of the plays has been the chief reason we've sought the office of Lord Chamberlain, and the plan for this publication has been the only bargaining tool we've had in securing and holding onto this office. We're not about to surrender the office of Lord Chamberlain and Mastership of Revels until we see the publication to its conclusion. I don't mind telling you, because I want you to know how vital it is to Susan and me so you'll devote your perspicacious eye to the emblazoning of every word, comma, and period."

"The most we could extract from the King and Robert Cecil was the right to print this ourselves under the name of Shakespeare, of course, and to suppress the attempt by other scoundrels to print inferior editions," Susan scowled, her forehead wrinkled.

"Earlier efforts were doomed to failure," Colton said. "There would've been no hope of accuracy. Many almost succeeded in stealing the right to print this very *Folio*..."

"William proved to be most clever," Susan nodded. "Once he achieved the office of Lord Chamberlain."

"Replacing the reckless Somerset." Phillip added.

"In late 1615, William had complete control over the substance of the only existing manuscripts of the plays written by my father. He turned down every satrap in the kingdom."

"Yes. Everything." Colton leaned forward with his emphatic right hand waving and eyebrows dancing, deliriously enchanted by the story he was finally hearing confirmed after his dedicated years of research and assumptions. "Including the office of Lord Treasurer, the most powerful office in England, except of course the King, in 1619, just so he could see the project through."

"But," said Phillip, rising in enthusiasm, "William wouldn't move from that seat, Lord Chamberlain, until he could have me replace him in his position. He was offered Lord Treasurer again in 1621 and would take it, I repeat, only upon the condition that I replaced him there. This time, however, my brother turned down both a seat on the Privy Council and the exquisite Hatfield Close up in Yorkshire. Later that same year, the King offered him the Lord Privy Seal. Again, he refused. This year the same offer and the same answer. He'll not retreat from his important post until he knows I may replace him there."

"Why didn't the King simply insist on your moving on? What possibly could you have had on the King to prevent him from controlling this project?"

"It was Sturm. Johannes Sturm," Phillip shouted gleefully.

"Sturmius," Colton said conclusively. "The Protestant rector at the Strasbourg Gymnasium. Yes...De Vere's great, intellectual friend received him with open arms on his visit there...later even begged Elizabeth to send an army led by Oxford when the Catholics were invading Strasbourg." Colton cast a puzzled look at Susan de Vere Herbert. "How could this German control King James I, especially since Sturmius died in 1589?"

"We believe someone gave him a manuscript or manuscripts that we do not have," Phillip explained. "It was written by Susan's father sometime in the eighties, we believe. It was a play or sonnets, we don't know exactly, dealing with a subject so intriguing that only Elizabeth and James knew its contents. Sturmius was to have it printed upon Elizabeth's death, or if de Vere was ever imprisoned by Lord Burghley. Sturmius died before either event occurred, but no one knows what happened to the manuscript or what its contents were. It could have been all a ruse. It's all rather vague."

Dr. Colton reeled.

"Ah, there's more! My brother received a letter in 1605, a year after Oxford's death. It was addressed to him as the Earl of Pembroke, but it also made reference to his sister-in-law," Phillip paused, nodding towards Susan, "Oxford's daughter. The letter prevailed upon William to pursue the office of Lord Chamberlain, and once he attained the office, he would receive a note describing where the manuscript was hidden—somewhere now in England, we assume. We've yet to receive the note. The King originally believed the note a hoax on our part, but he's coming around, especially since William has turned down so many positions. William has been reluctant to leave the office of Lord Chamberlain since he's waiting for the note, and most importantly, he wants to see the publication of the known manuscripts in this *Folio*. Indeed, he conspired with Jonson to slow down the process in order to await the message that has not come—besides their mutual desire to see the project through to virtual perfection." He paused. "Jonson also gets paid longer. We paid him even more to edit what became the First Folio, which took several years. By printing it we also could halt any other publication of the works."

"Why would that stop James from having control over your brother as Lord Chamberlain?" Colton persisted as he wanted to hear the reasons again.

Phillip blinked twice and laughed softly. "Because William led him to believe that he knew what was in the manuscript when he actually doesn't have the slightest idea—he has faked it all these years. It must be serious because the King suspects the content, and fortunately, he has always felt very favorably towards us, even before this brouhaha. Furthermore, we've seen all of the abuses of power perpetrated by the `wisest fool in Christendom.' Poor James can't resist spending money, and as all the lawyers of Parliament know it...so do we. Ironic for a man who is so," he issued the next words sarcastically, pausing as he glanced skyward, "so...next to God on high. But, fortuitously, he does care about our project dearly and he loved Edward de Vere for his artistic contributions. At a time when he was taxing everything that moved, he restored some of Susan's father's property and continued Oxford's annuity at the same level Elizabeth granted him—£1000 per annum."

"Incredible. Yes, James was generous to Oxford." Colton was teary eyed with admiration for the two brothers. "You've done all this for Susan and her father?"

"Yes," Phillip said smiling broadly, his cheeks reddening, "and for England and the world. We recognized greatness even though there was no way powers were going to allow Oxford to receive the credit. Besides," Phillip shook his head and said with a bitter low pitch, "Oxford dealt away the right to take the credit in his wretched bargainings with his father-in-law. William Cecil, Lord Burghley, was a conniving, perfidious man. Oxford, as he grew older, relented to more of Burghley's material demands—that's why Oxford lost large amounts of land and property to him. Furthermore, we didn't desire to have those egregious, infantile quartos published in his younger years and signed `E. of O.' to be the last word when such outstanding works existed and were acknowledged widely. Also, remember our mother, the Countess of Pembroke, was the greatest champion of poetry in the country and had written remarkable dramas herself."

"Of course, the small tome published before they assigned the Shakespeare moniker was infantile by comparison," Colton said. "It's the artist as young man, inferior."

Susan stared into the distance. "My mother even despised Burghley for his manipulations. He plundered our estate. Fortunately, James restored many of the lands and property—particularly when he recognized all that my father had done for our culture, our language, and our nationalism. An emerging nationhood soon abated the bitter dispute between the Protestants and Catholics. My father cared more about `this England' than his own mere chattel."

"Yes," Phillip nodded in confirmation. "It's true."

"A patriot, *über alles*. Why did Oxford conceal this one manuscript with, of all people, Sturm? Was it the distance? Yes. De Vere had a network on the continent, even after he died. Sturm."

"*Sperm*" or "*sturm*," Veronica wondered. Her father had either just mumbled another odd sexual reference, or was about to add the "und drang" for the German phrase for "storm and stress." Veronica giggled in slight awe, more in wonder.

"Stuuuurm," he said again. Veronica leapt from the cot where she had been reading the speech she had just rewritten for the third time. Was he improving?

"Sturmiussss," he hissed. Veronica had heard the name before. What was it? *Sturmius*. Joachim Sturm, or something—Ian had mentioned his name as an intellectual de Vere had visited for some time while in Europe. She would have to tell him when he called. Maybe her father was improving. She glanced at her watch: 7:05 a.m. Where was the doctor? When would she hear from Ian? She couldn't wait to tell Ian about Sturmius. Surely her father must be improving.

"Father? Answer me! If you hear me, moan, say something. Sturmius!"

She stared at the tubes coming from his nose and heard the soft breaths leaking through his dry mouth like old fireplace bellows. He didn't respond to her voice. Warm tears spilled down her cheeks.

Chapter Twenty-Two

Ian's earache intensified, a reminder of the ailment only days before while in Stratford-Upon-Avon. He had taken every precaution against the wind and cold except to care for this most valuable aspect of his well-being. How could he have forgotten earmuffs?

Wistfully, he thought of Veronica. He could picture her engaging, confident grin. Like any newly stricken, normal man, he, too, could be muddled enough to forget earmuffs, he reasoned. Consumed by the desire to sleep, his emotional state was battered even after the brief nap.

"Gentlemen, I'm having a problem with my lughole," he said, "and I hope we return soon so I can have a doctor observe it."

Wainwright cast an amused but curiously puzzled look at his comrade in the front seat. "It's probably from all of this sitting. You may want to get out and stretch for a minute."

Ian realized he'd communicated poorly. How to tactfully correct the error? "I had problems with this same ear only three days ago. The doctor administered some kind of powerful eardrops and it seemed to be better within a few hours. The other ear has given me no problems." A moment of frozen silence ripened into hysterical laughter.

Doerflinger looked at Wainwright, repeating with mock asperity. "You may want to stretch for a minute. *Doctor* Wainwright!"

"I must learn the langua—" Wainwright was interrupted by the radio.

"Forsythe to Wainwright, can you hear me?" came the clear, sharp voice penetrating the frozen airwaves.

"Yeah. Read you loud and clear. You okay?"

"We're just around the bend, about two hundred yards up from you, but we've had a complication. At first I thought it was you guys. Some damned idiot shot up the mountain and crashed against our plow. The doctor is attending to him now. The rest of us were not hurt, although the plow is bent somewhat. We can drive back but the plow is dragging in the center."

"Who was that fool behind the wheel?"

"I'm not sure yet. He appears to be a man in his early thirties. He's unconscious—no seat belt. You fellows need to walk up here. I'll drive down only if the plough doesn't scrape. Otherwise it'll take a few minutes to remove it and by then you'll be here."

"We'll be right up. We'll be walking in single file on the opposite side of the road from your lane."

"We'll see you in a few minutes," said Forsythe. The radio clicked to white noise.

"I was afraid that would happen." Wainwright shook his head in disappointment. "I hope your ear isn't hurting too badly for a short walk."

"There's no alternative," Ian said. "It's becoming painful again. What must we carry?"

"All we have here is the lights, the camera, and a box of film. Each of us has a small suitcase right next to the gas canister there." Doerflinger pointed towards the orange can next to the left rear wheel casing as he opened the door.

"I'll handle the camera and the film box. Steve, you bring the suitcases along. Ian, if you can handle the lights?"

They converged at the trunk of the Jeep as Wainwright flipped on his flashlight. "One of you guys lift that reserve gas tank—it's

heavy—and you should find some tape rolled up underneath."
Doerflinger groaned as he lifted the tank partly off its rack.
Wainwright said, "I'll tape the flashlight to the top of one of the suitcases. It'll give us enough light to make our way up."

He grabbed the tape and proceeded to wrap it around the entire suitcase, a small grey Samsonite, attaching the flashlight on the first turn. Doerflinger yanked the ski mask off the top of his head and handed it to Ian. "You need to wear this. It'll give your ear some protection."

Ian couldn't refuse his help. "I'm most grateful." Pausing, he pulled the mask over his head and immediately felt relief from the frigid wind in the affected ear. "It makes some difference."

Wainwright handed Doerflinger the suitcases. He rolled the tape back in the corner next to the reserve tank where it made a dull knock against the full contents of the gas can. He then loaded two light stands, not heavy but a bit clumsy, into Ian's arms, stretching them behind his head like he was carrying a World War II bazooka or pipe on a construction site, and handed him a small case containing the lights themselves. Then Wainwright grabbed the camera and film box, set them on the packed snow next to the Jeep, and shut the door with a thud.

"Steve, you take the lead," Wainwright ordered.

The men walked steadily in single file on the right side of the road towards their short destination. As they rounded the bend, Ian loudly exclaimed, "I must return to the car. I didn't lock my door." It might provoke more information.

"It doesn't matter," Wainwright said. "The only thing in there is that five-gallon reserve gas tank and a first aid kit. The car won't go anywhere until the snow melts. Even then it may be a problem until we get a thaw."

"Yeah, the right front axle is probably broken. We felt the right wheel hit a rock before we hit the tree," Doerflinger observed. "We were lucky Richtol was the only one hurt, and he probably wouldn't have broken his leg had it not been for his cancer."

"Cancer?" Ian yawned again even though he was immensely curious. He'd not heard Richtol tell Dr. Barlowe he was a cancer patient.

"He told us he has bone marrow cancer and he wasn't supposed to make the trip," Wainwright commented acidly, "but he failed to tell us that until we were half way up the mountain. There was no turning back."

"A trip too good to pass up." Ian tested for more information.

"Yes. He's a most insistent character," Wainwright said. "He knows how to achieve his ends—a typical, relentless, skillful old incubus. There they are..."

At the end of the curve they could see two sets of headlights. One set was pointing down the mountain along the road with a swirl of snow penetrating the beams. The other beams were also pointing towards them, one below the other, as if the car was turned over on its side. As the trio approached the scene, bodies darted in front of the lights interrupting the beams, throwing an eerie, otherworldly aura as if aliens had landed. They were about to lift a man on the stretcher into the back of the Rover. The disabled car, a Jeep, was tipped next to the ditch with two large scrapes down its side. Forsythe and Dr. Barlowe were the only rescuers on the scene.

"You're just in time to help us," Forsythe said.

"You're a sight for sore eyes," Doerflinger said, setting his load down next to the Rover.

"As well as ears." Wainwright laughed and pointed to Ian. "Our friend here has a very nasty lug—eh—earache." Doerflinger laughed, and Forsythe and Dr. Barlowe cast a momentary glace at him during his outburst.

"This gentleman has a concussion," Barlowe said. "Mr. Searls, we're taking you to my room for care and observation."

The thin, dark-haired man said nothing. The doctor had secured a bandage squarely in the center of his forehead, just above the two wrinkles between his dark eyebrows. His eyes were glazed as if he was semiconscious, and he moaned a meager acknowledgment.

Was this the man with the stolen artifacts? Ian noticed that the film crew expressed no open acquaintance with this particular man, perhaps not wanting to compromise their knowledge in front of the whole group.

The men lifted the stretcher and placed the patient across the back seat. Wainwright and Doerflinger bent to retrieve their equipment while Ian and Forsythe walked over to examine the wrecked vehicle as it lay tipped over on the driver's side against a sturdy oak, almost as if it might tip back to all fours in the right wind.

"I bet it would run if we tipped it back over," said Forsythe. "We have enough men here to do it—probably take only two of us the way it sits—but I don't want to risk any more problems. Barlowe's going to have a full hospital ward as it is. Ian, how's the ear?"

Ian started to blurt out that it was bearable when the strategy to stay near Richtol hit him like a bolt. "It's bear...uh...barely tolerable. Regrettably, I'm afraid it will need some attention as well. A doctor warned me about neglecting it a few days ago in England, and I didn't heed his warning in the excitement."

"I'm certain Barlowe will treat you after we take care of Mr. Searls," Forsythe assured him. "Follow us up to his room. Richtol is there now—you can stay in the adjacent room."

"Did Searls have any luggage? Who is he with—the Shakespeare-Oxford debate or the Holmesians?" Ian asked anxiously.

"No, he hasn't any luggage. He says his wife was supposed to be here already, and he was late from a business trip in New York, too," he grunted as he climbed up from the ditch after checking the back door that was either locked or jammed. "Spend a few days. I radioed Laura for a Mrs. Searls, but there's no one listed under that name."

"Sounds like a dirty weekend scheme to me," Ian said. "Extraordinary the lengths one will go to for a cover-up."

"Gents," Forsythe called to the other two men, "I believe Searls's Jeep will run if we can move it over on its proper side without getting injured. We aren't going to have room for everyone since the doctor insisted on coming back with me—and it's a good thing he did." Forsythe idly kicked the back tire.

"Let's all go back in yours. I don't need any more patients," Barlowe shouted, pointing to the Rover. "There's no point in running the risk of further injury."

"Searls said it's about out of gas. That's why he was driving fast—to increase mileage," Forsythe said, shaking his head in disgust. He crunched a path back to the Rover after examining the damaged snowplow. Barlowe leaned out the front passenger door, glaring impatiently. "The doctor's ready to go," Forsythe said. "Let's try to do this in one trip. I believe we can make it. Wainwright, can you crouch in the back there with the camera and lights? Have...what's your friend's name?"

"Doerflinger."

"Son, I'm going to ask you to wait down here in the car and I'll come back. I don't want anything to happen to you while you're here, so wait by the Jeep. I don't want you to come at me with a lawsuit if something happens, so think it over carefully. I would prefer to risk one person, rather than two or three of us by overcrowding."

"I'll ride on top," the young man yelled cheerfully. "Nothing will happen."

Barlowe shook his head in heavy doubt and turned to Wainwright. "Forsythe won't go for it. He'll want a signed release. He's dreadfully afraid of lawsuits."

"I'll be responsible," Wainwright said. "Steve's a talented guy. He'll hold on to the luggage rack."

"I don't have a release," snapped Forsythe.

"You have my word," Wainwright said firmly. "We've been out here for some time. I promise you no one will sue if something happens—which it won't."

"Just this once," Forsythe relented.

"Cool," Doerflinger said as he climbed on top and spread his body supinely across the top of the Rover.

Forsythe turned to Ian before heading to the driver's seat. "As for Searls, he better not sue because Barlowe hates lawyers, too. Besides," he looked again at the snowplow, "it was all Searls' fault. Somehow I don't believe his story anyway. He's on a greater mission than—what'd you call it—a filthy weekend?"

"Right," Ian chuckled clutching his ear. It started to hurt even more when he laughed, but the misuse of the expression and Forsythe's utter fear of court both struck him as oddly amusing. He must have had a dismal experience with the American justice system.

Ian went to the back seat and curled himself into as relaxed a position as he could on the floor. Searls was limber, as if he was about to sleep. Overall, they were a motley group of survivors.

"Hold his stretcher so he doesn't slide," Barlowe instructed Ian. "Make sure his body doesn't roll, although we should have no problems since we're headed uphill."

The endless snowfall had erased all evidence of the Rover's tracks from the drive down. Plodding along at about fifteen miles an hour, the dented plow would occasionally scrape pavement or rock. Forsythe mentioned that the vehicle had been in a skid when it hit the plow and the back end of the car, causing a bend in the plow. Searls' vehicle had then spun around completely and tipped over gently next to the ditch after scraping the entire driver's side against the snowplow. "If he'd spun in the other direction, he would have plunged to his death about two hundred feet into a rock pile below," Forsythe concluded.

As they came within sight of the inn, they heard a loud cheer from above. Ian had almost forgotten about Doerflinger and laughed, again clutching his ear. "Now you guys know what kind of kid I have to put up with on this project," Wainwright said.

They finally approached room 408. Dr. Barlowe sneezed as he turned the key in the lock to his room, black bag in hand. Inside were two beds framing an old, grey nightstand with a red reading lamp splashing light across the room. Ian strolled in behind him, followed by Wainwright, Doerflinger, and Forsythe carrying the newest patient to the neatly made bed nearest the door. Barlowe sat on the other bed, untied his heavy, black boots, and stripped off his outer clothing before heading to the basin to wash his hands.

"All I need is a cold," he said. "Ian, stretch out on this bed so I can treat you with ear drops. I'll do that after I've checked Richtol and Searls. I'm going to give you a couple of aspirins, too. By the time I've completely checked on Richtol and Searls, you should be feeling better. Then you may return to your room if you'd like, or stay here, but I will want to examine you again right before I retire."

"Where's Richtol?" Ian actually remembered where he was told the geezer would be, but he wanted to hear it again to be certain.

"He's in the next room, through that door." Forsythe pointed to the old, brown wooden door connecting the two rooms as he completed the transfer of Searls's sleeping body to the bed. "Spread his legs out a bit."

Ian moved the legs while Doerflinger began to remove the man's shoes and socks. Searls was totally unconscious.

"Searls should sleep quite well tonight," the doctor said and stepped towards a closet next to the door to the other room in the suite. "I gave Richtol a painkiller as well. Ian, as far as I'm concerned, you may sleep in that bed and help me if you hear Searls awaken or if he has any kind of trouble. I'm going to sleep in my bed next to Richtol's. He's a cancer patient and I do need to watch him since he can't seem to remember how much of each medication he's taken. I'm going to have to figure that out in the morning. His prescription bottles are scattered throughout his suitcase and he's not much help. Says his tea is all he needs."

Plopping the boots in the empty closet, the doctor then carelessly hurled his trousers and shirt on top of the coat, sweater, and scarf he'd just discarded in a pile on a small, pool-table-green felt sofa in the corner. He stood in his white long johns looking for the entire world like a rotund toddler wholly unconcerned about appearance. He retrieved a tube of eye drops from his suitcase on the floor and squirted a drop in each eye.

"Right." Ian clutched his head as if the pain were worse, although it was steady and mostly bearable. Feigned pain was his ticket to remain. "I do believe it's becoming intolerable."

Forsythe looked at his watch. "It's nearly three. I'm going to show Mr. Wainwright and Mr. Doerflinger to their rooms upstairs. I'll not bother you gentlemen until you've had a good night's sleep. If you need me, call me at this number, Doctor." He scribbled on a piece of hotel stationery next to the light on the nightstand and reached across the bed to hand it to the doctor. "Otherwise, I'll leave you to a sound sleep."

"Fine. Goodnight to you, gentlemen. It was quite an experience," Barlowe whispered as he opened the door and entered the adjoining suite.

"Thank you all sincerely." Forsythe waved at the other two men to leave.

"Goodnight," Doerflinger said and waved.

"Sleep well," Wainwright said.

Fatigued, Ian stripped down to his long johns, laid his head on the pillow, and turned out the light. Searls lay motionless while Ian stared at the dark crumple of jeans next to the nightstand where the doctor had dropped them. He reached for the trousers to check for a wallet or some means of identification.

Dr. Barlowe suddenly burst through the door and Ian quickly pulled his hand back to the bed. "I'm going to check the bandage, Ian. Please flip the light on." He crouched next to the trousers as Ian turned on the light. "I'll get to you next. Triage as usual, my friend." He laid a vial, a needle, and a tube on the nightstand.

"Doctor, it's most painful. My throat is also getting sore." Ian recalled the excruciating pain while at Stratford and tried to convey it now in his voice. "How does it look for him?"

"It's a mild concussion. The cut won't require stitches, although it will leave a minor scar for a time. He's young enough so it probably won't be too visible. Now, I found these drops for you, and I'm going to give you a shot of penicillin in case it's an infection as your doctor in England described. Here's a painkiller, hydrocodone, also. You'll be drowsy from it."

"Will Searls sleep well?" Ian asked.

"You betcha." Barlowe stared at the vial, then promptly stuck Ian's left arm as it lay next to his body. "I don't expect him to wake up until noon at the earliest. I'll be checking him throughout the night. There now, turn your head and I'll drop these in your ear. You should sleep well yourself. I'll try not to wake you when I'm in here, so I'll leave the toilet light on."

Ian thought through his plan. "Doc, I heard Wainwright say Richtol is irritable because of his cancer condition and is especially upset if he's around total strangers such as Searls, and I...."

"Believe me, I'm not going to give Richtol much leeway. I'm not even going to let on that you and Searls are in this room, and I don't want either of you in there. He seems to be very nervous and jumpy, and I don't want you guys, or anyone else, in there. He told me he's taking about a dozen pills, so he shouldn't even be on this trip. There must be some vital legal negotiation going on or he wouldn't be up here, unless he's one of those hardheaded types. Most of them are."

Ian nearly blurted a cheer at the doctor's unwitting complicity in not revealing their presence, since he was convinced that Searls was Richtol's contact, and the reason Searls had no luggage was simply because he already had the artifacts somewhere in the hotel—maybe the vital attaché case of Richtol's. For whatever reason, Searls must have been returning to the hotel and had already attempted to contact Richtol. Searls must have been concerned about Richtol's absence—brought on by the storm—and had jumped in the Jeep to set out down the mountain to look for the film crew. If he'd passed their disabled vehicle, the snow had obscured it, so maybe Searls didn't see it—especially since he was in a panic to return and the headlights hadn't lit up that side of the road. Evidently, Searls didn't know Wainwright and Doerflinger, and was fairly incoherent when they arrived with the film apparatuses, so he didn't associate them with Richtol who was already in the other room recuperating. Likewise, the two filmmakers evinced no indication they knew Searls. Ian believed this theory was as sound as any. The providential result of Barlowe not wanting Richtol in their room was crucial for Ian to gain more time if all this was the case. Was he jumping to illogical conclusions?

"Good night." The doctor rose and Ian returned the greeting.

As soon as the doctor shut the door, Ian reached for the trousers. He patted his hand against them, trying to discern the form of a billfold. There was none. He rose from his bed holding his head sideways so the eardrops wouldn't roll out, and felt the warm, comforting liquid tracking slowly down his aural canal.

Ian pulled a yellow ski jacket from the floor, but didn't find anything in the pockets. Next he retrieved a black woolly without a pocket. Underneath was a checkered blue and green wool shirt—L.L. Bean. He found a pen in the pocket and a folded white slip of notebook paper with some scribbling. It was all the man was carrying, unless someone had already removed his identification, but Ian was sure no one had had the opportunity to do so. He went over to the light from the bathroom and nearly staggered as he read the slip. He moved his head to a vertical position and some of the eardrops trickled out to his earlobe as he read, "Scarborough, Ian, tall, forty-fivish, English." Sliding the paper back in the shirt pocket as he'd found it, he rubbed his eyes. Who was this man? Where was he from? Why would Searls want to pursue *him*?

Sleep was overtaking him despite the shock of this new mystery. He yawned and shuffled to his bed. Whoever Searls was, Ian needed to avoid revealing his own identity, or even identifying himself as an Englishman, until he knew exactly what the man's role was in this matter. He resolved that he would not talk to him until he found out who he was. His height alone would betray him. If Searls awakened suddenly, he could pretend to be asleep. It was essential that he be awakened before Searls. He got out of bed, walked over to the adjoining door, and opened it slowly.

"Doctor," Ian whispered, "forgive mmm—"

"Yes," Barlowe moaned from the dark room where a sliver of light came from the bathroom, "I'm here."

"Forgive me for disturbing you, but I do need you to awaken me when you wake up tomorrow morning."

"I'll wake up periodically, but I intend to get up about nine. Is that about right?"

"Yes. If I'm feeling well, I simply must do some errands downstairs. Thank you."

"Good night," the doctor said with a trace of finality.

Ian went to his bed and fell asleep within minutes. He slept deeply and dreamlessly, soundly even, in spite of the stranger with a mission named Searls.

Chapter Twenty-Three

"I'm going to call him right now," Ian heard a voice firmly pronounce. "Tell him to come up here immediately. I don't want him to waste any time."

"I will. Now you lie back down in the bed. I will call."

Ian, groggy, was not awake enough to remember the names of the men in the next room, but he could recall that one was the doctor and one was the bloke with the concussion. No, the mucker was right here in the other bed in his room. The old lawyer who had cancer was in the next room. Daylight, intensified by the snow, beamed through the window. Snow still fell steadily.

"Hello, front desk? Dr. Barlowe here. Send Doerflinger up here. Yes. Would you be so kind as to send me a pot of coffee?"

"Order me some hot water and a teacup. I drink tea. I brought my own tea." The old man's scratchy, exhausted voice carried well from the next room where the activities of early morning had begun, a respite from the long night's adventures. "It's in the suitcase...and order milk and sugar."

"Oh, and tea service with hot water only, milk and sugar. Thank you."

Ian stretched. His ear was much improved but he would continue treatment to justify staying in the room—only without the pain pill. Still drowsy, he yawned. Richtol was the connection. He had to be, he thought. If he wasn't, and the action was elsewhere, then Ian knew it was risky undertaking any pursuit at all since there were no other clues. Doerflinger's coltish enthusiasm and willingness to confide had placed him squarely on the trail.

Dr. Barlowe stoked the fireplace and Ian heard him drop at least two logs on the flames. The busy doctor had probably forgotten to awaken him. He must remain perfectly still since the door to the next room was half open and he didn't want the old lawyer to hear his movements, or suspect there was someone else overhearing him. The dilemma was that he couldn't control Searls's noises in case he awakened, or moaned, or even broke wind. The crackle and roar from the fireplace might overtake some of the sounds. If Ian could hear it through the door, it must be a strong background noise in the sick man's room. Ian also felt the urgent need to visit the toilet.

"While you await your friend and your teacup, I'm going to take a shower," Ian heard Barlowe utter. "I'll leave the door unlocked. I've been looking forward to this hot shower for over twenty-four hours, my friend. I'm surprised you haven't commented on my need for it."

"One never complains about a doctor who makes such sacrifices while on vacation." Ian was shocked to hear the crotchety old man's generosity. "I'm grateful for your kind attention. I'm in considerable pain," the man's voice broke, "and under great stress. I must meet with a client here. I *must* have privacy when I do so. I hope you understand. We're filming an important deposition."

"I do understand."

Ian heard the doctor drop his shoes on the carpeted floor, probably beside his bed, which was located on the other side of Richtol's bed. "Once he arrives I'll be delighted to go to the lobby for the time necessary for you to consult with him. Call the front desk if you have any problems."

"I expect he'll arrive here in about thirty minutes. Doerflinger is to rendezvous with him in the lobby. I'll need an hour or more. It's a most sensitive case involving an SEC investigation. I'm grateful for your understanding. Oh yes, Doctor, you may bill me for all your trouble."

Ian wondered what SEC stood for. Was it really true? No, he hoped sincerely.

"No problem," Dr. Barlowe responded soothingly. "I'll be out in a few minutes." The bathroom door shut and the shower started.

Ian heard the man in the next bed move. He hoped Searls would not awaken soon. What if he was Richtol's "client"? How he wished he'd righted the wrecked vehicle so he could have searched it, or at least inspected it. Searls moved again. If he spoke, Richtol would surely hear him. Also, Richtol would likely recognize Ian from the night before because of his height.

Ian heard a knock next door. "Room service."

"Come in," Richtol yelled in a piercing, penetrating voice.

Above the shower dribbles, Ian heard the door creak open slowly and dishes rattle.

"Set it by the telephone here next to my bed. I'm not able to move, so you'll have to place it on the edge of the tray here on the nightstand. That's as far as I can reach, son." Ian detected a mellowing in Richtol's commands. Was it the morphine or whatever painkiller Barlowe had given him, or was it the realization that he was close to his objective?

Ian heard the tray gently hit the table. "Now, son, if you will reach into those trousers there and hand me my wallet, I'll reward you for going to my suitcase and checking in the pocket there for a plastic bag containing my tea. Wrapped around it is a small steel tea ball with chain. You may set it here on the edge of the tray next to the pot. It's just inside the pocket there."

Brief silence ensued, and then a rustling barely audible against the background of shower noises.

"Here you are, sir," a young voice replied.

"And there you are, sir." Ian imagined Richtol holding an American note. There was another knock on the door. "Come in." Searls moved again as Ian heard the room porter leave.

"You sent for me, Mr. Richtol?" The voice was unmistakably that of Steve Doerflinger.

"Yes, my boy, you must do precisely as I say or you and Mr. Wainwright won't have your story," Richtol commanded as Ian heard the shower go off. Now he would hear Richtol even better—but no, he lowered his voice and spoke more rapidly in anticipation of the doctor emerging from his steamy bathroom. "You and Wainwright bring the equipment up after you see the doctor, who is in the shower there. Go down to the lobby. I want you to go to the library—it's past the lobby near the shop—and you'll see a tall gentleman with a Sherlock Holmes deerstalker hat, a brown cape and a—and this is the distinguishing mark—a leather-bound straight pipe in his mouth with no tobacco in it. He won't be smoking it. You're to walk up to him, say hello, and then say," he paused, "'the English,' and he will reply `secretary.' He'll be reading a book."

Ian thought the artifacts were to be filmed there. *The English Secretary*. In his excitement he couldn't recall the author, but Oxford had contributed to it at the very least. His heart raced.

At that moment, the doctor reentered the room followed by a cloud of steam as it rolled across the ceiling. Ian could smell it. "S..S..Sorry, gentlemen," Dr. Barlowe responded. "I hope the room doesn't stay fogged up long." Ian thought, yes, what if the camera was affected? "I'll leave in just a minute."

"Steve's about to bring my client up. My client wants to film his deposition since we've made no provisions for a reporter here—and no tape recorder. It's that important."

"I see," the doctor responded nonchalantly. "Not a fan of depositions. I'll be gone. I'll be in the lobby."

"Steve will come and get you, Doctor, after we've finished," Richtol told him. "Now, Doerflinger, once you meet him, bring him right up. Do that exactly at eleven after you've helped Wainwright carry up the equipment. No time to waste."

Ian looked at his watch. It was twenty minutes until the appointed time. The door shut.

"I hope you get some rest after you finish the deposition," Barlowe said. "After all, we may be stuck up here for two or three days and I have enough medication for only that length of time. I searched through your suitcase this morning. You have enough of everything except Xanax and morphine. You'll run out late tomorrow."

"Doctor, I know you find this hard to believe, but I'm returning to New York tomorrow if I have to go down the mountain in a dog sled. This case is of utmost importance to my law firm and me. Nothing...nothing will stop me."

"You'll have to find someone to take you, and I'm going to advise anyone who tries that they are risking your life. If you're stranded for even a few hours, you'll suffer serious medical complications. You must expect that."

"I'll work up a release for Forsythe. That seems to satisfy him on most questions. Is there anyone in that room?"

Ian froze and tensed.

"No," Barlowe lied, "I'm keeping it open for any other medical emergencies, God forbid, that may develop today. We're in a room that was reserved for two other doctors who didn't show. We moved you in here because the fire was lit."

"Okay, shut that door before leaving. Is it still snowing?"

Ian heard footsteps approach. Searls moved his arm again and groaned, but apparently they didn't hear him. Who was Searls? He was certainly not the tall man in the library downstairs who, Ian now believed, was the bearer of nicked artifacts.

"It's a slow, stead..." Barlowe said, shutting the adjoining door completely.

Now what was he to do? Should he get up from the bed and try to listen through the wall to the next room? He heard the main entry door close in the next room. Barlowe was leaving. Ian was about to rise out of bed when he heard the key slip into his own entry door lock. Ian feigned sleep. It was Barlowe coming to check on his other patients. He turned his head towards Searls so he could watch to see if he was conscious. The doctor slipped in quietly and crept over to Searls's bedside. Barlowe had his black doctor's bag with him and checked the ailing man's wound by unwrapping the bandage. He seemed satisfied and softly crept over to Ian's bedside. Taking the eardrops from the nightstand, he skillfully squeezed a small drop in Ian's exposed left ear. Still feigning sleep, Ian flinched slightly. Ian could smell the doctor's coffee-tinged breath, so close was he to his patient. Barlowe sneaked back through the entry door and left the room. Ian looked at his watch. It was four minutes until the appointed hour.

His need to use the loo could no longer be delayed. He hoped the lavatory door was already open to prevent further sounds as he anxiously pulled on his pants. He decided he would use the wash basin since using the toilet bowl would make far too much noise. He tiptoed to the door that was indeed cracked open. As he unzipped his fly and relieved himself, he saw four standard-size clear drinking glasses, one of which had been opened and used. Here was the makeshift amplifier for eavesdropping on the activities in the next room. He recalled using the trick as a boy when he spied on his friends as they played a James Bond game.

Approaching the door between the suites, he placed the glass up to it and heard the entry door to the other room open with a squeak, then shut. No doubt Doerflinger and Wainwright had entered. He could hear the clash of equipment being set up for the shoot. "Over there," Wainwright ordered.

"I'll peruse the few documents here now before you shoot," Richtol said. "Hand me those." Ian held his breath in excitement.

The door shut again as Doerflinger likely left for the library. It was now nearly 11:00 a.m. For several minutes, Wainwright was apparently walking back and forth across the room positioning lights. Ian heard switch snaps as bright, penetrating light streamed under the door, and near Ian's feet reflected glare splotched the carpet, intermittently interrupted by shadows.

"I presume you're going to spread them over the floor." Richtol's piercing voice sounded like an impatient order.

"We'll film against the green carpet," Wainwright said.

"Have you kept your lips sealed?" Ian heard Richtol whisper, quietly for once.

"Yes." Wainwright's deep, baritone voice resonated. "I expect we'll have no trouble. I'm sending Steve out as soon as he arrives so he can keep watch in the hallway for a few minutes until we actually need him. As an extra precaution, we'll move the papers to the other room if someone tries to enter. Barlowe has two patients in the room but they're harmless. One of them is out like a light and the other has a miserable earache."

"What?" Richtol screamed, livid. "He told me no one was in that room. Lock that door!"

Ian removed the glass from the door and dashed back to his bed in case Wainwright entered. Searls had turned over and was now facing his bed. A board in the next room squeaked. Wainwright turned the key in the door with a firm click.

There was a soft knock at the entry door to Richtol's room. Wainwright marched across the room, opened the door, then shut it and bolted it securely.

"The English..." Ian heard Richtol announce.

Chapter Twenty-Four

"Secretary," an American, it had to be an American, replied. The last two syllables were not clipped but drawn out as Americans do. The reply was boastfully loud, like the triumphant consummation of a long-awaited event.

What the deuce was the significance of the password associated with the work entitled *The English Secretary*? Ian was familiar with the phrase and knew it carried a connection to Oxford if he could only retrieve it from his vast, but fatigued, memory. It didn't seem to have immediate importance. He sighed, sure it would occur to him momentarily.

A more urgent issue was before him, however. Instinctively, he felt like bursting into the room to interrupt the taping until he could form a judgment on the motive of the two-man crew. As he placed the drinking glass against the door to listen again, he dwelt on the implications of the fireplace. How simple it would be to destroy the artifacts as the British ambassador maintained was the miscreants' mission.

If their goal was to sell the artifacts, his penetration of their "film studio" could easily be countered by the use of a weapon, a firearm—these Yank criminals are famous for their ghastly penchant for violence—to kill or disable him. They could then continue their plans to transfer the nicked documents to a wealthy collector, Ian no more than a temporary obstacle to their designs.

But why was Wainwright filming evidence of their crime? Ian figured that the documentarian was paying Richtol as well as the

American who had answered the password "secretary." American telly pays handsomely for a good story. As he listened for a voice, he speculated quickly on who in America and in England could possibly have the money, the means, and the motive to execute such a daring venture—the two break-ins, the flight from the authorities in England, and the clandestine meeting. Surely Richtol was not acting alone. Furthermore, who was this fellow Searls? Why the secrecy?

"Cast a little more light on these in the corner," he heard Doerflinger, the cameraman, say. "And we need a filter on this one."

"Is it going okay, boys?" the churlish Richtol whined from his bed. Ian could imagine artifacts scattered over the entire room. There was no audible answer. Someone must have nodded.

"Go slowly, Steve." Wainwright's voice vibrated the drinking glass Ian held painstakingly still against the door adjoining the two rooms. He heard some sort of equipment being adjusted.

The soft whir of the camera was occasionally interrupted by a sharp crack in the fireplace. Wainwright, or his young partner, was probably snapping photos. These blokes were taking no chances, Ian thought, but he wondered about the lighting. Somewhere he'd read that old documents (if in fact they were documents) were highly susceptible to rapid deterioration if untreated. He hoped if they intended to retain them, that they'd taken proper precautions.

Suddenly the phone rang and Richtol answered immediately as if he had his hand on or near the cradle.

"This is Richtol," Ian heard him say. "Fine, Doctor. No, I've finished my tea and I'm in the middle of the interview. It's going to take longer than expected. If you would be so kind, do not enter for the next hour. Yes...thanks." He slammed down the receiver. "I told him categorically not to bother me even with a phone call. At least it gave me an opportunity to remind him not to barge in. McCann, open the door and place the `Do not disturb' sign on the doorknob. I don't know why I didn't think of it earlier."

Ian heard the door open and shut rapidly, and felt the brief suction against his own door as he leaned on the glass with his ear. So McCann was the courier's, the thief's name. Was it his real name? Was he indeed the American? He would have to assume he was dangerous.

Searls raised his head from the pillow and coughed. Ian noticed him cast a glassy gaze towards the ceiling. He had to do something to avoid this mysterious man when he awakened, which might be at any time. Standing with socks on the cold floor where there was no carpet, Ian looked for his shoes by the bed. It was time for action. He would bolt into the adjoining room and confront them using some means of force to extract from them their motives, rescue the artifacts, and determine their motives.

"That coughing was one of Barlowe's patients in the next room," Richtol moaned. "Damn, if only I wasn't put in this situation. I planned so meticulously to have my own room, even came up here once to plan. For that matter, we could've used one of your rooms. Let's get it over with, guys. Get it done."

Ian stepped over to the bed and quietly began to lace his boots over his wool socks. The doctor must have misplaced it. He noticed his cape, on loan from Sir Keith, which lay neatly across a chair.

If Searls awakened and discovered him, it certainly would interfere with his entry to Richtol's room. He reconsidered forcing the door open—it may not work, thus surely awakening Searls.

Then, as he completed lacing his boots, Searls glanced up at him from his bed. Ian froze, staring back at him and blinking. "Who are you?" Searls mumbled quietly. If he didn't know, then Ian would not increase his suspicions by answering with a British accent. Instead, he raised an index finger to his lips and winked. Grabbing his cape, he pulled it over his shoulders, inadvertently rendering an appearance of a blondish Count Dracula, confusing Searls even more. Searls's reaction was to roll his eyes once, shut them, lie back, and return to a drugged sleep.

Ian opened the door to the hallway and stepped lightly towards the lift. He punched the down button, waited, jumped on, and hit the "L" for lobby. When the lift door opened downstairs, he saw several people in the lobby across from the front desk. Dr. Barlowe was talking animatedly to Vernon, probably about the night's events after Forsythe had tactfully relieved the Texan of any duties for the second foray down the mountain. Both stood with their backs to Ian in the lobby, surveying the steady snowfall. He moved quickly up to the front desk. The ubiquitous, dependable night clerk called Laura was still on duty.

"Laura, I've been staying as a patient in Barlowe's room."

"Yes, Mr. Scarborough. Mr. Forsythe told me all about it. I hope you feel better." Would luck be with him? He felt awkward with his cape on.

"Right, well...I do have a bit of a problem. You see, I would bother Dr. Barlowe for a key to his room, since I see him just over there, but he admonished me not to leave the room until he returned. I locked myself out of his room since I didn't want to leave the door ajar and didn't get a key. I do so despise disappointing him, but I did need to return to my own room to fetch a book. Since my situation is frightfully boring, I thought I should have a go at a good rea—"

"And you don't want the doctor to know you've been out and about this morning. I'll give you a key so you can be back in your room within a minute. He's in 408, I believe..."

"Actually, we're in 410, the adjoining room. Mr. Forsythe may have told you a Mr. Searls and a Mr. Richtol are also patients in 408—which I know was the room assigned to the doctor."

She smiled. "No problem." She opened a drawer and handed him the key to 410. "You can leave it on the dresser when you leave."

"Lovely. Thank you," Ian said. "Oh yes, I need to bother you about two friends of mine as to whether they have arrived. A Retta Aldridge from New York City or an Englishman called Strawbridge."

She was quick on her computer. "Mr. Strawbridge called to say he won't make it at all because of the weather, and Ms. Aldridge, she's the television executive, and her entire crew have cancelled, too."

"You're a dear. Thank you," he whispered.

As he skipped back to the elevator, it opened to reveal Congressman Rogers, among many others, so Ian rapidly turned the corner and dashed for the stairs off the main hallway. Had Rogers seen him? Taking the steps three at a time, he was huffing with excitement and exertion by the time he hit the fourth floor. He searched his pockets to make sure he had the key to his own room in case he needed to find a sanctuary after his next adventure. Yes. It was in his left pocket.

Arriving at the door to 410, he glanced up at the transom window over the door and saw the bright lights and shadows flickering across the hallway ceiling above. Perfect, he thought, they were still working away. If the rooms were alike, there were no chain locks in his room or the connecting room. He hoped that was the case.

He took out his own room key so he could use it as a fake pistol under his cape. Using his left hand he inserted the other key quietly into the lock but froze when he suddenly heard the voices of Forsythe and Barlowe, who were just stepping off the elevator. A zinging fear made him bolt around the corner, frantically looking for a hiding place. He whispered a curse when he realized he'd absentmindedly left the key in the door. There was certainly no time now to return and retrieve it. Their voices got louder as they approached, and the door was only forty or so feet from the corner by the elevator.

"Searls is no big deal for now," Barlowe was saying. "If he shows any signs of worsening, we may want to take him down the mountain. I was supposed to awaken the Brit but I decided to let him sleep. You're sure Laura said she would be somewhere on this floor? If we don't find her, I guess I'll play doctor, nurse, and maid. Where is she?"

"I'll go this way and you go down there," Forsythe said.

Ian decided he would have to make a dash for the exit at the end of the hall. Were they looking for him? Damn that Laura. Who were they looking for? *She would be somewhere, and Barlowe would play doctor, nurse, and maid.* The chambermaid! Of course! Yanks and their hackneyed English, he thought, grinning wistfully. Evidently, Barlowe was about to turn the corner and see him as he heard his heavy footsteps approach. He crept down the hall towards the exit, every nerve rattling with each groan of the old hardwood floor. The worn, brass knob on the exit door was loose and he practically ripped it off as he dashed through the exit. No alarm, he sighed in relief.

Then he froze as he heard Forsythe yell.

"Here she is!"

The footsteps stopped, and then began receding in the distance. He heard some mumbling as he returned to the hallway. Apparently, the chambermaid in question had been in one of the rooms further up the hall. No doubt the two men were looking for her to service Barlowe's room later and were off to the elevator to return to the lobby. Before the doors slid open, Forsythe said to Barlowe, "I'm about to receive a radio report from the police as to who Searls is. We could have searched the Jeep thoroughly, but I raised them this morning on the ham. They'll call back in about fifteen minutes or..." The lift doors shut with a rickety slam.

Would the key still be in the door? Ian anxiously rounded the corner and saw the "Do not disturb" sign along with the key, securely in place. His heart pounded in eight-four time. He felt ridiculous with the cape over his long johns top, but he imagined how he would have felt without his trousers. That was it! As absurd as it seemed, Searls could not bloody well follow him if Ian collected his trousers and hid them. As he approached Richtol's entrance door, he decided to reenter his room to execute what he considered a simple, but essential, precaution.

Searls was still asleep. He'd turned onto his back. Ian grabbed the trousers, wrapping them around his hand tightly like a bandage to conceal the revolver he didn't have, thereby freeing up the cape for a better dramatic effect. There were no other trousers in the room, and Searls didn't have a suitcase or luggage. Searls was probably in his underwear briefs. The crew in the next room might be impressed by his use of cloth as a silencer from his make-believe revolver.

He stepped back gingerly into the hallway and swayed slightly as he came up to the entrance to Richtol's room—such tiptoeing disturbed one's equilibrium. Hesitating long enough to take a deep breath, he exhaled and opened the door.

Shocked eyes stared agog at him in the light-soaked room, creating an aura of actors who, having completed a gripping scene, are awaiting the curtain to fall. No applause here, though, just grimaces and gaping mouths. Ian swept a rapid glance over the floor carpeted with old documents—murky brown and yellow papers with dark scribbles of what surely was Elizabethan longhand. Here was the bone and booty of Hatfield House and Stratford monument.

"Doctor, pleee..."said Richtol, almost dropping a document in total surprise. He knew nothing about the tall man who'd just entered the room and certainly wasn't Barlowe.

Klieg lights brightly splashed over every corner of the room. Doerflinger stood near the center, between the two beds, carefully filming documents. Wainwright was using a Polaroid camera that sat on a stand only ten inches or so above another group of documents.

Two digital cameras swung from his neck, clanging and dangling as clumsily as if he'd forgotten their purpose, now that Ian had his sole attention. The newcomer, McCann, stood in the corner to Ian's right and was in the act of reaching, in all likelihood, for a weapon in an attaché case next to a small book case.

"Don't move," Ian barked at him, and McCann instantly stopped, folding his arms in submissive retreat.

"Who are you?" Richtol demanded.

"Mr. Richtol, Mr. Wainwright, Mr. Doerflinger, and Mr. McCann, I'm here on a mission of truth and the Crown. I insist on having those papers immediately." Ian hadn't really considered a definite escape except to go to his own room, which was open to anyone's query at the front desk. But he must secure the papers. He pointed his right arm towards McCann and in the most threatening voice he could muster, said, "Do not bother to arm yourself, Mr. McCann. I have a weapon and I shall use it on you if I must."

"He's from the other room," Wainwright said as he looked at the trousers holding a gun.

"But, how do you know us? Who are you?" Richtol repeated.

Good question, Ian thought. Who actually was he? To achieve his end was he associated with the British embassy (he felt he had some authority), or was he an investigative reporter? Was he first loyal to Britain, which would dutifully compel him to return the artifacts, perhaps for more centuries of concealment, or was he foremost loyal to the gallant cause of Edward de Vere, the Seventeenth Earl of Oxford? Or, perish the thought, were the papers substantiating the hand of William Shakspere of Stratford-Upon-Avon? Were their motives to destroy the papers or sell them to a tycoon, or were they truly Oxfordians? With his fatigue and general principle of assuming the worst, the Oxfordian identity for these four men, in spite of knowing Wainwright and Doerflinger, had not gripped his mind in the last twelve hours—maybe because of Richtol and now McCann. The tall Holmesian in his dark green cape must divine their purpose in the seconds ahead.

"I shall allow both of you to carry on your tasks while I pose some questions. At least you'll have recorded the documents adequately for posterity no matter your intentions. How much more, Wainwright, do you and Steve have remaining to finish your project?"

"How do you two know this man?" Richtol implored. He was seething, his mousy face crimson and his small lips tightening. "Did you two mastermind this?"

"Mr. Richtol, I'm in command here," Ian hissed through his teeth. "I must know exactly what is going on here. Carry on, gentlemen."

"He was part of the rescue team," Doerflinger said innocently.

"I have about a dozen more pages to shoot and I'm going back to shoot four or five over again," Wainwright replied. He bowed his head over a new section of documents using the specialized Polaroid as if he wanted to hurry the task before Ian went completely berserk. The camera made its characteristic whir and snap, the paper slowly spitting out the side. He would snap a photo with the digital camera while waiting for the snapshot to develop so he was assured of having a clear picture from no more than a foot away. As he rose from his crouch, his jaw quivered in serious apprehension.

"I'm nearly finished," Steve Doerflinger said.

"Mr. Richtol, I need to have a straight answer from you as to why you've engineered this project, and tell me what you believe the documents contain?"

"I prefer not to answer," Richtol said, mimicking Bartleby's reply. "I won't answer until I know who you are and who you represent."

"I'm pointing this weapon at you, Mr. Richtol. I expect an answer in thirty seconds." Despite his bravado, Ian decided he might have made a tactical error. He would have to carry out the bluff somehow at the appointed moment. He couldn't believe his audacious manner. "Out with it. Tell me."

McCann anxiously watched the old man lying propped on one shaking elbow near the edge of his bed, blinking nervously at the sixteenth-century documents spread over the entire floor. "Where's the cash? I've got to have my money," McCann shouted in clear American English, saving the moment for Ian by the distraction of the threat.

"Shoot me," Richtol's high, shrill voice demanded. "I'm almost dead from cancer, anyway."

McCann's long face strained with tension and his fists clenched. "Tell him, dammit...and tell me where my money is."

"Shoot me!" Richtol wailed. Ian did not move.

"Don't," Wainwright shouted, trapped from moving quickly in the minefield of precious documents.

Doerflinger kept filming, except he moved his camera towards Ian and McCann. Ian felt a strange penetration from the camera's eye as if it were invading his privacy. The entire embarrassing episode of his empty threat would be immortalized on film. But Doerflinger was stepping into a role as a film journalist at some risk.

McCann raised a hand. "I'll tell you everything I know. Don't shoot him."

Ian jiggled his "gun" at McCann. "Talk to me!"

"As best I can tell, Richtol and a group of people are interested in these papers because they prove that the Earl of Oxford wrote all of Shakespeare's works," the tall American sighed. "I was hired to steal these documents from their caches in two locations in England for," he glared at Richtol who was shaking his chin in rage, tiny white foam forming around the corner of his lips, "a predetermined sum of money, which I want now! I'm to return the documents after they've recorded them and there's a documentary on this subject in a special report airing on Wolf News television sometime this week—if only they could drive down the mountain, which they may yet try to do, although I'm not sure it's very wise. I'm returning the documents to a location in London. I was assured that they will be safely returned from there, but I won't know the exact location until I arrive there. I'm to leave today for the airport, and I *will*, even if by snowshoe—and *if I receive my money.*" He glared at Richtol.

Richtol was trembling with rage. "What if this man is from the British government, from MI5? We've put so much into this." In complete frustration, he slapped the nightstand violently, knocking the phone on the floor. It landed on one of the documents, tearing it slightly.

At that moment it occurred to Ian that the suspicions he had of them could have as easily been applied to him, maybe even more so.

McCann traced a smirk along his long, white, expressionless face. "He's not from the government. He's either interested in selling the documents or he's with us."

For the first time, Ian began to question how convincing he was in his cape, concealing the "gun" in the trousers wrapped around his right arm. Each second he bluffed or did not have his answers would diminish his shock and surprise. Suddenly, he thought of a way to test the motives of all parties. He was beginning to believe McCann, as dubious as he initially seemed, but Ian based his assumption on Wainwright's and Doerflinger's earlier hints of corroboration.

"We've time for some trivia, I hope," Ian stated matter-of-factly. "How many signatures did Shakspere leave us?"

"Six," Richtol answered, blowing his nose with a handkerchief from the night stand. Then the old man stared at Ian, his face alighting, incredulous with a celebratory expression, and eyes wide as if the sun had refreshingly appeared after a heavy rain. "You said..."

"Who was the Dark Lady of the sonnets if written by Edward de Vere and not Shakspere?" Ian finished the question as Richtol repeated the odd pronunciation of the Stratford boy's name twice.

"Shakspere! Shakspere!" He coughed from deep in his chest as he lifted his upper torso towards the other men. "Did you hear him? He's one of us. He *is*..."

"It was...Anne..." Ian paused and smiled thinly.

"Vavasor," Richtol and Wainwright harmonized.

Richtol was rocking with glee. "*The English Secretary* is by which author?"

Ian recalled his drive towards Stratford only last week before the wretched second trip and earache, fastidiously reviewing his notes before the debate that would never be here in upstate New York. His look of bewilderment transformed to bright, flashing eyes as he responded. "*Secretary*," he instantly recalled from his eavesdropping in the other room, but it took on its full meaning now. "*The English Secretary* is by..." He stared at the daylight through the window. Momentarily he'd forgotten it, so much had he attributed to his indelible memory. "...by Angel Day, 1588, with a tribute—uh—about a Muse from infancy, or some such as that...."

"I believe 1586," Richtol corrected him. "You are an Oxfordian, but I implore you. I can't reveal everything to you, except to say we're returning the documents, and according to McCann in his cursory glances at these documents through the last two nights here, we're sitting on the news story of the century—the most disturbing and important literary find in all history. Are you with MI5, or even the FBI? Who are you? Can we count you in, my friend?"

Ian moved towards the roaring fireplace and lowered his right "pistol" arm, which was beginning to strain with tension. "I'm confident that your intentions are to expose the truth and return the papers to England, a risky proposition, but I must be totally sure. I've had some fear that you intended to destroy or sell these treasures. How simple to sweep them into this fireplace, and then there would be no *corpus delicti*—no evidence. How easy, Mr. McCann, would it be for you to arrange for some agent of a vain, wealthy American tycoon to purchase these documents? When you two gentlemen have completed your filming so that the documents may be adequately interpreted, I shall stand beside this roaring fire and make sure they go back inside the attaché or whatever vessel you're transporting them in. I'm also going to travel with you, Mr. McCann, to assure myself that we return them safely. All I ask in return is that you allow me to break the story in London at the same time. You will leave your phone number with me, Mr. Richtol, and you, Mr. Wainwright—I presume—a press release here in the States, for I'm a newspaper reporter as well as an advocate of the de Vere candidacy for authorship. Now isn't that fair, Mr. Richtol?"

Richtol looked at Ian and McCann and shivered as if he were afraid to reply. He hesitated for several seconds and then smiled as if the penny dropped. "Yes. It's fair. But I want to know who you are and what paper you work for."

"I'm Ian Scarborough and I work for the *London Daily Times*."

Richtol raised his eyebrows and moved his head upward at the mention of Ian's name. Ian could see the man may have been shocked by the response. Or was it a nod of recognition? Abruptly, the old man wiped his forehead with the back of his hand. After a few seconds of silence, he cracked a scant grin, revealing brownish-yellow teeth. "Perfect," was all he said.

Ian was mystified by the curious silence and the wiry, ill man's reaction. It had been a bit too easy. Ian nodded nonetheless.

"Agreed," Richtol said. "Wainwright, write your home number on the pad here." Wainwright tiptoed to the bedside table and took the pad. "Don't write on the pad. Tear the sheet off first. It can be traced if you don't," he continued. He then gave his own home and office numbers. "Identify yourself as..."

"Arthur Golding." Ian laughed. From such rock-solid trivial knowledge sprang a cascade of trust and goodwill.

"Yes. Why not de Vere's Latin tutor and uncle?" The old man was now almost perky with delight. "I'll tell you the precise time I'm having the release delivered into the hands of the city desk editors of our major newspapers and network news. Let's go for a time in London, this Friday, of about 13:00 hours so we might have the five o'clock news on our east coast—that's before many 2:00 p.m. press deadlines. That should be plenty of time, four days, for your return."

"We will arrive when we arrive, Richtol," McCann said testily. "It's going to be hard enough to travel as a pair of tall males, especially if someone else finds us out before we're able to make some kind of getaway in this blizzard."

"Okay," Richtol agreed. "In that case, we'll synchronize the release of the news on both continents from your phone call. Not on a weekend"

"That's a wrap." Doerflinger lifted the camera off his right shoulder then stepped on the spaces on the floor as if they were solid beams and the papers were thousand-foot crevices.

"Got to get two more pictures." Wainwright hopped back to his prior position after passing the phone numbers to Doerflinger. He lifted the phone and photographed the slightly damaged document.

Doerflinger and McCann then began the process of carefully replacing each sheet in stiff plastic folders bearing small stickers marked with consecutive numbers in the upper right corners. The two men had skillfully laid the papers out in a fashion of concentric circles in clockwise order on the carpet between the two beds so they were in perfect sequence with the numbered folders. There were probably one hundred sheets spread over nearly five hundred square feet of room space. Where beds or furniture interfered, the men had simply interrupted the circles.

Ian remained baffled at Richtol's apparent shock upon hearing his name. Had he recognized it from music, a news byline, or the editorial—or was it merely the twitch of a cancerous mind?

Doerflinger and Wainwright returned the documents to a box and were handing it to McCann when the door connecting the other room started shaking. Then came knocking and a frantic voice screamed, "Open the door." It had to be Searls.

"We're not allowing anyone else in this room," Richtol whispered. "Barlowe is necessary, but—Scarborough, who's in there?"

Ian wouldn't reveal the discovery he'd made concerning his own name on the piece of paper since Richtol had reacted unclearly at the name Ian Scarborough. "His name is Searls. He was rescued last night after you were brought up here. He was attempting to drive up the mountain. Had he not been driving idiotically in such weather, he would probably have made it. We know nothing about him. He received a head injury and is on medication for a mild to moderate concussion. We don't know who he is. I thought he was somehow associated with your effort."

"A concussion," Wainwright repeated, "and he shouldn't even be out of bed. I'll call the doc after we've cleared out everything."

"Hurry," Richtol rasped as the door shook again. "Forget Barlowe! Too much is at stake. Hurry up."

The shouting from behind the door increased. "Let me in! Now!"

McCann prepared to close his attaché case and then stepped to Richtol's bed. "Let's not, in our haste, forget something."

"One small matter before I pay you." Richtol looked up at McCann's long, brooding face before gazing at Wainwright who was frantically placing the documents in proper order. "Wainwright, hand me document number seventeen. Gentlemen, I'm keeping it as proof! I suggest that all of you conveniently forget that I'm doing this, but I must have some proof in case the authorities subvert the whole project. Wainwright, make an extra photo of this document and hand it to McCann. I'll tell you what to do with it next time we talk."

Wainwright removed the document and handed it to Richtol after carefully remounting his camera and snapping a picture. McCann was growing exceedingly impatient. "Let's go!" He clenched his fists. Searls was shouting even louder from the other room. Wainwright passed the developing snapshot to McCann, who glanced at it, then stuffed it in his trouser pockets. Wainwright and Doerflinger glanced at each other in concern over this lethal-looking outsider who had apparently arrived before them. Ian noted their looks, thinking that McCann was the true mercenary.

"Steve." Richtol shoved a thumb over his shoulder. "Dr. Barlowe placed my attaché case behind this head board. Please retrieve it for me at once."

"Let me in." Searls was banging hard on the door. Probably he'd heard some of the conversation. Had he heard Ian's British accent? Doerflinger produced the same attaché case that they had so painstakingly removed from the Jeep at Richtol's insistence and handed it to the old man. Richtol reached inside his pillowcase and produced a small key that he twisted in both latches. He flipped the case open to reveal a hefty sum of marks and euros, some smaller quantities of British pounds, and some Canadian and American dollars. He handed the bundle to McCann, who shuffled hastily through the collection of older untraceable bills.

"I'll have ample time to count this in the room," McCann said. "If it's incorrect, I'll return. You wouldn't want that with this fellow on the other side of the door. I hope you've placed the right amount in here. Have you set up the accounts?"

"Yeah," Richtol moaned. "No matter what happens, you will receive the balance at the final destination. Do not...I repeat...don't stray from your instructions. Scarborough, you should be prepared to help when necessary or you shall not receive your story. McCann, buy his tickets as needed and I'll have the difference added to your remuneration at your final destination. If anything happens to me, my law clerk will have a number for you to call in England. Maybe it's good to have Scarborough along. If you're caught, you should simply turn over...no, give half the documents to him. I assume he'll be working on transcribing them." Ian nodded in agreement. "I hope you have an eye for reading this material. With you possessing them, we'll have some extra proof beyond these films and photos in case McCann blunders and is caught."

"Not going to happen." McCann nodded. "Let's go!"

"I must know what I am agreeing to," Ian protested. "How are we going? Where?"

McCann leveled his bony face close to Ian's. "You have little choice if you're going to have your story. But don't worry, because the risk isn't that great. We have a plan which should work well as long as we...." He stopped and lightly pushed him as the door shook violently. "No time. I'll tell you more downstairs in my room. We're gone."

Wainwright shivered in suspense. "Go!" he said and nudged Doerflinger.

"Yes. Let's..." McCann looked again at Ian and the four men scurried out the door. "I'll go to my room. Here's the number." McCann handed Ian a small card scribbled with the number 849. "Meet me there in ten minutes."

"Sorry, old man," Ian said, "I'm going to your room now, and then you're going to mine. We're inseparable for the days ahead."

"If you insist." McCann smiled grimly. "You've got to trust me soon, you know."

"I shall after we've a chance to chat about what's in the offing."

"I'm going to tell you in pieces for safety's sake," McCann rejoined. "In case you decide to report too quickly, I'll only tell you a little at a time—but I do have one immediate problem which we will discuss when we get to my room."

Ian and McCann dashed to the stairwell. As they rounded the corner they saw the door to Searls's room open slowly. Searls, crawling in his boxers, coughed and shouted, "Stop. I have to talk to you." He raised himself in one wooden movement and fell against the wall, then slid to the floor.

The two tall men—one adorned in a cape, the other in a suit, and carrying similar attaché cases—stopped briefly at the stairwell door to witness the poor fellow passing out. Then as they started up the stairs, Ian caught a glimpse of Dr. Barlowe coming from the elevator and sprinting to Searls's listless body. Ian hoped that the two film lads, who must have stepped onto the other lift, had not been seen by Barlowe. Any mention of Searls's disturbance might corroborate his version of what might have been overheard. The new problem for now was that no one knew exactly how big the story was except maybe Richtol or McCann, and Ian had the duty to unearth it upon returning to England. Ian would have plenty of questions to ask McCann when they returned to the room.

As they were moving through the stairway, Ian unwrapped the trousers from his arm and dropped them down the stairwell between the arm rails. They caught on the second floor and draped across the rail. "That was my pistol," he said. McCann nodded as if he couldn't have cared less. "And Searls's trousers."

McCann smiled mischievously. "Have you ever seen Searls before?" McCann asked.

"No, have you?"

"Never."

"I'm going to call Richtol before we leave and ask him if he knows who Searls is." McCann turned the key to his room and opened the door. "Now we can talk. We need a good four-wheel drive. I was going to use Richtol's vehicle, but I understand they wrecked it beyond immediate repair."

"Yes." Ian's quick mind fastened on an idea. Time to start bargaining. "If you'll tell me where we are going, I'll tell you where some transportation is most accessible to us. I must know your final destination in London."

"I won't know the final destination myself until we arrive in London, but we have several stops along the way. I'll only tell you that our first stop is Montreal."

"Where else?"

McCann stared Ian straight in the eye as he laid his case on the bed and knelt over his open suitcase to repack it. "Mr. Scarborough, I'm not going to barter with you. We're now in this together whether we like it or not. I'm not going to have you do anything that will jeopardize the mission. I've never injured a man, but I know how, thanks to my work for the last twenty-plus years. I don't desire to do any such thing, but the mission is all that matters, so you've got to cooperate fully. You'll get your story because you'll have ample time in another country, over forty-eight hours or so, to analyze the documents just as Wainwright's people will be doing here in the States over that same period. It's one of the reasons we're going to travel in different modes together—to give you time to work on the papers. Do we have an understanding?" He blinked once then snapped shut the suitcase.

"Yes." Ian was surprised at the man's candor and his own acquiescence. "I have a car for us. Searls's vehicle should be in running order even though it's currently standing on its side. It's only about a mile down the mountain. We should be able to tip it over and drive right down. Forsythe said it would run. The keys should still be in it."

"I hope you're right, and I hope the weather is better." McCann peeled back his curtains to see light snow falling. "I'm getting a weather update while I count the money." He looked at his watch. "Nearly two," he said as he flipped on an old, electric radio sitting stalwartly on the antique mantle above the vacant fireplace.

"...with the 'East St. Louis Toodle-Oo.' It's news time coming up," an announcer said.

"We should hear a weather report in five minutes. This is the hourly news, then there'll probably be a local weather broadcast."

Ian marveled at the man's coolness. He had to have been in the law enforcement or intelligence game in some capacity, he thought.

"I take it we're flying out of Montreal," Ian said.

"Yes. I hope we'll have no problem getting seats."

Ian worried that he would have to show his passport to this character next, and hoped his press credentials might save him if he were apprehended. On the other hand, he mused briefly on all the recent punters lured by the chase. Boone Phelps, the last of the hardcore investigative reporters, was as sleazy as this character. To freshen up his grey matter, he thought of Veronica Colton's debonair skill. And how was she doing? he wondered. Were the phones working so he could call her? He decided he might try in Montreal if he could distract McCann somehow. Instinctively, he knew the answer would be "no" if he asked.

McCann laced his boots and gathered his coat and parka. He wound his scarf loosely around his neck and picked up the attaché case and suitcase. "Here comes the weather segment," he said.

"...for Manhattan and vicinity, we'll have continued snow through tomorrow with accumulations up to three feet. The major portion of this blizzard is confined to a band stretching from Buffalo to Albany and south to the Poconos and northern Jersey. I-87 is now relatively clear, so is the New Jersey Turnpike..."

McCann's eyes widened in mock joy while he snapped off the radio and lifted his suitcase. "All we have to do, my friend, is make it back through New Paltz and to 87 and we're on our way. Excellent."

They went to the stairs and hustled their way down to Ian's room. Ian found it exactly as he'd left it the night before when the bizarre adventure had begun. He yawned, looked longingly at the bed he hadn't slept in, then marched himself to his suitcase and began loading his paraphernalia.

"I'm calling Richtol." McCann set his luggage on the love seat and picked up the old telephone on the nightstand. Ian heard Richtol's loud voice answer immediately.

"If you're able to talk, say `I can hear you fine,' and if you're not, say `speak a little louder.' Say I'm housekeeping." Ian could make out the buzz of Richtol's voice on `louder.' "We're leaving on foot in about five minutes. Scarborough has identified a reliable vehicle for us. He says the keys were in the vehicle." There was a pause. "Tell me, if you can, who's Searls? Do you know anything more?"

McCann looked at Ian and held his hand over the mouthpiece. "Barlowe's back in there. Richtol just sent him to the bathroom to wet a warm wash towel so he can talk." He uncovered the mouthpiece. "He is?" Ian saw McCann's face pale. "How do you know?" McCann leaned forward in great interest as if facing Richtol. Ian leaned forward, too, barely hearing Richtol's whisper. The old man spoke for nearly a minute. "Okay. We're leaving as soon as possible. I'll be in touch." McCann hung up the phone as if it were too hot to hold, then stood up mechanically and peered directly into Ian's eyes. "Barlowe just told Richtol that the New Paltz police identified Searls in a radio report to the innkeeper. Evidently, the F.B.I. called the police to track him down. Searls is an FBI agent. They say he's after you."

Chapter Twenty-Five

Ian sat in the nonsmoking section of Gate 24 at Montreal's International Airport reflecting on the previous six hours. Once the two men had reached the overturned Jeep, they had no trouble pushing it over on all fours again for the angle was just right. There was minimal damage to the vehicle except for scrapes. The problem was virtually no gasoline. So they decided to risk coasting down the mountain road where they might come within walking distance of a service station.

But as McCann steered down the mountain, it occurred to Ian that the spare gasoline tank they had lifted in order to remove the camera equipment held about five gallons, enough to arrive in New Paltz where they could fill up. McCann voiced his concern over the FBI man and that they were escaping with his vehicle, but Ian was beyond worry over the matter by the time they reached the freeway. A new wave of drowsiness had engulfed him—abetted by a warming purr of the heater working overtime against the cold, wintry outdoors. Sluggishly, he crawled over the space between the driver and reclined passenger's seat, huddling in the back to sleep as soundly as he'd ever slept without dreaming.

When he awoke, they were approaching Plattsburgh, New York, only miles from the Canadian border. The trip from New Paltz had taken four hours, though normally a two and a half hour drive. After a brief pit stop in Plattsburgh, they came upon the Canadian border. The customs officials asked them only for their destination, and warned them that there was another scourge of snow coming from the north. The authorities had evidently not been notified of the missing Jeep. Moreover, McCann seemed much more concerned about Searls's pursuit. Wondering aloud, he asked Ian if he thought Searls had been conscious and persistent enough to radio the state police.

Ian replied that he believed Richtol had managed that situation in conjunction with the faithful Dr. Barlowe. "Wily Mr. Richtol would have made the doctor consider him delirious to give him another tablet for his maladies. It was quite a wound and the doctor likely would have complied. I had heard the doctor say they might risk taking him down the mountain, given his injury. Richtol maybe would have suggested that I felt better and simply went to my room. I didn't check out, of course, and maybe Richtol will pay up. I'm certain Richtol would've said the film crew had finished the deposition, the client had departed, and you'd gone downstairs for a while after feeling better. If the police knew Searls was looking for me, why didn't they make more of an effort?"

"FBI and local authorities don't always work together," McCann observed.

Ian had momentarily forgotten about the valuable documents in the back of the vehicle, but by the time he saw the lights of Montreal, he'd sufficiently prepared himself mentally for the task of reviewing them while on the plane. They unloaded the car and wiped it clean of prints, though both had worn gloves. McCann left the key under the front wheel and they went to purchase tickets.

"McCann, where are we bound next?" Ian blurted.

"Munich," was the humorless response. "And the papers say it's covered with snow, too."

Ian squinted into McCann's dark brown eyes. "Why Munich of all places?"

"I can't answer that." McCann looked away at a stunningly beautiful redheaded lady who passed them on her way to use a pay phone. She bumped Ian's elbow as she went by.

"Pardon, Monsieur," she said.

"No problem," Ian replied as she picked up the phone. "That reminds me. I would like to ring my friend in London to enquire about her sick father."

"I'd prefer you wait until Munich. You'll have time there."

Ian could see lingering paranoia in the man's stern face. "You must trust me, you know. We're essentially after the same thing."

McCann blinked as though he didn't get it. "We're not after the same thing, friend. Let me assure you. We're not home free by any stretch of the imagination."

Ian resolved to test his motive by asking a series of questions concerning Edward de Vere. It had worked for him and Richtol at the hotel, so it should reveal something here about this strange, serious man. Was he a devotee or purely a mercenary?

"I was gratified to discover that Richtol is an Oxfordian. Had it not been for my reference to the Shakspere pronunciation I would've had to shoot him with my key."

"I suspected you weren't carrying a weapon, but I didn't care to take the chance. I figured I could grab..." He stopped. Ian thought "the attaché with the money," to complete his sentence.

"Have you looked carefully at these documents, Mike?" Ian pointed to the box sitting next to him on a small white table between the seats in a remote corner near their gate where they'd settled after buying one-way tickets.

"No. I only looked at sections as I photographed them. Richtol told me to make more photos as I traveled for him. You should take the photos for your paper. I'll give you the camera I used. I've got the needed film."

McCann's was not only uninterested in the question of the authorship, but he was being paid off—a mercenary to the highest degree. "Marvelous. I believe that would work well. Is it like the Polaroid Wainwright used? I hope it'll properly print in our paper."

"I'll try to phone Richtol now." McCann bolted to the telephone bank, intent on avoiding the traceable cell phone. "I've got to put my mind totally at rest concerning Searls. If they've stopped Searls, we'll have an excellent shot at making it all the way to London."

"I should be the one worried about Searls if the local authorities are correct," said Ian. "Have you got something to hide?" McCann didn't answer. He merely got up to go to a phone.

Ian again noticed a certain caution bordering on paranoia in the man. Was it justified? Richtol did seem like one who could control any situation, even in the face of such excruciating pain and suffering. Surely Richtol had used excellent judgment in selecting McCann. Ian recognized the high stakes involved, but McCann could be risking his position. He opted to assert the voice of rationale, of reason, of conscience.

"On the other hand, they could be tracing all calls to Richtol," Ian whispered to himself. Ian looked at the box of documents.

McCann returned. "Their phones are still down."

Ian was still staring at the boxes. "These papers are innocuous, as long as customs hasn't been alerted. Why would they suspect the documents to be reentering England? They'd anticipate the booty to be leaving the country. We've overcome the hard part."

"Yes." McCann nodded faintly and drew a deep breath. "It's just that I'm so apprehensive about returning to the general scene of the crime."

"You mean Stratford and Hatfield House?"

"No, England. I'm going to phone again in a minute. We'll be boarding soon and we've cleared customs by driving across the

Canadian border, but I want to know where we stand. We should be safe until we land in Munich."

"Yes, an unlikely locale for customs officials to be concerned about missing documents from the Elizabethan era. The danger is here in Quebec if the officials here have been alerted."

McCann dialed on his cell phone this time, using a telephone calling card of some kind as the announcement came. "Mesdames et messieurs, nous allons procider a l'embarquement immediat du vol numero sept-zero-un en destination de Munich. Les passagers handicappes ou voyageant avec des petits enfants sont pries de se presenter a la porte numero neuf..." McCann shook his head. "The cells are still down."

"Perhaps why we are not a priority for now."

"You're probably right. Well, we have first-class for you and coach for me."

"Really? How did I rate?"

"We need to be separated most of the time. I'm going to be riding in the back with my money, most of which I'll be relieved of in Munich, and you'll be up examining documents. But only if few people are up there. And if you do so, please examine them one..."

"At a time," Ian interrupted. "I know you'll find this incredible to believe, but I intend to sleep some as well, in which case I'll set the documents in your overhead compartment without fanfare. I'll be totally jet lagged if I don't get a kip. It'll probably be later in the flight."

"Nudge me if you find me asleep so I can keep an eye out. I'll try to remain awake, although I'm a little tired myself. It's always possible that someone on the flight is on to us."

Ian made for the first-class line. McCann followed with his attaché case containing the documents surrounding the money. He had been relieved when he passed through customs and no one said a word. The amount was sufficiently divided into large denominations so the other papers mingling with the money assuaged any suspicions.

As takeoff time approached, it appeared that no one would take Ian's adjoining seat, an aisle location on the left side of the 747. Only four other people occupied first class. He slid the box under the seat after carefully removing the top document for a hasty reading before takeoff. McCann passed him and cracked a slight smile.

While he buckled the seat belt, he lay the top document on the seat beside him, the glare from the plastic cover creating a problem reading it from that position since the plane's interior lights were hitting it from all angles. He softly clutched the document and held it under his nose to read. Because he had no magnifying glass it would be a slow process. The writing was in a very elegant hand, with certain dramatic flourishes in the capital letters and the pronoun "I" and the tails of Ys and Gs. It wasn't going to be easy to read the unfamiliar, ancient hand, he thought as the plane backed out onto the tarmac with an abrupt jolt. But he had practiced the previous summer while in the reading room of the British Library and at Hatfield House with Colton—reading the very hand of the Seventeenth Earl of Oxford.

It was quite legible once his eyes adjusted. "Wellcome, my Lord, what is the newes?" This page was obviously a continuation of another—yes, McCann had the first half of the papers.

Ian recognized the scribbling "Nrthmblnd" for what had to be: "Northumberland." Ian whispered and his eyes widened as the passage carried on. "Firste to the Sacred state wishe I alle Hapiness; The next News is, I have to London sente the heads of Oxenford, Salisbry, Blunt and Kent—the manner of their taking may appear at large discoursed in this paper hiere."

Ian recognized the passage from *Richard III*, although he couldn't place the precise act and scene. It was well into the play, since he recalled the mention of the towns (no small coincidence that the Seventeenth Earl preferred to name the town after his formalized peerage name of "Oxenford") after the defeat of Richard II. Indeed, Oxford had been to one of the sites of the battles. "Yes!" Ian whispered loudly against the roar of the engines as it dawned on him that this most likely was the first time since Oxford's death that a human being was examining one of the plays in the author's own original manuscript.

Sublimely conscious of how intensely he'd focused attention on the document, he laid it gingerly on the seat next to him. This trip could be his most eventful journey ever as he savored the thought of his possible impending achievement. Here was a find most reporters only hoped to uncover in a lifetime of reporting, and he'd been given the luxury of accomplishing such a feat on his second reporting mission. His luck had been uncanny.

In every instance where he'd tried to control recent events, some outside circumstance had stealthily interfered in his favor—even when it had seemed that he had lost or had no control.

Beginning with the earache that had plagued him in Stratford, straight through to his common pronunciation of the name for the Stratford man that had gained Richtol's confidence, things had gone well. By nature he was a methodical Englishman with an abundance of common sense, yet he was trusting, sometimes unassuming, even innocent in his approach to people. He'd never been one to advance his manner boldly. He had always taken a calm, methodical approach. That's why the hidden pistol ploy at the hotel filming was highly out of character for him. He now felt pangs of guilt and remorse over nicking the FBI man's trousers to impede his progress. Nonetheless, he smiled softly, nearly laughing aloud at his ingenuity and audacity. In the final analysis, he concluded, the ends do justify the means for such a noble cause as the liberation of the Seventeenth Earl of Oxford from his purgatory of silence for over four centuries.

He was reminded of an American film he had seen years ago, something about a ghost from the Elizabethan age that had been doomed to haunt Canterville Hall after being sealed behind a wall until World War II. Occupying American troops and a young English girl had charmed the tired old ghost, played by Charles Laughton, into giving up his haunts, and the denouement was that they gave him a grave with full and proper acknowledgment of his name. The movie was a bit of an American morale or propaganda film adapted from a short story by Oscar Wilde.

De Vere has been haunting works filled with a wealth of emotions, experience, skill, and charm only to be rejected by a world accepting most facile explanations—especially when the mounting drivel of scholarly exegeses had become wholly self-sustaining and intellectually incestuous. How devastated the Shakespearian scholarship world will be in a few days when Ian storms into Brad Vines office with the story for print. The rebirth should be in a spirit of further study, not angst to those who were devoted to the Stratford man, no matter their misguidance and unwillingness of treating it as a historical discipline.

Once the plane was airborne and the seat belt sign had been turned off, Ian retrieved the sheet from the seat next to him and reread the contents. As he flipped it over to find the passage from *Richard III* preceding that which he had just read, including the inscription "Scene Six," he detected a gentle tap on his right shoulder and turned to meet McCann's gaunt, passionless gaze.

"I need to consult with you about a contingency plan in case we develop problems. The flight attendants are beginning to serve drinks, but when the aisles are clear, let's meet so I can tell you what I've come up with. I'm still concerned about Searls. Sooner or later they're going to find his Jeep in the long-term parking at the Montreal airport. I hope he doesn't know my name, but we need to plan for such an eventuality."

Ian nodded and immediately blushed at recalling the slip of paper with his name scribbled on it. "Let's rendezvous as soon as you're served and the cart is on its way to the back of the plane." Ian noticed attendants filling a cart in the station between first-class and coach. One was taking orders, sans cart, from the lone couple on the right side of the otherwise empty first-class section with its wide, comfortable seats.

"I'll meet you then," the American said.

Should he tell his companion about Searls's note? He decided against it for the time being. It would only confirm what McCann had heard in his phone call to Richtol. Until there was some indication of a firm threat to their mission, he didn't want to jeopardize his access to the documents. In fact, he wanted to begin photographing the documents himself as soon as he had the privacy to do so, although he was not sure where, or when, it would be. An airplane was clearly not the proper place.

Ian returned to the document, searching for a direct clue to the Seventeenth Earl of Oxford—a signature or notation that would confirm the authorship of these manuscripts, original ones obviously, and certifiably by Edward de Vere. There were no such clues on either side of this particular document so he quickly reached for the box of documents and retrieved the next in line, slipping the first one back on top. As with the previous document, the only direct clue to him was the distinct handwriting of Edward de Vere. It surely had to be his work, and it was exciting to witness such a smoking gun.

Here was yet another passage in the same familiar hand: "And God forgive them that so much have sway'd your Majesty's Goode Thoughts away from me. I will redeem all this on Percy's Head, And in the closing of some Glorious Day be bold to tell you that I am your Son, When I will wear a Garment all of Blood and stain my favors in a Bloody Mask, which, wash'd away, shall scour my shame with it..." It had to be, yes, Prince Hal from *Henry IV, Part 1.*

The flight attendant gently tapped his tray. "Would you like a drink?" she asked with a trace of Québécois.

"No, thank you."

He continued reading the passage until it finished at the bottom of the page: "....if not, the ende of life cancels all bands, and I will die a hundred thousand Deaths Ere break the smallest Parcel of this Vow.

"KING: A hundred thousande rebels dye in this: Thou shalt have..." and the passage ended to be continued on yet another page.

Ian examined the back page to find nothing on the parchment except tiny cracks in the paper. In the overhead light, the plastic cover still glared back at his face. He glanced at a young couple across the way in first-class, clearly lovers most blissfully intent upon mutually admiring eyes and nothing else.

The flight attendant appeared again. "We have Coq au Vin or Beef Tips as entrees served with baked potato and asparagus or green beans almandine, followed by New York cheesecake. Which do you prefer?"

"Right. Coq au Vin and asparagus, please, and tea with dinner as well."

"I'll bring your spinach salad right out."

"No. If you do not mind, I would rather have it after the main course and before you serve the afters."

She nodded and moved on to the busy lovers. Ian inserted the document back in the box and began to retrieve the next one when he noticed McCann approaching.

"Let's talk back in the first seat in coach where we can see through the curtains."

"It doesn't appear to be a problem. The flight attendant is friendly and there's only that couple there." He rose as he unsnapped his seat belt and closed the tray against the seat in front of him. Before opening the curtain to follow McCann into the very empty coach section, the same attendant appeared from behind and gently nudged his elbow.

"Excuse me. Your friend may sit with you here if he likes for as long as you need him. We've such a light load of passengers, he can remain here 'til we land if necessary." She looked like a midget next to two Goliaths as she held Ian's entree steaming from a small, plastic tray.

"Thank you," McCann said and flashed a quick full smile, the first one Ian had seen. Maybe he wasn't some pernicious dropout from the American version of the Old Lags' Brigade or a prison sod. Maybe he could be trusted beyond the mere pursuit of the pot of gold sitting at the end of the rainbow arching to London from Munich. Maybe he could ask him why they didn't take a direct flight to London. Why was a flight from Munich safer?

McCann reappeared with his attaché case containing money and the documents. He had carried on his suitcase and stored it in the front of the plane, near the entry door where passengers usually hang garment bags.

"While you were parking the Jeep in long-term, I deposited a sum of money in a Montreal banking machine there in the airport. I'll be doing something a little different in Munich with the marks and euros. It'll leave us with American dollars and English pounds in the amount of about four thousand dollars total." McCann was leaning across the aisle as Ian listened intently. "No problems with customs. I'll give you about three hundred pounds and two hundred euros, just in case you need them for whatever reason. Once we pass through customs in England, I want you to return the remainder of what you don't spend."

Ian grunted. Now was the time to ask. "Why are we going to Munich first? It seems like a bloody circumbendibus. We could have flown directly to London from Montreal."

McCann locked his jaw firmly and the muscles in his cheeks twitched. "It's part of the plan," he pronounced through gritted teeth. "I pick up almost all tickets there. You'll have ample time to study the documents—with some privacy. I believe we'll have no problems on this plane. I'm not too concerned with Munich, but I'll be very concerned with England. The Germans are more alert to terrorists than any such small potatoes as us. If either of us has problems through customs, the other needs to create a diversion of some sort. The diversion may be as simple as interrupting the customs official and explaining that you dropped your passport in the hallway, or some such nonsense, even though it's hidden in your jacket. Hopefully it'll break their concentration and you can try some kind of good humor or sleight of hand. Otherwise, we have a doomed mission at that point."

Ian was baffled at the man's tendency to delight in esoteric details, most of which would insult even the average person's intelligence. Why was he so pretentiously secretive? He had to be in some sort of a bad way.

Ian sliced the steaming chicken and nibbled on the asparagus.

"As to my identity, I'm picking up a new passport in Munich in the name of Albert M. Shellabarger. We'll act as though we have just met, in case anyone sits nearby. I'll try to give you a chance to accomplish your task since Richtol has signed you into this project, in effect."

Ian contemplated protesting such an implication, but decided to hold his tongue.

"I'm not sure how to handle your situation," McCann continued, "since you have no other credentials. I may decide to keep the entire batch of documents in light of that fact. Once we're near the drop-off point I want you to do precisely as I say. You simply must do so. All I'll have is a vague, partial address and I'm not to know it myself until we're there. I've been assured that it's a safe place and we'll not be watched. The only problems we may have are through customs in England when we land."

"Above all, I want the story. I shall cooperate fully as promised. Not to worry."

"Mr. Scarborough, you'll have your story by Friday morning." He yawned deeply. "Now it's my turn to sleep. If the flight attendant says anything about my stretching out here," he raised the arms across the middle set of seats, "then tell her I'm on medication for heart problems and I'm not to be disturbed unless it's an emergency, or unless someone chooses to make off with my attaché case up here in the overhead compartment." He placed the case in the compartment and removed a blanket and three small, white pillows. He stretched out and spread the blanket over his long body, setting the three pillows near the armrest on the aisle seat. "If you decide to sleep, awaken me and I'll keep guard." He kicked his shoes off, letting them fall to the floor under the seats.

As Ian finished his entree, the attendant brought him the spinach salad and more tea.

"He must be your older brother," she giggled.

"He's not, although we have been accused of it," Ian laughed lightly. "He's a friend. He's going to remain there for I must awaken him for his medication in about three hours. He's a heart patient, you see."

"That's no problem. I'll tell them in the back that he's moved up here for the duration. If you want to sleep, I'll be happy to awaken him at the proper time," she offered.

"No. I'll be working the entire time until then. Thanks."

He returned to the pages of manuscripts for the rest of the flight to Munich through the short, calm night, flying east over the top of the world and high above his manicured homeland of England. Had he fallen in with the wrong lot? Had he betrayed some ancient secret known and protected by the royalty of his England? Were these misguided Americans involving him in a plot that would only cause him to get boobed in some indeterminate sentence and embarrass his father MP? Or separate him from his newfound fascination, Veronica Colton? Or was the truth paramount?

It wasn't necessary to dwell long on such questions. Now it was his duty merely to follow the scenario as dictated by this strange snoozing man. His conclusion was to accept his judgment to achieve his own noble ends—the fulfilling liberation of the good name, the real name of de Vere, behind the empty facade of the man from Stratford.

Chapter Twenty-Six

"Gentlemen," said the Scotland Yard inspector, who sported a black moustache and a gap between his two large front teeth which made his S's whistle, "the FBI has not been able to contact Mr. Ian Scarborough, nor has the British Embassy in Washington, except for a brief initial chat. Therefore, we unfortunately can't determine how effective he has been in his mission if in fact he's taken it upon himself, that is, to recover the missing artifacts." He paused to let the Minister for the Arts and the Lord Mayor of Stratford-Upon-Avon absorb his comments.

"Meanwhile, Mr. Vines has not published a story on the incident so we can only assume, tentatively of course, that Scarborough has no story to report or he would certainly have done so by now. As of this afternoon, about an hour ago, we have heard nothing from the FBI man since he is snowed up at the inn. Their telephones, including cell phones, are out of commission because of severe weather. They're equipped with a shortwave too old, apparently, to work sufficiently for any long-term communication."

The Minister for the Arts shifted in his chair to speak. "It appears as though we've reached some type of impasse in acquiring new information from the FBI, the British Embassy in DC, and Scarbrow," he couldn't pronounce the name properly, "or whomever the culprit may be. So then, what's the purpose of our meeting?"

The Scotland Yard inspector twitched his black moustache. He was a man who ridiculously prided himself in evincing command of vast detail when, typically, he rarely bothered with too many facts. This middle-level bureaucrat ("bumble" as they are referred to in England) wrapped his psyche in blinders and habitually reinforced his prejudices and notions by surface information shaped to fit his own theories, regardless of the outcome once across the finish line. The inspector could fashion any fiction to fit his theory. The current instance would be no exception, since it was relatively minor in his estimation next to terrorism defense.

"Scarborough's father is an MP from Devon and they're loyal Tories and patriots according to our sources," he whistled. "The young man will preserve those artifacts for Queen and country... so we believe. If he finds them, he'll discover a way to report to us in due course. As I reported, the telephones are out at the inn. This matter is of negligible importance unless the artifacts are worth something more than their intrinsic sentimental value."

The mayor of Stratford-Upon-Avon became furious over the latter remark, accidentally spitting a small bubble from his mouth as he began his reply. He slapped an open hand on the table in front of him, shaking the glasses and pitchers of water.

"Some sort of valuable artifacts were stolen from the church where William Shakespeare is buried—his monument, no less—and you are implying they have a *sentimental* value? Whatever they are, whether trinkets or documents relating to the most popular playwright in the world, they are priceless. The market value, from one billionaire to another, is indubitably inestimable!" He arose in anger. "Bullocks! Do something!"

The inspector virtually giggled and feigned a soft cough in disguise. As a further embellishment, he removed his handkerchief from his inside suit pocket and trumpeted his nose, somewhat convincingly, although the other two men weren't fooled in the least by such amateurish histrionics. Mr. Scotland Yard had never been in a position of having to confer with a local official. "What could the artifacts possibly be indicating if they've been secreted in a monument for all these centuries? It's as if you're fearful that Willie wasn't the man."

The Minister for the Arts, red-faced at the facile response, leaned forward to impart a serious demeanor. "I asked just such a question regarding the authorship of my able research assistant in my capacity as the chairman of the Royal Commission on Historical Manuscripts. She prepared a letter for me concerning the lacunae in the area of Shakespeare. I mailed the letter to Her Majesty's Office in the Royal Library at Windsor and they informed me that, indeed, there was no such evidence of further documentation on William Shakespeare. There is such a gap of biographical material on the man that there is a scholarly debate, albeit limited to the esoteric few, Scarbrow's friends and Baconian cranks. However, bear in mind: this doesn't mean that the monument, which was revamped in 1748, wouldn't still contain some manner of manuscript, undisturbed by the workmen at the time who may have reverently replaced it in its original position. They may not have noticed or even disturbed it since it was above the bust in the monument. Their work would have likely not been above the bust. I must tell you that I have reason to believe, because of its mere existence in that location, that it is no small beer. It's somewhat likely that it is the body of a portion of the original works, or personal effects, or some order of direct nexus to Shakespeare. Mr. Scarbrow, loyal Tory or not, would contemplate, as any reasonable man shall do when tempted, joining the miscreants who desire to sell the documents to a Saudi sheik. Or, not proving the case for his man, simply destroy them. *It is* a devilishly serious matter, I assure you."

The Scotland Yard inspector was now shifting in his chair. "I must come to the horses with you, gentlemen. The only clue we have is that whoever nicked the documents, trinkets, or whatever you desire to call them, was American or Australian and wore a deerstalker cap as Mr. Sherlock Holmes wore faithfully, and was going to a Holmesian affair in New Paltz, New York. He was assisted by a few men with British accents in this country, if we assume the men who perpetrated the crime in Hatfield are the same as those in Stratford. This is the extent..." His sibilance was interrupted as the door to the room opened and a young man slid a small black tray across the table under Mr. Yard's twitching face. On it was a folded envelope, which he swiped up, stopping in mid sentence to thank the man before continuing, "...of our knowledge as of..."

He opened the envelope, paused again, and read silently, then looked up.

"Gentlemen, this message relates that the FBI has failed in its mission, thus far, to establish a further connection with Mr. Scarborough as of two o'clock GMT, and in fact Scarborough has left the vicinity of the inn, apparently with the FBI's rental vehicle, as of some time yesterday morning or afternoon New York time. We're back to the off, I'm afraid." The news reported with his vocal susurrus was the final straw.

"It's imperative that I report this to the Prime Minister's office as I have been directed," the Minister for the Arts stated. "We must find Scarbrow."

"Gentlemen, I assure you that we're doing the utmost in this grave matter, and I shall establish a routine of ringing up both of you each morning to deliver updates." The inspector's grey pallor never changed in spite of the embarrassing moment—after all, it was the American FBI who had failed in the mission. "We're continuing the investigation in spite of this setback for the FBI."

"You'd better consider placing the matter on a higher priority," the Lord Mayor warned.

"Oh, we shall, we most certainly shall," the inspector whistled in a supercilious tone. "Now that the FBI has failed at our embassy's request, we'll alert our entire network."

Chapter Twenty-Seven

The late-model, white Mercedes taxi pulled up to the curb in front of the Hauptbanhof, the newly remodeled central train station in Munich. Two tall gentlemen, one an American with a gaunt, pale face, and one Brit with an expressive pair of blue eyes and a blond Beatle haircut, stepped out from the back of the car. Each carried an attaché, and the driver lifted two medium suitcases from the trunk as the American handed him the fare and tip. Fresh snow blanketed the ground, and the streets and sidewalks glistened with patches of melting ice on a bright, sunny, immaculately cloudless Bavarian day. The air was fresh, clear, and invigorating between wafts of diesel.

The giant, silver-steel clock, stark and spare, read nearly half past nine CET. Yawning mightily, Ian felt his sinuous back pop. How he longed for a rest at any hotel for one night, since he'd not slept well, and particularly now, burdened as he was with a double-dose of jet lag. But first, an important mission needed to be completed, he thought, as he sucked in pure, chilled air.

"So a train it is," barked Ian testily. "I adore them, but I wish you'd told me. I would've slept more on the plane since I should have ample time for research."

The trip through customs in the new Franz Josef Straus Airport had been routine. No unusual questions were asked. McCann seemed relaxed then, particularly since he knew the suitcase had no clues inside. Their only vital concern was with the contents of their attachés, which apparently weren't a source of scrutiny by the customs officials. Ian had been nervous, mostly from fatigue, but his luggage was the second one down the chute, calming him immensely.

"You will surely have plenty of time," McCann said. "Now we'll check which gate to board, but I do have to attend to one small matter first—I must find the men's room."

Ian noticed McCann's stride quicken as they moved through the remodeled airport, past the huge television showing a downhill ski competition. McCann moved as though nature was demanding urgent attention. Ian didn't suspect more than this motive, but he did want to keep up with his traveling companion at every juncture, so he followed him to within sight of the men's room and waited outside. McCann was familiar with the surroundings of the Munich Hauptbahnhof, demonstrated by his directed gait towards the precise location proclaiming "Herren."

Ian remained nearly one hundred feet away from McCann across the large center section of the building with the schedule boards. A stout, old Bavarian rail station worker in a blue work suit pushing a luggage cart nearly scraped Ian's leg as he set the attaché filled with the boxes of documents on top of his own luggage and softly propped his knee against the attaché so he would maintain contact with it. The open station was cold in spite of the warm feeling of bustling traffic going to the platforms and up the spiral stairway nearby. There were cozy shops, and a yellow post box at the top of the stairs in the center of the station.

Ian counted about a dozen train tracks leading into the station, and gazed at the large clock denoting the time of 9:40 a.m. He yawned and thought about Searls at the Mohawk Inn. Had he found his way out of the "infirmary"? Had the escape car been discovered in Montreal? Had the old buffer, Richtol, usurped the FBI's efforts as Ian had assumed? What would Laura and Forsythe think of his leaving early and not checking out? Fortunately, they had worn gloves in the FBI Jeep, but he did worry about some inadvertent telltale clue.

Ian turned around after another hasty yawn and caught sight of McCann running up the spiral stairway with his black attaché under his arm. He was in a mad dash as he jumped up the steps three at a time. Ian picked up his own suitcase with his left hand and held on to the attaché of boxed manuscripts in his right while clumsily sliding McCann's suitcase towards the stairway. At the very least, he had to keep McCann in sight and, if need be, chase him in case of some escape. Ian didn't want this mysterious, secretive man to abandon the only Englishman who could report this earth-shattering discovery to a receptive world. This wasn't a matter for Americans to report alone. Ian Scarborough had earned the right to represent England. After all, it was indeed a purely English scandal involving highest of royalty—from Elizabeth I to, maybe, Elizabeth II.

Ian shouted at him in the hope that an English voice would penetrate the patina of Bavarian patois. Then he saw him embrace a young woman with red hair and a striking doll face, chiseled as if from a pale balsa. She was holding a bundle that looked like a baby. Ian observed the firm, macabre countenance of Mike McCann lighten and relax into a beaming smile, like a husband arriving home from the office after a grueling day. He was awed by the transformation into a gentle, refreshed appearance—so much so that Ian found that his arm rose, preparing to wave and speak, then felt abominably foolish at his silly gaffe and dropped his arm. It was what one did in Italy or France, not Bavaria. He saw McCann chat hastily with the woman, kiss the baby inside the bundle of blankets in her arms, and then hand her the entire attaché case.

She gave him a smaller attaché case, which he set on a glass counter normally used for sealing and stamping envelopes. He slid a thick file folder from beneath the front of his jacket and placed it in the smaller attaché. He removed his box of manuscripts, smaller than Ian's collection, and moved it right into the new attaché. Then she gave him a small, white, plastic wrapper that he slid with one slick motion into his overcoat pocket. Ian watched his mouth form the simple word "Danke." They conversed a few more seconds, probably in German, and he kissed her again before bounding down the stairway two steps at a time. The woman carried the baby back into the recesses of the upper floor of the train station and disappeared.

"You may now refer to me as Herr Shellabarger," McCann said and smiled, tapping his coat pocket. "Don't worry. All documents are accounted for inside this case. They'll be interspersed with copies of old letters written in German. I'm now a Bavarian English professor headed for a lecture in Cambridge and," he produced two tickets in his free left hand, "here are tickets north to the English Channel, already bought and paid for."

"I see," Ian said, puzzled at the vision of a morbid, serious man transformed to openly embrace his lover. "You've, um, excellent contacts in Munich."

"All part of the plan, my friend." McCann continued to smile engagingly. "We didn't want her to have to go to Frankfurt. I look forward to the last leg of our little journey. We'll board in about five minutes on Platform 10."

As the two men made their way to the gate, Ian said, "When will I ever have the opportunity to ring up England? I'm also in dire need of that camera you promised."

"I need to phone Richtol," McCann said, "but our only chance will be if the train has a phone. We'll be on an InterCity train. I'll give you a camera, which has a close-up attachment, when you're to use it."

"And when might that be?"

Ian, fatigued, was becoming impatient with the mind games. He knew he needed to look no further than the signs on the side of the first-class car they were entering. The final location listed was "Hoek von Holland."

"The Hook of Holland," he fairly whined. "We'll not be arriving in time for the hovercraft to Dover. You're not going to tell me we're going by ferry, are you?"

"That should give you ample time to sleep and finish your research," McCann said. They climbed into the brightly lit first-class car and Ian took a seat after setting his luggage in the overhead. "It's best that you know as little as possible, but I've decided to tell you this much—we'll have a private berth on the ferry. You'll then have the whole night to photo documents, if necessary. I want you to get as much of this story ready by Thursday evening as possible. You, my friend, are allowing our project to go so much smoother than anticipated."

"What do you mean?" Ian glowered as McCann placed the suitcases in the overhead.

"You *are* a reporter, aren't you?"

"Right. Of course."

McCann returned to his seat, staring blankly at the passing countryside. He sat for a few minutes pensively, and then abruptly got up. "I'm going to check the train out, particularly for a phone."

Ian removed the top box from his attaché and began perusing the entire top page. The verse was totally unfamiliar to him. Furthermore, he was having a problem reading the legible, highly elegant handwriting because the paper on this page had faded much more than the others. Some words had disappeared altogether:

S___ the stem and breath __ and close thine eyes
___ lift the small corolla. Gently ____ aside.
Blue Iris wide embrace the spinning stem cap.
Cast aside as carefree and gyrate low

to hug the earth then transform downward on she goes,
And further still to see the cold face gleaming.

And one day to tenderly recall, far away,
sewed as casual current of thought, rose to stay,
renders s_______ bonding encounters fresh meaning
through mere retrospect of a blossom during spring.

Ian shook his head. He couldn't recall a poem like this one, obviously an incomplete verse. Because of his recent rereading of them, he remembered all the poems from his studies. This was not one of the published ones. Was he looking at something never revealed? His heart pounded as his trembling hand almost dropped the page. Was this the work of the young Edward de Vere?

A stately young woman with long black hair entered the first-class compartment as the train pulled out. Ian barely noticed her as she asked, "Entschuldigung bitte, ist ein platz frei?"

Ian did not respond immediately. He rarely noticed surroundings when he was composing, much less in this most unique instance, *reading* what he strongly believed to be early poetry of the true author of the work ascribed all these centuries to Shakespeare, the genius without a past. Here was the solution in his shaking, excited hands. No distraction as inviting as a beautiful fräulein could take him from this gem. He finally nodded and abstractedly noticed her sit down in the far corner, and then lay her dark coat, likely mink, gracefully across her lap.

His body shook in excitement, and his face lunged closer to the page like a pensioner needing glasses. Now the significance of finding the documents took on a meaning more profound than their mere sentimental and commercial value. Even larger than the works being attributed to the Seventeenth Earl of Oxford was that there was more of it—even if it only consisted of this more than likely incomplete verse about flowers and a "cold face gleaming." That "cold face" had to be in a grave—yes, the writer smells the corollas, closes his eyes. What's this about a blue iris, another flower—blue, no less—embracing another flower? The other flower hits the earth and then transforms. It must be decaying, yes—and penetrates the earth to the grave. The next set of lines is much clearer. Later the poet recalls, in another location, that moment when he stood over the grave and dropped the flower. Why "rose to stay"? It must be a double meaning. Right. The verb "rose" referred to the *rising* thought, and the flower dropped into, or on, the grave was a "rose to stay"—a naked allusion to revival each spring.

He looked up at the young German girl, who by now had removed a black sweater to reveal a lovely torso in a blue blouse. He pictured her as an opera singer. Her dramatic white face contrasted with her long, black hair and prominent eyebrows. She crossed slender legs encased in black boots. She was out of breath and probably grateful to have found a roomy compartment in which to relax. She looked at Ian and smiled softly as he looked into two of the largest blue eyes he had ever seen. Now he openly stared at her eyes—dark-blue, natural fathoms of cold invitation.

"That's it. `Blue iris' is a reference to the eyes with the jeu de mot on iris, the flower—just like rose, probably, a double-meaning." Ian blurted this out just as McCann slid the compartment door open and beheld the new passenger with a look of consternation on his face—like an adult catching two children in an act of abandon and devilry.

She blinked several times in bewilderment before pronouncing in flawless English to Ian, "Did I interrupt anything?"

"Not at all." Ian laughed madly. "I was thinking aloud."

"Entschuldigung sie," McCann said with a slight bow of his head. "Mein Freund ist krank mit fieber."

"Fieber?" she replied, looking with disdain at the lanky Englishman before her, laughing under his breath, hands shaking in the purest, uncontrollable delight over his startling discovery.

McCann nodded and she rose to collect her coat and purse. He slid the door open and she dashed out indignantly.

"What did you tell her?" Ian's nose snorted to halt the laughter.

"I told her you had a terrible fever. I wanted her out of our compartment while you work."

"What kind of bloody confidence trick was that? She was perfectly harmless. She actually helped me understand this poem."

"You know how important it is to keep this quiet." McCann's serious demeanor was enhanced by plastic glasses and a colour change to his eyes, evidently with blue contact lenses, his eyelashes still wet from putting them in. His hair was also a darker shade of brown.

"You're a master of disguise," Ian said. "Quite adept."

"Fits the passport."

"Will it be necessary for me to disguise my identity?"

"That's why I've got to phone Richtol, so I can get a handle on whether we're being followed or not. I'll try further up in first class. There are phones there." McCann sat in a seat across from Ian and propped his long feet carelessly on the box of documents. "Keep working."

From his overcoat next to him, Ian removed the note pad he'd been using on the airplane and began copying the poem. If there was this new work, incomplete and "out of iambs" as it was when written, surely there would be more. He desperately needed the camera. The Polaroid would be perfect for viewing the pictures instantly. It had worked well for Wainwright. The question McCann hadn't answered was when he would be able to begin photographing. Probably not until the night ferry.

As he completed his meticulous copying, his mind played the tune he'd been working on for the last few days while lying in the clinic in Stratford, while riding up the lift to visit Veronica, and, for a long time, while traveling in the limousine to the inn. It was flavored Dowlandesque. The tune fell in an alternating minor to major key like so much of John Dowland's Elizabethan lute music, and like so many of his compositions, he'd worked on this one in patches. Now he noticed the convenience of the incomplete verse before him—it had a haphazard beat with some lines having six feet. To make it fit all he needed to do was supply fresh words for the illegible ones. He hummed the tune, a melody which for these several days had been like a leaky faucet in his mind, and indeed noticed the fit even without knowing what two of the words were. "S____ the stem and breath __ and close thine eyes to lift the small corolla. Gently ____ aside." Hmmm, he thought, I'll have to embellish Lord Edward's piece thanks to the illegibility of the decaying sheet.

It was nearly 11:45 a.m. He had to finish the papers so he could return to the exquisite composition. How incredible it was that he was motivated by this wave of creativity as much as his discovery of de Vere's newest work. In spite of his drowsiness, he felt alive and fresh, as if the world was about to be his again.

Inspired, Ian grabbed the box from under McCann's feet and slid it his way. The next document had composition on both sides. It had to be a play, he surmised, from the format of the names with the attending lines. Like many other documents he'd read during the flight, the passage was a familiar one. Bottom's desire to roar the lion in *A Midsummer Night's Dream*:

> Quince: You, Pyramus' fathere; myself, Thisbe's fathere; Snug, the joiner, you the lion's part; and I hope here is a play fitted.
>
> Snug:Have you the lion's part written? Pray you, if it be, give it me;

for I am slow of study.

Quince: You may do it extempore; for it is nothing but roaring.

Bottom: Let me play the lion too. I will roar that I wille do any mans heart good to hear me. I will roare that I will make the Duke say `Let him roar again; let him roar again!'

Quince: An you should do it too terribly you would fright the Duchess and the ladies that they would shriek; and that were enough to hang us all.

All: That would hang us, every mother's son.

Bottom: I grant you, friends, if you should fright the ladies out of their wits they would have no more discretion but to hang us. But I will aggravate my voice so that I will roar you as gently as any sucking dove. I will roar you an 'twere any nightingale.

Quince: You can play no part but Pyramus; for Pyramus is a sweet-faced fellow; a propere man as one shall see in a summer's day; a most lovely, gentlemanlike man. Therefore you must play Pyramus.

Bottom: Well, I will undertake it. What beard were I best to play it in?

Quince: Why, what you will.

Bottom: I will discharge it in either your straw-colour beard, your orange-tawny beard, your purple-in-grain beard, or your French-crown-colour beard, your perfect yellow.

Quince: Some of your French crowns have no hair at all; an

The text ended.

Ian giggled like a child. Before him a passage, one of his favorites, from the first play he'd ever seen as a boy with his mother. McCann looked at him with annoyance, his eyelids blinking rapidly over contrived, glassy eyes. "I hope you're having a damn good time," McCann said.

"I'm finding excerpts from most all the plays. I discovered a few of the so-called `fatherly' sonnets and a new poem never read before, I suspect, because he never completed it. This is marvelous. If only I had time to copy it entirely...properly," he sighed, "and photograph them."

"As I said, if you're rested up, you should have enough time for all you need to do. Now I'll mention one thing I've put off telling you. Have you come across document number sixteen yet?"

"No, I can't say that I have." Ian leaned forward intently. "There are no numbers."

"Richtol used a pencil and placed it in the upper right corner. Under our plan," McCann said, drawing a deep breath and puffing it towards his companion's now serious face, "you're to withdraw number sixteen and keep it after we made our drop-off."

"What's special about document number sixteen?"

"Only Richtol knows, and soon, you'll know."

"What am I to do with it?"

"Retain it for safekeeping, of course, just like Richtol kept one."

"Of course. The scientists and scholars will need to analyze it to the core, date it, test it, examine it. We have to keep one as insurance—in case the world doesn't accept the photos." The legal implications had quickly crossed his mind, but he knew ti was best to follow the scheme. He had no choice for the moment, he thought.

"Richtol's left no detail unattended in this quest, believe me. He gave me those instructions to give you during this little, leisurely train ride. He mentioned it quickly on the phone when I called his room from your room."

"Clever. Quite clever."

"Also, the authorities are directing the search overseas on the assumption it was an American behind this. I'm convinced they wouldn't expect anyone to re-enter England with the stolen contraband, and especially on a ferry across the channel. If they were to suspect a mode of transportation, they would look to a quicker mode," McCann raised his palms, "when, in fact, to analyze the material properly a slow boat is most advantageous."

"Suppose someone in Scotland Yard is thinking the same way and has alerted Interpol and anyone else, domestically and overseas?"

"I've worked on taking care of that as well, my friend. While you were otherwise occupied in Montreal I made a most important phone call, which I hope we'll see the results of once we're near the Hook of Holland."

"How so?"

"I'd prefer to show you, not tell you, since it may not be achievable. You have..."

"Tickets." The German conductor dressed in dark blue slid the door open, speaking in English. "Tickets, please." Obviously, he'd heard them speaking. Ian quickly covered the document he was currently examining by moving a portion of his coat carefully over it as though looking for his tickets. The two men leaned forward over the folded table and pulled tickets from their shirt pockets, handing them forward. The conductor punched them.

"What time will we arrive in Hoek van Holland?" McCann inquired with a German accent.

"Koln is about an hour away, so Hoek van Holland—we should arrive at about 8:15."

"Where are we now?"

"Approaching Mannheim. We have a nine minute wait in Koln."

"Danke," said McCann. The conductor slid the door shut and the compartment warmed after cold air had infiltrated the room from the hallway. McCann turned the lever for warm air.

"You should have no problems. I'll return to my studies," Ian said. He began to feel immersed in work the way he'd felt while composing or studying in school or writing a review.

The next page he picked was covered with a clear, legible hand, a poem he did not recall ever seeing before—an unusual stanzaic form for the works of Shakespeare, as the world may refer to him for only a few hours more. His heart raced as he read such an uncharacteristic poem:

Before the Journey

This orb shall lose a countenance so pure,
by love, thy strength transfers to us a cure
for grief and sorrow—we replace with joy.
Thy new life gained, eternal—ne'r destroyed.
My tears for now like rain to rivers flow
astride swells, swirls to fathoms deep below
wher warmthe entraps from rays of sun above
to rise skyward immersed in fusing love.
A simpler, briefer broken-spirit clan
mourning, knows greed can not exceede Godd's plan.
You own such love, no hint of avarice,
a heart so grand, a tongue of sage advice,
a balm for wounds, warm pillows for a cheek,
praise for the strengths, encouragement when weak.
You'll be there still in whispers through the wind.
We'll know, we'll hear 'till soon we meet again.

That day's encore when all new life begins,
entwined hearts on the bridge where this life ends.
Such rich reunions, travel, walks and talks,
unveiled mysteries and clues no more to stalk.
Rewards distilled from precious qualities,
kisses full, gracious generosities.
While brewing storms may pound this aging face,
your love resounds inside my heart's deep bass;
a heart of love borne from a soul so great
through veins which pulse the wondrous gift of faith.

E. of O.

"There. There it is!" Ian jumped from his seat. While there was hovering stress, the rhyme pattern not wholly consistent, a sixteen-line (not fourteen-line) sonnet followed by the ten-line stanza all in couplets. It was still superb. His cursory critique halted upon seeing the simple signature "E. of O." It was all he needed. "A signature!" he yelled, incredulous. "He signed it."

"Let's see," McCann stood to examine it. "What's the poem about?"

"It's a spiritual poem, probably dedicated to his mother. The problem being that he wasn't too keen on his mother marrying within days of his father's death—a la Hamlet." Ian scratched his head. "His mother died when he was nineteen, though. Possibly, upon her death, he made her into more of a saint than she actually was."

"Or it was a lover, maybe."

"No. That's not correct, because he refers to her dying soon. It must have been his mother on her deathbed, and he wrote this about her to cheer her up, cheer up the immediate family, or cheer himself up. Or he simply forgot about her transgressions and wrote of her nobler qualities. Or," he sifted some air between his lips for emphasis as he spoke rapidly, "she was about to die and recovered. That's probably it. It appears to be a poem he wrote in his early years—before he helped his uncle, Arthur Golding, translate Ovid."

"Incredible, isn't it?" McCann leaned forward and tilted his head in a gaze of curiosity.

"Right." Ian slowed his cadence and sat. "This is a brilliant discovery." He began copying the document, so excited he began bending his left leg back and forth like a four-year-old boy anxiously in line to see St. Nick.

McCann recovered from his own rare display of reverie. "While you're absorbed in your work, I'm going to the dining car. Want anything?"

Ian didn't answer. He flipped the sheet over to reveal the simple dedication printed in the young Earl of Oxford's graceful hand: "To Regina If Ever The Plague Consumes Her Noblest Of Worldly Spiritts." His heart fluttered and tears of adulation filled his blue sparkling eyes.

So, Edward de Vere expressed a platonic, reverential love for the Queen of England. She was his surrogate mother figure—at least so it might appear. Did it ever become more than that, as some have hinted? Maybe the answer was within this body of old, fragile documents. The idiosyncratic, primary epic poem he'd just read made him more curious. Was this the early Edward de Vere? It had to be. With an immense flourish of energy, adrenalin flowing, he began to copy the page when he noticed a very light, virtually imperceptible, dot over each beat in the meter. Maybe, he thought, this was an early version of a later primary epic. Since a primary epic was defined as an epic poem dedicated to nobility, the Queen in this case, it's entirely possible he updated it from time to time in order to remain in the Queen's good graces, or simply to have it ready to dedicate to her for the entire kingdom to read and cherish her with. He was mystified by this oddity. These discoveries raised more questions, and emphasized the vital importance of scholarly pursuit of the early elusive works of de Vere. Shakespeare scholars would have their hands and eyes full if only they could ever defer to de Vere. Removed of prejudice, they would be delirious over such meaningful tasks ahead. Once having seen the other side of the mountain of research, they would gain a whole new perspective to receive a fresh breath of academic respect, not disdain, at their collective folly over the nonwriter Shakspeare. Their cottage industry would be a mansion.

As he finished writing, he decided to lay this poem aside for further analysis, in spite of his earlier promising himself he would do no such thing for the sake of security measures. His artistic intuition prevailed. There was something deeper behind the making of this verse than he had yet determined. Where were any new sonnets? Why were the verses somewhat primitive? Were they all young Edward de Vere? Were there more documents elsewhere in England?

Ian looked up from his work to notice the train slowing. They were entering Mannheim in late afternoon. Would they have trouble re-entering customs once in England? Could they pass through the "green" queue without having a spot check? Or should they go through the "red" and declare, say, two bottles of brandy or two cartons of fags? They had had no problems in Frankfurt whatsoever. The authorities probably couldn't care less about an English-speaking bloke with no terrorist intent. He yawned as he saw the white signs in black letters proclaiming "Mannheim." Were authorities on full alert for a particular re-entry into the country with purloined artifacts?

His back ached from crouching over the small foldout table in front of his seat. He folded it up and stretched his slim, spindly legs towards the seat across from him. A dark outline of a face formed on his closed eyelids. He envisioned a wide mouth, a hint of an underbite, little make-up, brown eyes, a dark elegant nose, long dark hair, high cheek bones, slender figure, small breasts, compact forehead, and smooth, creamy legs that climbed and climbed becoming part of the buttocks. The clacking of the tracks were hypnotic ticks of time reminding him he'd known her less than a week, yet he could see her features vividly. Upon his return, it would be so necessary for him to tell her he'd missed her dearly for these last four or five days. He saw her in a dark blue form against the full blackness of his eyelid backdrop with her open smile, as his head propped on his left arm and he fell into deep sleep.

Chapter Twenty-Eight

Veronica arrived at the hospital room a half hour early to find Aunt Joan sipping a cup of coffee and studiously filing her fingernails.

"He muttered even more through the night. Something about 'pee helps.' How odd it all is. He never, ever uttered such trash before. He woke me several times." She rubbed her eyes. "I only slept about four hours."

"Has one of the doctors been in?" Veronica asked, removing her coat.

"Yes, more good news. His blood pressure has dropped some. Dr. Slade will be in this afternoon."

Veronica smiled and raised her eyebrows. "First, he comes out of the coma for about three hours. Then he asks to see Sinclair. Then he asks to see the tall musician. Can't remember his name, but insists. Then he asks for Richtol, who has worn the phone out. Then he asks for Phelps."

"Then he goes out like a light again. Should we allow him to see anyone?"

Veronica shook her head. "Admiral Sinclair is unavailable. I've tried to reach him. Ian and this Richtol are in the States. Wasn't Richtol one of his old army buddies? And Phelps took me to lunch yesterday and said he would like to have about five minutes with him if he asks. I'm not a fan of his, but he said he would probably ask for him if he awakens. He's a vile reporter."

"I will ask the doctor when he gets here, or you can. I'm inclined not to, but he is so insistent on seeing certain people."

"Phelps said he might come by to see him today."

"Well, only if Tyler insists."

Tyler Colton turned away from the long line of Elizabethan commoners and peasants sprinkled here and there with a dollop of merchant class and minor nobility. He reached for one of his ever-present cigarettes, the recessed filter Parliaments, and staggered to the north transept of Westminster Abbey for a quick smoke. If he was dying, he mused, he might as well enjoy his favorite bad habit—even though it probably helped send him along to his conclusion. He kept wondering why all these perambulations through history? Most of life had been waiting arduously and patiently for something to happen, no matter how much effort he'd made. Cruelly, death was the same frustrating plodding of seconds, if that was what it was to be. He reached into his pocket for some matches and felt a small piece of crumpled paper. A short, spry, dark-haired man with a prominent goatee appeared from behind a large, tabular monument and flicked a lighter for him as he approached.

"Lord Burleigh asked me to keep an eye on you," he said. You've been snooping around quite a bit in our century." The flame from the lighter cast light on a swarthy face with a smile as genuine as could be. "You may smoke here in this corner."

"Sir Francis Walsingham, Burleigh's assistant and chief spy. So I have the distinction of being followed by you personally."

"It's my duty, my job, my life. If the Catholics win, I lose all three—same as Burleigh, Raleigh, Leicester, and all other good Protestants."

"Phillip Sydney, too?"

That, dear fellow," he said, gesturing towards the long line approaching a bier, "is what remains of Sir Phillip Sydney, the most honorable man of the day."

"Oh. That's the funeral procession. What's the date?"

"Fifteenth of February, 1587."

"Yes. I smell incense."

"Thus, no one will detect your cigarette."

"Or the stench of a body dead and decaying for nearly four months. We've got modern politicians adept at such legerdemain as this production," Colton said, pointing to the sinewy line of hundreds.

"Only we are better at it."

"You are, indeed. No adverse press. No oversight. Great freedom to manipulate. Make young Sydney the most heroic war figure ever slain. Deign to inflate his conservative image, his Protestant credential, and further accentuate his bravery on the field in the Low Countries fighting Spain. The fool would still be living had he worn his leg armor after hearing that a fellow officer was quixotically doing without as well. All this hype over Sydney was timed to delay the funeral until the day Elizabeth finally has Mary, Queen of Scots, beheaded—tomorrow!"

"Brilliant, isn't it?"

"Even the pusillanimous press of our day would see through this. If you and Burleigh hadn't convinced the Queen to recall Oxford—God help you if he'd been a hero in Flanders—from his leadership of an army, then the Spanish might have killed him, who you despise, rather than your beloved Sydney."

"We can't control everything," Walsingham said, shrugging and looking away in embarrassment.

"You're lucky enough, though. Thomas Knyvet made Oxford lame in their duel. He almost did the job for you."

"Oxford had no business rodgering Knyvet's sister, Anne Vavasor. He would never have gone to the Tower of London for long confinement had he possessed the good sense not to impregnate her."

"Both events are well documented in the sonnets: 'Speak of my lameness, and I straight will halt.' Or, '(I), decrepit.... made lame by fortunes dearest spite.' The Dark Lady of the sonnets was none other than his mistress, Anne Vavasor."

"Sydney himself almost came to blows with him over the tennis court fiasco.

Oxford did what any nobleman would have done. Sydney had no royal blood. What a breach of etiquette in calling Oxford a puppy. Oxford was rightfully inflamed."

Walsingham looked around desperately as though the marble floor would yield a stolid response. "Well, uh, it all goes back to Sydney's unsuccessful wooing of Anne Cecil. She deserved him, not a wild, wanton weasel like Oxford."

"Burleigh wouldn't approve of Sydney. He would only have Oxford's royal blood in his family, not to mention the lands and money. He knew he could obtain it all by having Oxford marry his daughter."

"Wrong. Oxford asked him to sell properties in order to raise cash for his staggering debts, his spendthrift lifestyle, his thespian endeavors, his travels, his publishing."

"You placed Oxford on the commission for the trial of Mary Tudor. You wanted his unpopularity with Catholics because you knew that was the last remaining support he had, and it was waning. But even the Queen couldn't bring herself around to having Mary executed until your little cabal prevailed. What kind of Christians are you?"

Colton scanned the floor for a discreet spot to drop his cigarette and recognized a crumpled piece of paper that had fallen from his pocket when he'd earlier searched for matches. It was then he recognized the section of Westminster Abbey where they were standing. Oxford's cousins, Francis and Horace (Horatio of *Hamlet*?) de Vere, supreme war heroes both in the Low Countries, were to be buried in 1609 and 1635, respectively. Oxford's son, Henry, the Eighteenth Earl, was to be buried there as well, a victim of war wounds. Beside the large tabular monuments and tombs, there would mysteriously appear a slab of stone floor with the simple phrase, "Stone Coffin Underneath," carved neatly into it for the whole world to forever wonder. It was the only true mystery in the Abbey, except for why the statue of Shakespeare deserved to be placed about one hundred yards and decades away from this spot. There had been no notice of Shakespeare when he died, especially by his fellow writers and playwrights.

He picked up the crumpled paper and read aloud, "Phelps, try tomorrow."

He awoke. In his long battle, Colton's senses had been affected greatly. Besides an annoying hum in his ears, like the drone of a not so distant commercial truck on the highway, his eyesight was blurred and it felt as though his eyes could not focus for more than a second or two on an object—the greater the distance, the more significant the blur. His sense of smell was virtually gone.

Before him now was a smaller, leaner version of Falstaff, but without the Elizabethan attire. The white beard was neatly cropped and the face had a tameness lacking in the cast about gaze of Sir John Falstaff. It appeared to be his friend Admiral Arthur Sinclair, although he looked leaner than he remembered him.

"Tyler," Colton heard the man say in a gruff, whispering voice. "I'm not going to bother you long. I hope you can make it, dear old egg, but whatever happens, I've loved you dearly as a friend and I do sincerely thank you for everything. Thank you for seeing Phelps this morning. I've been out of touch, as have you, but have you heard again from Richtol?"

Colton's eyes widened and he stretched his mouth to whisper, "Yes. Young Ian...British Museum...Montague Street...to his father's flat...today, tomorrow or next day...he...returns...with papers... Richtol called...last time I was awake...he said Ian, not P....helps. Phelps." He puffed forcefully.

"Yes, splendid, old fruit. But why not Phelps?" Phelps as Sinclair couldn't resist asking.

"Wrong...too aggressive...you wanted Ian...so...did I...Richtol agreed...finally...Ian and a...tall American...return tomorrow...tall Mc…Mc...can't recall name...got the papers."

"I know you're tired. In case I can't return soon, thanks for your friendship. I love you. I must go. I shall return soon. Rest well. Cheers."

Phelps dashed into the bathroom, removed the beard and wig he'd rented from Disguise the Limit(ed) in Soho, then stuffed them inside his Barbour jacket and dashed out to see Aunt Joan just returning from the café. He thanked her for giving him a few more minutes again alone with her brother, and reported that he had fallen back asleep, but had been talking haltingly and nonsensically.

Chapter Twenty-Nine

The odious sight of Veronica Colton embracing another man caused him to quiver. This must be a dream, he thought, and if it is—I must wake up...too shocking. The two bodies were huddled together in a prayer stall in Trinity church.

"I failed in my religion, my faith, most of all," the specter of a man moaned while he gripped her right shoulder. "I lived my youth only to please Her Majesty. I couldn't bear her dissatisfaction. But I had no morals, no responsibility. I allowed a desire to please others to take precedence over my judgment. I surrendered my possessions to the throne and Burghley. My life alternated between confusion when serious and dissipation when I was not."

"We may yet salvage the title. The world always will own the works," Veronica said. "You're going to meet someone soon who will change that much for you."

Suddenly rebounding from the vision as if nothing had elicited jealousy, Ian found himself strolling towards the couple with a violin tucked snugly under his chin. He was playing the melody he had been composing, the rueful tune tugging at his sleeve these recent days. He slid the bow deliberately across the strings, and would have sung along if only he could remember the words. The lyrics were from something he'd recently read. The melody sounded too maudlin on violin. Well, after all, it was a song about a flower on a grave, settling through to the casket and corpse. Indeed, maybe it should be mournful. He felt a stir and heard movement.

"We're nearly there," a voice announced from above.

He opened his eyes and recognized the obtuse expression of a man he had seen before. Now acutely awake, and enough to remember, this was McCann's metamorphosis as a German English professor with blue eyes, formerly brown, peering through round plastic-rimmed glasses.

"Where are we?" He stretched his long body and realized his left arm was totally asleep, paralyzed. The arm fell limply from his head like a brick to his lap. He had used it as a pillow. He rubbed it against his leg for circulation. "How long have I been asleep?"

"Friend, we're only some thirty minutes from Hook of Holland and I've been preparing us for our journey on the ferry and beyond. Remember, we'll meet some British immigration officials for the passport check in about a half hour or so. I'll go to the front of the line. You'll go through nearer the end of the line. We should have no problems, it's only a checkpoint."

Ian squinted at the lights of Rotterdam flashing across his window. Groggily, he rubbed his face and felt traces of heavy impressions made from the seat's rough texture. His arm still felt as though it were weighted by a bowling ball. "I've been asleep for three hours?"

"That's about right," `Professor Shellabarger' answered. "We have a few things to do once we get off this train. I talked with Richtol. He's remained free of suspicion. The telephones are working some back in New Paltz, although the snow is still coming down. Wisely, he decided to remain at the inn."

"Is the FBI making a fair treat?" Ian asked.

"We have a problem. They established that you've left the resort in the Jeep, although they don't know where you went."

"*I* left the resort in the Jeep?" Ian shook his head angrily. "*We* nicked the Jeep. How did they miss you in this bloody escapade?"

"Now calm down, man. It seems that Searls was only after you, not me. No one knew I left because I never checked in and didn't meet anyone. You're a member of the press corps. You can get away with it. Richtol did see that you got checked out, but it appears Searls and his buddies are only chasing you in the States. Oh, and they're taking Searls to a hospital. A Professor Vernon and the owner were looking for you, but Richtol checked you out through some inexperienced guy at the front desk. They were short-handed because of the storm."

Ian's mouth dropped open. The British authorities would be looking for him as well. His eyes squinted in confusion as a limp wave of helplessness and weakness spread through his joints. What would become of him if he were caught transporting stolen documents?

"Don't worry." Ian sensed that McCann was enjoying his control over him. "I have a man here who'll solve the problem."

"What...who is this man?" Ian asked as a slumping, old man wearing sunglasses quietly entered the compartment clutching a black Polaroid camera. His unkempt curly, white hair and clothes were in fashion some thirty years ago—a worn black turtleneck and bell-bottom corduroys with a black patch proclaiming "The Spider Murphy Gang."

"This guy," McCann said, "is going to photograph you so we can change your passport to an American one. He's an expert at such matters. He'll only need a photograph and about five minutes or so before we leave the train in order to give you a new passport. You should use it at the checkpoint we're going through before stepping on the ferry, and again when we reach Harwich. Since it is an American passport you must say little, but if you talk, talk like us. Your name will be William B. Todd. This is only a checkpoint coming up, so you'll have no problem. It'll be a rehearsal for Harwich."

Ian chewed his lower lip anxiously. "What if I'm questioned?"

"You're receiving an all new identification. Don't worry."

The old man said something in German or Dutch, brushed Ian's hair back off his forehead, snapped about ten photos, and then left the compartment to go down the hallway—maybe to the wash basin to prepare the doctored papers.

McCann smirked with contentment. "He got on at Dordrecht after I phoned him from Koln. He's tops according to my source."

Why were they only pursuing him? Ian recalled his encounter with the British Embassy. Whatever the result of the conversation on Saturday before the telephones went down, he would now be wanted far and wide since he'd stolen the Jeep and was the only person known to have left the inn. Had Searls been suspicious of the others? Possibly, but the film and evidence had successfully been secreted away to Wainwright's room. One lone FBI man, injured as he was, would hardly be able to efficiently search the entire resort in his condition. Furthermore, film could be hidden virtually anywhere. Doerflinger could carry the film separately down the mountain, obviating any need for the principal players, Richtol and Wainwright, to attract suspicion. Richtol had probably adamantly stuck with his deposition story. Why had Searls been chasing him, a reporter interested solely in reporting? A confused sense of panic struck him. Were these characters setting him up?

"Now, Ian, if you'll change into one of my shirts or sweaters, I believe we'll get the desired effect for the passport picture. Also, comb your hair a little more off your forehead, even more so it'll stay in place. Oh yeah, go shave, too. You'll have a five o'clock shadow in the passport photo, but that'll help."

"What if I am caught?" Ian whispered and shivered at the prospect.

"If you do all I say, you won't be. As I said, you'll need to speak American English. Can you do that?"

"I hope so," Ian said with a flattened accent. "How's this?"

"Better," McCann laughed haughtily. "By the way, your passport will show you born in Rhode Island. They don't pronounce their Rs—much like some of your folks in the eastern half of England. You don't need to say much on this first trip to the ferry. It's the unloading at Harwich that's crucial."

"That's one way to do it. I'll say Harwich like it's spelled instead of Hair-rich." He mimicked McCann's pronunciation, which was the typical one said by most Americans.

McCann opened his suitcase and retrieved a shirt, blue and green plaid with thin yellow stripes zipping throughout, probably his own. "This should fit perfectly since we're about the same size. Try it on. We'll switch luggage except for document sixteen."

"Which I haven't found yet."

"You'll have all the time you need after we board the ferry."

The old man returned, silently handed McCann a large manila envelope, and then immediately turned about face. Expressionless, he slid the train compartment door shut. McCann tore into the envelope, removing a worn, but shiny, green book with gold lettering spelling "PASSPORT" and featuring the ubiquitous American eagle symbol holding arrows and an olive branch. He flipped it open to the photo and nodded approvingly. "They told me he was the best!"

Ian took the passport and stared at his visage against the light brown background of the compartment wall. Noting his stern eyes, cold and glassy, as though annoyed at a bothersome, drunken, persistent beggar, he instantly recalled the nuisance he felt at the time the photo was snapped. It wasn't, to him, a convincing fake passport photo, but the passport itself had a very used feel to it. The back cover was bent and some sticky substance had been spilled over it at least several months back. He flipped to his picture again and read the name typed in black: "Todd, William Brannon." The light blue eagle, replicated from the gold eagle on the front cover, overlay the photo and the printed matter perfectly. The colour photo revealed little of him below the chin but it gave the viewer the impression he was wearing a white sweater, which he had been wearing until changing into the blue shirt. On page four he saw his new name and address in Providence, Rhode Island, and the listing for his closest relative, "Elizabeth Bethea Todd," presumably his wife, at the same address, 1219 Benezet Avenue, Providence, Rhode Island.

An entry from the previous year showed a landing at the Frankfurt airport, an entry into England a week later at Dover, and a US Customs entry a week after that at JFK Airport. There was a fresh entry, three days before, for a landing in Vienna.

"Has this been stolen?"

"I don't think so. They just know what they're doing. Oh, Mr. and Mrs. Todd are usually in Mexico this time of year. You're a music teacher at a high school who has visited an old friend who now teaches in Vienna. The two of you had been to the opera there and you're now going to catch some musicals in London. After all, it is the height of the theatre season."

"Brilliant." Ian took the credit cards and drivers license from McCann, which all looked equally authentic. "Much the mark." He shook his head. "No. It's been nicked."

McCann ignored him as the train came to a halt. He emptied all the paraphernalia from his luggage. "It's almost time, buddy. Let's switch. My luggage looks American. Yours looks European."

"Where are the documents?" Ian's voice skipped excitedly to a nervous falsetto, as he uncannily felt a gradual comfort with McCann's elaborately placed artifices.

"I forgot to tell you," McCann said and patted his shoulder. "They're now all safely encased in our luggage. I loaded them while you were snoozing. Oh yes, I doubled up our deerstalkers so one rests inside the other and I stuffed them in your suitcase."

"That's it," Ian exclaimed. "I nearly forgot to tell you. That's the reason we could be stopped. It was the reason I was stopped at Kennedy. I was wearing my deerstalker. It's the only clue they have, more than likely. We *must* lose them."

"Who stopped you in Kennedy?" McCann's voice sounded tight, clipped.

"Some gent with the Federal Bureau," Ian replied. "He seemed most interested in singling me out, and the only reason was my deerstalker—no...no...I..." Ian was genuinely shocked at the thought, lips trembling, voice terse. "I'm tall and I was arriving from England! They may be very hot on our trail!" Ian dumped his belongings into McCann's baggage.

"Not really according to Richtol." McCann scratched his unfashionable center-parted, professorial-style hair. "We do need to be cautious, though. I'm thoroughly satisfied with my decision to call Mr. Passport Man. How does it feel to be a Yank?" He smiled slyly. "Well, it's time to go. Agreed. We'll leave the hats behind." McCann unzipped the suitcase and retrieved the deerstalkers. "I'll pay the passport artist and then we're on our way."

After McCann gave the old man an envelope of cash, which he counted then went to his section of the train, the two men left the train and stepped onto the platform. McCann crushed the two plaid hats into a ball. Ian regretted the sight of McCann tossing them cavalierly into a wire trash bin attached to the outside wall of the train station. Clearly, it was the last stop before a short trek to the docks and the waterfront where a long walkway went towards the entrance to the ferry. A couple of hundred people of various nationalities, sizes, dress, and purposes made their way steadily up the platform that wound to an area where the foreign exchange kiosk and passport control stands were located. Those who needed carts went to get them before they were all taken. Ian and McCann separated in order to practice for Harwich. McCann queued up first, occasionally glancing back at Ian. Ian thought of them as two giraffes in a line of zebras. How obvious were they to the authorities, Ian wondered. There was only one other fellow as tall—probably a merchant marine of some European origin who had a yellow beard the length and regal magnificence of George Bernard Shaw's. His girth easily exceeded both of them together.

Ian was nervous, although he'd been told that the passport control effort was strictly to make sure everyone had credentials for the long ride through the night across the English Channel. Once they arrived in the port of Harwich, above the Strait of Dover and just north of the peninsula called the Naze, they would meet their true test. Ian flipped his passport open near the respective control areas, Dutch first, British second, and handed them the passport. In both cases they barely glanced at him. The Brit official held the document for only about two seconds. If only this mission were completed, he thought. If only the newspaper was on the street proclaiming the revolutionary news he hoped soon to deliver.

As they hiked up the platform McCann joined him and whispered, "You'll find the Polaroid with close-up attachment and directions in your luggage."

The two men found their cramped berths, but they were far better than the alternative on some ferries, which was to sleep in the lounges or the movie room, or even on the floor. McCann was intent on going to the disco lounge for drinks. Ian stayed behind and worked on the documents through the long night. McCann seemed to require little sleep, never hampered by jet lag, in direct contrast to Ian's battle for enough sleep and his inability to overcome the debilitating confusion of different time zones.

He opened the attaché and removed the old parchment. He gently set the papers down on a small dresser at the foot of the bed. He moved the dresser so he could hover above the papers while seated on the bed. In this position, the overhead lamp lit them. Not a comfortable approach but one he would work with as long as necessary.

The document before him was a bona fide Shakespearean sonnet, with the three quatrains and a couplet rhyming "abab cdcd efef gg." Again, the love theme was expressed as if to a mother lying in her grave:

Dark eve before the day of virgin birth
observed increasing years from time so young
when seeds below sown deep within the earth
inspired the first jonquils from here so sprung.
Thy buds from which arts blossoms have full bloomed,
but one was pick'd to decorate the skies
sunshine yellow envied by jaundiced blue
to paint verdant the grass above thine eyes.
In me thy see'st my withered, tattered leaves,
drooping petals, brittle stem, starved roots creape
to search the soil among the legacies
awakening memories within your sleep.
If my kernels are whisked away by birds
then grant this Will endless bouquets of words.

[Signed] Earl of Oxenford

The signature and elegant hand were unmistakable. Remarkably, this startling sonnet, never published, was an explanation to the incessant speculation concerning the so-called "Will" sonnets. And it confirmed the pseudonym "Will" while accomplishing the play on words for the legal term of the same spelling. It also extended the jeu de mots to the Elizabethan sense of the word "will," meaning "romantic love" or, even a sexual meaning—at least there was room for interpretation on that point. Ian recalled the controversy over the "Will" sonnets and was satisfied now that the woman in the grave was, again, Elizabeth I. She was so definitely the cynosure of all that was the age, particularly the arts and literature. She'd been one of the movers and reasons behind the conspiracy to associate the works of de Vere with "Will" Shakespeare, and here was the Earl, writing after her death in 1603, begging her for a restoration of his good name through the singular means he could express futilely to a deceased Queen—his art, his "endless bouquets of words."

Who or what was this "sunshine yellow envied by jaundiced blue?" Henry Wriothesley, the Earl of Southampton, of course. The "W.H." of so many sonnets, inexplicable when ascribed to the man of Stratford, but so manifestly evident when associated with Oxford, especially in this verse. Southampton had contracted a bad case of jaundice at one stage of his life after serving a prison term for his involvement in the Essex Rebellion. He was the Earl of Oxford's favorite because of their identical education (Burghley's wardship, St. John's College-Cambridge, an MA, followed by a law degree from Gray's Inn, and eventually becoming a patron of poetry and drama). Also, he'd been a colourful and dashing young man like de Vere (who was 23 years older).

As he weighed the poem, Ian detected a hint of sarcasm in the tone, as though the Earl of Southampton was still able to give life and the Queen could only elicit memories that he, Edward, could only extract from the grave. Of course this blatant sarcasm was reserved for the last couplet.

Casting his eyes vacantly in deliberate thought, he recalled the earlier poem—clumsy, unpolished, less directed, not in the strict sonnet form. If it was made for music, as well as for Elizabeth, it definitely was created much earlier in the (true) Bard's career judging by the lack of urgency and levity. It was likely the precursor, in thought and execution, to this superb sonnet, which, in spite of a few awkward rhythms (Ian mused, like the sprung rhythm of Gerard Manley Hopkins), accomplished all the poet set out to do.

Buoyantly, he flipped the parchment over with the intention of placing it in the "read" stack since he'd completed his handwritten copy. There appeared on the back the words, "To His Majesty, James I, upon the death of Her Majesty, Elizabeth." Eyes widening in dumbfounded surprise, his face whitened as his heart skipped a beat and his hands trembled. The handwritten notation was not signed or initialed, but it was indeed in the same hand. Lord Oxford intended this sonnet for James, obviously for the purpose of imploring him to consider giving the works a life, at best under his own rightful name, at worst under the pseudonym "Will Shake-speare." At any rate, he wanted the works to be published, and James ultimately (as Ian recalled from a portion of Dr. Colton's copious research) granted his wish along with restoring much of his land as well as renewing his £1,000 annuity (and likewise, but without solid evidence, here or before, a simultaneous annuity of equal amount for Mr. Shakspere of Stratford).

The historical sophistry was evaporating—at least as to the motive and the struggle to have the manuscripts published. Where were the remaining parts of the manuscripts, since all he'd read were paltry, random samples of the complete works and glimpses of new ones? Was McCann needing to execute yet another break-in? Did he know where to look, as he clearly did when executing this mission?

As if on cue, McCann entered, looking ever so the German English professor. "I'm going up for a bite, do you care to join me?"

"No, thanks. Too enthralled with what I've found," Ian pronounced, practicing his American English. "You won't believe this. Look at the signature and dedication on the back."

McCann nodded, just mildly impressed. "After dinner I'm going back to the disco and have a beer. Come join me if you care to. Your American is improving. Just don't use words like 'enthralled.' Say `amazed' or `shocked.' Keep it simple...more common. We're not so sophisticated, you know."

"Yes, `laid-back' you call it."

"Just a tip. We've got to get ready for `Hair-rich...almost carriage.'"

Ian burst out laughing, feeling better. "Har-witch," he enunciated.

"I'll be back later."

Ian waved and picked up the next available document in the stack. The handwriting on this one was illegible. Had air penetrated the encasement where the documents had lain for over four hundred years? McCann had told him on their long drive to Montreal that the encasement was airtight, bolted down by the best of screws, and held together by some sort of glue that required careful opening. It was also precisely sealed with a thicker parchment as a wrapper.

It was labeled number one, so it must have been riding on top of the other documents—dark yellow, virtually brown. The ink had blended with the brown so only a few words were readable—"sight" "solstice," "within darkness," "thy spare rods were," and "awkward instants (or instances?)." A sonnet form, but nonetheless, illegible. Ian hoped the photos would be adequate. Perhaps some sort of enhancement could ameliorate the legibility for sixteenth century handwriting experts to study. After all, if the authorities don't acknowledge the documents and refuse to hand them over for scholarly study, only the photos would be available.

He looked at his watch, which read 10:00 p.m., as he set the page gently in the stack of read copy. He decided it was absolutely urgent to begin loading the film into the special Polaroid and snapping pictures. Oh dear, he thought, I'm not one of those individuals who can stay awake through the night in the face of jet lag. "I'll probably run out of petrol at about 3:00 a.m.," he muttered. What if McCann would take the photos? No. He had spoken to him about his poor photography during the ride to Gatwick. Besides, if Wainwright and Doerflinger were experts (and he believed they were), then this action would be superfluous. But the shots would be vital for the newspaper. He never dwelt on the suitability of Polaroids for a major London daily. "I'll leave it to the photography department to have a go at it," he blurted in a halting whisper. Reading the instructions, he snapped on the attachment touted to reproduce documents in perfect legibility, and holding the camera ten inches above the subject (as instructed), began photographing the documents he had read.

The process took nearly an hour since he had to wait for the film to develop the required ten or fifteen seconds after each shot. Time was further consumed with sliding in new film cartridges and the necessity to rephotograph those documents that didn't come out well—a tedious effort. Wainwright was a master indeed to have finished the business within an hour. Ian also painstakingly checked off the number on each page, making the task infinitely more boring.

His heart sank when he realized there was no document number sixteen. There were the numbers before and after it, albeit in a random occurrence since no one had bothered to place them in perfect order after photographing them, but there definitely was no document numbered sixteen.

Ian wanted nothing more than to storm out of the quarters and locate the saturnine McCann, but he didn't dare leave the documents behind in the room, even for a minute. Angry surges warmed his body. Why didn't McCann simply level with him instead of engaging in these wily manipulations? Was sixteen being held to ransom?

After he'd completed the work and cooled down emotionally, he fell back on the bed and stretched out, having painfully cramped his back during the final process of rearranging the documents in the proper order. Wistfully, he conjured a lucid memory of Veronica. As soon as this is over, no matter how dreadful her father was, he would insist upon her going with him to his cottage by the sea in Torquay,

Devonshire. If she resisted, he'd suggest a chaperon, maybe Admiral Sinclair. He'd joined Ian, his father, and uncle on so many other occasions he was now a fixture. They'd often gathered this time of year—the weather normally splendid in spite of intermittent storms off the channel.

His back ached more as he tried to curl his legs onto the short bed. It had been a grueling trip, what with his spells of jet lag, nervous tension, an ever so mild but nagging ear throb, and now an ache in the center of his back. Could he accomplish his mission in time to have it ready for the presses?

The door to the berth opened to reveal the reddened face of McCann. He was squiffy.

"What ya doing?"

"I'm taking a brief rest. Just now I completed photographing the entire set of manuscripts. There is no page numbered sixteen," Ian said, forgetting the American accent.

"I can definitely help with that little problem." McCann was most assuredly smashed as evidenced by his lighthearted mood. Ian considered the man's remarkable swings and wondered if he was stable.

"Well, I think it's important that I know." Ian rose up from the bed, unfolding his arms from behind his head. He didn't want to display anger, which might incite him to withhold the document, but he simply needed it and would have it, with firmness, now.

"I've shecreted it away until you finish work on all the documents," McCann slurred as he weaved his head about fluidly.

"That's ludicrous. Please, stop your charades. I've been most cooperative, haven't demanded to know whom else you work for or why you have done certain things. I've trusted you as if you have had this entire matter..." Ian stopped abruptly, realizing that the instructions to withhold document sixteen were all part of the plan—probably suggested by Richtol in his brief phone conversation while they were at the hotel packing their bags for their escape. "Will I have the document in time?" Ian stared at the inebriated man intently.

"Friend." He paused and issued a long, low, deep belch. "I'll get it to you this morning during the train ride. That'll keep you hard at work."

Ian glared at his forced companion, even as he came to realize that McCann wasn't merely following orders, but was also incapable of bending them. Ian would have to comply with each step or he wouldn't receive the reward.

"Very well. I understand. I'll work away the next two hours. But I shall...I *shall* have it."

McCann silently nodded and left, going back to wherever he was drinking, probably in the noisy lounge, while Ian carried on with his copying and reading. He discovered nothing more of significance, no poems or excerpts of plays not previously published, until he reached the last document at about 2:40 a.m.

Through red, squinting eyes, he found what he believed was yet another new sonnet dedicated to the Earl of Southampton, according to an inscription on the back in the hand of Oxford. Fortunately, it was entirely legible, probably occupying a position near the bottom of one of the two boxes during those long silent centuries. Ian reread and copied it through tears of exhaustion and sympathy for the writer.

Thy youth was spent like mine in studious deed
while delving in young man's pleasurous gaits
—unharnessed, jolting, gallant stallion steed
below the open window where she waits.
As age advanc'd you found a new crusade
Within Essex which cross'd the chase of ease.
Processions hiss above the traitor's grave—
"Accessories deserve same fate as these."
When casting wistful glances oe'r my way
recall my hoofs have trod that barren inn

where empty time makes void both night and day
and lonely thought solicits long passed sins.
Inspired then by reflections on my will
prevail upon the turnkey for a quill.

E. of O.

Ian screamed loudly, "Yes. Brilliant." What more proof was there that de Vere adored the Earl of Southampton? After all, it was dedicated to him on the back with the brief inscription, "I have done muche, I shall endeavore to do more."

Southampton was the "fair youth" of the sonnets. The "traitor" was the Earl of Essex—Essex who "crossed," with Southampton as an accessory, in the "Essex Rebellion" his "chase of ease" (the chase of an easy life, of chasing the fair sex, as well as a jeu de mots on the French for chair)—"crossed," or negated—hinting a canceling of his easy life, as well as any possible legitimate chance at the easy chair of the throne. It also meant to "keep," Ian thought.

But, Essex arranged for the Lord Chamberlain's men to enact *Richard the Second*, de Vere's own play of intrigue and insurrection, on the eve of the rebellion, hoping to stir the masses to join in. The play was not performed, however. The next day, Essex and Southampton, accompanied by over 300 swordsmen, marched through London shouting, "For the Queen! A plot is laid for my life!" as they accused Lord Cobham and Sir Walter Raleigh to be the plotters against them.

De Vere served at the trial as the senior nobleman and may have played a central role in arranging for Robert Cecil, the Lord Treasurer, to implore Queen Elizabeth to commute Southampton's sentence to life imprisonment. Essex was executed. James I freed Southampton from the Tower upon his first act as King following Elizabeth's death and his succession. Mysteriously, Southampton was again later imprisoned the day following Oxford's death. Had Southampton had a hand in the placement of the caches of documents? Did he know where they'd been placed by Oxford? Did Southampton do it himself with a few of his trusted comrades? This might never be answered, Ian thought.

While contemplating this sonnet, he soon fell fast asleep in the tiny cramped room, probably as confining as Southampton's cell. Just before his slumber he concluded that the Queen had fully approved the sanctions against publication by the nobility, and yet she had clearly valued the very writings that she prevented from being published. Oxford was at the fulcrum of this entire conflict.

Such irony was more than Ian could handle, except in the private chamber of his dreams. The ferry rocked him to the steady beat of iambs—"Once inspired by reflections on my will, prevail upon the turnkey for a quill."

Chapter Thirty

Ian followed McCann from a distance, carrying their paraphernalia, and looking like all the other mostly weary travelers steadily marching up the platform towards the customs checkpoint at Harwich. The bland, grey walls of officialdom eerily impressed upon Ian the urgent nature of their mission, and the serious consequences of being detected with the documents. He had been rehearsing a question in American English that he would use upon passing through the checkpoint. "Where can I get the train from Harwich to London?" he would ask as he handed the official his passport, pronouncing Harwich and London phonetically. There would be no hint of a short 'u' in the capital city. "Thanks," Ian would curtly reply after hearing the response.

McCann instructed him that if they were stopped and searched, he should cooperate and immediately contact a barrister at a London telephone number—a direct line to him. Ian placed the number inside his left back trouser pocket. He was curious to know the identity of the barrister, but he knew if it came to that he would call his own legal expert instead.

"The train leaves at seven-forty, in about fifteen minutes. We arrive in London's Liverpool Street station at about 9:00 a.m."

"Which class ticket should I purchase?"

"We're going coach. It's less conspicuous and there will be lots of commuter traffic," McCann said as if Ian didn't know that first hand. He grunted to stifle a reply to such condescension.

"If you're stopped and searched, I'll go ahead," McCann continued. "If you're stopped but not searched, then you'll need to board the same railroad passenger car as me, only we'll stay separated. Once on board, if you need to communicate with me, rub your eyebrow three times and cough loudly, and I'll meet you by the toilet. If I believe you're being followed, I'll not move, in which case we'll rendezvous by one of the elevators at Russell Square tube station. I'll block your follower and prevent him from getting on the elevator as you enter, then I'll jump on with you. When we get off, you can follow me. I've scouted the area well. We'll meet at the concrete oval in the center of Russell Square if we're separated for any reason. Otherwise, we remain within a few feet of each other. Understand?"

"Right."

"Oh yes, we change trains in Manningtree at 7:54."

"Yes...where's document number sixteen?" Ian was frustrated to be totally at McCann's mercy.

"That's the reward I'll give you once the train starts rolling, after we've changed trains in Manningtree. I'll buy a newspaper and pass it to you as you go to the toilet. Richtol says it has much you'll need for your story...all in sixteen."

McCann went through the green line first. The young man asked if he was traveling on business or pleasure. "Pleasure," McCann answered tersely.

"How long do you intend to stay?" the British customs official asked calmly from a perch on the wooden stand.

He almost blurted out a fortnight, trying to accommodate the British usage. "A... for...two weeks."

The young man returned his passport and McCann went through, glancing briefly back at his traveling companion. He reestablished his grip on his larger suitcase, which now held the attaché of documents surrounded by a padding of clothes.

Ian nervously approached the same young man five minutes after McCann had walked through. "Are you visiting for business or pleasure?" he asked, flipping the passport pages.

"Vacation," Ian answered according to McCann's coaching, rather than "holiday." Then he asked in his practiced, flat American English, "Where can I get the train from Harwitch to London?"

"Bear to the right, then to the left," the man directed with his hand, "down the ramp, carry on a bit, and you'll find the station, sir."

"Thanks," Ian answered and grabbed the American passport, slipping it back into his shirt pocket.

"Have a lovely visit." The official evidently didn't notice his discomfort.

Ian breathed deeply in relief and glanced about nervously. There were steady crowds of people in front and behind him. As he rounded the corner up ahead, he saw a customs official break from the crowd and walk towards him. The man, in his thirties, stared at him, looked around, and walked directly up to him as he took a pen from his shirt pocket and reached for a small pad in his back pocket. Ian, spellbound, froze on the spot. The short man blocked his path. Ian noticed McCann at a newsstand near the platform, out of earshot but in plain sight through the morning's foggy drifts pouring out from the quiet track. McCann was not, however, looking at Ian at that moment.

"Mr. Ian Scarborough?"

Ian quizzically looked around trying to avoid acknowledging his own identity, and then shook, petrified in fear, sensing weakened knees and wrists.

"I'm sorry?" Ian realized he had fallen into his natural British accent and faltered. "I..." he stammered, trying to correct his accent, but it was too late. "I'm most certainly not..."

The man grinned admiringly. "I thought it might be you. I recognized you in spite of all these years. I've seen you many times in concert, including the Isle of Wight festival years ago when I met you while on the security detail. I don't wish to inconvenience you, but how kind you would be to autograph this piece of paper for my son. He's got your albums, CDs, and even a photo I took of you. I've passed these things on to him since your music is a crowning work. I do hope I'm not a bother."

Ian smiled in relief as he set his luggage down. "It's no bother at all. Please, though, I do so adore my privacy. Don't tell others." Ian clutched the pen and began writing. "What's your name?"

"John...address it to Nigel, though, if you don't mind." The man giggled. "We'll make him into a 'Ghostie,' too."

"I don't mind, not at all. Please do take care not to mention to anyone you saw me here. I'm meticulous about my privacy. It's such a luxury to have only one fan arrest my progress that I don't mind doing this for you, but don't tell anyone else you saw me—especially at this port since I come through very often on business."

"I shall not," John said. "Nigel will be gobsmacked over this. Thank you loads."

"No problem." Ian smiled graciously and picked up his luggage. "I'm happy to accommodate you."

"Would you like me to assist you with your luggage?"

"No, I should manage quite well."

"I insist." He reached for the larger piece.

"No, my doctor tells me I need to exercise more so this is a part of my regimen."

"Well, you have given my son his meat and drink," he grinned. "I play `Fishing' at least once a month for him. Do keep up your good work at the paper. Cheers."

Ian nodded and strode rapidly towards the train station at Parkeston Quay. His upper lip began to sweat with anxiety. He saw McCann about one hundred feet ahead on platform one where the second-class cars board. He was holding a copy of what appeared to be the *Guardian* with its characteristic style of headlines.

Hopefully, Ian thought, McCann had not seen the encounter since it would only complicate matters. He purchased his ticket and moved to a spot only a few feet away from the ticket window. As he set his luggage down on the cold, grey pavement, the air surged crisp and dry across the platform. Ian felt a sudden urge for something warm to drink. A cup of cappuccino would do rather nicely, so he clutched his luggage and walked into the nearby buffet. The station clock showed 7:29. Perhaps the caffeine would help alleviate the jet lag, he thought, as he succumbed to a yawn. The cappuccino machine was broken, of course, as in every train station café in England, so he ordered a regular coffee with cream and sugar. As he stirred the cup, he noticed McCann's head peering through the buffet window. Ian knew with certainty that he must do something to separate himself from the man as soon as they got the documents to their final destination. If there was any indication whatsoever of wrongdoing, he would have to rely upon his role as reporter to extricate himself from a knotty legal dilemma of appearing as an accomplice.

"What am I thinking?" he whispered to himself. "I *am* a bloody accomplice." Could he fall back on his role as an ad hoc courier for the British government? Suppose the ambassador had given up on him once he'd discovered his flight from the hotel? How much faith did the ambassador have in him? For that matter, how much faith did Ian have in McCann, Richtol, and whoever else was involved? McCann was a mercenary, a man who would conceivably murder for money, and probably had at some point in whatever career he'd made for himself—likely CIA or the mob. Those blokes are utterly ruthless.

He sipped his coffee and looked again at the ghoulish giant glancing at him. McCann trusted no one. He had obviously been in England many times before since he knew this train line better than Ian did. Ian had only been on it once before when he was a cheeky lad of twelve. His father had taken him to Harwich to meet his aunt that sparkling summer's day after her extended holiday on the coast of Denmark.

Ian finished the hot cup of coffee as the train pulled into the platform and the announcement of its arrival boomed over the speaker. He yawned again and lifted his luggage. As he left the buffet, he saw McCann enter the second-class car. Ian leapt onto steps at the opposite end of the car and placed his luggage in the space between the somewhat worn second-class car seats and the wall. McCann intentionally looked away out the window from the other end of the car, but Ian could discern his furtive eyes darting towards each passenger as they entered, trying to estimate if they were being followed. The whistle sounded and the train slowly began its journey to Manningtree—a fourteen-minute ride with two stops included.

The train stopped at Manningtree and the two men emerged from the car at each door simultaneously. McCann looked at the television screen listing the platforms, and then flashed a thumb and forefinger. Uncharacteristic for a Yank to use those fingers, Ian observed. A typical American uses the index and middle fingers for the number two—an obscene gesture in England.

The train to London's Liverpool Street station arrived within four minutes, and Ian transferred to the second-class coach of the new InterCity train with its comfortable sea-blue velvet seats and a table—perfect for reviewing document sixteen. McCann went to the corner seat after setting his baggage in the compartment by the entrance. Only one other individual, an old man holding an unlit cigar stuffed in his mouth, shuffled into the coach using a cane and sat in the seat in front of McCann, lifting a tattered paperback and soon lost in his book.

As Ian set his luggage in the rack above the seats, he suddenly felt a cramp in his right leg, another clear sign of ongoing fatigue. He needed document sixteen to revive his tired spirit.

When the train began to move, he rubbed his eyebrow and coughed while staring at McCann, certain that he was watching. His traveling companion reacted immediately, stepping quickly to the toilet at his end of the coach, and remained inside for about two minutes. When he opened the door, Ian moved steadily towards the toilet while McCann stopped at his baggage rack to feign adjusting his suitcase. He laid the copy of the newspaper on top of the empty rack above, whispering, "Voila," to Ian as he passed by.

Ian stepped into the toilet, completed his duties rapidly, and returned to find McCann vacating the rack area. Ian snatched the newspaper from the rack and returned to his seat. He opened the *Guardian* and scanned the headlines, pretending to be truly interested in its contents: "PM Falters In Latest Poll." Another headline proclaimed: "Chunnel Accident Claims Two Lives." His jaw dropped at a headline in the bottom left-hand corner: "American Journalist Predicts He Will Solve Shakespeare Break-In." Ian's eyes rolled in disbelief as he read:

> Investigative reporter Boone Phelps, of the *International Herald Tribune*, alleges in an exclusive to that paper this morning that he has narrowed down to one suspect, by name, the perpetrator of the recent break-in at Trinity Church in Stratford-Upon-Avon. The break-in occurred last week at the monument above the grave where William Shakespeare is buried. New Scotland Yard authorities allege that the crime involved the search for artifacts or documents relating to the Bard's manuscripts.
>
> The article also alleges that an American masterminded the

apparently successful incursion into the monument. Phelps believes the man is currently in the United States, possibly heading for England, and has probably sold, or will sell, the documents to a wealthy collector. While the article did not mention the man by name, Mr. Phelps believes he is a tall, slender man who carries an American passport with fake identification, and may have hired British ex-convicts to help carry out the scheme.

The report did not altogether rule out the possibility of the man traveling in England or on the continent. But Mr. Phelps believes the American and the missing items are now in the States. Mr. Phelps, who was instrumental in breaking the story on the Flick Affair several years ago in Bonn, said he is pursuing leads through a variety of sources and would continue to search for the man's whereabouts in order to discover the contents of the stolen artifacts.

Meanwhile, officials at New Scotland Yard have reported no clues, and apparently they are very interested in talking to Mr. Phelps about the matter. Mr. Phelps has not been available for comment in either the London or Paris offices of the *Herald Tribune*. However, the byline for yesterday's story was Paris.

Publisher and editor John Angleterry declined comment except to say Mr. Phelps was still working on the story and may have left for America.

The chief of police at Stratford-Upon-Avon, Inspector Lester Morton, confirmed that Mr. Phelps was held and questioned the night of the break-in because he had witnessed the crime.

"Mr. Phelps was released shortly thereafter because he could offer very little description and merely reported that he had somehow followed the perpetrators into the building as they were committing the crime."

The mayor of Stratford-Upon-Avon, Heath Bentham, commented, "Whitehall wasn't interested in this audacious looting of the

National Trust. Unless it's terrorism or arms smuggling, the government is uninterested."

Ian's mouth went dry. As soon as he broke out of his catatonic state, he shook his head and looked up at McCann, who raised his shoulders slightly in puzzlement at the shocked expression on Ian's face. The train was slowing for a stop at Weeley station and McCann stepped softly down the aisle, his small suitcase now in hand as a precaution.

Ian couldn't believe the complete spin—a bald lie that Inspector Morton had told about Phelps. Always, the police present the fact that they nicked their man, but never that they nicked the wrong man. If not for Veronica, Phelps would still be in the boob. Morton tried to spin the story as though Phelps were caught during the first, `shilly-shally' break-in. How incredible that Phelps was now about to compromise their position. Heavens, they might go to prison for years thanks to his efforts! The idea of their being caught smashed him fully in the face for the first time. Dejected, he lowered his head, now filled with doubts and confusion. Was Phelps really off to the States? What was worse was the placement by McCann of a photo of document sixteen, rather than the actual document.

"I'm curious as to why you seem so startled," McCann hissed at him. "Is the document not inside the newspaper?" Only a mother with two small children were seated in the corner—the son begging his mother for a Disney World colouring book.

Ian couldn't hide his expression of disbelief. If all Phelps said was accurate, and based on what he himself knew or suspected about McCann, he was on the mark. He actually considered not telling him, but decided it could jeopardize the goal if he did not do so.

"You didn't read this newspaper closely, I can see," Ian remarked flatly.

"I turned to the center of the paper and placed *it* in the center, holding it with my thumb and forefinger while I read the next page over, the obituaries." McCann reached for the paper, now resting on Ian's lap. "It is there, isn't it?"

Ian opened the paper to show the photograph of the document, not the document itself as he'd promised, signed "Edward Oxenford" near the bottom. "The problem is," Ian said, staring intently into McCann's blinking eyes, "there is an American reporter who has written an article, as of yesterday, in the *International Herald Tribune*. He's discovered enough about you to heat up the investigation apparently going on. Read this, you swine. And, by the by, where is the actual document?"

"You'll have it when we arrive. Trust me." McCann blinked irritably as he read, sweat forming on his upper lip.

The full thrust of the dilemma now hit Ian as he watched the mysterious man across from him shift nervously in his seat. "You shouldn't be the worried one," Ian said in measured tones in what he offered as his best imitation of an American accent, "for I am the tall American, according to my passport. Did you, did you set me up in case they discovered it was you? Is Todd the name you use here in England or is that your real name? I must know, now!" He grabbed McCann's shoulder and pulled.

"I...I...didn't set you up. Your passport came from our friend on the train. He always has a half dozen or so. Believe me."

"I might believe you if you tell me what you're about to do. I'm not at all happy with these charades. I'm not even positive who you work for, and who Richtol works for. For all I know, you could be associated with some terrorist organization interested in selling these documents for arms money. I want the truth."

"I am not `Todd' nor have I ever used his passport. We're about to deliver these documents to a location in London where they will be safely returned, I've been assured, within a few hours of our leaving them."

"What's the location?"

"I don't know yet."

"How do we get there?"

"By tube, by taxi, and then on foot."

"That's barmy."

"It leaves no tracks. We're taking a taxi outside the tube and it'll take us to our appointment close by."

"So we're returning the documents to the rightful owner—Whitehall. Are you sure they'll be returned properly?"

"Yes."

"Who are you returning them to?"

"We won't know until we arrive at the train station. It's been prearranged by Richtol. I'm telling the whole truth. I'm merely carrying this task out as a job...following orders. That's it."

"How do you know these people aren't with some sort of extremist group or that the documents will be delivered to the proper person? Suppose that some group is going to sell them for their largest fundraiser ever?"

"On that you must trust me, but I'll say that I've known some of the people involved for many, many years. They're sincerely interested in having the documents safely returned. They are after the truth, like you."

"How do you know I'm after the truth? What if I decided to make off with the documents and sell them to the highest bidder? They're priceless, as you know. What if you decided to scurry off to Munich with them?"

"I trust you," his eyes softened. "You won't destroy or sell them. I know. Nor will I. I've too much at stake."

Ian exhaled deeply. The lady in the corner with the children was looking at them curiously, a hint of suspicion in her eyes. McCann stared out the window as the train drew into Great Bently. Ian resolved then to gain some modicum of control. He had nothing to lose and all to gain. He needed to regain his identity.

"Understand I'm taking control of this project. I am now Ian Scarborough again. I want my identification materials back in my possession, especially my press credentials." Ian decided suddenly on a ploy. "I'm going to try to ring that reporter, Boone Phelps, since I know him and I was partially responsible for his release in Stratford. He's a press associate of mine. I'll ask him—no, I shall demand of him that he throw the authorities off the track for the next twenty-four hours so I can get my story. You know I have an interest in accomplishing that objective. So you and I must cooperate. I'm going to deliver the papers myself. You may go with me, keeping a distance between us, or you may abandon the project and return to safety. It's entirely up to you. If you're being paid at any juncture, I shall send you the money in whatever currency you desire. These are the most important papers in the world at this moment and I'm not risking their safe delivery to an anxious public. Do you understand?"

McCann gulped slowly as if weighing the proposition. "The only request I have is that you allow me to accompany you so I can pick up the balance of my fee. It'll be waiting in my getaway car when we make our rendezvous."

"I have no problem with that as long as you realize that if you're caught, you're to say that I've held you so I could escort the documents back to England and get my story. How do you intend to deposit your sheaf of notes?"

McCann looked confused. "Sheaf of notes?"

"Your bloody money," Ian barked impatiently.

"I have bank accounts with Midland, Bank of England, and Lloyd's. It's all set up in four separate foolproof identities. I'm making several smaller deposits and keeping the rest to buy some stock. I'll sell the stock once I've returned to G..."

"To Germany," Ian finished McCann's inadvertent leak, corroborated wholly by the article and the scene at the Munich Hauptbahnhof.

Sweat formed on McCann's upper lip and Ian waved his hand as if to dismiss the matter. "Now, I'm going to the toilet to dispose of the credentials of one Mr. Todd. He's served his purpose. Thank God the customs officials evidently don't read the *Guardian* or the *Herald Tribune*, or if they do, they don't connect the facts with any communications from their superiors." Ian rose and marched to the toilet.

When he returned, McCann was still sitting, staring vacantly at the sunny Essex countryside as they approached Colchester. With a deep breath, Ian firmly spelled out the scheme to him.

"We'll go with your plan, but you carry the suitcase with the documents, I'll carry my larger suitcase since it has mostly clothes in it. You can return it when we get to the taxi so we can make sure we've consolidated all the documents for their return. I must read the photo of document sixteen now since I've only an hour before our arrival in London. I'm going straight away to a telephone once we've arrived. I want the real document sixteen by the time we arrive."

McCann nodded and returned to his seat. The train was entering Colchester as Ian opened the section of the newspaper that held the photo of the document. He folded the newspaper in such a way as to have the photo rest comfortably in the creases he'd made three-fourths down the span of the newspaper. The writing was entirely legible. McCann's use of the specialized camera was indeed expertly practiced.

It read, "My very good brother to whome I write so swiftly following the expression of my very own grief over the death of her Magestie. I briefly interrupt my gloomie sorrow to cast about for resolutions to all of the woes I have been subjected to, which only you, my brother as Lord Treasurer, could possibly offer comfort. As I have related to His Magesty, I am willing to foregoe the rightfull authorship and title of all plays and sonnets, which is consistent with the wishes of your departed and dear father, in return for the complete restoration of my land and property as well as the continuation of the annuity granted to me by the beloved Mistress we have lost to God's kingdom where she will reign in most lofty position of that heavenly state and where we shalle soon be reunited. I accept the continued annuity after seventeen years of receiving the amount with humble gratitude. My only remaining desire is to wishe that the Lord Chamberlain's players, herineafter the King's Men, will bestow upon the world to whomsoever be solicitous to view, the plays as I have written them including `Othello' and `Palamon and Arcite,' the which are near completion. I yesternight sent by courier the manuscripts for "The Tempest" and "King John's Charter" with divers sonnets, plays and songs as may be inserted. I descry the tide of fortune, ever mindful that my works shall sail the seas of playhouses through the abiding and steady vessel now nominated The King's Men with her full sails blown by the breath of our Master, James I, by his providential and judicious star. I take my leave this 12th of July from my House at Hakney, 1603 with infirme yet grateful hand,

Youre most assured and loving

Brother.

[Signed] Edward Oxenford

"Yes!" Ian exclaimed and looked up to find a young man in a business suit sitting across from him as the train stood at the station in Colchester. "Yes!" He repeated the simple affirmative several times, nearly laughing as the young man quizzically blinked at him. Ian dropped the newspaper in his lap and laughed loudly. "I'm sorry," Ian said in a falsetto, then thought quickly of a score he'd noticed on a sports paper at the stand in Harwich. "I was beside myself over the rugby match."

"Birmingham?" the young man asked.

Ian hesitated, and then picked up the thought. "Yes. They won, didn't they? I made over fifty quid on it."

"They are brilliant. Murray is my personal favorite."

"Right." Somehow, Ian needed to pry the original, magical document from McCann before they arrived in London. He turned to look at the map of the Northeastern Line on the wall over his head. He would prevail upon McCann to guard their possessions once they stopped in Ramford, the last stop before London. That would give him about ten minutes in the toilet with his Polaroid to snap off as many photographs as the remaining film would allow of this singular historical document. Unable to contain a desire to set this important procedure in motion, he stood up and bolted towards McCann as the whistle sounded and the train jerked into movement.

Intrigued by his companion's behavior, McCann's face brightened in mild enthusiasm himself. "Good news, eh?"

"Smashing."

McCann nodded. "What's the big deal?"

"Document sixteen is everything and more than what you promised. It not only confirms the authorship," Ian whispered in even lower tones, "it suggests there's another play which has been suppressed all these years, presumably about the Magna Carta. It's brilliant, yet gloomy" (Ian had to use a word right there from document sixteen which was attributed to Shakespeare as his invention as an adjective) to read how our man gave up his legacy."

McCann seemed mildly impressed, nodding slowly. "You're wanting to photograph again. Isn't one enough?"

"It is not. If something happens to it between here and my paper's office, I want an extra photo. It's vital. Pull the original document out, place it in this newspaper, and take it to the loo for more photos. I'll watch our baggage whilst you're in there." Ian thought of one more detail. "When I'm on the telephone at the station, leave the baggage with me and dash over to the bookstall. I want you to buy a copy of the *International Herald Tribune* and ask the vendor if there are any copies remaining from yesterday. Also, buy several other London papers—the *Financial Times*, the *Times*, for instance. I want to see how much coverage my friend is receiving and how big our problems are. We're much too tall to be traveling together. I'm tempted to take a separate taxi and live by the consequences of following your taxi."

"No." McCann was adamant, pursing his lips tightly together. "I've changed enough of my plans. You must trust me!"

"Very well, but you could be making a very dear mistake."

Ian returned to his seat, contentedly staring at the gently undulating Essex countryside only a few miles west of Braintree and Castle Hedingham, named after the castle where the seat of the Oxfords dominated, today the cozy town of comfortable believers in their earl as Shakespeare. He was thinking about the boy removed at such a young age from that castle, who wrote the works ascribed to William Shakspere of Stratford-Upon-Avon. The prominent, the significant Earls of Oxford would become prominent and significant again. This singular talent, who might have retained fortune and fame if he hadn't left the castle, if his father hadn't died early, if his mother hadn't remarried (as in *Hamlet*), if he hadn't suffered the masterful Machiavellian manipulations of his father-in-law, Lord Burghley. But then, if all that had not happened...

He pondered those tumultuous times and recalled a parable of such told by the hallowed sage, the late Malcolm Muggeridge, in a memorable discussion on Christianity with William F. Buckley Jr. When Buckley asked rhetorically how one could love a God who might take from us a seven-year old girl, Muggeridge replied with an anecdote in his ingenious, charming, captivating way: "There is, you see, this elderly lady, who in the eternal shade, meets William Shakespeare and asks him, `Why did you have to put poor Hamlet through so much? Why didn't you merely kill him at the end of Act I?' Shakespeare replied, `Because, madam, without the other four acts there would have been no play.'"

Chapter Thirty-One

London's Liverpool Street station had been refurbished of late to take on a modern look at eye level, and an elegance in the uppermost reaches of the main station worthy of the early part of this century. The loftiest corners of the ceiling featured flying buttresses, miniature versions of the famous ones surrounding Paris's Notre Dame Cathedral. The arches, with red trim and white lacework decorating the buttresses, emanated from elaborate white columns with a brown trim at the top. Platforms 10, 11, and 12 had been reconstructed and included television modules that listed the various arrivals and departures. The East Anglia line arrived only two minutes late, at 11:30 a.m., and emptied out a small crowd of passengers, two of which were tall men wearily carrying their respective luggage, walking approximately one hundred feet apart.

McCann had instructed Ian to approach the new ticket windows across from platform 11, as he himself was instructed to do. Upon reaching the door to the window stalls, Ian was to turn around immediately and march quickly towards platform 10 underneath the television console. Since they had stepped off platform 12, this was not a great distance, no more than two hundred yards, from the coach car they had just departed. According to McCann's instructions from Richtol, the contact receiving the password was to watch for a tall man with luggage to meet him under the television console at the entrance to platform 11 after almost entering the new ticket room directly opposite.

McCann watched from near platform 12 as Ian nearly reached the door, then turned around with his baggage swinging as if suddenly remembering to retrieve something left behind. As he did so, Ian caught in the corner of his left eye a short, scruffy old man circling under the television screen at 11 and staring up at the console. He was holding a pipe in his hand, and wore black earmuffs with a blue ski cap atop his head. He was dressed just as McCann said he would be. He hadn't shaved for days, possessing the air of a vagrant. Where did McCann get these sods? Ian shivered to think what archways these people occupied.

McCann, no more than sixty yards away, could almost hear Ian say the mystery word "Zelauto," which Ian had explained to McCann was nothing more than the title of one of Anthony Munday's works dedicated to the Earl of Oxford. Now he repeated it to the short, smelly tramp, and McCann whispered it to himself as well. The contact was then to respond by stating the suite number to which the documents were to be delivered.

"What of the address?" Ian had demanded of McCann.

"I have the address," McCann had answered curtly. "I'm not giving it to you until I have the suite number."

McCann waited until the information exchanged, and then bolted towards the newspaper stand when, as agreed, he saw Ian head towards the telephones for a call to Vines, and a short call to Veronica, to tell her he was on the way with the story. McCann bought several dailies and the *International Herald Tribune*. There were no copies remaining from the prior day, however. He stood about fifty feet from where Ian was telephoning and scanned each paper thoroughly. Nothing in them referred to Shakespeare or any "tall American."

Ian approached and murmured, "Phelps is here in London, according to my editor. I told him I had the story of my lifetime, and his, and I would be in the office this afternoon about fivish." It was 11:55, Ian noticed. "Is that a reasonable time to expect?"

"Yes. It should be no problem at all. You could be in by as early as one if all goes according to schedule."

"Anything in the newspapers?" Ian nodded at the pile of papers next to McCann's suitcase.

"Nothing. Nothing at all, unless I missed something in a rush."

"Right. I'll follow you. In case we're separated, tell me again, which underground stop are we going to?"

"Russell Square. I'll walk slowly."

"Right." Ian was intimately familiar with the tube stop since it was the one he traveled for his occasional guest lectures on composition at the University of London, and he had sometimes frequented the nearby British Library's reading room, before the move to St. Pancras, to peruse documents by Lord Burghley or Edward de Vere. His father's flat was also nearby, although it was closer to the Holbern tube station. One of his favorite pubs was around the corner from the Russell Square tube stop, where he had often gone with his late wife when they were dating. He'd never been back, since he couldn't bear the gloomy thought of happy times spent there, a popular pub for students.

As an afterthought, Ian recalled that Sherlock Holmes first took lodgings at 24 Montague Street. Bloomsbury Square was designed and laid out, ironically, by the Fourth Earl of Southampton, Thomas Wriothesley, Henry's very own son.

Ian caught his breath during the underground ride through King's Cross-St. Pancras where they transferred to Russell Square on the Piccadilly line. The dash down the tube as they transferred only made him short of breath again. He couldn't wait to return to his apartment and freshen up, or at least go to the office in Derry Street and begin writing the story. That's what I shall do, he thought. Vines has a nice shower in his office and I'll have a go at it before I sit down at the processor. No, I'll hand over the photographs first. I should be back in good favor with Vines again. The fatigue and jet lag were still making him nervous and mentally confused. It had been a strange, grueling trip. All he had to do was follow McCann, the Deutsche English professor, and remember Suite 200 for the address, to which McCann would lead them very soon. The subway doors slid open to the familiar sign proclaiming "Russell Square."

Ian saw McCann leave from the next car and turn left for the "Way Out" to the lifts up two small flights of stairs. He followed some forty feet behind, taking the steps two at a time. Upon approaching the lifts, he saw McCann standing near the front of the crowd awaiting entry on the left, so Ian joined the back of that crowd. Everyone got on the lift and remained facing forward as the door behind Ian, the last person to step on, closed with a low clatter and the obnoxious warning beeps. After about ten seconds, the door opened and the aggregation of tube travelers poured out into the hallway leading to the exit. Ian pushed his luggage through the turnstile and slipped his yellow tube ticket into the machine that promptly digested it and released him to the other side.

Outside the entrance, the bookstall vendor was pulling his wares closer to his stand to protect them from a heavy shower that must have started only seconds before. The west wind was driving the cold rain in a slant. Ian's eyes searched about for Mike McCann's tall figure, and there he was hailing a taxi. A black cab pulled up and Ian saw McCann's gangling neck stretch above the roof of the cab.

"We're taking this taxi," he shouted. "Come on!"

Ian leapt to the auto in three healthy strides, banging the larger suitcase on the back of his knee. He winced in pain as he opened the door, laying the baggage inside, and then piled into the corner opposite McCann. He didn't hear McCann tell the driver the street address.

"Have you given him the address?"

"Yes. It's close. Driver, I want you to take us as near to the entrance as possible."

They drove past Russell Square after leaving Guilford Street, then took a left onto the east end of Russell Square, which was Woburn Place. The traffic was light as they cruised left again at Bedford Place, halfway down the south end of Russell Square. The entire Bloomsbury area was one of the historical mainstays of literary London, and number 24 Bedford Place was the first address where T.S. Eliot had lived. They stopped at the entrance of Bristed House, an address most familiar to Ian. It was the address for his father's flat.

"What're we doing here?" Ian demanded. "Is this...?"

"This is the location where we make our delivery, according to what I've been told," McCann replied coolly while handing the driver a ten-pound note. "Keep the change."

"This is my father's London address. You can't."

"What was the suite number our man gave you at the train station?" McCann asked, as he lifted his luggage, now lighter from their rapid shifting of all documents during their short ride from Russell Square. Ian was struggling with luggage from the opposite side of the seat.

"Suite 200," Ian said loudly. "Something's amiss. The suite numbers are only in the thousands. We need another digit!"

"I was instructed to add a 7 to whatever it was. So, tell me, Ian, what suite does your father occupy?"

"2007." Ian dropped the suitcases on the wet pavement in disgust. Rain splattered him, but he didn't seem to notice. "We can't deliver these papers to my father."

"Why not?" McCann laughed. Ian flashed back instantly to his remark about the "surprise" when they arrived in London.

"He's a member of Parliament...he knows nothing about..."

"I was told you know the code we need to gain entry to the front door. As soon as the buzzer sounds and we enter, I expect you to take the elevator to the second floor." McCann unzipped his suitcase and slid a load of manila envelopes out as they stood huddled under the dry copula next to the clear glass security door. "I've been told there is a healthy-sized mail slot in the door at Suite 2007. After you've inserted the papers inside these manila envelopes, slide them through the slot. Remember, your fingerprints are all over the documents. Your father is on the floor of the House of Commons this morning. When he returns, he should find a note from you inserted along with the documents asking that he immediately telephone the authorities at Scotland Yard and that you've accomplished your mission."

"I'm not going to involve my father," Ian protested loudly. "I'm hiring the nearest taxi and taking them to the office."

"Do you know the number to the entry switch?" McCann blinked swiftly.

"Yes, I certainly do." Ian's felt his cheeks flush.

McCann reached inside his overcoat and produced Polaroid photos of yet another document. "I selected a document the crew in New York never saw. I've been holding it for you in case we ran into any problems communicating. If you do carry through, if you simply go inside, I'll see that you have it. Here it is, in perfect condition." He lifted another manila envelope out. "In this one you'll find a photo of the one document Richtol kept. It's perfectly legible. Otherwise, every photo I've taken will go to another newspaper, not yours. In fact, I was originally supposed to deliver these and a photo of sixteen about ten minutes ago to that reporter who is on to us—Phelps—in front of the British Museum." McCann's face became rigid and taut. "I'm going to visit him soon if you don't carry out your patriotic duties."

Ian wondered if he was bluffing about Phelps. "I'm not going to subject my father to this and be a part of some bizarre con..."

Ian gripped his baggage as he prepared to move into the driving rain past McCann, to hail a taxicab, when he saw the inimitable figure of Boone Phelps emerging from the corner at the end of the street. Unmistakably, it was he, even though his black umbrella was sometimes covering his face. McCann may have been telling the truth.

McCann pulled Ian by the collar when he saw the American reporter heading their way. "Act now, my friend."

"Ian, wait. That man's got the documents," Phelps shouted. Dropping his umbrella, he broke into a full run from about 100 yards away. "He's the man. I recognize him. Hold him!"

"You don't want him to have the story, do you Ian?" McCann tugged his collar.

Ian hesitated, looked at McCann, and then turned to press the switch with its numbers two-zed-zed-seven-nine-one.

"Whatever you do, McCann, don't allow him inside. I'm cooperating. That is definitely Phelps," Ian said frantically. He punched in the numbers of the code and the door buzzed.

Phelps was a dozen yards away.

The door continued to buzz. "Good luck," McCann said nonchalantly, and thrust the envelopes of new photos onto Ian's luggage, which he'd just swung through the door. "If those documents aren't returned to the proper authorities and I'm caught, *you're* an accomplice. If they are, you're a hero. It's that simple, buddy."

He thrust one particular envelope into Ian's hand. "This is a photo you should keep for insurance. Have a good life."

"Ian, stop, stop, stop!" Phelps crossed to their side of the street, barely avoiding a moving van. He slapped both hands on the side of the slowing vehicle, but by the time it passed, Ian was already in front of the lift, now a most welcome sight.

The lift was luckily on the ground floor and opened immediately. He set the luggage on, thankful to be alone, and pressed the button to go up one floor. As he did, he saw Boone Phelps being jostled by Michael McCann. He heard shouts as the door shut and wondered if he'd made the correct decision.

When the lift opened, he scurried down the hall to the doorway of 2007. He rang the doorbell twice and unzipped both pieces of luggage, the attaché and the suitcase, tilting them flat to the floor. No answer. His father was in a meeting at Parliament. He worried now about whether his father had been cued on this matter.

Nervously sliding the first set of manila envelopes through the slot six inches above the bottom of the heavy wooden door, he remembered suddenly that his father had threatened to block it up because of his fear of IRA mail bomb attacks. Fortunately, his father had been remiss in doing it, for he heard the documents land with a soft plop on the thick carpet inside the door.

The sound of the lift door closing jolted him. As he shoved the last envelope through and it landed with a light thud, he said a quick prayer that they had not been damaged, biting his lower lip. "God, help me if my father doesn't return these shortly. I'd better ring him as soon as I have an opportunity."

Swiftly, he stabbed a hand through the wads of clothes and found his note pad. He jotted down a message to his father as to what the documents were and concluded, "Father, do take immense care in having these most priceless documents delivered to the Ministry of Cultural Affairs or Scotland Yard. You'll hear about them on the news this evening, or at the latest, in the morning. Please explain to the Ministry, Whitehall, and particularly the British ambassador to the US that I accomplished my mission by delivering them to the most competent MP I know for preservation by the National Trust-—although I feel the contents may render new meaning to the title `National Trust.' I shall phone you shortly. Ian." I do believe he's at Parliament today, Ian thought. I'll call his office and his cell phone, both numbers that he had at his own office. He zipped the suitcases closed and exhaled a sigh of relief. Now he had only to file the story and have the photographs prepared to publish for the world to see.

When the lift opened to the ground floor, he saw no one at the glass door. Approaching the door, he saw what had to be droplets of blood mixed with rain puddles on the sidewalk below, peppered over two sidewalk squares. Shoe tracks were everywhere. An old man appeared behind him from a ground floor flat.

"These homeless yobs are becoming a bloody nuisance," he growled. "Did you see the fight out there?"

"No, I was upstairs. I heard it and I've rung up the police." Ian couldn't believe he had issued such a line. Maybe he could make it in McCann's world.

"I called as well," the bald pensioner angrily replied. "I think they went on to another location. Probably bloody winos. I'd lay odds on they're habitués of Bedford Square."

"I do hope they've got on with their business," Ian replied truthfully, casting around to find no scrapping Yanks. "I'm off to work since I've been out of town for a time and I need to hail a taxi. I left my mobile in my attaché this morning and my telephone has been out of order in my flat..." Oh dear, maybe he wasn't good at lying after all since he saw the old man eying him from tip to toe. Finally, he waved his hand in a come hither.

"I'll be happy to ring one for you," said the old man returning to his flat. "There are always plenty at the museum."

Ian stepped back towards the glass door and saw a bobby on foot coming from the direction of the same corner Phelps had rounded. The helmeted figure under a ubiquitous black umbrella forced Ian's line of sight to a blue Volkswagen Jetta that had pulled up and stopped in front of the door. In the driver's seat was a waving hand attached to the welcome arm and body of Veronica Colton. Ian waved back and opened the glass door as the bobby approached her car. He yelled to the old man as he shut the door, "Never mind the taxi, sir. I've just made my connection. Thank you."

The bobby heard him say "thank you" and asked Ian about any altercation. "The pensioner inside saw it. I was upstairs in my flat and didn't know it was going on." Ian held the door open for the officer. "Just to the left there at the door." Meanwhile, a small crowd was forming.

Ian set the suitcase in the back seat since there were no longer any priceless papers inside, only notes and photographs. He leapt into the rider's side front seat to hug Veronica long and tenderly until a car screeched behind him honking loudly.

"I missed you, love," he uttered, kissing her on the cheek.

They embraced again to a second blast of horns.

"I really missed you," she said, driving south towards Great Russell Street. "Where should I take you?"

"To my office. Here, carry on, and then turn onto Tottenham Court. You're not going to believe what I have to report this afternoon for tomorrow's paper and tonight's telly," Ian was anxious to tell someone, but especially Veronica with her fetching smile and gentle, crackling laugh. "I tried to phone from the train station this morning. Aunt Joan wasn't there and no one answered."

"I was out picking up this car Dad had rented. Did you get your business done with Phelps?" she asked.

"Business with Phelps? I saw him coming down the street just now and avoided him."

"Yes?" Her smile disappeared. "He said he was going to meet you at your father's flat and send you out to meet me. Did you not meet him?"

"Not really." Now Ian was completely puzzled. "I avoided him. I didn't want him glomming onto my exclusive. What is going on?"

"Ian, father came out of his coma about thirty-six hours ago, for nearly four hours. If father is correct, he and Phelps had a long talk.

According to Phelps, you have all the proof in the world our man wrote the works."

"What?" Ian, delighted at the news on Colton, flinched, however, at the connection of Boone Phelps. "He's better? What was Phelps.... That means...Phelps talked to your *father*?"

Veronica could appreciate his delight at her father's recovery, but why the confusion over the activities of Phelps, who was merely reporting the good news?

"Why did Phelps say he and I were meeting together at the flat?" Ian asked.

"He said my father and Mr. Richtol talked and agreed that he and you were to share the bylines in this story. Apparently, they were behind all these break-ins, confidentially."

"True, except there's been nothing said about the sharing of stories," Ian barked. "Phelps was merely trying to figure out a way to help take credit for this story. The man will stop at nothing."

"He said he hoped to get to you before the authorities did. That they were looking for you and he knew you were trying to return the documents—after you got your story. He said he was going to turn in the documents for you."

"That explains the article," Ian said.

"What article?" she enquired.

"It appeared this morning in the *Guardian* and in yesterday's *Herald Tribune*. He vaguely describes a tall American who has in his possession the stolen documents. That's whom I've been traveling with over the last three days. Phelps was apparently the man's original contact, or he figured all this out when talking to your father and got squeezed out of the deal for some reason. Evidently, Phelps was supposed to meet the man at the British Museum. How did Phelps acquire all his informa—" Ian's gears turned as he watched Veronica frown.

"That idiot!" she shouted. "That's why he insisted on speaking to my father alone. Dad mentioned he was worried about a project he was working on which started before he suffered the stroke. His speech was slurred and Phelps was having trouble understanding him, he said, but apparently not much if..." She paused at the unthinkable—that Phelps would actually take advantage of a dying man in order to get his story.

"Tell me, how well does your father know this man by the name of Richtol?" Ian asked, leaning forward. "How does he know him?"

"Very well, of course. Dad and he are old friends. They served in World War II together here in England...US army intelligence. He's been calling the hospital twice a day since father had his stroke, except for maybe two days or so. He finally talked to him, a few minutes before Phelps had his private visit."

"Phelps nearly exposed us for the sake of scooping the story himself," Ian said, his face burning red. "While he was trying to throw the authorities off by having them believe the `tall American' was still in the US, he did it so he could be the first one to find us and threaten to turn us in if we didn't give him some of the glory. He's totally unscrupulous."

Veronica shook her head and raised her voice contemptuously. "He told me he thought he could find you if he talked to my father alone for about ten minutes. Father told me that after Boone left, he thought he might have made a mistake in talking to him. Father said he'd talked to him about this project briefly a few weeks ago. He's still heavily medicated. He couldn't remember what he'd told him exactly, or when. He said Admiral Sinclair came in to see him, and I know he didn't. Father said Sinclair told him that Richtol had changed plans and was allowing Phelps to help return the documents. When Phelps called me this morning and asked when you expected to arrive, I told him that as soon as I heard from Vines, who would hear from you.

I made the mistake of believing him, and Dad made the mistake, especially since he didn't know him well, of telling Phelps all the other changes Richtol had made. So apparently, Dad had something to do with the break-ins."

Ian was silent, trying to absorb the Colton-Richtol, and seemingly, Sinclair connection with the break-in and documents. He grunted once, looking for a change in subject. "Is your father still conscious?" he finally asked.

"He was when I left a half hour ago." She turned right on Southampton Row at Ian's right hand motion. "He's in for an hour, then, oh, out for two hours. It depends."

"As soon as you deposit me at the office, I want you to go to your father's room, even if your aunt is there, and have him stay awake so he can watch the evening news—even if you have to medicate him more. I'll phone him briefly, but only if you think it won't excite him too much. Remain there. Don't, under any circumstances, *do not*, *do not* allow Boone Phelps back inside that room. Ring security and have them station someone on the floor if need be. He'll either try to gain more information from your father for his story or he will, " Ian smiled slyly, "do what I believe will place him on a piece of string. I wish we'd left him in the Stratford nick. I wonder how he figured out the scheme."

"Piece of string?" she repeated inquisitively.

"In big trouble," Ian spoke in deliberate, measured tones. He changed his mind as he raced over all the contingencies. "Maybe he'll not be a problem, but I want to be sure. Let's return to my father's flat."

"Your father's apartment?"

"He obviously lied about that as well. Tell me precisely what he said. Why was I there?"

"He said you were meeting with your editor there. That you and he were in agreement, and asked me to park by the British Library and wait while he made sure you were there. He said he had to meet with the same editor, and if he didn't return in precisely five minutes, I was to drive by and pick him up. He said parking was easier at the library."

"Why did he have you drive?"

"He said he was taking some kind of drug for a migraine and it affected his vision. That sneak." She smacked the steering wheel and inadvertently tooted the horn. "Obviously, he figured he could lend some legitimacy to his plan by having me along in case you saw him as he arrived. He told me to meet him at the front of Bristed House, the flat. How could he do this after all I've done for him?" She took a left back onto Bloomsbury Way. As she approached the turn slowly back onto Bloomsbury Square and then Bedford where the apartment was located, she shook her head in disbelief. "He knew Dad, in his awful condition, would tell him what was going on. The very idea of taking advantage of a dying man. How easy to play his hunches on someone with both feet in the grave."

Ian patted her shoulder affectionately. "When did you learn to drive in London? Well done."

"Yesterday, when father was finally able to tell me he'd rented a car and they were about to tow it from the QE II Centre parking lot *and* after I convinced the towing company not to remove it. The company didn't charge us for the days it sat there. I had to pay the parking fee, though."

Ian coughed and laughed simultaneously, covering his mouth. "You certainly know how to deal with these situations. You would make a cunning barrister."

"Thanks."

"So, one can say Phelps was originally designated their reporter. Why? Sinclair and your father know me so well." They turned the corner towards Bristed House. "Phelps is surely around here somewhere. He's probably trying to gain entry."

"Judging by the spectacle ahead, you'd make a good psychic."

They peered down the street to see a crowd of people surrounding a bobby and a man kneeling next to the steps by the glass door. The bobby was handcuffing the man and speaking into his shoulder radio. The street was filled with the screaming sound of an alarm blaring inside the building, a penetrating high-decibel shrill. The man was Boone Phelps, protesting his impending incarceration and questioning.

"He should be accustomed to this routine by now," Ian laughed.

"And I don't intend to lift a finger in his defense since I'm *not* a barrister," Veronica said. "I hope he rots in jail."

"Just the same, I'll rush by and make certain he didn't damage the door to my father's apartment." Ian motioned at her to slow the car down and stop about fifty yards past the spectacle. He would have to cleverly maneuver through the crowd past the miserable, pleading "burglar to be" in order to make sure the documents were safe. Maybe he could ask someone—the flat manager perhaps—if the miscreant had successfully entered the flat.

The confusion of the small crowd, now beginning to disperse as the rain abated, allowed Ian to slip in unnoticed. He purposely slanted his black umbrella towards Phelps, who was arguing still with the bobby.

"There are valuable documents inside this building, inside the MP's apartment, and you're preventing me from salvaging them. You'll be sorry." His voice was high-pitched, pitiably insistent. "You just don't understand. The MP isn't at home and those documents are sitting there. They're the Shakespeare documents. The government is interested in returning them."

"You American reporters can't go breaking into any place you deem necessary. Just now I received a report as to your activities a week ago in Stratford. Now," he shook him as a police car drove up, "see here. We can't have you lurking about an MP's quarters."

"I had to do it," he shouted.

"Just like you'll have to spend the night at our expense," said the cop.

"That'll be the last attempt for him," a man in the crowd standing next to Ian said. Ian turned around to find the old man who'd called the police. "The bloody Yank came back after fighting with this other fellow and tried to break into Scarborough's flat."

"Did he succeed in entering?" Ian asked.

"Not at all," the pensioner said and smiled. "Scarborough sloshed him on the head with his attaché...just returning from Parliament. He's a Tory, you know. He'll have him on toast!"

"Brilliant." Ian walked steadily back to the car, laughing loudly at the imagined sight of his father's heavy attaché crashing down on Phelps's head as Phelps was working the code for the lock. His father was evidently up in the flat and he would call him directly.

"We're off to see Vines straight away," he said to Veronica.

"Yes, sir," Veronica said and saluted as she pulled out, satisfied that Ian appeared to be in an immensely victorious mood. Her arms and knees tingled with the delight she'd experienced only upon hearing her first speech years back being delivered earnestly by her boss, but this foreshadowed greater thrills—an appetizing slice of literary history in the making.

Chapter Thirty-Two

"De Vere Revered! Shakespeare Smeared! Sphere Shakes Weird!"

Typically trite, corny attempts at iambic pentameter spread across the newspaper poster stand outside the Russell Square tube station the Friday the news broke.

"Bard Scarred! De Vere Cheered!"

The tabloids were having their way. The day bore a circus atmosphere similar to a day following on a close, nasty national election. People on the street, in the tube, or by the tea tray were conflicted on how the British institution called Shakespeare could be toppled, yet most welcomed the new man, since much more was known about him with a stronger connection to the works.

The various headlines over Ian Scarborough's bylines in the conservative *Times* were less bombastic and more penetrating:

"De Vere Wrote Works Of Shakespeare, Cover-Up Over Four Centuries."

"New Works Discovered In Oxford's Hand!"

"Reporter Refuses To Discuss Details On Discovery: A New Shield Law Issue?"

"A History Of The Seventeenth Earl Of Oxford."

The newspaper ran the front-page news stories and all the photographs of the documents Ian had supplied. The most in-depth reading was the report Ian filed with his own analysis on the impact of the discovery, the implications of the corruption leading to the Shakespeare hoax, and the general facts concerning the locations (but not very precisely) of other manuscripts, letters, and artifacts by Edward de Vere, the Seventeenth Earl of Oxford, true author of the works attributed to "Shakspere" of Stratford-Upon-Avon. The next day, Vines had granted him the latitude of an editorial because of the deadline, so Ian editorialized liberally. Entitled "The Shakespeare Hoax and Its Perpetrators," the article was cast to the broad reading public and reprinted in newspapers throughout the world:

> This is an account of corruption at the heart of government and the Crown for over four hundred years. Not hand-in-the-till corruption, or the kind involving sex and morality, but corruption of the intellect, the arts, history itself. It's the most pernicious type of corruption, since what appeared originally as outright lies to a public that either did not know, or did not care, about an author's relationship to his works, eventually became accepted, unblinkingly, as the whole truth, with a developing cottage industry of academia, government, and tourist trade. A lie to be perpetuated through the ages."
>
> Edward de Vere, like many court figures and nobility of the Elizabethan Age, occupied his time with his many considerable talents: falconry, jousting, tennis, travel, and literature. His prolific activity in the Elizabethan literary field is well documented from an early age in his life, from the help he rendered to his uncle's (Arthur Golding) translation of Ovid's *Metamorphoses*, to his activities as a court poet, to his oversight and production of plays under the inherited title of Lord Great Chamberlain, to his oversight and production of plays as the inspiration of the earliest generation of Elizabethan playwrights.

Since it was highly unfashionable for an earl to publish works under his own name, the earl stopped doing so in his teens. Undaunted, he continued to compose poetry and write plays, finding praise among the courtiers as simple as in Gabriel Harvey's toast: "Edward de Vere, thy countenance shakes a spear." This was a reference to the earl's personality, but if one wonders about the substance of the praise, one only has to read from the same address Harvey gave during a Queen's Progress at Cambridge: "Thy splendid fame, demands even more than in the case of others, the services of a poet possessing lofty eloquence. Thy merit doth not creep along the ground, nor can it be confined within the limits of a song. It is a wonder which reaches as far as the heavenly orbs."

At the center of Harvey's panegyric stood the simple toast (hasti vibrans) and the residual effect was the *nom de plume* of "Shake-speare." A frequent use of jeu de mots on the noun and verb `Will' gave birth to William. Shake-speare was not a common name in England, so it served the purpose of creating a certain laughter at court, among the few, as an inside joke even while remaining distinctive enough for the benefit of the uneducated and unsophisticated public who cared when the plays were performed under that name.

One man who understood the habits of the merchant class, since it's from whence he came, was William Cecil, Lord Burghley, Lord Treasurer under Queen Elizabeth. Most pivotally, he was the guardian of young Edward de Vere after the death of his father and sudden remarriage of his mother (echoed in *Hamlet*), as well as the father-in-law to Edward. This latter aspect was crippling to the young earl. Cecil gained noble title through the marriage, gained access to the earl's holdings, and controlled Oxford's purse strings, giving him complete insight into Oxford's day-to-day activities. Even when the Earl of Oxford was away from his wife, Burghley's daughter, the treasurer relied on the expertise of Sir Francis

Walsingham, his top spy, to report on Oxford's every move.

Not only was Cecil relying on information about the earl because of the relationship with his daughter, he was also concerned, possibly obsessively paranoid, about his flirtations or even embracing Catholicism in an era when Elizabeth was also paranoid rightfully so about Mary Queen of Scots. Burghley could justify surveillance on his own son-in-law based on this matter alone, even when the Queen granted complete personal favor to Oxford. The steady deterioration of his son-in-law's relationship with his daughter encouraged Burghley to seize the opportunity to appropriate lands, control activities, and eventually imprison him, especially after Oxford formed a liaison with Anne Vavasor—the Dark Lady of the Sonnets—now identified! (Burghley is also the consensus among virtually all scholars as the model for Polonius).

One of the vital activities with which Burghley was charged was regulation of the written word, the proprietorship of all state documents. Burghley understood the impact of records, as evidenced by an astoundingly meticulously handwritten log of his day-to-day activities. For one with doubts, a trip to examine them at the British Library or Hatfield House will suffice in providing ample proof.

Once Burghley decided the works should never be ascribed to the Earl of Oxford, his manipulations weren't so difficult. He controlled the history since he controlled all, and wrote much, of the primary source documents of that era.

Since the pseudonym "William Shake-speare" was being attached to the publications of *Venus and Adonis* and *Rape of Lucrece* with Oxford's blessing, and since it was taboo for a nobleman to be involved with writing publicly performed plays, Walsingham needed to find someone with the name who would consent to accepting an annuity, £1000 per year, for the use of their name for posterity. This individual needed to have some financial means and needed to be somewhat literate, since a poorer man might compromise the truth by virtue of prima facie illiteracy. Preferably the man must be located some distance from London, thus Stratford-Upon-Avon, so the myth might be nurtured along after Oxford's death and the Stratford man's death. A man with a name similar to `Shake-speare' would, therefore, be ideal if he were younger than de Vere to allow more time to erode the truth *and* build the case for the impostor while the plays and sonnets were being edited and compiled for a complete and later publication.

So Londoners who may have suspected de Vere, based on leaky court gossip, would eventually accept the Stratford man—especially if he had some sort of established interest in London theatres, while Stratford's citizenry, mostly illiterate and uninterested in the stage, would readily accept Mr. Shakspere's absence in London as his time for writing plays and sonnets. While this Shakspere was in London enjoying his wealth, Londoners believed he was busy with stage presentations and writing more plays—the start of which he'd allegedly scribed in Stratford-Upon-Avon.

All this time, while both men were living, neither apparently knew each other. But to make the scheme work, Edward de Vere had to consent somehow to the conspiracy. This he had done in 1586 after the promise of a lifetime grant of £1,000 per year (while sitting as the senior earl at the trial of Mary Queen of Scots). This amount, equal to over £200,000 per year today, allowed him to live comfortably for the remainder of his life.

Throughout the two men's lives, nothing penetrated, at least for recorded history, the veneer carefully constructed by the most skillful and powerful man in England, Lord Burghley—except for one small detail. De Vere was sly enough to place documents in highly secret locations throughout England and the Continent, so whenever they might be found they would reveal the hoax to a world waiting for substance—for the man who wrote the most widely-read works in history, except for the Bible and Agatha Christie.

The documents in Trinity Church were placed there, in all likelihood, by De Vere's son-in-law, the Earl of Montgomery, since he had retrieved them from Theobalds House, (where de Vere had hidden a batch) in 1603 before or soon after Robert Cecil traded the estate to the King for the Hatfield estate. They hid some in in the wall of the old palace while it was being transformed into stables.

Montgomery, Phillip Herbert, probably felt the documents could best be preserved by placing them in properties that would survive for years. The bust in Trinity Church would, ironically, be a perfect candidate, as would Hatfield House, given its long history of royal owners. For those papers capsuled in Trinity, they naturally had to hold on to the papers for embedding them at that location since it didn't have a monument until about 1623.

The documents published in this paper this morning, and shown simultaneously late last night in New York by Wolf News, are those taken from the Trinity Church at Stratford-Upon-Avon, where Shakespeare is allegedly buried, and Hatfield House in Hatfield, north of London, on the estate of the Marquess of Salisbury. These are probably a small part of the documents scattered across England and in a few locations on the Continent. One document, not published by this newspaper and not shown on WNC, cites the highly specific locations of the remaining secreted documents. That one document has been retained by the documentary team, according to New York attorney Randle Richtol, legal counsel for Wainwright Productions which filmed the documents for sale to WNC. Wainwright Productions maintains they're holding the document until such time as they have full permission to film the documents in the other locations listed as they're being excavated.

Richtol maintains that the team has returned all of the documents, except the one listing the locations, and his client will treat the remaining document as "a protection of a source for future news." He said it would be returned "at an appropriate time." He also stated in a news conference preceding the broadcast that the documents were "stealthily obtained through breaking and entering the Trinity Church and Hatfield House, but, the documentary team, my client, did not know the source. They only recorded the documents, not aware of who perpetrated the crime or gave them access to the papers." He would comment no further on the subject except to say it could make an interesting test to the law, but "if the government in America or Britain desire to test the law," he and a "large and expert team of pro bono lawyers are fully prepared."

This reporter returned the documents after tracking down clues at the scenes of the break-ins and receiving a request from Whitehall through the offices of the British ambassador to the US—particularly after logistical complications prevented law enforcement authorities from converging on the rural New York resort hotel where the film crew recorded the documents before having them secreted away. (See adjacent news summary for these events.)

Richtol did attest that the document the crew retained cited one location as being the Royal Archives at Chartsworth. "Apparently, the Royal Family has allegedly continued the practise of covering up the matter, from Elizabeth I to Elizabeth II," the attorney alleged in his press conference. (This reporter had a torn photo which only showed the one location).

The reasons are compelling for the Royal Family to have done so, in spite of the truth behind who wrote the works—tourism in Stratford-Upon-Avon brings well over £150 million a year to England. Indeed, some believe the town will be devastated now that the truth has surfaced. The countless Shakespearean scholars and professors throughout the world will have to revise virtually all of their beliefs, not to mention their courses and publications. It gives them a new task, namely that of structuring the creation of the works around Edward de Vere, a man whose life fits many characters and events in the plays and sonnets, as has been advocated with grueling research and strong circumstantial evidence by the de Vere Societies of England and Europe, and the Shakespeare-Oxford Society of the United States. One American scholar in particular, Dr. Tyler Colton, has dedicated his entire adult life to research on the subject of Oxford as the author. Dr. Colton suffered a massive stroke recently while delivering a speech in a debate filmed for later broadcast on television in this country.

Of course, Whitehall has been interested in the documents from a legal standpoint, not devoid of the issues written above, relating to the public good. At the New Scotland Yard, it is a facile matter of bringing the perpetrators to justice. According to Inspector Thomas Burns, "After the film company has had its day in court in the States, we expect to put them on the judgment call here for their part in the matter, so we might discover who committed the crime. Their mere possession of the stolen valuables makes them accessories to the crime, shield law or no, in the US as well as here."

Nonetheless, the secret is out. The most revered name in all of English literature, William Shakespeare, has been destroyed in the wake of the revelation the Seventeenth Earl of Oxford, Edward de Vere, was the true author. The documents returned yesterday to a member of Parliament, who then handed them to the Ministry of Culture and Scotland Yard, reveal much about the man, but even more about further works. Three new sonnets were discovered and one additional play, which appears to deal with the events surrounding the signing of the Magna Carta in 1215 at Runnymede. In fact, after further analysis of photographs of the documents made by this newspaper, it appears the play dealing with the rebellion of the nobility may have been a part of the original *King John* but was suppressed by Queen Elizabeth and King James. This appears to be true, especially since the play may have been considered dangerous in the wake of the Essex rebellion in 1601, and may explain furthermore why the Pope and King John are portrayed in the original play in a sterile characterization because of the so volatile religious issues surrounding the throne during both reigns. Of course, all speculation may be resolved by eventual release of documents from the various heretofore hidden locations. There may even be a play developed around Robin Hood.

At any rate, the newly discovered works, as well as portions of manuscripts and important letters regarding the cover-up, according to its reluctantly willing conspirator-nobleman, should offer scholars whole new avenues in developing the body of works. As recalcitrant as these scholars may be, such revelations should be viewed as a literary gold mine for the new works to be fully reassembled after years of reposing in their disparate locations throughout Europe and the British Isles.

The most absorbing element of the plays and sonnets printed in photographs (taken via Polaroid and an L-221 close-up attachment) on the following pages is that they evince a concrete nexus to the life of Edward de Vere. While literally hundreds of pieces of circumstantial evidence have indicated Oxford was the author, without a "smoking gun," a *corpus delicti*, the question was merely academic—so much so, only academia debated the issue.

A most significant document, even though it was not a manuscript—not even a manuscript of a new work—was a document referred to by the researchers as simply Document 16. The document is featured in the singular photograph on the front page and is the best proof, the ultimate corpus delicti. Here, the Earl of Oxford expresses his intention of giving up all rights to his written works. It is signed by him.The text is printed below that photograph.

As for the retained document by barrister Richtol and the film crew in America, it is essential because it establishes that there are other locations with locations listed. It is so essential because it furthers the investigation into the affair. The locations, most likely, will reveal more manuscripts and important letters in de Vere's hand, conceivably more new plays and sonnets. They will also confirm, res ipsa, as one more scintilla of empirical evidence in behalf of Oxford.

The sole requirement remaining is some form of cooperation from Her Majesty's Director of Royal Archives in finding related documents, such as those in Lord Burghley's or Elizabeth I's hand, further corroborating the cover-up of the Oxford name as author. Will the government, in the name of veracity, allow scholars and qualified reporters to research the archives—and especially with utmost celerity since any delay would only create an incessant anarchy of break-ins in churches and castles throughout England? Are there also documents that have been discovered in the past by various individuals who have either sold them or destroyed them or even given them to the government for their conspiratorial safekeeping? The government should answer these questions. Members of the public with any knowledge of artifacts should come forward and give them daylight so the hoax may end after these four centuries.

There is no need for a cultivated society, no matter how steeped in history and tradition, to continue presenting a facade over the face of the world's greatest author. The scars on the Seventeenth Earl of Oxford's face as a nobleman, and as a man, have been there always for the public to see, but now they will be intensively examined, tirelessly scrutinized. The blemishes will be unimportant in these modern times when cast in the light of the accomplishments of Edward de Vere in literature, as well as in the extraordinary life he lead. The nobleman's downfall came partly as a result of historical circumstances, most beyond his control. In spite of these obstacles, the works were reassembled and salvaged through the process of the gaining of the title of Lord Chamberlain of the Royal Household to his son-in-law and then his son-in-law's brother—the earls of Pembroke (William Herbert) and later, Montgomery (Phillip Herbert), respectively. The consummation of his legacy demands his name be assigned de jure by historians to the works. Anything less would be a gross insult to the nobleman's most considerable talents. It is the proper thing to do.

A culture that no longer measures its art by a high standard also begs for correction of the error. A society that tolerates, even promotes, the sophistry of a life as void as the Stratford man can only lose the lessons of art in drawing from the verisimilitude encountered in a life as active and variegated as was Oxford's. Now the ideal role model is fulfilled for scholars and students to study in detail for years ahead. With the revelations of further primary sources of the plays and sonnets, more crackling inspiration will radiate from the genius reflected in this source of enlightenment. A splendid interest shall be rekindled. The flame will grow from this initial spark of rediscovery behind the earl's life and works, burning throughout the cultural world.

If the economic development and tourist trade issue is paramount—as it shouldn't be—then trade will not be interrupted but can only be enhanced. Tourists will swarm the sites where Oxford drew inspiration: Castle Hedingham, Hatfield House, Bilton Hall (near the Avon in Rugby), the Inns of Court, the site where Hackney House stood, Windsor Castle, and as mentioned by the American lawyer in the interview with Wolf News television (the only location Mr. Richtol specifically answered as being a location from the list retained by the American film team, except the Royal Archives), the tombs in Westminster Abbey next to Aubrey de Vere and Horace de Vere marked by the simple phrase on the floor: "Stone coffin underneath." It's the only such mystery in the Abbey.

This mysterious stone should soon no longer obstruct truth.

Now that this vital literary legacy in history is being fully restored, the words of Lord Kenneth Clark resonate from the recent past in measuring the earthshaking data unearthed in recent hours: "Western civilization has been a series of rebirths. Surely this should give us some confidence in ourselves...it is the lack of confidence, more than anything else, that kills a civilization. We can destroy ourselves by cynicism and disillusion, just as effectively as by bombs." Confidence as an advancing civilization shall allow us to view the truth, no matter the result, for the truth was bottled up far too long by cynical and disillusioned leaders disinterested in properly advancing civilization.

Chapter Thirty-Three

The morose tune Ian was playing on the Yamaha on a stormy afternoon was begging for lyrics. He had held the tune for nearly a week since his exposé. His muse was in labour and now he sat over the keyboard plotting the melody. If he could deliver the music, he would dress it with the lyrics from one of de Vere's early poems, probably the most posthumous aid in the history of music.

A heavy rainstorm off the English Channel was pelting the rectangular, pink-coloured concrete house, called simply "Southwest House" by Ian's father when they bought it together in the mid seventies. It overlooked a large rock only a few hundred yards out in the bay, barely visible through the downpour and swarming with seagulls fighting for a dry perch. Torquay had the little plaintive sound of gulls soaring above today.

Ian saw a black taxi cruise cautiously up the short driveway and he asked his cleaning man to open the door. Ian was expecting him. The motorcar disgorged a bearded mariner in the good form of Admiral Arthur Sinclair.

"Arthur," Ian shouted as he entered. The old man shivered once from the cold, removed his large rain hat, and dripped fresh rivulets of water onto his grey, protruding beard, looking like a mop before the next floor sweep. Ian helped remove his rubber fishing mac, revealing a dry, vintage leather vest, cord trousers, and a beige shirt—perfect attire for unpredictable Torquay.

"One can't even see Thatcher Rock this afternoon," he complained as he removed his galoshes. "Ahh, well now, home and dry, Ian.

"Home from home, well enough, but not dry." Ian smiled, striding towards him.

The Admiral laughed almost to a characteristic deep cough. "This morning when I awoke, I was inclined towards taking the yacht from Brighton. But a voyage out of the harbor and down the channel is much like my relationships with women in these years—young enough to carry on, but too old to have it off."

The two men laughed amply and greeted each other with a rough hug.

"It was lovely out this morning. I walked over to Babbacombe and back before lunch," Ian said. "There wasn't a cloud around then."

"I'm afraid it'll be bucketing down on us through tomorrow and Sunday." Again, he shivered. "We're in for a quiet time. It's probably what you need."

"What will you have to warm your bones?" Ian asked, motioning him towards the soft, white sofa which commanded the best view of the sea, the outer edge of Torbay, and, occasionally through the driving rain, a glimpse of Thatcher Rock now pummeled by fifteen-foot waves just beyond the park Ian and his father had anonymously donated to the Council of Torbay. They had paid £85,000 apiece to own the property, and enjoined their neighbors to buy the seven and a half acres across the road to prevent further development. It ensured a splendid view and enhanced property values for everyone.

"I'll have a brandy. Those sandwiches on the train left a lot to be desired. A brandy should make me forget them."

"Have a cigar if you'd like." Ian opened a box for select guests only. He never smoked and rarely allowed anyone else to do so on his property, but the admiral was a notable exception.

"I shall have one this evening. Thank you, dear chap. How does it feel to be a celebrity again? Has it hit you yet?"

"Just barely. It's like always here, though. The fishmonger in Torquay asked me yesterday afternoon if I was composing songs. The lady of the Ristorante Costa Fiorita acknowledged my newfound achievement and congratulated me. She was very restrained. These people are quite lovely and considerate here. A retired couple with a dog bought a pint of bitter for me at The Hole last night when Biggles the gardener and I went in. Very restrained, I'm happy to say."

Ian didn't let on that he felt that special tinge of fame nonetheless—a feeling of knowing a little more "of being inside the kitchen" than anyone else, an exclusive feeling like when he heard one of his compositions on the radio or in a lift. A gift had been returned to him, but he was humble enough to realize it could be taken away with time. He knew how to handle it. Acknowledge it only to one's self and closest friends, but realize his body and mind were still basically the same as before.

"Most people will be kind, especially here," Admiral Sinclair noted.

"I'm going through a bit of mental and emotional fatigue, somewhat like my father does after a campaign is completed, after all the crowds are gone. It's not unlike the atmosphere after the band broke up. There is a certain drive lacking now, not to mention the sporadic sleep I had on the plane, train, and ferry, and the abominable jet lag. When I've sufficiently recovered, I need to write an article on the behind the scenes aspect."

"You should save the `how it was done' for a book, you know," the admiral advised, taking the brandy tumbler from Ian. "Don't allow Vines the privilege of running that copy except as an excerpt. Do consult with your barrister about it, but I believe he can't hold you to such an assignment."

"I shall. It could mean I'll resign from the paper anyway. It was merely a job, a security blanket. It basically paid the living expenses in London and the upkeep here."

"I've always wondered why you took such a job."

"Boredom." Ian sat on the opposite corner of the couch with his long legs crossed and stretched out in front of a glass table. "Sheer boredom. But it wasn't worth the trouble, the criticism from Vines, not to mention the so-called modern pop artists. I despise boredom."

Ian reached over and playfully slapped the admiral's arm, rather uncharacteristically. "I talked to Veronica this morning as she was attending her father in his cubicle. She related to me everything her father had told her last night before he slid back into a coma again. You've always told me the truth, even after the fact. Can you now?"

"Please explain." Sinclair looked away nonchalantly. Ian recognized his friend's apprehensions and leaned backwards in the sofa to put him at ease.

"Don't panic, old fruit," Ian said. "The book will not mention names or compromise your noble efforts in any way whatsoever. And besides, I'm not going to publish it until the governments of Great Britain, Belgium, Italy, France, and Germany allow us to examine the locations. Thank God for the bloody EU for once. Actually, maybe I'll write two books. One on how it was done, and the other a scholarly tome on the new works with an American coauthor who may popularize the book there." He pointed in the southeast direction across the bay past Peignton. "She should have ample access to her father's papers."

"How can you expect the governments to comply?" the admiral sighed. The admiral seemed resigned.

Ian asked himself, was the revelation of de Vere as the author destroying the cause and crusade? Were they deflating because the campaign was nearly complete, even though fulfilled beyond wildest expectation?

"My father tells me the Prime Minister is meeting with the Queen on Tuesday morning about the matter so they might spin it towards enhancing the tourist trade—New Cool Britannica. The locations of the concealed documents are supposed to be in walls and floors of old castles, churches, and government buildings—Lancaster Castle, Warwick Castle, the Tower, situs impregnable—and why would any tourists avoid Stratford? The Royal...Shakespeare (ahem)... Theatre still draws the best actors and actresses in the English theatre. The Trust is still there. Granted, the birthplace and Anne Hathaway's Cottage have suddenly become meaningless. The Avon is lovely. Trinity Church is picturesque even with a famous nonentity supposedly buried there. The whole trap is charming, and they know how to cope with American and Japanese tourists. The kitsch industry will still thrive. The exciting phase is about to begin. The campaign is won. It's time to execute the research, the discoveries, the truth."

"What does your father think will happen?" the admiral asked.

"He thinks the PM will convince her, based on the uproar among the hoi polloi. The upper classes are gobsmacked, silent, but it is the middle class—teachers, researchers, students, bookworms, pensioners—who seem to be expressing the loudest protest thanks to a media that won't leave them alone about it. This certainly isn't the poll tax problem, or the war, but there are enough people anxious to see the new plays and read the new sonnets that it's making a difference. There were nine letters to the editor this morning in the *Guardian*, and I'm bringing back my old dependable agent for a speaking tour. One of her employees is superb at commanding fees for such venues. She can book nice venues for me as well."

"The revelations on Yank telly that indicate yet another play and another sonnet only add to the furor. Your evidence didn't identify those, did they? Clearly, Richtol kept the one document on the other locations, but he's shared it with you," the admiral said.

"Right." Ian smiled. "Your trusted friend McCann gave me one more very important photo of a document Richtol kept before we parted company. He was holding it hostage in case I didn't perform my duty. It was the Sturm letter. The evidence from the film crew is supposed to appear in the Sunday papers. Vines is e-mailing me a copy of the Associated Press account when it arrives this afternoon. I hope we can trust McCann."

The admiral tried to change the subject. "I certainly hope Tyler heard about that before he kipped down. I was amazed to learn he'd ever awakened. I hope he realized the mission was accomplished beyond expectation."

"He did, although he couldn't articulate it. Veronica said he nodded and his eyes were extremely bright in spite of his condition. It was probably too much for him." Ian shifted a crossed leg. "I saw a poll in the *Times* and most of the public had not heard of or seen Shakespeare's *King John*, but when asked if they wanted to see a never before published or produced work, they shouted a roaring `yes' to the tune of about eighty-seven percent."

"Not every school boy at Eton has ever read *King John*, but the fact that it now includes the one and only Magna Carta makes it a whole new play, doesn't it?" the admiral said.

"Most definitely, though it may have been an early version expurgated by the Crown," said Ian, "and imagine, to think this soliloquy by this character about the `new soil, thou art three-piled loam awaiting fresh toil' for `her benevolent Grace Queen Arabella' should play well in the States, too. That transparency and is it possible a Robert, Earl of Huntington, revelation...?"

"Of Sherwood Forest!" the admiral interjected, his eyes lit.

"The Robin Hood plays...as well as the discovery of the New World. How arresting!"

"Yes, those marvelous, but jejune, plays that apparently became refined into a solid work, repressed all these years." Admiral Sinclair shook his head, sniffing the brandy tumbler.

"Father says most MP's are supporting the PM, so there is a consensus. By the way," Ian lifted his eyebrows superciliously, "did you plan the political aspect, too?"

"You've been thinking entirely too much. Two books, you leave your work, American girlfriend, this so-called manipulation we've allegedly schemed...I am..."

Ian's voice rose as he interrupted. "I shall not hold it against you. I desire simply to know, dead cert, the truth so I can reconstruct the story without jeopardizing you, Veronica, if she is in on it, Dr. Colton, anyone else. How far does it go? Who was McCann? Can I describe him in my text at all? Will he appear stiffed in some alley in Soho some night if I allude to him? Or will I? When did the manipulation begin? Where did Boone Phelps go wrong? How did Phelps discover you were in it? Why wasn't the government more successful or more alert?" He had ticked the questions off on his long, bony fingers and held them open as if anxious for answers. "I do deserve some answers merely as a friend who is grateful to have been the one to capture the Holy Grail. My ego isn't so big that I need to be spared the details on how I was used for the mission. I am, dear friend, most humbled to have played such an instrumental role as the central figure in the project. I *have* made some history, you know. I simply need to know how I've done it, accidentally as it may have been. What are the outer bounds?"

The admiral coughed as he sipped another bit of brandy. "If you will fetch me some more of this, I shall tell you as much as I know. While you're replenishing, how is Colton?"

"Veronica says the doctor is not very optimistic. He believes more clots have formed. It's probably only a matter of days, and I'm thinking you and I better leave Monday morning instead of Tuesday. There's an early train to Newton Abbot that changes for the 9:20 InterCity. I'll bring the bottle over here." He set it on a coaster and strolled over to the large bay windows where the rain was pelting a staccato rumble against the glass. From this angle, the hoary form of the rock outside in the distance, edged by a small tree-lined cliff, gripped his view momentarily.

"Ian, dear soul," the admiral began, "there was no conspiracy on our part to have you involved, except towards the end after you met Richtol in New York. Originally, in early December, I tried to sell you to him as the man we needed for the stories right before the break-ins—the first of which we discovered was a hoax, thanks to one of McCann's minions leaking the information at a pub and tipping off the authorities. He was bragging to some tart who sleeps with a married London bobby. No one knows who he is. It could have been the cockney bloke. Oh yes, please don't reveal any names or descriptions in a show-and-tell book. You fell into a most convenient situation by some small luck and much perspicacious skill, according to your new friends in New York. I had a phone chat with Richtol last night, who judged you a godsend under the circumstances—their plan was in some disarray. You managed at the end of the day to convince Richtol you were the best reporter here for the simultaneous release of the scoop, but I couldn't sell you to him originally, especially after he'd concluded Phelps was the man. Richtol had some control, he felt, over Phelps, and he failed to remember you again until you two met in that hotel room. Colton would've agreed to have you, of course, and we would have out voted Richtol, but he was thoroughly convinced the minute you blurted Shakspere. In that room, you were always Colton's choice. He knew you were one of us. We should've included you from the start. But there was hesitation on his part since he wasn't sure how long Vines would keep you around. When he allowed you the editorial space, I called Richtol and begged him right after Richtol read your op-ed. He didn't want to undo what he'd done with making an initial contact with Phelps. He felt he had time with McCann's circuitous route back to England. Richtol is very sick, too, but always a boorish, truculent character." He paused to sip his brandy. "Phelps was on standby and really knew little initially."

Ian remained fixed at the bay window, his back to the admiral, not wanting to stop the flow of words.

"See, Richtol was headstrong about Phelps's credentials. He'd met him once at a speaking engagement after the Flick Affair. Colton talked to Phelps about a week before he arrived in London and nearly signed on, but he told me he wanted to give it to you. I never got involved with Phelps or met McCann. I wanted to stay out of the legwork. Phelps never even heard my name, I'm sure. After I met Phelps in Stratford, I knew he wasn't the man for the job. After Vines assigned you the coverage in Stratford, and my knowing your keen interest, I wanted you more than ever on it. Richtol is Colton's barrister and a very close friend as well as a member of the Oxford Society. Richtol and Colton served in World War II together in the American OSS. Richtol is dying of bone marrow cancer and decided to gift a large sum of cash to the project. I contributed as well. The total amount was about £150,000. Richtol found McCann, not his real name, in the National Security Agency where he was stationed as a code scrambler in England and Germany. His twenty-year career was halted a few years back when he was suspected of aiding a German company's selling of nerve gas to the Iraqis."

Ian grunted and curled his lips as if tasting an off tin of kippers when thinking of McCann.

"It seems he became desperate for money because of a series of rather rapid romances, culminating in a serious liaison with a Munich crumpet who calls herself an artist—from Schwabing. She became pregnant, he took his retirement to support his new family, and then found this opportunity."

"Where is he now?" Ian asked. He began to pace.

"He's taken what money he didn't spend in the mission and some he's saved to retire in the village of St. Johann im Pongau, Austria, near Salzburg. They're running a small ski shop. Richtol's best friend knew of the place, and Richtol got someone to manage all the legal work. He felt we could depend on him to complete the mission, although he was threatened just the same that his wife would be implicated in some sort of drug-running scheme if he didn't perform. McCann was a dependable sort until his mid-life crisis struck. Richtol doesn't divulge too much, and with the matters involved in the US concerning the film crew and Wolf News, there's not much use in pursuing more about McCann. I didn't ask much. I know that Richtol assured Wainwright that he had a scoop, which should remain confidential, and the agreement was that after they filmed it, they would run it only on the day when your story ran. That's what they did, as promised. It was a bullet in the ratings in America."

"And after I rang him as code name Arthur Golding, Oxford's uncle" Ian said, still looking away from his friend. "That was the arrangement we made while in New York to cue them."

"Yes."

"What about the timing of the break-ins?" Ian asked.

"We had to have McCann break in the night after the hoax, since we believed, correctly as it turned out, that the Stratford authorities would have their guard down. They must have thought no one would try such a thing the night after. McCann himself called in the fake fire alarm at the Royal Shakespeare Theatre. It was the perfect diversion for a good forty minutes. McCann knew exactly where to penetrate the section above the bust once he was inside. Oxford's people, probably the Herbert brothers, wanted something placed there upon erection of the monument. Amazing chutzpah. But we'd originally planned for the break-ins both to occur on the same night—actually the night of the Hatfield break-in."

"So McCann has accomplished his mission. He was a dodgy sort. I didn't know whether to trust him completely," Ian said, and looked the admiral directly in the eye. "For example, he hands me an envelope containing a photo of document 17 on the locations of another document, which Richtol kept. I only receive the top portion showing Chartsworth. Was that Richtol's instruction or McCann's rogue work? I'll ask Richtol when we chat."

"Yes...well. We've a local resident checking on him just in case he tries to tell all. If he tries anything at all, well, his wife knows what would happen. McCann is very much the pig in the middle."

Ian sat down on the couch and rubbed his chin slowly. "How did you discover there were indeed papers inside Trinity Church and Hatfield House? Did I have it right assigning the execution of de Vere's desire to hide the artifacts to the Herberts and daughter Susan?"

The admiral rubbed his chin. "I'll tell you all I know. You got pretty much all of it right in your editorial. Some of what I'll tell you here is speculative, but I think I'm close to being spot on."

"One of our scholars found a letter in Strasbourg from Oxford two years ago that identified a diagram and a site for, quote, `some works and letters by the Earl of Oxenforde the safekeeping by

Johannes Sturmius at the Strasbourg Gymnasium and for release after Oxenfords death or imprisonment.' It had a precise mention of an exterior wall, we found out later, at Theobalds House, Lord Burghley's large property north of London. This location was where Oxford spent much of his youth and training. A hiding place there would be perfect since he knew it so well and had easy access... however, the letter had a clear diagram but no reference to a building and its location."

"The letter also referred to a letter to Susan de Vere with the same location in the wall in her father's collections, which I thought might still survive in the British Library. I wanted to have it researched before the move to St. Pancras. Ironically, the paper was right there in the British Library, accidentally given to our young scholar by the clerks during the preparation for the move to St. Pancras. It was either too important to release to anyone, and they knew, or no one knew its value without the other letter to Sturmius. Probably in the old days, the former, later days, it was the latter. We may never know. Robert Cecil had intercepted it, we believe, failed to destroy it, and it evidently was secreted in the library somehow and only found its way out during the stressful move. The letter to Susan also related a later letter from Sturmius would indicate a precise location on a property without naming it. This letter found by our researcher from Sturmius to Susan named Theobalds House, as I said. Incidently, the letter may have triggered a two day incarceration of the Earl of Southhampton upon Oxford's death, since Southampton may have known where most of the works were hidden but didn't talk, or at least tell all. That arrest was particularly mysterious and we'll probably never know why precisely."

"Perhaps Robert Cecil was not quite the administrator that his father, Lord Burghley, was. Walsingham and Burghley were masters of deceit and manipulation, and long dead by then, as you know. Why he didn't act on it? Who knows? It may have been a simple oversight on his part. His days were as full as his father's."

Ian shook his head at this scenario and the possible strange twist of fate.

"Only the name of one location was known then, thanks to the letter to Susan-- Theobalds To repeat: The diagram was in the Oxfrord letter to Sturmius. It indicated a likelihood of being inside a wall and was marked precisely. I couldn't match them to a building. He rubbed his nose and poured a bit more brandy.

"Sturm died long before James the First, and possibly the letter we found in Strasbourg was forgotten by whoever had the responsibility. Regardless, the Sturm letter from Oxford sat there in Strasbourg for centuries. That's the photo McCann handed you before you left the materials at your father's flat. When we discovered it in Germany, I contacted Richtol, who contacted Colton, who contacted me, and so we triangulated and set on our scheme."

"How did the documents get to Trinity Church and the monument as well as the outbuilding at Hatfield House?" Ian asked. "I presume they wanted them out of Theobalds when the King acquired it from Robert Cecil in exchange for Hatfield House.

"Yes. Now, aware of the modus operandi, we found an indication in a document from the Earl of Pembroke, William Herbert, suggesting they found out about de Vere's letter to Sturm and the instructions, simply enough, from Phillip Herbert's (the Earl of Montgomery) wife and Oxford's daughter, none other than Susan de Vere. She simply told them of the secret location at Theobalds which was told to her by her father, shortly before dying. No letter was needed. They probably fetched the papers and held them until an opportunity came to conceal them again. Meanwhile they hired Ben Jonson to edit and copy all of the manuscripts."

Ian raised his hand to interject. "Ben made money from Burleigh, then off of the Herbert brothers and Susan and achieved even more fame with his intro to the First Folio. You say an indication in a document from Pembroke. Did it indicate Hatfield House and the monument in Trinity?"

"We found a cryptic letter in Montgomery's collection that indicated both locations precisely, which only made sense in context of the knowledge of hidden works, especially at Theobalds," the admiral replied. "Since it said nothing of what was to go in there, we had to assume it was artifacts given the pattern now established at Theobalds. 'Arms coat the words' was the phrase, as I recall, for the area above the bust. Cryptic. But, the coat of arms embrace the manuscripts, the words, where they were hidden compactly. An earlier letter referred to the 'new structure' at Hatfield as 'to replace the site at Theobalds.'

It indicated a precise location but made no mention of artifacts. That letter was about 1605 as I recall. Given what was found there, it lead me to believe the Earls and Susan placed portions already copied for use in the First Folio, if and when they achieved control."

"Robert Cecil was having the old palace re-built as stables at Hatfield estate and a lapidary had probably been paid handsomely by the Earls and/or Susan for the insertion in the wall during construction or under a pretext of repair. So, one or both brothers engineered the transfer once they found out the King was taking Theobalds in exchange to Robert Cecil for Hatfield House. All of this would have taken place in about 1605, about one year after Oxford's death."

Ian formed a large grin. "Yes. The 'incomparable pair of brethren' became even more incomparable."

"Now, all this happened during their quest for the crucial post of Lord Chamberlain of the Royal House," said the admiral. "In late 1615, they did succeed when Pembroke achieved the position. They may have held all the remaining documents which Susan and. Montgomery had in their possession until 1626 and the publication of the First Folio. After then, they would have contacted Sturm's people for placement in caches on the continent or some had been placed already and they had more placed in England as well. We assume this knowledge was given to them by Susan verbally. About that time, the initial monument to Shakespere was erected or refurbished in Trinity Church and they found a way to insert another collection which Johnson had edited and completed in the section above the bust in the monument"

"Refurbished?" Ian said as he raised his brows.

"Originally, the monument may have been of Shakspere's father, John, a grain trader and Mayor of Stratford. The "pair of brethren" may have been responsible for the vague language below the monument and used its carving as a pretext for lodging the documents. All of this is based on some speculation, but it's clear that Susan, her husband and brother-in-law were dedicated to publishing the First Folio properly and preserving the artifacts in places which might not allow anyone in power to apprehend given the uncertainty of power in the Kingdom—especially the locations on the continent as arranged by Sturm's people."

Ian nodded. "No one had come forward, as probably planned by Oxford, Susan, the brothers and Sturm, to announce the locations revealing the truth."

"Or, whoever it was became petrified at the thought of such consequences, yet, Sturm's people went ahead with their plan, we believe. We'll see what's on the continent soon, we hope, once Richtol lists all the locations, which should take a fortnight or so.."

"Who else was involved besides you, Richtol and Colton?" Ian raised an eyebrow and cocked his head to the left.

"Naturally Wainwright and his people, and Ms. Aldridge at Wolf News."

"I completely forgot to ring her," Ian said at first with wide eyes and then squinted as he started to ask if contacting her was part of his anointment in coverage of the authorship question.

The admiral quickly interrupted. "Doesn't matter. Wainwright got the footage for her. At any rate, I told Vines I believed you were hot on the story and were close on the miscreant's tail, because I said that you'd seen or heard about some Sherlock Holmes clue. Actually, I leaked this to Vines so that he would not allow you to cancel the New York trip because I believed you would get back on the trail there. I told him yet another reporter had some hard information that the suspects would end up at the debate at the inn. Naturally, I didn't want to give up my cover and jeopardize my position in the scheme."

"So, you see, I was trying to place the story under your byline all along. I knew you had it planned anyway. Colton briefly suggested to me before he arrived in England that Phelps go there with Wainwright for the filming as a backup to the original plan, and I did not, could not, have Phelps as the reporter getting the scoop after meeting him in Stratford and Veronica telling me about his escapades in the Trinity Church. I firmly believe he would have blown the story. So, I convinced Vines to leave you on the story. He actually listened to me. You have no idea how close he was to putting you out on the street. It's the reason I had trouble convincing Richtol, even though he loved your editorial, as it appeared right before our project began."

"So Vines nearly did sack me," Ian mused, "and Phelps nearly got the story anyway."

"Almost." The admiral cast his eyes about the ceiling. "Our mistake was failing to prevent him from seeing Veronica and her father. The man stores an insatiable appetite for even the most excruciating detail, and will go to great lengths to achieve his ends. To ask the one incisive question in the limited time he was in the room alone with Tyler—" He shook his head. "He asked that poor man, 'Where and when are they sending the documents now?' He figured they were documents because he'd observed pillaging of the cache in Trinity Church at the cost of going to jail. He made the bald assumption that Colton was still involved somehow, and in testing it out, he got his answers, even though Richtol had already contacted him clandestinely through a phone call three days before—while you were flying to New York—asking that he meet McCann, without giving his name, in front of the British Museum. He's was a great journalist, but he's lost subtle aggression. The very idea of donning a beard and imitating my voice in front of Colton just to reconfirm the timing and the rendezvous." The old salty dog coughed, requiring a quick sip to soothe his vocal chords. "That's how he presented himself to poor, old, drugged-up Tyler—he imitated me. He assumed, correctly, that I had something to do with it. He knows how to probe. He spent much of the last few days trying to find me so he could make me talk. I presume he reckoned that if he couldn't find me to discuss it, then I was guilty of being a part of it."

"Incredible. Aunt Joan swore to Veronica that you came by to visit the day before my return. And so Phelps was designated for the pickup in front of the British Museum," Ian said.

"Richtol said he was the only major investigative reporter on the beat. So Phelps planned to take the papers to his office, with McCann, work up the story for the *Tribune*, return them to Colton's bedside, *and then* report their presence there to the Yard. After all, my boy Richtol had made the last contact with Phelps without my final consultation and the day before you met Richtol. Phelps was only told by the contact that he would need to meet McCann, described simply as a tall American with a briefcase, near the British Museum or Bristed House in the afternoon hours on either Thursday or Friday. McCann never knew to whom the documents were supposed to be delivered. He only had a vague description and some password—Richtol was big on that—and evidently didn't figure that out until he saw Phelps at Bristed House, containing your father's flat."

"Colton gave a clearer description of McCann to Phelps when Phelps was disguised as me. This was right after Richtol had called Colton—just after he came out of the coma—to update him on the plan for you and McCann to go to your father's flat at Bristed House. Richtol had been calling twice a day since Colton passed out, except, of course, when the phones were out at his hotel in New Paltz. Phelps desperately wanted the story. Phelps was very jumpy after a no-show at the British Museum on Thursday by you two. That's when he turned to impersonating me at Colton's bedside. To cover all angles he prodded Veronica to tell him when you would arrive. Richtol never told him you were on the case and with McCann. He assumed it as a worst case. He took a calculated risk, all the way. So much so he's in the nick."

The admiral raised his eyebrows dramatically in conclusion and pronounced, "The lag will spend some time writing from the nick. He'll be in the boob for his attempted breaking and entering."

"I haven't seen a mention of it since the day he was nicked. I assume so," Ian observed. "He even convinced Veronica to give him a ride to my father's flat as he assumed I was going to be there with McCann. Being with Veronica, he hoped I would trust him, then confront me with a sharing of the scoop. What was to guarantee that I would discover the papers and even return them?"

"In the face of the blizzard, nothing. Just before the phones went out, we'd told Richtol to seek you out once he'd arrived and they had successfully filmed and photographed the documents. Remember, he likely forgot who you were until you went through that routing on Oxfordian trivia. After all, he was handicapped by the accident, his drugs, his illness and having to worry about filling in for Colton on details here. You, obviously, followed him back to the inn and positioned yourself in the next room with a FBI bloke," the old mariner roared. "Marvelous! Brilliant! Tossing his trousers!"

"That was incredible," Ian smiled. "The FBI man had a piece of paper with my name scribbled on it. I had no idea who he was."

"He was merely looking for you to enquire as to whether you had made progress and help you, as per the request from the British ambassador and probably not entirely in order for jurisdiction of Yank Department of Justice—but probably a wink and a nod. But, fortunately, he never quite made the contact. He was restrained from trying to follow you by the doctor, since he was in bad shape. As a result, he believed you made off with the papers for their safe return to England—which you did to your father, no less, and thus honored the request by the British ambassador. The ambassador made the mistake of forgetting that your loyalty to your newspaper is equal to your patriotism. Her Majesty, I assume, did not expect you to publish. The FBI never even knew of McCann. All they knew was height. Both of you are tall. Richtol told McCann that you could deliver them to your father's flat in London, not to tell you that they would go to your father's flat, and for you to split up the papers so no one could be tempted to steal all of them. McCann would receive his money, in toto, upon their safe delivery to the assigned address, which neither of you knew completely until you both arrived thus the raggedy man in Liverpool Street station with the number." The admiral rose with a soft grunt. "Pardon me, Ian, but I'll continue after I'm back from the loo."

Ian raised his eyebrows as it suddenly hit him. The slip of paper in Admiral Sinclair's hand: "P helps. Try tomorrow." Phelps! It had nothing to do with incontinence. He'd almost forgotten the note. Ian concluded his close friend had been prepared to stay with Phelps at least right until the stroke occurred. As he said, Ian thought, it was after he'd met Phelps when his friend had doubts. And, Ian smiled grimly, who but the admiral knew the number of Ian's father's flat? For now, maybe forever, Ian decided not to bring the matter up.

The admiral returned. His voice echoed from the hallway as he marched towards the brandy table. "Richtol changed the plans because we didn't totally trust McCann and we didn't trust Phelps at all. We trusted you—particularly after your father told me the foreign secretary's office called him to ask how to telephone you. I'd phone your father making small talk to make sure I knew his whereabouts for the days ahead. I'd mentioned you'd be in New Paltz at the inn since he doesn't always know your movements. I knew you had a legitimate escape for returning the documents—you would be acting on behalf of the government. We think the FBI fellow at the airport was on the trail when he acted on the clue of the Sherlock Holmes cap sitting on your skull, and you said you were going to New Paltz for a Holmesian birthday celebration. I'm sure that was how the foreign secretary's office came to know you were going there—after the FBI interception at Kennedy. Since we knew the ambassador had more or less deputized you, in spite of only one brief communication according to him, we assumed correctly that you would read your role as being the safe *and sanctioned* delivery of the documents back to the government. Thus, you were perfect for the mission. We were worried about you making it to New Paltz and back to London, though, even secure in our knowing the route had been planned carefully by Ricthol, McCann, and me."

"Again, why didn't Richtol react favorably to me when I entered his room?" Ian questioned.

"Dear fellow, remember how you burst into the premises. McCann could probably sense you were harmless...but the rest of them weren't certain, although Richtol was adjusting to you, that is, whether you were the right chap. He was afraid you might be MI5 or the British embassy or even FBI. That fake pistol was the meat and drink." Sinclair laughed again. "What a smashing entrance! Richtol changed his mind about you after your trivia game. The penny dropped. Shakspere, indeed. The problem was I had no way of communicating with Richtol after the phones went down there, and by the time they were back in order, you were on the Continent."

"I was as fearful of them as they of me," Ian laughed sheepishly. "It was a special moment."

"I quite concur."

Ian shivered at the thought of all the cock-ups that could have been. "So where did McCann find the passport forger?"

"Passport forger?"

"Yes. There was this old Dutchman who boarded the train somewhere in Germany or Holland and devised an American passport for me. It was easy. He carried a camera and gave me an assumed name, American, called Todd. Later, when I read Phelps's article on what he'd pieced together, I was convinced—oh dear, what fatigue will do—that McCann intentionally wanted me to be a `tall American' since McCann was then assuming the disguise, skillfully I might add, of a German professor. I was horridly terrified. I took control of the project at that point, so to speak."

"That's ghastly...intriguing. McCann brought his own fellow over from Germany to work on this project—probably some toby from Munich. We found a similar fellow in Soho. He was the geezer you met in the Liverpool Street train station, a punter in deep debt, one of Richtol's old army friends. It's likely McCann had all kinds of little criminals. It's all too mysterious."

"So, you knew nothing of the passport photographer?"

"No—and it could be a problem if he kept any copies. I shall have McCann's neighbor check it out in St. Johann. McCann's neighbor is a drinking companion, so we should be able to stay informed.

We gave McCann some free reign. Richtol has done much legal work for this fellow. If I'm not mistaken, there's some sort of family connection, possibly with McCann's parents. Richtol developed an international law practise after the war—was stationed in Germany with Patton at Munich after the OSS."

"Richtol was a challenge. We had to go through this puerile word game on books dedicated to Oxford while I was standing there rigidly as if I had a pistol."

"You knew the two blokes filming. How did you know them, by the way? Your rock days? That confused Richtol momentarily."

"I was part of the rescue mission. Richtol paid no attention to anyone since he'd been injured. There were no introductions. Because of lack of room in the rescue vehicle, I chose to stay with the film crew in their car at the scene of the crash while the innkeeper, doc and others drove Richtol back up the mountain. I bluffed with them as though I knew very little and one of them told me enough to let me know they were indeed there to film something concerning the authorship question. Also, Richtol was so adamant about his attache coming with him, in hand. I knew it had to be cash or artifacts, or both. He also was determined to get the film crew, us remaining in the car, back up the mountain."

"Well, lad, you did indeed make the connection with Randle Richtol entirely on your own."

"What sort of barrister is Richtol?" Ian asked as though he'd forgotten.

"Much of it having to do with the US military overseas—mostly European—criminal and civil matters."

Ian abruptly stopped pacing. "You know, I haven't hesitated to ask you, and you have been more than forthcoming, but every bit of information makes me even more the accomplice." He wasn't sure he wanted to know more as he looked at his surrogate grandfather in a totally new light.

"Ian." The admiral detected Ian's dour shift in attitude. "I believe you know about enough. Richtol is dying of cancer. Colton isn't long for this world. They have little to lose. It was all a 'busted play' as Colton said, using an American footballers term. You and I are the best of chums, and no obstruction of justice or misprision charge will ever separate us, since one will never be filed. We're not going to be implicated—certainly not you. You're a hero at Whitehall, in spite of your reportage. You gave the valuables to the Crown. Furthermore, even if I'm implicated, that is as far as it will go. You are home and dry."

"My father?"

"Your father is a bit green over your marvelous success again, but he was more than happy to cooperate with me on the return of the papers. I merely informed him they might be coming at any day. I urged him to take responsibility over them in light of, as I put it, your brilliant success as an investigative reporter, dash, patriot. As I told him, I knew he'd return them promptly." Ian blushed as the admiral smiled very proudly at his accomplished friend. "Your father did his duty and asked no questions."

"I rang him as well. How much did Colton's blood clot have to do with the timing of the scheme?" These revelations about his father were now instantly reassuring him. Ian ignored the seemingly legitimate argument one could make that he'd been used by his friends. The success of reporting the truth behind the mask of William Shakspere dominated all else: his fame, his wealth, his mission of stimulating the masses. He had summoned forth a new feeling of deep contentment for truth that was the victor in revealing Shakspere's secrets."

"It was pivotal. A 'busted play.' Tyler was scheduled to intercept the papers and hurry them off under his arms and eyes to an old, remote hotel near Hay Tor, in Dartmoor, just miles from here—near Newton Abbot. He was to hire a car to take him there and convalesce for a few days while he wrote a report for presentation at the upcoming debate in America. That is, if the proof was going our way. The American film crew had planned to meet him there and film in another room. It had been an elaborate plan, carefully conceived. The incident at the studio, his brain hemorrhage, created much confusion since we felt his scholarship was essential—so the entire cache would have stayed in England. Richtol was quite adept at reading old documents. He was the other party to our knowledge, besides me, and had studied Marlowe at Cambridge, so we had no other choice."

"Richtol did not want to stray too far from his doctors, and I do believe this is the barrister in him,so he felt his part of the bargain could only be fulfilled by having the papers come to the US. With Colton out of the picture, he gained greater control, so we agreed to have McCann carry them to the US and that meant paying him more."

Ian cocked his head as though still unsatisfied, but he did recall Colton's warning about something exciting. Maybe he would have been invited to Hay Tor since he'd told Colton he'd planned to come here to Torquay being nearby. Maybe it all could have been done here, he thought.

"Ian," the admiral groaned as if searching for words, "it never occurred to me to invite you in on the story until all the pieces fell into place. It was Phelps by Richtol, and we were not happy with his choice." Was the brandy surfacing some trace of guilt over not holding on for Ian from the beginning? "After all, it was two sick men and..."

"Thee makes three," Ian grinned unctuously, imploringly. "What sort of scoundrel have I been mouching about with all these years?"

"I didn't underestimate you. Phelps was not the man for the job. I knew it. He's lost credibility in much of the press, especially now.

It's why only his paper and the *Guardian* carried the 'tall American' story." He tried to change the subject. "What a ruse."

Ian leveled his eyes at his longstanding friend. Why not bring it up, after all? "Explain the 'P helps. Try Tomorrow.' Not a note to loo before the cue, but a note to contact Phelps."

"I'd firmly decided to have Colton call Phelps and tell him the story was going nowhere. This was after your luncheon with Colton, and I presumed he'd be open to keep Phelps off the story. I wanted him to contact Richtol, and he didn't since he suffered his stroke. I called and had a long chat with Richtol the morning I met you and Veronica at the hospital. I'd pretty much succeeded to end Phelps as our contact at that point. Richtol was supposed to call Phelps at that point but could never find him before the phones went out at the inn. So I'm not sure it was effectively stopped except Phelps didn't know the documents were going to Richtol in New York."

"And he wasn't halted." Ian still wondered to himself as to why it would be set forth in a handwritten note. Maybe Colton had become forgetful. Maybe Arthur was reinforcing his verbal instruction. Ian would pursue it no further.

Ian whirled around from his slow pacing and smiled brightly. "Arthur, you're forgiven if you had doubts about me. But you're too riveting. You're quite a schemer for a man who came up to admiral."

"That's how one gets there. I never informed you, but I ploughed at the Royal Naval College…too much plonk and fanny on the Isle of Dogs. My academics were poor. Damn good thing the war came along for many students like me."

The two men laughed like schoolmates sharing a rude joke. Above, the pelting rain and thunder soared as the admiral tossed back his brandy with a jerk.

"You're achieving a rare form." Ian took the tumbler for another refill without asking the desideratum.

"I'm the only survivor, at least in some reasonable state of health, to tell you the story. Colton executed much of this. He had already paid McCann a deposit and told me later it was Richtol's money. I believe they were determined to accomplish this mission whether I agreed to it or not. Expediency. I suppose it's why I don't fault Elizabeth and the Cecils too much. They were building a nation in very perilous times. Expediency."

Ian handed him the glass as the telephone rang on the nearby bookshelf. It was Veronica.

"Ian, I had to call."

"I hope it's not dreadful news." Ian ground his teeth, expecting her to report her father had died.

"No. I do expect the worst soon, though. I wish I could be there. I wish you were here. Anyway, I have an exciting piece of news from Brad Vines. He doesn't have your number there."

"Oh, yes."

"A pensioner has come forward with a few remnants of what appears to be the *Love's Labour Won*" play. He said he'd found it accidentally one morning after the London Blitz among some ruins at Gray's Inn where it had been shaken largely intact from inside a support. He didn't know what it was at the time and quickly set it in some old drawer, then forgot about it in the confusion during the bombing. Vines paid him a sum and is going to run it in tomorrow's edition. He's inviting anyone else who has knowledge of similar documents to come forward immediately."

"Extraordinary!"

"He says your father told him, as well as one of the minister of cultural affairs assistants, that the government is going to cooperate in locating the other documents, and opening the inquiry on our man Oxford."

"Hold, my dear, while I tell the admiral. Arthur, splendid news..."

Chapter Thirty-Four

High above the trees of London's Hyde Park floated the griffon vulture, riding thermal air like buoyant waves of water. The baby blue sky above reflected on the crowds of roving animals below as the bird scanned, his penetrating eyes searching for a proper carcass. There must be one. It was a cold January day so something would die. God would provide.

Tyler Colton was more puzzled at the sights on this day than he had ever been before. He recognized the griffon vulture circling above, totally out of its geographical range. Only he, among all the people surrounding the tub-thumpers at Speaker's Corner, saw it and knew its closest habitat as being the coast of Spain. It was clearly the inimitable griffon. No other vulture in Europe had the characteristic brown body and the white feathers on the neck and head. He'd seen one on Torremolinos on a Sunday morning years ago. Two German boys had told him of the legend they believed as told by one of the local barmaids: "The bird was searching for the next overdosed teen, homeless person with an expired liver, or a drowned partygoer. Otherwise, the birds flew to the bullring in Barcelona on a Sunday afternoon."

Dr. Colton wasn't as concerned about the legend. He was more baffled at the baby pram he felt jolting him—more so when he recognized the woman who was pushing him. It was his late mother. He'd lived too long to revert to this odd dream, but at least he could see his mother.

A grey-haired, impish man ahead on the sidewalk stood on a wooden crate just beyond the steel rail as his mother pushed the carriage up the green hill on the black asphalt, which led like a neat, dark ribbon from the wind-whipped Serpentine Lake's café where they'd been for lunch.

"We're each streams running into the ocean," said the short, spry fellow with darting leprechaun eyes moving slowly on the wooden crate as he spoke to a small crowd. "All one religion."

"That means we are all wet," a tall, bald fellow with a prominent red beard pronounced, eyes rolling lugubriously.

"Why don't you dry up?" another heckler shouted nearby.

The audience, getting bored now, was turning to pounce on other prey. There was a ridiculous black racist in the next crowd when the religious speaker made the bold remark, "Our goal in life is to annihilate the little self. We must become humble and childlike again."

The tall bearded one pivoted upon hearing this, his whiskers extending in parallel with his furled umbrella brandished like a sword of crusading pontification. "I'm from the Royal Society for the Prevention of the Annihilation of the Little Selves and if you don't watch it, you'll be visited by the Big Self."

The crowd roared with laughter as applause broke out. The herd turned back.

"Why are you bothering to listen to me today?" the speaker asked.

"I'm doing it purely in the charitable tradition of this recent Christmas season," said the Great Beard. "Merry Christmas, Barry."

"You should listen to me," Barry rejoined. "There is substance here. In a sound system you don't pay attention to the sound speakers, you should pay heed to the producer of the sound, even though he's far away."

Great Beard pointed to a desolate spot on the Serpentine, near the café, far away in the expanse of the park. "Why don't you go stand over there? We can hear you better." The crowd laughed again. Colton laughed. He looked up to admire his young mother. What's she doing here? he thought. She's more beautiful than I could ever remember.

"What you should do, Barry, is join the Freemasons," another heckler kindly advised. "You're saying the same thing, really."

"No," Barry protested, "they wear aprons, don't allow women, bare their breasts, and such silly things."

"You're down on them because the members are wealthy and successful, unlike you," Great Beard observed. "That's the truth of the matter." Great Beard stomped away, feigning disgust, much to the amusement of the crowd.

Colton began to cry. He felt his mother push him to a spot near the triangle, closer to the Marble Arch, where a crowd was gathering to hear another speaker. As they were approaching, Tyler stopped crying mid breath, arrested by the sight of himself. It must have been only a few months ago, yes, two summers ago with Randle Richtol. They had briefly met a tall, gaunt-faced man where they stood near the back of a crowd gathered around a commanding African college student dressed in a suit eloquently articulating the beliefs of Dr. Mangosuthu Buthelezi and the Inkatha Party. Richtol was handing the tall man a book. It had Sherlock Holmes mentioned in the title with gold letters, which he grasped and held under his arm. The man strode to the cavernous pedestrian walkways leading to the intersection of Bayswater Road with Edgeware Road and Park Lane. After about five minutes, the man emerged at the Marble Arch. Another ten minutes went by as the child watched the two men, who gave the book away, chatting nervously with each other and staring at the man who stood several hundred yards away under the Marble Arch. Then the tall man left the monument, retraced his steps to the two men, and nodded approval. The tall man and Richtol left together, the book still lodged safely under the tall man's left forearm.

Colton watched himself take short steps towards "Barry the Unitary" and then slowly stroll towards the café at the bottom of the hill and the edge of the Serpentine.

Then mother and young son glided over to a small cluster forming where a young, female student and an old man, a professor, stood in front of a worn, brown podium. The people were curious about a sign the old man hung around his neck proclaiming "Shakespeare Was the True Author."

"My colleague and I have come down from Hertford College this cold but sunny Sabbath to make the case for the man who gave the world so much—Mr. William Shakespeare of Stratford-Upon-Avon."

The small crowd hissed and laughed. Two elegantly dressed older women shook their heads and walked away.

"I shall like to begin by reciting the known facts about Mr. Shakespeare. He was born on 26 April 1564, and an entry of license for marriage was issued to him on 27 November 1582. On 28 November 1582, a bond of sureties for marriage was issued to him, `William Shagspere on thone partie, and Anne Hathwey of Stratford.' On 26 May 1583, Susanna was christened as were Hamnet and Judeth on 2nd of February 1585."

Colton's tiny mouth yawned in a fleeting, oval puff. He kicked his left leg excitedly and threw his right arm towards the vulture. The griffon should be licking his chops at those two blathering anachronisms, he thought.

"On 11 August 1596, Hamnet was buried. On October 20 of the same year, a grant of arms was made to John Shakespeare. Also, sometime that year, the sheriff of Surrey issued a writ of attachment against Shakespeare and others. In 1597, a collector from Byshopsgate failed to collect a tax from William Shakespeare as he was also unable to do in the two following years. The exchequer also finds him delinquent in 1599 and in 1600."

"He sounds like a man after my own overtaxed heart," said Great Beard, who had slid into the midst of the ever-growing crowd. A ripple of laughter prompted the professor to pause and look around helplessly as if deciding whether to dignify the heckling.

"Well, mark my words, sir, it's about this time. He negotiates for New Place in 1597, one of Stratford-Upon-Avon's best homes. It cost him the tidy sum of £60, and that should have placed anyone in a tight way at the time. In fact, we have a series of letters involving primarily Mr. Richard Quiney and his desire to borrow money from William Shakespeare. The Bard wasn't only a great writer, but a businessman who involved his money so widely he made the occasional faux pas with the tax collector like any other businessman of then or now. In May of 1602, he profits enough to purchase property from William and John Combe of Stratford. So, he obviously was a shrewd businessman in spite of troubles with the taxman."

Great Beard raised his beard and umbrella like an elephant preparing to spout water from his trunk. "Yes, and according to the *Times* article, he was hoarding corn the whole time. Do you have any evidence he found the time to write?"

Again, the crowd laughed. In 1598, he *was* cited for hoarding, Colton thought, frustrated since he could only mumble and kick.

"Yes, my dear sir, if you will allow me, or I should say my young friend here, Evelyn, from the drama school to carry on. She'll be less tolerant of your rude interruptions."

"It's my duty," Great Beard smiled eloquently, "since most of these dear, patient people are too speechlessly mortified over your argument, purely nihil ad rem."

"In May of 1603, a license for the King's Men, an acting company, lists Lawrence Fletcher, William Shakespeare, Richard Burbage, Augustyne Phillipps, and others as players in the stage plays. In March of the following year, Shakespeare is listed as one of a group of, presumably, actors receiving a red cloth in a proceeding for King James through London."

However, thought Colton, the detailed account mentions no *actors* in red. Was he even an actor?

"That same year," Great Beard blared, "Willielmus Shexpere, spelled S-h-e-x-p-e-r-e, and Willielmum Tetherton sue Phillipum Rogers over a small debt in Stratford."

"Good show," someone said to Great Beard, nodding with a grin.

"And the next year, S-h-a-k-e-s-p-e-a-r leases some tithes, spelled t-i-t-h-e-s," Great Beard continued. The young girl was becoming visibly frustrated.

"In May of the same year," she huffed, "a fellow actor by the name of Augustine Phillips wills `to my fellowe William Shakespeare a thirty shillings peece in gould, to my fellowe Henry Condell one other thirty shillinge peece in gold...'"

"In 1608, Mr. Willielmo S-h-a-c-k-s-p-e-a-r-e, it is spelled, secures the arrest of one Johannem Addenbrooke for a debt and the suit proceeds through 1609. In 1610, he buys a freehold in Old Stratford," Great Beard shouted.

"Well, what of it?" The professor was red-faced, angry.

"Nothing, because he was too busy to write. In the year after, he and a Richard Lane and Thomas Greene are involved in a lawsuit concerning tithes in Old Stratford, Byshopton, and Welcombe. The next year he gives depositions in a suit concerning third-party marital problems where he firmly identifies himself as being from Stratford-Upon-Avon."

"Well, in 1613 he bought a house in London." The young girl lifted her nose pertly.

Great Beard shook his head defiantly, mockingly, and raised the pitch of his voice accordingly. "Well, we next hear from him in 1615 when Thomasina Ostler alleges in a lawsuit that your man Shakespeare, Augustine Phillips, and Thomas Pope, original shareholders of the Globe Theatre, are generosis defunctus—that means dead. But we know that William S-h-a-k-s-p-e-r-e, his preferred spelling, is very much alive in Stratford at the time. He dies in 1616, when the will is executed, sans manuscripts, sans unpublished literary property, without even a single solitary book of any kind. If it were not for Johannes Sturmius, Susan de Vere and the Earls of Montgomery and Pembroke, Burghley's conspiracy might have succeeded forever!"

The professor was thoroughly outdone with the bearded one. He stepped rapidly towards him and balled his fist. "I'll destroy you, you charlatan! My life is built on him. You can't take it away, you pervert!" He grabbed for his beard and the large man dodged.

Colton's mother began pushing away the baby carriage containing her kicking, screaming son who was staring straight up at the griffon. The bird was recklessly soaring down at him. Why? He was a baby under full protection of his mother. He glanced over at his older self who was heading for the tunnel, the underground pedestrian walkway that networked under the streets and the Marble Arch to the sidewalks and buildings across from the park. Old man Colton was terrified, clutching his head, screaming a terrifying yelp like a dog hurt on a night deep in the woods. Baby Colton was screaming, kicking, frantic to gain the cover of the tunnel as well. They passed the old man who uttered in a low, desperate voice, "I'm not going to make it. I wanted so much to see my work completed. I can't make it."

His mother grabbed the old man and trailed him along. Baby Tyler Colton saw the griffon floating down less than fifty feet away. They were almost to the entry of the tunnel. If only they could make it. "Your work's done. You did well, so well, son," came her soft whispering voice brushing his ears like the gentlest of feathers.

The griffon made an uncharacteristic alarming call, like a disturbed American blue jay. It was closing the gap rapidly.

Mother and sons dashed down the steps and into the depths of the pedestrian subway in the nick of time. The griffon hit the top edge of the tunnel, squawking vehemently, bounced onto the pavement, and flapped its wings as if they were broken.

The old man collapsed as his mother held his arm over her shoulder and pushed the baby carriage down the passageway. She miraculously steadied the old man and the carriage as they scrambled down the stairs. The carriage teetered once, with baby Colton shrieking screams of terror.

She stood at the foot of the stairs with the old man mumbling while he hung over her shoulder, the baby screaming at the top of his voice. She and the baby saw an utterly black, dark void up ahead. There was no air, but the three felt strangely secure, comfortable in the chamber. They felt peace, a balm for all of life's arduous pain, a healing for the multitude of scars suffered in life.

"I'll take us there," they heard his mother say. "All to be at peace. You performed magnificently, son."

At the end of the tunnel was a small light, growing with each step they took. A light blue star grew larger in a misty shroud. There were shadows, then softly discernible figures walking gently towards them. The trio was reassured as they heard soft, whispering voices echo, "We've been waiting for you." "You are safe now," another said. "Mother came along to escort you here. She's missed you," a voice splashed across his ears in a quiet, reassuring tone. He didn't see a face or a body, only a vague figure, a form, but it was undeniably his father. It was as if he were seeing his soul, he vaguely conjectured.

Sniffing, he smelled an airy shroud of foggy vapors like that rising from a waterfall, refreshing and pure. He'd never felt such invigoration and comfort, yet he had a desire to know absolutely everything, to know things he'd never before been curious about. Sakharov's concept of the Zero Lagrangian inexplicably crossed his mind. Profound thoughts filled his fertile mind on several levels, fulfilling emotions deep and raw. Was the ivory-billed woodpecker really extinct? Who were the Melungeons? What's behind the mystery of space and time?

"Mother, Father, I have missed you so," he sobbed in a full-hearted joy, reaching for them, a warmth penetrating his entire being. It was as though he'd had a long-time illness and now, at least, the full reinvigoration of recovery. "You're so good to me."

"We have someone you've been anxious to meet, and he's so anxious to meet you. You have given him a mirth that nobody can contain," his mother said.

"Dr. Tyler Colton, you liberated my tortured, imprisoned legacy." Colton heard the voice of Edward de Vere. "I shall tell you the entire truth about my life beyond the basic facts unearthed by you and your friends. It's my sole meager means of beginning to adequately thank you in this time we now have."

"Vero nihil verius," Colton said to the dark, misty shape beside him, now embracing him with warmth. The Latin was from the legend on the de Vere coat of arms: "Nothing truer than truth."

Colton's mother uttered words blown like hyacinth fragrance across her lips, past the two embracing men's faces. "You've each made the other immortal."

The misty shroud around the four beings was lifting—the light was brighter, now incandescent. Multitudes of cheering throngs shaped the distance...applauding.

The following sheet music is composed by Ian Scarborough (J. Timothy Tatum) and Edward de Vere with some minor tweaks by Ian Scarborough (your truly) in lyrics for the first page and entirely by Ian for the second—rough draft though they may be.

Oxford's Revival
By Timothy Tatum
(Lute Song)
*First Verse Lyrics by Timothy Tatum
Lyrics On Second Verse by Timothy Tatum
Acoustic Guitar (Plucked)
*Some Additions by Aaron Tatum
℗ Copyright 1990 by Timothy Tatum
Synths: Clarinet
+ Strings (Strings In Middle of Fourth Line)

OXFORD'S REVIVAL
BY TIMOTHY TATUM
(LUTE SONG)
2ND VERSE
FIRST VERSE LYRIC ADDITIONS
SECOND VERSE LYRICS
BY AARON F. TATUM
℗ COPYRIGHT 1990 by
TIMOTHY
TATUM

Dedication and Acknowledgements

As noted, this book is dedicated to my late wife, Maria Reichel Tatum, ever patient and lovely, to my late mother, Inadene Rogers Tatum, a saint and lovely, and the late Mr. Charlton Ogburn Jr., who gave me magnanimous encouragement and written permission to utilize his earth-shattering and detailed research providing the chief facts in this work of fiction.

I presented a few fictions as historical fact (the Sturmius connection as repository of caches, the caches of documents themselves, the new sonnets and lines from new plays) to provide one small leap of faith for those empirically-minded souls incapable of recognizing the abundance of circumstantial evidence in Mr. Ogburn's *The Mysterious William Shakespeare* (Dodd-Mead) 1984, and other more recent works.

Oh yes, thanks to the late Joseph Sobran for his incisive review of Ogburn's book in "National Review" and giving me the pleasure to start this intellectual journey. Joe was a good friend. His *Alias Shakespeare (Free Press)* 1997 was very helpful. Joe was a superb writer. So valuable has been my close friend Charles Beauclerk, author of numerous excellent books, including *Shakespeare's Lost Kingdom* (Grove Press) 2010. His advice, counsel and friendship always served me greatly, as did his great knowledge of the issue. All of his books are so well-written and researched. Do read them.

Thanks to my brother, J. Timothy Tatum, for his compositions and their use (see enclosed sheet music), along with his considerable computer skills. Thanks to my other brother, Lloyd R. Tatum, Esq., for his patience with me on legal questions that necessarily arise when characters do what they inevitably do outside of the author's vain attempt at control. My father, Judge F. Lloyd Tatum (Ret.), also contributed on criminal law questions and how the F.B.I. operates, since he was an agent before his practicing legal career.

I heartily thank former editor Scott Whaley, of the *Chester County Independent* and all the staff there who allowed me to re-launch my most read and longest running work, the column "A.F.T.erthoughts" for over 10 years. It was revived from my undergrad days at the University of Tennessee Martin. I spread the circulation of the column to about ten other papers and it forced me to meet a deadline each week while keeping my writing skills at a healthy level.

The Stratford-Upon-Avon constabulary was kind enough to give me a tour of their jail—so gratifying to visit without committing or being nicked for even a misdemeanor. Early discussions of my project fell on the ears of then Oxford student, John Considine, now a professor at the University of Alberta and a leading world-renowned lexicographer. My good friend Steven N. Weed performed yeoman's work in reading the earliest manuscript with constant and sage advice.

World famous guitar genius Joe Walsh gave me insight way beyond my experience in a band as a teen and in the studio briefly, with his invite to a recording session (a place I had not been to in over 40 years) and general knowledge of conduct as a reigning rock star and songwriter, which he shall always be to generations of fans. Also, the long friendship of the former bass player for Roy Orbison, Terry Widlake, and his recently departed wife Margaret who ran the Sherlock Holmes Pub in Nashville for the years after Orbison and Terry's bands. This wonderful couple brought a part of England over when they established the pub and Terry shared insightful stories of a popular touring band and his role also as road manager. Worth mentioning is Mr. Pigeye Jackson for a first-hand look at playing and singing in karaoke sessions before, usually, small audiences on three continents. An irascible character, he is. He and I, we both play by ear, would have never understood some fundamentals of music from an early age without the conversations with my uncle, composer and music teacher, Wayland Rogers.

Various medical questions were answered with fitting terms of art by several doctor friends: the most recently departed Dr. Jesse Cannon, Dr. Robert Casey, Dr. Tom Mullady, Dr. Phillip Langsdon, Dr. Stephen Goodwin and the late Carolyn Benson, a cousin and superb intensive care nurse.

On matters spiritual, Pastor Will Miller, and the historian Ronald C. White, whose excellent book on Lincoln and recent on Grant, emphasizes the importance of one's relationship with God—especially as an element of one's character.

Judge Hugh Harvey gave me ideas on how criminals might smuggle old documents, given his years on the bench and clever perspectives. The late Walter P. Armstrong, Esq. was helpful not only as a fellow Giant Rat of Sumatra (and Baker Street Irregular, no less) but as an Oxfordian with great articulation. Various attorneys lent their knowledge, usually on the nature of evidence and fact, whether they realized it or not, including David Hardee, Patrick Martin, Gerald Easter, Jim Garts and Elliott Costas (who guided me to this solution of self-publishing as he has done with his own work). Cursed be you literary agents with your short attention spans and reluctance to represent a book questioning the authorship of Shakespeare.

Thanks to all of the Giant Rats of Sumatra of Memphis, who had the first taste of this book as many of them suffered through my one act play as participants and audience, many years ago. The plot was virtually the same as the one presented in this novel, though with a few glitches as is always the case in a one-time, unrehearsed production, but executed, nonetheless, with amazing aplomb.

Thanks to the late Jeremy Brett, who truly captured Sherlock Holmes as best as one can, for his insights into Holmes's nature. He took valuable time with me. The late Sir Ian McGeoch, Admiral (Ret.) in the Royal Navy, and his charming wife, Somers, gave me the lay of the land at Castle Hedingham. The very (from my perception) English family of Roger and Diane Simpson were helpful in various ways they might not know except to write that of an American glancing at the inner workings of an exceptional and kind family.

Thanks to certain members of the Shakespeare Oxford Society of the US, and particularly to the De Vere Society of the UK—too many to mention but why not a few in spite of being impolitic by doing it: Joe Peel, Esq. (assistant Tn. Attorney General), Michael Pisapia, Esq., the late Verily Anderson, the late Dr. Noemi Magri, the late Grant Gifford, Esq., the late Richard Roe, Esq. and Katherine Chiljan. Many of these have or had excellent written contributions and lectures on the subject. A most sage man, the late James Hardigg is someone I simply looked up to and listened closely to always.

An excellent blog site is ShakesVere, set up by author and superb researcher Mark Anderson. You'll find advanced discussion of the issue with the top researchers featured.

Many years ago, after my late wife and I spent a delightful four days at Mohonk Mountain House in New Paltz, New York, I thought, what a delightful place for a mystery setting. A quick phone call a few years later and I had questions answered by staff on weather emergencies, procedures and limitations. They were wonderful.

The late Robert Morris, formerly of the National Security Agency, gave me as much knowledge as he could without violating security on matters regarding Interpol and international policing at the end of the Cold War.

I would be remiss if I didn't include, last but not least, various teachers from high school through grad school. The late Miss Nancy Johnson was the local Shakespeare expert, and a good one, in Henderson, Tennessee. I'm sure she's tumbling in her grave over my faith in De Vere as author. The late Dr. Stephen Mooney was a Poe man and a poet who helped me bring out the "id" kid, as he put it, involved in writing. Various professors at the University of Colorado, where I received my Masters degree, always encouraged me to be creative, as bland as the subjects were.

Thanks for general support from my excellent neighbor Carter Wynn and my good friends Scott Forrester and Eugene Perkins.

It has been a long trip but I am happy this project is seeing the light of day. I hope you enjoyed reading it at least a tenth as much as I did in writing it. In your future reading on the subject, remember to look at some of the smaller arrows that point to Oxford as author: Baptista Nigrone's name, the extraordinary source of the names Rosencrantz and Guildenstern, the common precepts of Burleigh and Polonius, and, as you see in my plot, the uncanny coincidence of the Earls of Pembroke and Montgomery in their crucial roles in publishing of the First Folio. These are only a few, stubborn facts to overcome when Oxford is the candidate for authorship vs. Shakspere.

"O good Horatio, what a wounded name
(Things standing thus unknown) shall live behind me!
If thou didst ever hold me in thy heart,
Absent thee from felicity awhile,
And in this harsh world draw thy breath in pain
To tell my story."

About the Author

I'm a writer of fiction and non-fiction, having sold short stories to the Memphis daily (The Commercial Appeal), as well as a syndication of Texas weeklies called the Dallas-Ft. Worth Press Service, Inc. Non-fiction has appeared in Memphis Magazine and weekly columns for ten Tennessee weeklies over a dozen years entitled "A.F.T.erthoughts." As a student, my poetry appeared in the Tennessee Poetry Journal, founded by the late American poet Stephen Mooney, who taught me while an undergrad at the University of Tennessee-Martin. I was Features and Fine Arts Editor all four years for the student newspaper. I began "A.F.T.erthoughts" there my freshman year. I had a double major in History and Political Science and virtually enough hours for a major in English.

After graduation I worked production and headlining on a daily. I've a Masters from the University of Colorado. I interned for the U.S. House of Representatives one summer and later in Denver for then-Senator Gary Hart. While in government, I wrote or co-wrote such thrillers as the Final Report to the Governor (then-Lamar Alexander) on the Memphis Jobs Conference and the Foreign Trade Zone Application for Memphis.

I was President of the Shakespeare Oxford Society of North America and member of the De Vere Society of England. I'm former President (First Garrideb) of the Giant Rats of Sumatra—a Sherlock Holmes Club. I live in Memphis and travel to the U.K. from time to time, usually for a couple of months. My late wife was from Germany, so I network on the continent as well.

I was stand in for Joe Don Baker in the original "Walking Tall" film. At age sixteen, as keyboardist with Blu Revolution, we recorded a rock demo and gigged in the area. Today, as a hobby I play flute and harmonica while singing at karaoke—where the other band members show up sober and play precisely. From time to time I play on friends' recording sessions.

I'm semi-retired from an insurance business of over thirty years.

25423979R00264

Printed in Great Britain
by Amazon